Love Lives

Love Lives

Josie Lloyd & Emlyn Rees

WILLIAM HEINEMANN : LONDON

First published in the United Kingdom in 2003 by William Heinemann

1 3 5 7 9 10 8 6 4 2

William Heinemann
The Random House Group Limited
20 Vauxhall Bridge Road, London, SW1V 2SA

Random House Australia (Pty) Limited
20 Alfred Street, Milsons Point, Sydney, New South Wales 2061, Australia

Random House New Zealand Limited
18 Poland Road, Glenfield
Auckland 10, New Zealand

Random House (Pty) Limited
Endulini, 5a Jubilee Road, Parktown 2193, South Africa

The Random House Group Limited Reg. No. 954009

www.randomhouse.co.uk

A CIP catalogue record for this book is available from the British Library

Papers used by Random House are natural, recyclable products
made from wood grown in sustainable forests.
The manufacturing processes conform to the
environmental regulations of the country of origin

Typeset in Palatino by SX Composing DTP, Rayleigh, Essex
Printed and bound in the United Kingdom by
Clays Ltd, St Ives Plc

ISBN   0 434 00844 3 (hardback)
ISBN   0 434 01121 5 (trade paperback)

For Tallulah – may you always love life

Acknowledgements

With special thanks to special agents Vivienne Schuster and Jonny Geller, as well as to Euan, Doug, Carol 'The Engaged' Jackson, Kate, Emma, Diana, Sarah, Gill and all at Curtis Brown. Thanks to everyone at Random House, especially Andy McKillop, Kirsty Fowkes, Kate Parkin, Georgina, Justine, Mark, Ron, Karen and Glenn. Many thanks to our friends and family for their incredible support, particularly Bob and Barbara Wines for so much, Richard and Anne Rees for lending us their home and for coming back safe and sound, Catherine, Moose, Liz, Ralph and Kirsti for keeping an eye on us in the Wild West, and Philip, Jenny and all at the Packhorse Inn for making Southstoke a great place to write, and to Anne Lloyd for the feedback when it mattered most.

Chapter I

Jimmy opened Rachel's bedroom door as quietly as he could and peered inside. There his dad's girlfriend was, half hidden under the double duvet, alone on the double bed. In the half-light of the new day her thick black hair lay tousled across the pale-yellow pillowcases, reminding Jimmy of the clumps of seaweed that got tossed up on to the beaches during the winter storms.

Rachel had redecorated in here six months ago. Gran's old rose-patterned wallpaper had been too sickly sweet for her taste. It had been like sleeping in a box of chocolates, she'd complained. So now the walls were a neutral cream and Gran's crinoline dolls had been relocated from the dressing table to a cardboard box at the back of the white laminated wardrobe.

It made Jimmy sad, the way his gran's past had been so easily wiped out, but at the same time he was glad that Rachel had fixed things up the way she liked. This was her home as much as his now, and he knew his gran was never coming back.

Calm, Jimmy thought, that's what this room felt like now. It had a clean, sweet smell to it, a combination of fresh laundry and aromatherapy candles, which the rest of the flat lacked. Plastered with posters, Jimmy's room smelt of deodorant and cigarettes. A jumble of toys and clothes, his stepbrother Kieran's room smelt of nappy sacks, Calpol and milk. Both had a busyness to them, which made relaxation outside of sleep almost impossible. But this

1

room, neutral as doctor's waiting room, exuded nothing but calm.

And calm was what Jimmy needed right now, which is why he lingered in the doorway, vainly hoping that the room's essence might somehow filter through him and unravel the octopus of nerves that had writhed inside him from the very instant he'd woken up.

The source of these nerves was simple: Jimmy was in love. Jimmy was in love with Verity Driver. Jimmy was in love with Verity Driver, even though Verity Driver barely knew who Jimmy was. Jimmy was in love with Verity Driver, even though Verity Driver barely knew who Jimmy was, but Jimmy didn't care. Jimmy was in love with Verity Driver, even though Verity Driver barely knew who Jimmy was, but Jimmy didn't care, because Jimmy was going to make his move.

And what's more, he was going to do it today. He really was.

Only, in the same breath, he worried that he wouldn't. Because sometimes Jimmy only *thought* he was in love with Verity Driver. Sometimes Jimmy only thought he was in love with Verity Driver because he wanted *someone to fall in love with*. Sometimes Jimmy thought that if he *only thought* he was in love with Verity Driver, then he shouldn't say anything to her until he knew for sure.

It was a complicated situation, he was aware.

Only sometimes it got more complicated still. Sometimes Jimmy wondered whether he actually knew what love was. He didn't mean the kind of love he felt for Kieran, or the kind of love he felt for Rachel, or even the kind of love he sometimes – rarely – felt for his dad. He knew all about that. That kind of love was just there, background, like bricks in a wall. It wasn't something Jimmy ever gave much thought to. It wasn't something that could soar like a bird or plummet like a stone. It wasn't an emotion that could be stretched one way or the other and yet remain the same. It wasn't, in other words, the kind of emotion that overwhelmed Jimmy whenever he thought about Verity Driver – the kind of emotion he'd never experienced before, the kind that left him confused and ecstatic and terrified all at once.

Was that love? Jimmy hadn't a clue, but that's what he was going to find out. Was it real? He'd soon discover that, too. And if it was, would Verity care? Well, that's what today was all about for Jimmy: certainty. By tonight, all would be revealed.

But not just yet. For now, he'd stick to his routine. He'd act like nothing out of the ordinary was going on. He'd put Verity Driver and all thoughts of love to the back of his mind. He'd keep it fresh for when it really mattered.

Jimmy crossed the room and set down the steaming mug he'd been holding on Rachel's bedside table. Weak white instant coffee slopped over the mug's edge and down its side. He watched it spread outwards across the table's embroidered cotton cover, like a mud splash on snow. And although the thought did enter his head that this might be a bad omen, he dismissed it immediately.

Over on the windowsill the arc of red lights on the baby monitor flared, picking up the sound of baby Kieran coughing in his sleep in the room next door.

Rachel responded with a deep sigh and her brow pinched into a frown that she'd wear for the rest of the day. Her 'Mummy' frown, she called it, whenever she saw it captured in photos, swearing blind that it hadn't existed before she'd discovered she was pregnant with Kieran. 'All right, love?' she asked Jimmy, noticing him there and rolling over on to her side so that the duvet bunched up around her. Her accent had an easygoing Welsh lilt to it, even though she hadn't been back to her home town of Fishguard for more than a decade. Jimmy had always thought that little Kieran was a lucky kid, having a woman like this to lullaby him to sleep at night. Jimmy's own mum hadn't been around to do the same for him. That had been down to his gran, who'd brought Jimmy up – what with his dad being out and about, neither here nor there, for most of Jimmy's life.

'I brought you some coffee,' Jimmy said, nodding at the mug, noticing that the glowing turquoise display of the prehistoric Sony Digicube next to it read 8.05 a.m.

Rachel rubbed the sleep from her tortoiseshell-brown eyes and looked him up and down. She tugged the sleeves of her white cotton pyjama top down over her exposed upper arms. 'What's the big occasion?' she asked. 'The T-shirt,' she prompted, as he stared blankly back at her.

Jimmy looked down at the old Iggy Pop tour T-shirt he'd borrowed off his dad. ('Neat family heirloom,' his friend Tara had grumbled at the time. 'All my parents have in the way of rock and pop memorabilia is a photo of Michael Jackson with some chimp.') 'What about it?' Jimmy asked.

Rachel smiled. 'Just that you've ironed it so hard that poor old Iggy looks like he's had a facelift.' Her eyes flicked down a notch, taking in Jimmy's shop-fresh, blue-black combats. 'New trousers, too, aren't they?' she observed.

Her question was a loaded one. Jimmy hardly ever bought himself new clothes. What little money he allowed himself went on social necessities like hanging out with Tara and co. down at the Sapphire, or paying off the talk and text time on his phone. The rest of the cash that came his way he stuck straight into his deposit account, safe for the

4

future. That's how his gran had brought him up, to take responsibility for himself, and Rachel knew it.

'New-ish,' Jimmy responded noncommittally, deciding against getting into the whole story about how Tara had given them to him cheap after she'd shoplifted the wrong size from Denny Shapland's shop over on Tudor Square the day before.

'What's her name, then?' Rachel asked, reaching for her coffee.

'Eh?'

'The girl you're out to impress.'

The accuracy of Rachel's guess took Jimmy by surprise and, before he could prevent it, a blush had crept up on him and prickled across his cheeks. 'I'd best get going,' he excused himself, ducking forward and kissing her on the forehead, catching a hint of the sweet perfume he'd bought down the market last Tuesday for her thirty-sixth birthday.

Outside in the hallway, a memory surfaced in Jimmy's mind of his dad pitching up on the doorstep the year before, deep-tanned, crew-cut and beaming. He'd had a half-empty bottle of tequila cradled in one arm and an eight-months-pregnant Rachel in the other. 'Meet the new love of my life, kiddo,' he'd announced, blue eyes shining. 'And get yourself used to her, because she's going to be staying for a while.'

Jimmy wished his dad would treat her better. The old man had split a couple of months after Kieran had been born, off to Portugal on the promise of regular bar and building work. He'd been full of promises of his own to move Rachel and Kieran over just as soon as he could, but – a weekend trip to Lisbon aside – he hadn't come good on any of them yet.

Out in the corridor Jimmy paused and checked out his

reflection in the full-length mirror. The stolen combats hung baggy on his slim waist and, too long for his legs as they were, swamped his ankles, so that only half a white Nike tick showed on each trainer beneath.

He toyed momentarily with the idea of beefing himself up with the grey woollen crew-neck he wore whenever he went out fishing on Arnie's boat, but decided against it. If he wore the jumper, then the retro black leather jacket that Ryan's sister had given him after the funeral would have to go.

He shuffled his shoulders inside the heavy black garment, which he wore most days like a second skin. Anachronistic, Tara called it. Made him stick out like an operatic aria on a hip hop compilation, she reckoned, next to all the other kids' Hilfiger, Reebok and Nike gear.

But Jimmy liked it that way, looking different, letting everyone else know that he wasn't the same as them. That's what had always drawn him to Ryan: the fact that he'd dressed different and thought different.

Lifting the veil of his dark shaggy fringe, Jimmy tried out a smile on himself, but then he wiped it off again. It had made him look apprehensive, like one of those Jehovah's Witnesses who turned up on the doorstep from time to time. And, today of all days, he could do without that kind of negativity.

He ran his hand across his jaw. Not bad, he thought, for a week's growth. The stubble – adolescent and fluffy as he knew it was – still managed to make him look older and wiser, like he'd lived a little more than he really had. Maybe he should keep it going for a few more weeks, he considered, grow himself a mini-goatee, or maybe even go for the full Che Guevara.

Sadness crossed Jimmy's face as he remembered Ryan

sticking up that massive red-and-black poster of Cuba's finest on the Wreck's wall early last year. Ryan had been stoned and it had taken him six or seven attempts to get it straight, but eventually he'd managed it. 'There,' he'd said, flopping back down on to the old mattress and staring up at his handiwork. 'The Unholy Trinity.'

At seventeen, Ryan had been a little old for posters, but posters there'd been, plastered all over the Wreck – the name they'd given to the disused and boarded-up cliff-side chapel they'd been hanging out in for years. 'A practical necessity,' Ryan had called them, 'an invaluable aid in covering up the continents of damp which have made it their business to colonise our den of iniquity.'

Next to Che Guevara had been one of Ryan's hero, Howard Marks, the renowned Welsh dope smuggler. And beneath him there'd been a butter-wouldn't-melt grinning head shot of Britney, culled from some teen magazine, upon whose forehead Ryan had painstakingly drawn a series of crude, rude cartoons.

'No one's really worth following, Jimmo,' Ryan had pronounced with a sigh, staring up at Che, 'because nothing's really worth fighting for – not in the long run, anyway.' He'd turned to Jimmy, who'd been sprawled on the torn maroon leather armchair they'd liberated from a skip down in the town. 'The most charismatic revolutionary of his era and look where he's ended up,' Ryan had concluded, 'stuck between a convicted Welsh felon and an American pop princess.'

Ryan had then winked at Jimmy, the same way he'd always been winking at people. Ryan had never acted anything other than smarter than the people he'd mixed with. His near-black eyes – almost impossible to outstare – had always let others know he saw right through them.

He'd been able to silence people twice his age – teachers, shopkeepers, you name it – without having to speak.

Jimmy had respected Ryan so much that he'd got into the habit of never questioning his pronouncements. His friend's confidence had been like a fire against which Jimmy had warmed himself over the years and the last thing Jimmy had wanted had been to douse it with doubt. So instead, this time as every time before, Jimmy's response had been to nod his head and to smile.

Which had been good enough for Ryan, who'd started to skin up a joint. He'd been coming out of his Jim Morrison stage at the time. His hair, naturally dark like Jimmy's, but thin and needle straight, had hung low across the same jacket that Jimmy was wearing now. Jimmy smiled, remembering how, two weeks later, Ryan would have lopped off his locks, buzzing his hair down to grade two all over and ditching his gypsy earring in favour of a stud through the centre of his lower lip.

Reinvention, that's what life had always been about for Ryan, living as many lives as possible in the little time you had. Jimmy had loved him for this back then, for teaching him that you didn't have to be a passenger all your life, and for showing him that you could take the wheel whenever you wanted and choose your own road. Even though Ryan had only been a year older than him, he'd been a mentor to him, bigger than anyone else in his life, and certainly bigger than his dad.

Turning his back on his reflection, Jimmy continued down the hallway into the kitchen. He swigged down the rest of his tea and swilled the mug out under the hot tap, leaving it to dry on the stainless-steel draining board next to last night's plates and cutlery, and the ever-present row of plastic bottles and bibs and other baby paraphernalia.

Something hooked his attention, and he glanced out of the window and saw a gull hovering there in the wind, barely five feet away. But then, no sooner had he seen it than it was gone, sheering upwards, leaving nothing but swirling clouds in its wake. Jimmy was seriously into his photography and he wished he'd had a camera to capture the sight, but now it was too late.

The living room's threadbare brown carpet was patterned with the stubborn stains of twelve months' worth of tipped bottles and thrown bowls, all courtesy of baby Kieran and his growing appetite for destruction. Jimmy navigated his way through the minefield of second-hand Fisher Price and Tomy toys and other baby clutter, and on into his bedroom.

On the upturned tea chest next to Jimmy's box bed was a lava lamp in the shape of a space rocket, a cracked Jack Daniels promotional mirror and a framed photo of Tara, Ryan and Jimmy, the day Ryan had jacked an Alfa Romeo from the Royal Inn's car park and had Schumachered it all the way along the coast as far as Lyme Regis.

A nihilist. A bright kid, but a waster nonetheless. A dirtbag, a loser and a bloody shame. A kid who'd lost himself through taking too many drugs. That's how everyone in the town thought of Ryan now. A young man whose life had ended in tragedy, driven to suicide by the lifestyle that had taken him over. That's what the coroner had concluded. But Jimmy knew different. Ryan had been his best friend and Jimmy knew the truth about him better than any of them.

T-shirts and socks overflowed from the wicker basket by Jimmy's bed. Pringles tubes, chocolate wrappers and crushed Tango and Coke cans were scattered across the floor, next to copies of *NME*, *Uncut*, *The Face* and a variety of school textbooks and second-hand, mostly American, mostly modern paperbacks. Jimmy liked to read and liked to learn, the same as he liked to listen at school. But these were things that he wouldn't admit to anyone except his closest friends, in case people thought him soft.

The shelves on the wall above his bed gave the room a sense of order, stacked as they were with Jimmy's precious film magazines, all of them lined up in chronological order.

Alongside them, every bit as neat, were the boxed video diaries which Jimmy had shot using the camcorder he'd borrowed from Clive down at the Youth Centre. Their labels faced outwards, some of them dumb, liked *Ain't Life a Beach?* and *Stoned* and *2 Stoned: The Sequel*; but some of them were serious, like *An On-Off Season* and *Fisherman Blue*, the latter of which – 'A short film about the end of a traditional way of life' – Jimmy had sent off along with his film college application forms the month before. He was ambitious. He wanted to make something of himself. He wanted to come back here in ten years' time and for all the people who wrote him off now to see him and stop and point and whisper and stare.

He took the three small paces needed to cross the room and grabbed his Marlboro Reds and Zippo lighter from where he'd left them on the windowsill, behind the curtain out of the disapproving Rachel's sight. He reached across the square wooden desk that housed his cranky typewriter. The machine whirred in protest as he pulled the final page of his English *Macbeth* essay off it. It was a sound Jimmy liked, because it was a sound that meant something was finished and something else would soon begin.

It was icebox-cold on the cast-iron balcony outside Jimmy's flat. Last night's storm had been a bad one and the wind was

10

still up. It howled in from the great grey slab of sea to the east and hissed in Jimmy's ears, slapping like something solid against his face as he knelt down to unchain his scratched-up BMX from the rust-freckled railings. He pulled his baseball cap from his pocket and tugged it down tight on his head.

From up here on the ninth floor of Carlton Court – the hulk of crumbling Sixties concrete Jimmy had called home for all but one of his seventeen years – he could see clear across North Beach's half-mile curve of platinum-blonde sand to the harbour and the town of Shoresby itself.

Aside from the gulls and the waves, and a lone walker visible down on North Beach, little stirred in the town. The windows of the pastel-shaded seafront town houses, hotels and B&Bs were grey and unlit, as if someone had forgotten to colour them in. It would all change soon, of course, once everyone was awake. But for now, only the shops on the High Street – whose striped awnings rippled in the wind above their brightly illuminated doorways – signalled that the town was inhabited at all.

Jimmy took his bike down in the lift and out through the shoddily decorated reception. And then he was out of there, off along the Croft, the road that followed the curve of North Beach, running fifty feet above it, before terminating in the High Street.

Fast as he could pedal, with the wind in his face, he forced his way past the swinging hanging baskets and 'Vacancy' signs of the guest houses, and on past the shut-down burger bars and Mr Whippy Head ice cream parlour, before cutting through the empty Pay & Display car park where he'd spent most of this summer's evenings practising skateboarding, before he'd got yawned-out by the whole damned thing and had flogged his board to

11

Tristan for a bunch of CDs and the bronze Zippo lighter that now jiggled in his pocket.

It wasn't till he reached the High Street that he stopped and dismounted. He leant his bike up against a Victorian lamp-post, ducked into Wilson's the newsagent and picked up the November issue of *Total Film* from the rack and a bottle of Diet Coke from the fridge.

'How's your gran?' Bob Wilson enquired as he ran Jimmy's stuff through the cash register. 'You still visiting her?'

'Every Wednesday and Friday,' Jimmy confirmed.

Bob nodded his head in empathy. It was cancer that had taken his Elaine from him five years ago, the same as it was cancer that had got Jimmy's mum less than a year after Jimmy had been born.

'You give her these from me,' Bob said, reaching above his head and selecting a box of Milk Tray from the shelves behind him without even looking. He slipped it into a brown paper bag and handed it over to Jimmy. 'But don't let the nurses see, mind,' he warned, 'or you'll get me in trouble.'

Jimmy didn't have the heart to tell Mr Wilson that his gran was too far gone these days to care much about chocolates one way or the other. 'Thanks,' he said, tucking the box into his black-and-white Adidas gym bag.

Back outside, Jimmy cycled on another twenty yards before pulling up next to a green park bench, which had been set into a gap in the black railings, facing out to sea. He propped his bike up against its wooden slats and looked back across the street.

There, next to W. H. Smith, was the wide white front of the Grand Hotel. He swallowed, all ideas of calm now forgotten. The Grand was where Verity Driver lived and she'd be coming out of there soon, ready to go to school and sit in the same English class as him at nine thirty, and open the same book at the same page and discuss the same W. B. Yeats poem, which he'd pictured her reading as he'd read it himself over the weekend.

Jimmy and Verity had been at school together since they'd been five. He'd known her for most of his life. Or rather, he'd known of her. He'd never actually hung out with her, never been invited to one of her birthday parties, or sat next to her on the bus.

But he knew plenty about her. He knew she liked wearing pink, but looked better in red. He knew she mostly wore her hair down, but sometimes looked great with it tied up. He knew a flash of her green eyes could turn his head from a hundred yards. He knew she always took a packed lunch to school with her and never ate the crusts on her sandwiches. He knew she'd had good-looking boyfriends over the years, but that the latest one, Tim, had stopped walking her home from school, which probably – *hopefully* – meant they were no longer an item.

But these were things that anyone who'd grown up near Verity Driver could have known about her. What Jimmy wanted now was more. So why hadn't he made a move on her sooner? Could it have been because he was shy? Sometimes he thought that was the answer. Sometimes he did feel awkward in front of girls he was attracted to. But he'd had girlfriends before. He wasn't even a virgin. So it couldn't really have been that.

Could it, then, have been because Ryan had always thought that crushes were dumb, and had further stated that he and Jimmy were too young to get fixed on one girl? Could that have been why Jimmy had kept his feelings for Verity hidden over the years, because he hadn't wanted to appear uncool? Or could it have been that since Ryan's death – nearly a year ago now – Jimmy had felt too screwed up to risk getting involved with anyone new?

It could have been. It could have been any of these things. But Jimmy wasn't going to let any of them stop him any more.

He felt unsuccessfully for the CD cover through the stiff material of his gym bag. He'd burnt it for her, using one of the computers at school. The tunes on it (mostly chart-friendly garage and R&B) weren't his kind of thing. But all the girls he knew (with the exception of Tara and Steph) were into it, so chances were Verity would be as well.

Doubt hit him. Maybe giving her a CD was too over the top? Maybe it was laying his cards on the table too quickly? Where was the mystery, where the intrigue, he now worried, in such a bald statement? Maybe he should forget that idea for the time being. After all, he didn't want to look desperate. But then again, he had to mark himself some-how, and the CD showed thought, right? A little care? Yeah, he'd give it to her, but just do it with a bit of chat so as to make the gesture less corny. Something like: *Hey, Verity. How's things?*

Good, Jimmy. Yourself?

Yeah, good, you know. I did this compilation over the weekend and . . . you should listen to it . . . here, I'll tell you what, why not borrow it?

Thanks, Jimmy. That's really sweet.

And then he could ask her out. This Saturday night and – who knew? – they could be sitting right here after the pub, his arm round her shoulders, her eyes staring into his, and him leaning his head towards her, feeling like he was falling into her, and then kissing her so tenderly that he'd feel like he'd gone to heaven.

Then a great certainty swamped him: it wasn't going to happen. It hit him like a bullet in his guts. Verity Driver walked like a model and was top of her class, and she could sing and she could dance, and she'd only ever looked past him and not at him. And even if she was sometimes quiet, even if she sometimes looked nervous, or – the same as Jimmy – acted awkward, as though she didn't quite fit into this town . . . Even then, what did he have to offer her? What could he show her that she hadn't already seen?

Jimmy lit a cigarette to calm his nerves. He took out his phone to see if he had any messages. There was one from Tara, a few minutes old, asking him if he wanted to hook up at the Jackpot Café for a pre-class coffee, but he decided he'd better not reply. She'd only want to know where he was, and once she found out she'd guess straight away what he was doing here. And then she'd be over in a flash to persuade him to do anything but. Because Tara didn't like Verity. Because Tara thought Verity Driver was stuck-up and prissy.

The growl of a car engine cut through the noise of the wind. Jimmy saw a sky-blue Land-Rover Discovery twenty yards up the High Street, driving towards him at about one mile an hour. Tourist, Jimmy thought automatically, not only because of the flashiness of the car, but also because he could clearly see an ordnance survey map held up against the dashboard by whoever it was who was sitting in the passenger seat.

As the car drew parallel with him and came to a halt, the inevitable happened: the passenger window hummed down and the passenger – a woman in her thirties with the kind of styled blonde hair that Tara would have called 'newsreader', but Jimmy just thought of as plain fit – leant out. She smiled at Jimmy in the same way that Marianna

Andrews, Jimmy's boss at the video store on South Parade where he worked part-time, always did whenever she was about to ask him to cover an extra shift or run an errand in the rain.

Jimmy spoke first: 'Where are you trying to get to?'

'Is it that obvious?' the woman asked, smiling again, only differently this time, with her whole face instead of just her mouth.

'The map's kind of a give-away,' he said, mellowing towards her.

Flipping open a titanium-cased electronic organiser, she read aloud, 'Harbour Cottage, Number Four, Quayside Row. Do you know where it is?'

Jimmy's gran's great friend Arnold lived two doors along. Jimmy was surprised at the address, though. Judging by her car and her clothes, he'd had the woman down for one of the pricey apartments built into the old town walls. He peered past her and saw a thickset younger man drumming his fingers on the brown leather steering wheel.

'Well?' she asked.

Jimmy toyed briefly with the idea of giving her wrong directions, just for the hell of it. He and Ryan had always been doing that as kids, competing with each other to see just how far from their destinations they could con the tourists into going. But he wasn't a kid any more and the woman looked like she'd had a long enough start to her day already. He checked his watch. Yeah, he thought. Why not? Chances were he was going to be waiting here at least another half-hour anyway before Verity showed. He could risk it and – who knew? – perhaps it might tip the karma balance that Tara was always on about in his favour. He scuffed out his cigarette on the pavement and clambered on to his BMX. 'Follow me,' he said.

He pedalled a further ten yards along the High Street, before peeling off to the left and freewheeling down the steep cobbled length of Crackwell Street. When he reached the bottom, he glanced back over his shoulder to check the Land-Rover was still with him, before swinging left into the harbour car park. Ten yards more and he skidded to a halt at the top of the path that led down to Quayside Row, the boatyards and the harbour proper.

The Land-Rover pulled up behind him, and the man who'd been driving got out and stood with his hands on his hips for a moment, surveying the view out to sea. He was two or three inches shorter than Jimmy and was wearing a tired old pair of jeans and a heavy red and black checked jacket with the collar turned up. He grinned out across the water at nothing in particular, just looking happy to be here.

Jimmy turned back to the car to see the woman striding purposefully over towards him, the wind riffling like invisible fingers through the fur on her coat.

'It's the one with the rusted cockerel weathervane,' Jimmy told her, pointing down the path to the terrace of pastel-coloured cottages, 'and the pale-blue window ledges.'

'Thanks,' she said, but there was a note of apprehension in her voice. She glanced between the car and the cottage as if she were mentally gauging the distance. 'Can't we get any closer?' she asked.

'No,' Jimmy told her.

Her gaze kept moving, sweeping past Jimmy and not stopping until it reached the harbour master's office over by the car park entrance. Next to this squat red-brick building was a closed barrier and beyond that a variety of vehicles could be clearly seen parked down on the quayside. 'What about them?' she asked.

'They belong to the fishermen,' Jimmy told her. 'And the

sailing school people. But it's off-limits for tourists. There's not enough space.'

The short man said in an Australian accent, 'Don't sweat it, Ellen. It's no real distance anyway.' He turned to Jimmy. 'We've got a few heavy bags in the back here,' he said. 'Any chance of you giving us a hand with them?'

Anxious to get back to his vigil opposite the Grand, Jimmy checked his watch, but he was still all right, he reckoned. 'So long as we're quick,' he said, following the man round to the back of the car.

Five minutes later and the three of them were standing on the mossy cobbled path outside the cottage, with the heavier of the man's and woman's bags on the path beside them.

'Thanks,' the man said, reaching out his hand to Jimmy, 'I'm Scott, by the way.'

'Jimmy,' Jimmy mumbled, shaking Scott's hand. The wind was stronger here and Jimmy pulled his cap down tighter still on his head. 'Not very good holiday weather,' he commented.

Scott shrugged. 'We're not here on holiday.'

'No?'

'No. We're shooting a documentary.'

Jimmy found himself staring at them. He buzzed with excitement. Film . . . TV . . . this was his thing. Contacts, that's what his media teacher had told the class it was all about. And that's the one thing Jimmy had been missing. But now here they were – two of them – walking into his life. His mind started working on how he could swing this accidental meeting round – maybe shadow them or something – to boost his chances of getting into film school. 'Yeah?' he finally asked, trying to sound casual, determined that they wouldn't perceive him as unworldly and overawed. 'About what?'

18

The woman – Ellen, Scott had called her – was staring at the front door. 'Lost Soul's Point,' she said without turning round.

Jimmy's heart dodged a beat. His skin prickled and he could picture the colour draining from his face. Lost Soul's Point was the tourist trail name for the suicide black spot up on the cliffs overlooking North Beach and the town.

'You heard of it?' Scott asked.

Jimmy nodded warily. Who in this town hadn't? The drop from the cliffs to the rocks below at low tide was nearly two hundred feet. And the drop from the cliffs to the sea at high tide was just as fatal. Since Jimmy had been alive, there'd been maybe ten suicides up there. Most of them had been men and women from up-country, people who'd ditched their cars up on the cliff-side. Most, but not all.

'Then you probably know the story behind it, as well,' Ellen said.

Again, Jimmy nodded. Every kid in the town got the legend passed down to them by older kids in the primary school playground: something about some crazy rich girl throwing herself off the cliff a hundred years ago or more; something about her having done it because she'd been ditched by some bloke; something about his ghost walking the cliffs at night, forever damned for what he'd done to her. Something that smelt a whole lot like bullshit, in other words.

But Jimmy didn't give a damn about the legend right now. He just wanted to know that there was where their interest in Lost Soul's Point ended.

'Well, we're here to do a history of it,' Ellen continued, encouraged by his attentive silence. 'We want to cover the legend and then we want to look at the modern victims as well, to examine the lives of the people who've committed suicide up there in the last few years and to ask what drove them to it and to this place in particular . . .'

With each word that Ellen spoke, the sparks of excitement inside Jimmy faded and died. *Victims* . . . the word reverberated round his skull. *Victims* . . . like Ryan . . . These people were here to investigate Ryan's death. They were here to find out why Ryan had done what he'd done.

Ellen picked up on his shift in mood immediately. 'What?' she asked.

Panic was building inside Jimmy. What was he doing even talking to these people? How could he have ended up talking to them about *this*, the one thing he never wanted to discuss with anyone ever?

'Are you all right, mate?' Scott asked.

'I –' But Jimmy couldn't speak. He looked between Scott and Ellen. Their eyes felt like searchlights on his face. He had nothing to say. Not to them. Not about Ryan. He felt dizzy, breathless, like the air was being sucked from his lungs. 'I gotta go,' he said, turning his back on them and hurrying away.

Chapter II

'Was it me? What did I say?' Ellen asked Scott, as they both watched the boy cycle away. He'd been so helpful, so why had he gone silent like that?

'So much for charming the locals,' Scott replied.

Ellen glanced at the young Australian by her side, suddenly remembering all the positive things she'd said on their long drive down here from London. 'Thank you,' she called out after the boy. But it was far too late and her voice was lost in the wind.

She turned to see Scott failing to hide an amused smirk. 'Oh, get on with it!' Ellen exclaimed, pushing the Australian playfully in the direction of the car.

Beside the cottage's scuffed front door, Ellen groped inside the wooden post box until she found the key. So much for the friendly welcome note, she thought, as she waggled the old-fashioned iron key in the lock, but the door was swollen with damp and wasn't budging.

She let out a growl of frustration and glanced towards the car, but she was determined not to rely on Scott for help yet again. She might be nearly ten years older than him but, at thirty-four, she wasn't past it yet. Standing tall in her fake-fur coat, she twisted the brass handle again and heaved her shoulder against the door. It took a few more hefty pushes before the door suddenly gave and she fell down the step into the living room, twisting her foot on the way.

Inside, the cottage was so lopsided it would've made her feel like limping, even if she hadn't fallen. The low plaster ceiling sloped down at an acute angle and the staircase looked as if it had collapsed drunkenly against the wall, so that the only way to climb up would be to skulk up sideways.

'Jesus. It's minute,' said Scott, pushing in behind her with one of the camera cases and heaving the oversized chintz armchair out of the way to make room.

With two of them in the doorway, the cottage felt horribly oppressive.

'It's . . . er . . . quaint,' said Ellen, searching for the right word, as she surveyed the dusty arrangement of dried flowers in the fire grate and the dresser crammed with an audience of sour-faced china figurines. 'It'll just have to do.'

Hobbling across the threadbare rug to the far corner of the room, she pushed aside the bead curtain and peeped into the tiny square of kitchen. An ancient gas cooker was wedged level with a telephone directory and a tap dripped against a green beard of limescale in the sink. 'Ah!' she said ominously. She turned back to face Scott, blowing up over her face in the idiosyncratic gesture she'd kept, even though her fringe-heavy bob had recently been replaced by a sleek blonde crop. 'OK. So we'll get the rest of the stuff in,' she said, injecting as much bravado into her voice as she could, 'then we'll have a cuppa and work out what to do.'

'You're the boss.'

By the time they'd lugged in all their equipment, Ellen was sweating as she hauled her bag up the stairs. Pushing down the latch on the arched wooden door, she dipped her head and stopped on the threshold of the first bedroom, her nostrils filling with the acrid smell of damp. It was then that her positive attitude cracked and the picture of rustic charm she'd drawn in her mind finally crashed around her like a broken mirror.

Instead of the sunlight-infused sanctuary of her imagination, complete with a gigantic iron bed, sumptuous homemade quilt and tasteful soft furnishings, what lay before her was more like a nun's cell; the white walls faded to a dull grey, with no decoration except for a tin crucifixion sculpture, which looked like a misshapen cake mould.

With a sinking heart, Ellen threw her Burberry holdall on the high single bed, but it bounced off immediately, as if the lumps beneath the nylon bedspread had angrily repelled it. As she watched the bag thump on to its side, there was the unmistakable chink as something – no doubt her bottle of bath oil in her wash bag, or worse, her perfume – smashed deep inside.

Steeling herself not to lose it, Ellen stepped over the bag to the sash window where a net curtain twitched in the cold draft. Edging past the dressing table, where a forlorn lace doily was Blu-tacked, she yanked aside the curtain and unfastened the brass clasp, thumping the heels of her hands against the flaking sash window frame until it yielded and flew upwards. Then she thrust her head through the open window and, leaning on the wide sill, took a deep breath.

Below her there was a thin strip of cobbled road before the thick harbour wall, but from the bedroom window it felt as if Ellen was right on the edge of it, looking down a dizzying fifty-foot drop to the harbour floor. There, the cold tide nudged the fishing boats afloat, their lengths of chain emerging from the mud as if connected to a sinister underworld below.

Looking up to where the mud turned into a sweeping arc of sand, she could see a concrete ramp dotted with heaps of nets leading to a jumble of masts and machinery in the boatyard. Along the path there was an abandoned fish and chip van with one wheel missing, then a tiny stone chapel, which was completely overshadowed by a concrete reinforced cliff rising up to the front.

Behind the ornamental gardens and railings at the top she could make out a row of ostentatious Victorian houses, their windows lifeless behind the cast-iron balustrades. Beside them was a crumbling art deco building that was probably once a cinema or a bingo hall, but was now boarded up, and along from that an ugly Sixties block dominated the view, a tidemark of dirt visible halfway up the pale concrete wall. Beyond the town the land stretched up, patchy grass punctuating the furrows of dark mud, where a lone horse grazed.

Ellen took another lungful of salty air and sighed, feeling a pang of homesickness as she thought about Jason. He'd be at the airport right now on his way to South America for his latest adventurous filming expedition. Spot the difference, she thought gloomily as she surveyed the sleepy off-season seaside town before her.

She didn't begrudge Jason the obvious excitement and satisfaction he'd found since his rainforest wildlife series had come off, but Ellen couldn't help feeling peeved at how unconcerned he seemed to be about being apart from her. And, if she were really honest, she was jealous.

'But you'll be away too,' Jason had reasoned last night, in the bedroom of their Clerkenwell apartment.

'It's not the same,' Ellen had replied, rubbing moisturiser into her face and glancing behind her at Jason in the long wardrobe mirrors. He'd been fresh from the shower, a tan sarong wrapped loosely round his slim waist, as he'd stood by their handmade teak bed, fiddling with the small ebony pendant he always wore on a leather thong round his neck. Even undressed, he'd looked cool, in the eccentric way that was all his own. There'd been something sexy about him, an aura of untouchable manliness that Ellen had always found irresistible. He was the same age as her, but Ellen had always had the feeling that Jason wouldn't age. He'd always looked the same, as if he were deeply comfortable in his tanned olive skin, with his smiling grey-green eyes behind long, curly lashes. But his most distinctive feature had always been his untameable mane of deep auburn-brown curls, which Ellen had watched him tie back in a band.

The smooth linen duvet in front of him had been covered in neatly ironed piles of Ellen's shirts and trousers, and a messy small jumble of his shorts and T-shirts, which he'd been about to pack.

'Oh Jase, stop,' Ellen had begged, turning round and walking to his side. 'At least let me iron your things.'

Jason had chuckled at her concern. 'Believe me, where I'm going there'd be absolutely no point in having anything dry, let alone ironed.'

Ellen had looked down at him shovelling the clothes into his ancient rucksack, and had felt childish tears welling up. She'd had a bad feeling about Jason going off on this trip all week and now it had got to the night before them both going their separate ways, she'd felt desperate to hold on to him. At least when Jason usually went filming she was at home in a place he knew, but with them both away they'd be more disconnected than ever.

'Don't look like that,' Jason had said softly, drawing her into his embrace. 'The month will fly by.'

'You see! You won't miss me at all,' Ellen had blurted out accusingly, looking up into Jason's face.

His jaw was usually covered with stubble, his eyes sleep-starved, but last night he'd been groomed and clean-shaven, and he'd looked like the man she'd first fallen in love with over a decade ago when she'd been a graduate trainee at the BBC and he'd turned up one day with a camera crew.

'You want to bet?' he'd said so tenderly that her petulant mood had instantly dissolved. 'I'll miss you all the time. Particularly this bit,' he'd said as he'd pulled aside the edge of her thick white robe and had kissed her neck. 'But then again, I might miss this bit a bit more,' he'd continued as he'd traced soft kisses down her collarbone and Ellen had started to laugh.

Then he'd hooked his foot round her ankle and effortlessly tripped her up so that she'd fallen softly on to the bed. As he'd landed gently on top of her, he'd pulled open her robe and continued his descent, and Ellen had looked up at the soft pools of light from the designer up-lighters she'd installed in their room, relishing each kiss and trying not to mind too much that her neat piles of clothes would have to be refolded. After all, she'd thought, this one was going to have to last her.

Now Ellen closed her eyes briefly, breathing in the sea air as she savoured the memory of last night. 'It's going to be fine,' she said out loud. 'Be calm. You can do this. You can –'

But she didn't get any further, before her ears filled with a terrifying scream, as an enormous seagull swooped towards her, its sharp yellow beak open, its beady eyes shining as it missed her by inches. Ellen froze as it arced away from her before wheeling back, obviously intent on making another malicious swipe.

'Shit!' Ellen darted back inside the window, banging the back of her head on the bottom of it, as the seagull swooped past. Slamming the window shut, she leapt away, holding her head as she turned to see Scott in the doorway. 'It's like a fucking Hitchcock movie!' she said, as the seagull shrieked with victory on the other side of the window.

Scott shrugged unsympathetically. 'I've got bunk beds,' he said, flicking his head in the direction of his room. 'And

26

there's no phone socket, which means our fax and e-mail are busted.'

'Oh, God. This is a disaster,' said Ellen, hauling up her holdall from the floor on to the bed. 'I'm so sorry. I should never have trusted Joy.'

Ellen might have known that Joy, the most unhelpful production secretary on the face of the planet, the woman whose only mission in life was to see Ellen fail, would find the smallest, most inhospitable place in the entire town, just to wind her up. Now she felt angry for not paying more attention to details like this herself.

She'd assumed that renting a cottage would be the logical thing to do, since she would be travelling between Shoresby and London on an ad hoc basis each week, spending days at the editing suite in Soho so that she could finish off the other programmes, while sorting out the shoot in Shoresby. And since Scott was short of freelancing work, Ellen had suggested that he stay down here the whole time, as a sort of low-paid holiday. Joy, though, obviously hadn't had comfort at the forefront of her mind.

Considering that Ellen thought of herself as fairly easy-going, it had come as a shock when Joy had taken an instant dislike to her when she'd joined APWW, the small independent television production company, a few months ago. Joy had made no secret of the fact that she thought Ellen had insufficient experience to take over Amanda's role, dismissing Ellen's previous job at the BBC. Coming from an editorial rather than a directing background, Ellen knew there was a grain of truth in Joy's opinion, which was why, even though she now felt thrown in at the deep end, she was determined to make this trip a success.

'Look, I'll see if I can sort something else out,' Ellen said, sensing Scott's disappointment and following him down the stairs. Finding the pre-set office number on her phone directory, she punched in the call command.

But there was no reception. No reception on the state-of-the-art mobile she had bought specifically for this trip.

It had been a long time since Ellen had been in a phone box. The ones near her flat in London were covered with graffiti and the phones had mostly gone (it being the part of Clerkenwell that was still to up and come). Therefore, finding a functioning old-fashioned public phone was a novelty. So was trying to do business in a metre-square office.

Wedging her boot up against the glass and the phone on her shoulder, she pulled off her pen lid with her teeth. Then, opening the plastic folder and jostling all her notes to make them balance on her thigh, she dropped some change into the slot and dialled the office number.

She could imagine Joy in the small kitchenette in the tiny West End office, scowling at the phone as she took her time squeezing out the teabag in her mug. Eventually, she answered, and, after the briefest of pleasantries, Ellen got straight to the point. 'There's a couple of things. We need permission from the American owner of Appleforth House to film there and on the land near Lost Soul's Point. But there's no permission letter here in Amanda's notes.'

Joy did one of her dismissive sniffs. 'You've got everything there is,' she said. 'If something's missing it's not my fault.'

'I'm not saying it is, but could you chase it . . . if you have a mo—?'

'I suppose I'll need a fax number for you, then.'

'I'll get on to it right away and phone you one later this morning,' said Ellen, relieved that she'd clinched a commitment out of Joy. 'And . . . um . . . one more thing?'

'Yes?' Joy said, her voice loaded with irritation.

'Did you have a list of Bed and Breakfasts or hotels here? It's just that the cottage is a bit on the small side for both me and Scott –'

No sooner were the words out of her mouth than Joy interrupted indignantly. 'I got you the cheapest accommodation I could find. *You* said *you* wanted to save on the budget so that you could do the extra filming down there –'

'OK, OK. I hear you.'

It was true that Ellen had pushed through the idea of including the full story of the suicides at Lost Soul's Point in a series of documentaries about the myths behind British landmarks. Amanda, the series producer, who'd left Ellen in charge, had already made several programmes around the country and had only wanted Ellen to supervise a few shots of Lost Soul's Point with a tiny voice-over. And then to fill the rest of the programme with interviews with people in Shoresby. But Ellen had argued that including a full account of the story of the nineteenth-century girl who'd thrown herself on to the rocks after having had her heart broken by her lover was a sure way to bring a touch of class to the programme. And with the reconstructed drama she had in mind, the programme would spring to life.

But now she was aware of the vast gulf between the discussions she'd had in her office and the reality of being here. She'd been so eager to pull off her first project that she'd flippantly dismissed anyone's help and had batted away Amanda's scepticism about filming in the autumn, when the light was bound to be dreadful. Now, she'd barely been in gloomy Shoresby an hour and already there seemed to be a million problems.

Ellen pressed the receiver against her forehead, feeling completely out of her depth. She knew she shouldn't call

Amanda, but she was the only one who'd been here before when they'd researched the series six months ago. Surely a few words of encouragement couldn't do any harm. Ellen took a deep breath and dialled. 'Amanda,' she said. 'Look I'm sorry to call you at home, but –'

Ellen stopped immediately. On the other end of the phone Amanda let out a strained gasp.

'Oh, my God!' Ellen exclaimed, her notes falling off her knees and scattering like a snowdrift on the phone box floor. 'You're not . . .'

'No. Just Braxton Hicks.'

'Who's he?'

'For God's sake . . . Pretend contractions . . .' Amanda puffed. 'Bloody painful. What is it?'

'Nothing. It's nothing. Nothing at all. Go back to your . . . I'm . . .' Ellen replaced the receiver quickly. 'Fine,' she said, finishing her sentence aloud, as the money clunked down into the phone. Ellen bit her lip, listening to the wind punching the side of the phone box.

What was she doing calling Amanda? Surely the whole point of being in charge was just that, to be in charge, even if it did mean feeling scarily alone. Annoyed with herself for being such a wimp, she scrabbled around to pick up her notes and stuffed them inside her folder. After all, how difficult could this really be?

A greasy chip packet whipped in a whirlwind by her feet as Ellen hurried out of the phone box and set off to find the hotel they'd passed on the way into town. Standing still, she couldn't remember whether she should head up the cobbled road, or whether they'd come round on the road to the left. Plumping for the tarmac option to the left, she put her head down and headed off.

Soon, though, as the road headed up and away from the

harbour, she was completely disorientated. Stopping by an estate agent's, she looked at the pictures of shabby bungalows and holiday caravans for sale, and all the optimistic things she'd said to her friends about basking in the restorative powers of the sea air now seemed silly and naïve.

Crossing over the road into a race of skipping leaves along the pavement, Ellen was narrowly missed by a four-by-four towing a rattling boat trailer, followed by a post van. Ahead, beyond the open trapdoors in the pavement, where a publican was taking in several barrels of beer, Ellen could see that the road widened out into a main square where the shops were starting to open.

She instinctively clutched the leather wallet in her pocket and flicked the edge of her Selfridges store card as she walked through the town centre. But it looked as if she'd have to try very hard to find anything worth buying. Granted, there was a typical seaside surf shop, called Wave Cave, but other than that, the whole town seemed to have had a style bypass.

Well, it's certainly a challenge, Ellen thought, edging past a couple of woolly-hatted old ladies chatting outside the post office and noticing a pretty alley running down the side of Woolworths. With a bit of sunshine and a clever camera angle from behind the holly bushes in the churchyard, she might just succeed in making this place look vaguely decent.

Stopping by the church with its witch's hat spire, she realised she was at the top of the cobbled street and had been on a pointless detour through the town. Still, at least she now had her bearings and she recognised the High Street where they'd stopped in the car earlier by W. H. Smith. As she looked down the front, she could see the sign for the Grand Hotel swinging in the wind.

The only thing for it, she resolved, as she hurried towards it past a Chinese takeaway and a shop crammed shut with semi-deflated beach toys, was to be professional. She would get the filming done and get out as quickly as possible. As soon as she had a fax number, she was going straight up there to check out Lost Soul's Point and finalise her filming schedule.

She was brought out of her thoughts by the sight of the boy she'd met earlier. He was next to a bench a little way down from a wrought-iron shelter, hunched down in his leather jacket, furtively smoking a cigarette as he leant up against his bike. Ellen could see him clearly from her side of the road, but either he was so engrossed in what he was thinking as he scuffed the toe of his trainer against the pebbled concrete, or he was deliberately ignoring her. Ellen almost called out, but then she changed her mind, lowered her eyes and headed on.

It seemed so long since Ellen had been a teenager that she had no idea what it must be like living in a town this size. For all she knew, the boy probably regarded her as some nosy city type.

Well, that was exactly what Ellen wasn't and she would prove it. She was here to be sympathetic about the suicides that had happened and to make the legend of Lost Soul's Point interesting again for everyone, including the locals. That was what she was going to do: capture the romance of the place and bring history to life.

Ellen had been thinking, when she'd seen the impressive Georgian façade of the Grand Hotel, that she'd throw caution to the wind and book herself in on her own credit card. But now, as she walked through the door, she immediately had second thoughts and started to wonder whether she could make the cottage cosy after all, despite Scott's reservations.

Inside, there was certainly nothing grand about the hotel as its name suggested. A tall mahogany plant stand was by the door, but instead of a leafy aspidistra adorning it, an ice cream tub filled with stagnant brown water caught drips from the leaking porch roof.

As she walked further inside, Ellen could see a visitors' book resting on a carved wooden lectern opened at an ominously blank double-page spread. She could smell the faint odour of cigarettes mixed with a sickly tang of pine air freshener as her footsteps echoed on the tiles. She stopped by the reception desk and looked up at the panelled staircase and around to where the space opened out into the lounge. There, the only sign of life was a grand piano in the huge bay window which was stacked with open music books, the stand light illuminating the shiny white keys like a cartoon grin.

Timidly, Ellen pressed her palm on the brass dome bell on the desk and heard the loud chime echo out in the hall. When nothing happened, she looked behind her at the pictures on the wall by the staircase. Several reproduced sepia photographs showed scenes of rotund women in bathing chairs on the beach. Another showed horse-drawn carriages crowding the market square and well-to-do gents in top hats walking ladies in fine dresses. Ellen peered more closely at the images of Shoresby in its Victorian heyday. Maybe she should do some shots of these, she thought, to show how the town must have looked when Appleforth House was still thriving.

She was so engrossed that she jumped when she heard the door behind the reception area burst open and she looked round to see a girl stepping through.

The girl was holding a piece of toast in her hand and, when she saw Ellen, she covered her mouth and tried to chew faster. As she came forward to the desk, Ellen noticed that the girl was strikingly tall, with pretty, wide-set green eyes. Everything about her, from her make-up-free complexion to the rope-like plait of thick chestnut hair hanging down her back, was exceptionally neat. It was only when she put her hands on the edge of the desk that Ellen saw that her fingernails were bitten right down.

'Can I help you?' she asked, in a well-spoken, clear voice, fixing Ellen with a disarmingly aloof stare.

'I'm here with a television company. I'm going to be making a documentary up at Lost Soul's Point –' began Ellen, slightly thrown by the girl's manner.

'Would you like a room?'

'Actually, I was wondering whether I could use your fax machine. If you have one?'

'Of course.' The girl nodded and stepped back a few paces, pushing the door ajar. 'Mum!' she called through the gap. 'Is it all right if –'

She was cut off by a small, busty woman who marched in a businesslike way through the door, straightening the starched white collar beneath her bulky checked blazer. The woman had the same green eyes as the girl, but none of her feline grace. Her freckly cheeks were flushed and three parallel stress lines burrowed across her forehead. 'Don't shout, Verity,' she scolded in a hissed whisper, shooing the girl out of the way, before turning to Ellen. 'Welcome to the Grand Hotel, Shoresby,' she said, licking her fingers and vigorously flipping over pages of an oversized notebook on her side of the desk. 'How can I help?'

'She wants to use the fax machine,' mumbled Verity, her haughtiness now completely evaporating in front of her

34

mother. 'She's already explained. She's from a TV company.'

Verity's mother looked up, forgetting the notebook, her eyebrows rising with instant curiosity. Then she smiled and proffered her hand over the desk, as if Ellen were a long-lost relation, or a famous guest.

Ellen smiled back and avoided eye contact, her attention diverted by an old couple who were walking arm in arm down the stairs. They nodded good morning, but the woman ignored them, still gripping Ellen's hand.

Ellen was used to people mistakenly being impressed by her job title. When they found out she was a television director, they assumed that she could get them on to the small screen in an instant. She always found this slightly embarrassing and was ready with a spiel to dispel any ideas that her job was in any way glamorous. She certainly didn't feel glamorous right now.

'I'm the hotel manageress, Cheryl Driver,' said Verity's mother, introducing herself with a satisfied tut, as she finally let go of Ellen's hand. 'Cheryl with a sh, although I'm not very quiet,' she added with a self-deprecating laugh.

'Ellen Morris.'

'Mum,' Verity said, with forced patience and Ellen could hear the frustrated embarrassment in her tone.

'Shouldn't you be getting to school?' asked Cheryl, not turning round.

Ellen watched Verity push off the wall back towards the door. But for a split second her eyes met Ellen's and she smiled shyly.

'That's my daughter, Verity,' said Cheryl conspiratorially, darting her hawk eyes between Ellen and the door through which Verity had disappeared. 'She may seem surly, but

35

that's just her temperament. Oh yes,' she continued smugly, 'my Verity's quite something.'

Ellen nodded, as Cheryl lifted up the flap of the reception desk and walked through it towards her. 'Can I offer you some breakfast?' she asked.

At that moment Ellen realised that not only was she starving, but Cheryl's friendly offer was the first nice thing that had happened to her all morning. 'Thank you,' she said gratefully. 'That would be wonderful. You see, I've only just arrived.'

'Then you've come to the right place,' assured Cheryl. 'Let me tell you a little bit about the Grand.'

Chapter III

On the other side of the door, Verity tipped her head back against the wooden door and closed her eyes. She'd had her fixed metal braces removed the week before and she couldn't get used to the sensation of her unencumbered teeth as she bit down on her lips.

Why did her mother *always* have to do this? she thought, as she listened to Cheryl through the door. It was bad enough that she'd totally butted in when Verity had been just about to sort out the TV woman – Ellen – herself, but worse, her mother's whole manner was just so embarrassing.

Verity could hear through the door that Cheryl was trying to sell Ellen the benefits of staying at the Grand, reciting verbatim the bullet points on her latest amateurish home-produced pamphlet.

'And obviously here's the drawing room,' she heard her mother saying.

'Who plays the piano?' Verity could hear Ellen Morris ask.

'Oh . . . Verity. She's always been an exceptionally talented child.'

Child? Verity cringed. She wasn't a *child*. She'd just had her seventeenth birthday.

'She sings too. There's not one person in the whole town who won't tell you that she's got the voice of an angel.'

Stop quoting other people's CD sleeve notes, begged Verity silently, but her mother was on a roll.

'I mean there's so many talent programmes on the television nowadays – people signing up left, right and centre to become pop stars and there's no doubt in my mind that Verity would beat them hands down, but she won't enter. Well, you see, opera is more her forte, as well as the piano, obviously. I've told her that a talent like hers mustn't go to waste. It's so frustrating, but I try to encourage her rather than push her . . .'

Verity felt her stomach clenching up as she stared ahead at the dormant fax machine on the office shelves and thought about how her mother must look to someone as worldly and sophisticated as Ellen. Ellen was just the type of person Verity hoped that she'd turn out to be one day. She had that kind of confident ageless style that nobody had in Shoresby. Even her make-up looked classy and, despite the fact that Ellen was obviously so much older than her, Verity felt dejected at how far away she was from ever achieving anything like that kind of look.

Now, by the mere fact that she was related, Verity was bound to be tarred with the same small-town snobbery that her mother had perfected to an art form. Well, one thing was certain, she thought, darting through the small office door into the dining room, there was no way she was going to have any more embarrassing encounters this morning.

Slipping silently between the tables, which she'd laid up with fresh paper cloths only half an hour earlier, Verity could see that the breakfast on the long table remained more or less untouched, except for the cornflakes which the mad professor and his wife picked at like sparrows. Verity glanced in their direction. They were in the far corner at their usual table by the window near the fat sisters who were studying guidebooks and waiting to devour their daily fry-up. Even though there were several other diners, a couple of old men reading newspapers and a sad lady with an Agatha Christie novel, the only sound was the odd chink of cutlery on cheap china.

Ever since her parents had taken over the hotel six years ago and Verity had watched *The Shining*, she hadn't been able to shake the creepy feeling the guests gave her, especially off-season when all the oddballs and pensioners came to stay.

Why anyone would want to come to a dump like Shoresby in the first place was a mystery to Verity. Once the schools had gone back and the tourists had left, it was the dullest backwater she could imagine and she couldn't wait to get out. Anywhere would do, just so long as she didn't have to live with strangers any more.

Verity sped onwards, trying to keep her scorn for the guests from showing on her face. Some days she could ignore them, treating them as moving wallpaper in her home. On other days the polite institutional hush of the dining room made her want to scream. *Talk to each other*, she wanted to shout. *Make some noise. Live a little!*

But Verity kept quiet. She'd learnt long ago that it was better to keep her opinions to herself. It annoyed her mother more that way.

In a few seconds she'd reached the kitchen service door, which swished against its felt lining and she flattened her palms behind her on the door to still it.

In front of her – a world away from the pink-carpeted cleanliness of the restaurant – was the vast, cluttered kitchen. Above her, rows of giant pans hung down from the maze of clanking water pipes on the ceiling. A few dusty, dimpled, stainless-steel units lay unused in one half of the room. In the other half, vast wooden cupboards with wonky doors stretched along the walls to the cavernous sinks. On the back wall, beneath the windows dripping with condensation, rows of tomato plants flourished unseasonably and a feather danced in the thermal above the gas heater.

Yanos, the kitchen porter-cum-waiter, was wiping the grease from the edge of two giant plates, where the sausages, eggs and fried potatoes destined for the fat sisters were piled high on a sea of baked beans.

Behind him, at a huge stove, Verity's father, Russell, was whistling in a loud builder's tremolo in time with Tom Jones's song 'Delilah' on the radio, as he flipped over rashers of sizzling bacon in a pan. Off-season, he liked to cook breakfast for the guests himself, instead of paying Rudi, the chef, who was never at his best in the morning and Russell regularly referred to himself as Shoresby's fry-up king. As much as his wife's face betrayed the stress of their chosen profession, Russell's wrinkleless complexion failed to mask the inner boy inside him. He never took anything too seriously and was ready to play a practical joke at any second.

'Hang on, princess,' he said, stopping Verity on her path to the stairs in the corner. 'Breakfast coming right up.'

'I've already had toast, Dad.'

Russell Driver was in his late forties and had lost most of his hair on top, but what did remain was fixed in a rebellious curly ponytail at the nape of his neck. He'd once been the town's karate instructor, but despite having the tall, slight frame he'd passed on to his daughter, his metabolism had caught up with him lately and a large rotund belly stuck out over the top of his low-slung jeans. 'I heard you playing,' he said, as Verity stopped at the bottom of the stairs. 'Up early, weren't you?'

'I've got the exam coming up. Remember?'

Verity wanted to remind him that she didn't get up at the

crack of dawn by choice. It was just that it was the only time she could practise in peace when the guests were still asleep and she could be guaranteed some privacy.

'What do they want to test you on this time?' her father asked, reaching into the bread bin and plucking two pieces of economy white from the bag inside. 'Sounded perfect to me.'

Verity smiled wanly at her father. He wouldn't know the difference between Brahms and Beethoven if his life depended on it. His idea of music appreciation was rocking out with an air guitar to Dire Straits, or, more embarrassingly, dropping Pink Floyd lyrics into the conversation when he was trying to sound profound. She'd often got the feeling that even if she were to sit down and assault the piano keyboard with a mallet, her dad would still lead blindly enthusiastic applause.

'It's not perfect,' she said. 'At this rate, I'm not going to pass.'

Russell snorted and laughed loudly, as if she were joking.

'I've got to go, Dad,' Verity said. 'Treza will be here any minute.'

At that moment one of the old service bells rang in the kitchen. Verity and her father looked up at the ancient Victorian contraption above the service door and then back at each other. Even Yanos looked up in alarm.

The bells were hardly ever used, but Verity knew it could only mean that Cheryl was showing off to Ellen instead of walking through to the kitchen herself. She must be in her absolute worst Cheryl Driver, Grand Hotelier mode.

The service bell rang again, more impatiently, as Verity bounded up the first flight of corner stairs, which led up to the top of the hotel.

41

'But what about your butty?' called her father, holding up the bacon sandwich on a plate.

'You have it,' Verity replied. 'You know you want it,' she teased, bobbing her head down from the top of the stairs to see her father roll his eyes in mock frustration. He was just about to take a bite out of the sandwich when Verity saw her mother swooping into the kitchen from the other end.

'Ah, ah,' she chided, marching across and swiping the plate from her husband's hand. 'That'll do nicely for our new visitor, Ms Morris. Poor woman is famished. I rang for Verity. I think it would be very useful if they had a chat. She's a television director, Russell. She seems so professional and nice with it. That's the true mark of success . . .'

Verity didn't stay to hear any more, slipping away, up the carpeted stairs two at a time, past Eva and Katia, the chambermaids, and on to her bedroom.

Everyone in the town admired the front of the hotel and its uninterrupted view over North Beach, but Verity's room faced the opposite way. From her seventh-floor window in one of the old suites she'd been allowed to move into on her sixteenth birthday, she looked over the shiny corrugated air-conditioning pipes that snaked over the different levels of the hotel roof. Below her, across the asphalt polka-dotted with seagull droppings, she could see the abandoned chairs on the cast-iron fire escape that lay broken and tangled together as if they'd been in a fight. Then down into the hotel car park, where a family of stray cats lived among the cylindrical bins.

Beyond, over the old town walls where the drunks held court outside the amusement arcade, she could see the humped tops of the green buses in the bus station and, further on, the wide triangle of wasteland between the train tracks, where a group of travellers camped each summer.

Verity knew that people in school thought she was spoilt

living in a hotel suite, but none of them, apart from Treza, had seen the reality; that the room, with its shabby early Eighties floral decoration, was so vast and cold that in the winter months she could see her breath and the condensation froze in sheets on the inside of the windows at night.

But Verity didn't mind. She was as far away as possible from her parents and their claustrophobic flat next to the boiler room in the basement. Her mother regularly threatened Verity with her imminent incarceration back below stairs once Russell had magically transformed Verity's room into a honeymoon suite, but Verity knew she was safe. Firstly, the hotel was a financial sieve and there was no way her parents could afford to renovate the room properly and repair all the damage caused by the burst pipes a few winters ago. And secondly, no honeymooners came to Shoresby – only the odd hen and stag parties and her mother refused to have them in the hotel.

Despite all the space in her bedroom, Verity spent most of her time in the bathroom, where the MTV she could get on the oversized television in the bedroom was linked up to some surprisingly good speakers above the bath. It was only there, with the door locked, that she felt she had any privacy and could forget all the strangers doing the strange things that people did in hotels, in the rooms below her.

The bathroom window had a wide sill and she'd rigged up a kind of window seat there with several pillows and blankets. Verity liked to sit here at night, looking over the rooftops to where she could see a glimpse of the cliffs beyond North Beach. It was here that she wrote her diary and composed poetry, not that she would ever show anyone any of it. And it was here, now, that Verity found her mobile phone, which lay on the cushion.

Picking it up, she checked for text messages, but there was nothing new. She screwed up her nose with disappointment. She'd been hoping there'd be one from Treza, telling her when she'd left home. Until recently, they'd always walked to the bus stop together. But since Treza had started seeing Will, their morning journeys to school had become more and more infrequent until, in the last fortnight, they'd almost stopped altogether.

Verity picked up her diary, walked into the bedroom and knelt down by the stack of schoolbooks by her TV and video stand and dialled Treza's phone. Ripping open the Velcro strip on her bag and pulling up the top flap, she glanced at the photos of her and Treza inside the clear plastic pouch and ran her fingertip over the pictures of them both crammed into the booth in Woolworths.

Even with their heads pressed together and their tongues sticking out at the camera, they couldn't have been more different from each other looks-wise. Where Verity had dead-straight chestnut tresses, Treza had inherited her mother's Maltese looks and had a bob of tightly coiled jet-black ringlets. Verity was gangly and flat-chested with long legs and tiny hips, while Treza was short and curvy, and would never need clever bras.

But it was more than physical differences that separated them now.

Verity looked away from the photos. They were only taken in the summer, but it already seemed like years ago. She couldn't put her finger on when everything had started to change, but a few months ago she wouldn't have had to call Treza, she would have known what she was up to every second of the day. Now that was Will Macdonald's responsibility.

'Hi, there,' Treza answered breezily.

Even her voice sounded different these days, thought Verity bitterly. Of course, both Verity and Treza had been out with people before. But the boys they had dated had been just that: boys. None of them had been serious. Not like it was between Treza and Will. For one thing, Will had left school and had a job, which meant he had a car and money to go out with. And for another, Treza had – she'd confided in Verity only a few weeks before – *slept* with him. As in all the way.

All Verity had done was some heavy fumbling with Tim, her last ex whom she'd broken up with two months ago. It hadn't worked out on account of the fact that he was a terrible kisser and because Verity had refused to have sex with him. She was saving herself and she'd thought that Treza had been too. Except that now Treza had found the person she'd been saving herself for.

Verity was all too aware of this new gulf in opportunity and experience between her and Treza and, as a result, she couldn't help feeling immature and silly, as if somehow she'd been left behind. And she didn't want to be left behind. Not by her best friend.

'Hey. What's up?' Verity said, deliberately trying to sound normal. 'You nearly here, or what?'

'Not exactly . . .' said Treza. Verity could tell by the catch in her voice that Treza already had an excuse. 'It's just that Will wants to run in one of the cars . . .'

Verity sat back and hugged her knees as she listened to Treza enthuse about Will's latest two-seater that he was restoring in the classic car garage where he worked. Absent-mindedly, Verity gazed at the corner of the room where she'd set up a kettle and toaster on the side table. It would do for now, but one day she'd have a flat of her own and wouldn't that be bliss, she thought.

'Verity?' Treza sounded concerned and Verity realised she'd stopped listening and had been childishly chewing on the end of her plait, relieving the dull ache left over from where her teeth had been imprisoned.

'I'll see you there, then,' Verity said, immediately hating herself for sounding so stiff.

'You *do* mind. I knew you would,' said Treza, sounding upset.

Verity straightened up. She didn't want Treza's pity. 'I'm fine.'

'Look, look, it doesn't matter,' Treza hurried on. 'I'll get Will to drop me off at yours as usual. I'll see you in a minute –'

'No!' Verity interrupted, swinging round, so that her plait flipped over her shoulder. 'Don't be silly, Treze, you must go with him. Don't worry about me.'

Treza let out a hum of indecision.

'Seriously,' said Verity, meaning it.

'Are you sure. Sure sure sure sure sure?'

'You're my best friend. Now go go go go go! Have fun!'

Verity ended the call and stared at the phone, her false good humour dissipating into a disappointed sigh. Her comment about Treza being her best friend sounded hollow in her ears and she felt foolish for saying it.

None of this would matter if she had an older sophisticated boyfriend of her own, she thought miserably. But what chance did she have? She wasn't nearly as confident as Treza, or as pretty.

Slowly, Verity packed the rest of her books into her bag. There was no point in wishing for the impossible.

Verity's mood hadn't lightened as she headed up to the bus stop in town. She was still busy persuading herself that walking alone was fine after all, when she saw Jimmy Jones waving to her from the other side of the street and her heart sank even further. She put her head down, as if she hadn't seen him and hurried on.

She didn't want to talk to Jimmy, not that she'd ever really spoken to him before. He was in her English class and was always fairly quiet, but that was because he was probably stoned half the time. He hung out with Tara and those other dope-heads, and while he'd never done anything to spite her, she knew Tara made fun of her behind her back. Last summer, as she'd passed the Sapphire, she'd seen Tara doing a stupid impression of her singing the aria from the Puccini opera that had won Verity the school prize.

Jimmy's bike's front wheel was wobbling, as he caught up with her. 'Hi,' he said, jumping off his bike and falling into step beside her. 'Verity. So . . . how are you?'

He was grinning at her in a very strange way. She was so used to seeing him look bored that it took her by surprise. He was wearing the same grubby leather jacket he always wore, and his pink cheeks were dirty with stubble. He looked as if he were going out for the night, rather than to school. Maybe he was going to bunk off and wanted to butter her up to make an excuse for him. Maybe that was why he sounded so over-friendly. He probably thought she was some kind of soft touch with the teachers.

'I'm fine,' she said, walking quickly on.

'Going to school, then?' he asked, catching up with her almost immediately.

Verity threw him a sceptical glance. Of course she was going to school. What was he *on*? 'What does it look like?'

'I thought I could walk with you,' he said.

'But you've got a bike,' she pointed out. 'And I catch the bus.'

'I'll go with you to the bus stop, then. Do you always go this way?'

Why was he being so *weird*? 'Yes, Jimmy. This was the way to school last time I looked. I walk down the High Street to the bus stop. That's what people do when they catch the bus.'

They walked on in silence for a while until they rounded the corner by the churchyard.

'You were good in the play,' Jimmy said eventually, as if they'd been talking all the while.

Verity stopped and turned to him. 'That was last term.'

Jimmy shrugged. 'I know, but I haven't had time to say anything before. I haven't seen you,' he said, then stuttered on, 'I mean . . . I haven't seen you alone.'

Verity had seen Jimmy nearly every day since the school play, so why was he waiting until they were alone? They'd never been alone before. Not as far as she could remember.

Jimmy smiled and shrugged again. Even though he was squinting against the light, Verity could see now how blue his eyes were. He didn't look half so much of a drop-out when he smiled.

'I didn't think you were into that kind of thing,' she said, feeling guilty now for being so sarcastic a minute ago.

'I like plays. I could never act, though. I'm not confident . . . not like you are.'

'I'm not confident. I'm just used to it. If you're saying words you've learnt by heart, they're like a mask,' Verity replied. 'You can hide behind them.'

'Well, it doesn't come across that way.'

'Thanks,' she said, realising that this was the start of the first real conversation she'd ever had with Jimmy. Maybe there was more to him than she thought.

Suddenly he grinned, as if remembering something. 'I

thought you might like this,' he said, reaching inside his bag. He wobbled his head with embarrassment as he tried to extract something from the pocket inside. Eventually he pulled out a small carrier bag and handed it to her.

'What is it?' Verity took a step back, wondering if this was some practical joke, where she'd accept the bag and it would turn out to have something gross inside.

'Nothing much,' he said, shaking the slim package until she took it.

Verity didn't know what to say. She was about to open it when there was a loud roar and Denny Shapland sped past them down the road on his scrambler motorbike and pulled to an elaborate stop outside his surf shop, Wave Cave. Distracted, Verity stared down the road and craned her neck to get a clearer view of Denny.

Even though she saw him every few days on the way to school, Denny, who was without a doubt the best-looking guy in the whole town, never failed to rouse her interest. He had money and he had style – albeit of the designer surf bum variety. But at least he was fashion conscious and took care of himself.

Now there was an older and sophisticated man indeed, thought Verity, watching as he cocked his leg over his bike and took off his helmet. Despite the time of year, he had a deep tan and sun-streaked wavy brown hair. She watched as he stopped and ran his hand through his hair, before unlocking the door of his shop. Everything about him was just so . . . so cool, she thought, disappointed that he'd stepped out of sight.

Wrenching her attention away, realising that she'd been absorbed in taking in every detail of Denny's arrival, Verity turned back to Jimmy, noticing that she was still holding his package in her hand. But Jimmy had gone. Perplexed, Verity looked around, but there was no sign of him. How odd that he should just disappear and she hadn't even noticed.

Without bothering to open the bag, she stuffed it into her school bag and walked towards Denny's shop. She'd just had an idea and it was much more important than Jimmy Jones and his bizarre gifts.

Afterwards, Verity decided that fate moves in the strangest ways. While she was busy resenting Will for taking Treza to school in a sports car, all the time he was providing an amazing reason for Verity to be dawdling alone past the door of Denny's shop. Dawdling, that is, at the very moment that Denny turned the 'Closed' sign to 'Open' in the door and happened to look through the glass directly at her.

It was at that moment that everything changed for Verity. It was as if in that private moment when his eyes met hers, a whole new world opened. And, of course, there was the all-or-nothing smile she flashed at him. That couldn't have hurt either.

'Hi,' said Denny, lounging against the door frame, a curious grin on his face.

Verity nodded, the burst of confidence that had got her this far suddenly deserting her.

But Denny didn't seem to notice. Instead, he flicked his head to the dark interior behind him. 'Why don't you step inside, Verity? There's something I want to show you,' he said, before turning and walking away from her. But in spite of his apparent confidence that she would follow, Verity was rooted to the spot, thinking only that *he knew her name*.

Verity hadn't been in Denny's shop much. If fact, she could only recall being here once or twice, when Treza had encouraged her to push through the throng of teenage groupies who lurked around the door on a Saturday and step inside to browse the rails.

On those occasions Verity had spent her time glancing furtively at Denny to see what all the fuss was about, but she'd never actually spoken to him. She wasn't like the girls in her school who flounced around discussing the merits of Australian imported sweatshirts and competed with each other to get the latest funky gear at a discount from Denny's shop. Neither did she want anything to do with the crowd of boys who gathered to enthuse over extreme sports videos and wince in contented unison at the horrific wipe-outs.

Verity looked nervously up the street. She couldn't run away, not now. Not after he'd invited her in. For a split second she longed for Treza to be with her to do all the talking, but then she remembered where Treza was and stepped inside.

Denny had done up the shop like the inside of a cave and the walls were covered in stone effect cladding. Two large, expensive-looking televisions hung from the ceiling and carefully angled spotlights illuminated the circular racks of clothing below. This morning, though, the televisions were off and the pumping music, for which the shop had a bad reputation, was silent.

'Close the door, will you?' said Denny, rubbing his hands together. 'It's freezing out there.'

Verity smiled weakly and feebly pointed to the street. 'My bus will be here . . .' She fizzled out as her eyes met Denny's.

He was probably in his mid-twenties, but still young to be as successful and rich as he was. Leaning back against the glass counter with his arms folded across his lithe torso, he looked like a man totally at home. His Police sunglasses were pushed up into his hair and his cheeks were flushed from where he'd been riding the motorbike. Despite the time of year, he was wearing long surf shorts and his toned tanned calves were crossed as if he were casually leaning against some kind of Caribbean beach bar. MTV, was all Verity could think: he looked like a model off MTV.

What was she doing? This was crazy, she panicked, coming to her senses. Denny was way out of her league. She must be out of her mind.

But it was too late to run away now.

Forcing herself to be brave, Verity quickly pulled the door so that it clicked from its stopper. It closed behind her with a conspiratorial whisper, sealing her into Denny's world.

There was a moment of silence as Denny stared at her. Verity looked down at the carpet.

'I'm getting new stock in,' he said suddenly. In an animated turn, he pulled some glossy catalogues off a pile by the till and spread them open on the counter. 'I wanted to know what you thought.'

Wow! Verity wanted to gasp, but she knew it would make her sound pathetic and girlish, so instead, she tried to act nonplussed as she asked, 'Why me?'

'Well, you know, you're a girl and you've got good taste,' said Denny, flipping over some pages.

She waited for Denny to turn round and tell her he was joking, but he didn't, and Verity felt the adrenalin rush she got every time she sang in front of an audience without drying up.

It was almost as if she were watching herself from the corner of the room in slow motion, as she moved towards Denny. As she got closer, she could smell his musky after-shave. She looked at his profile, tracing the line of his immaculately manicured goatee beard and dreamily wondering what he'd be like to kiss.

'I've got to get my orders for the summer stock in. I was looking at beach wear,' Denny said, pushing the catalogue along to face her. 'What do you think?'

Verity could tell that her whole complexion was pulsing red, but Denny didn't seem to notice. On the contrary, he seemed totally serious and, realising he required an answer, Verity took the last couple of paces and stared down at the catalogues. 'Nice,' she mumbled, looking over the pictures of sun-drenched blondes draped over surfboards in cut-away swimming costumes.

'The thing is . . . you've just given me a fantastic idea. If I got some samples in stock, would you model them for me?' asked Denny.

Verity stiffened.

'I mean, nothing funny . . . all very tasteful. It'd be good to have some authentic pictures for my new website. . .' Denny stopped as he caught her embarrassed glance. He clicked his tongue over his bottom lip. 'That's a no, huh?' he said, as she stepped away from him. 'Your parents wouldn't be too pleased?'

'No, no,' said Verity quickly, 'it's not that.' Although that was most of the reason. She couldn't imagine what her mother would say if she found out that Verity was modelling bikinis. It was more to do with the fact that she couldn't imagine baring that much of her flesh in front of anyone, let alone Denny.

There was silence as Verity looked at her hands. She'd known all along that she was out of her depth and now she just felt like a fool. Her brain was telling her to run away, but her legs wouldn't obey her.

'I'm sorry,' Denny said, breaking the tension. 'Really. I mean we hardly know each other and I get you in here and ask you to model . . .' Denny let out an embarrassed laugh and made a spire out of his fingers over his mouth. 'What must you think? Look, forget it, OK? Forget I ever asked. Is that a deal?' he said, stooping to search out her eyes.

Verity nodded. She couldn't hold his gaze. Surely he could see that she was a sham. Why would Denny ever think that she was anything other than hopelessly naïve?

Denny closed the catalogue and rested his hand on the cover. There was a long pause.

Verity held her breath.

'You know, Verity,' he said. 'You shouldn't believe what everyone says about me.'

At that moment the waterfall feature that Denny had rigged up to gush over a line of surfboards at the back of the shop started with a gurgle. Verity jumped and Denny laughed. Embarrassed, she adjusted the strap on her bag.

'It's just that around here, people tend to pigeon-hole you, you know?' Denny continued.

She knew he had a reputation for hanging around all the tourist girls who came in the summer and everyone knew he was a bit of a show-off on a surfboard. He'd certainly been out with stacks of girls, but right now, with just the two of them together, none of that seemed to matter. 'I don't really listen to what people say, Denny,' she said, her voice catching.

'Good,' he said, as if deliberately lightening up, wiping away his vulnerable admission with a cheerful smile.

Verity smiled back.

'You know, I think you and I are quite similar,' he said. 'People look at you and see a successful, talented person and yet they don't see the real person underneath. They expect you to be this . . .' Denny rubbed his fingers in the air '. . . star all the time. In here it's my job to watch people,' he continued, tapping his temple. 'I have to tell how they're going to react . . . what they're going to buy, what their motivation is.'

'I hadn't thought of it like that before,' she said.

'I watch people. And sometimes I get to watch you as you come past here with that girl . . .'

'Treza.'

'Whatever. And I can tell just by looking at you that you're so much classier than all those other girls around here. It's the way you hold yourself. Your posture, your height. I mean, you're stunning and I bet you don't even realise it.'

'Don't,' Verity said, starting to blush.

Denny waved his hand in dismissal. He smiled reassuringly at her, as he deliberately tidied up the catalogues. Verity felt light with the implied respect in his little gesture and she could feel herself smiling at him. There was a pause.

'I'd better . . .' Verity pointed at the door and started towards it. She was acutely conscious that he was watching her. She was nearly at the door before she heard him laugh. She turned. 'What?'

He glanced down at his hands, shaking his head. 'I know it's a long shot,' he said, 'but . . . would you go out with me some time? Just you and me?'

Verity was so shocked that she finally lost her cool and gawped.

'Nothing heavy,' he went on, 'I mean . . . you probably already have a boyfriend and I don't want to tread on any toes –'

'No, no,' Verity blurted out. 'I'm not seeing anyone . . . right now.'

Denny grinned at her and even his eyes seemed to smile. 'Right,' he said, stroking his beard. 'Right. Well, um, how about this Saturday night?'

Verity grinned back and shrugged. 'OK. Saturday's fine.'

Verity stood on the pavement outside Denny's shop, feeling as if she'd just stepped out of a virtual reality ride. 'Wow!' she finally allowed herself to say out loud, before swinging her bag over her shoulder and setting off down the street in a run.

By the time she reached the bus stop – just in time to see the back of the bus disappearing into the distance – her head was pounding with so many implications of her meeting with Denny that she decided she didn't care whether Treza was with Will or not, she had to tell her what had happened.

Stopping, she crouched down and pulled open her bag to find her mobile phone. It was only then that she saw the carrier bag that Jimmy had given her. Unwrapping it, she found a home-made CD and turned it over in her hands. Why on earth would Jimmy Jones give her this? she wondered, checking the name of the R&B bands on the cover. It wasn't exactly the kind of music she expected him to be into.

She picked up her phone but, now she thought about it, decided she wouldn't call Treza. She was too excited and Treza was bound to put a damper on it. After all, Treza hadn't talked to Denny. She didn't know how different he was, how charming and how understanding. No, Verity thought, heading off to school on foot, she'd keep Denny Shapland to herself for the time being.

She was still grinning twenty minutes later as she walked up through the residential cottages towards the top of the hill. Even when a crazy-looking dog started barking furiously at her from behind a window, she didn't alter her pace, or stop grinning. Whoever said that dreams never came true?

Chapter IV

Ned Spencer woke to the frenzied barking of his half-mad, one-eyed collie dog. He groaned, picturing the delinquent animal cheerfully battering himself against the cottage's bay window downstairs, no doubt intent on terrifying some hapless passer-by to death. 'Shut up!'

It would have been a scream, but with his face wedged into the pillow, Ned's words came out muffled. Not that it mattered: they'd been more of a plea than a command. Ned knew his limitations in relation to the dog. He was aware that even if he'd shouted at the top of his voice, he would have been ignored. Because as well as having been blind in one eye since birth, the dog had developed Ned-orientated deafness in both ears since.

Wobbles, as in *collie*-wobbles (Ned's daughter's idea), was two years old. Working on a ratio of seven to one, this made him an adolescent in canine years, Ned had calculated, thereby explaining the creature's current anti-authoritarian streak. It was a phase Wobbles was going through, Ned was convinced. The barking, the battering, the drooling and the occasional leg-humping were all symptoms which he'd shed as soon as he exited his doggy-teens and became a mature and responsible member of society. Which let Ned off the hook of dealing with the problem now.

As the barking continued, and the smog of his hangover began to dissipate, Ned concentrated instead on what the day ahead held in store for him. He had to be up at

Appleforth House to supervise a delivery of flagstones and their accompanying black slate insets at eleven (the supplier had already delivered the wrong sizes once). But that aside, he could think of no pressing reason to be at the building site any time sooner. And should such a reason have slipped his mind, he knew that Dan, his foreman and right-hand man, was more than capable of taking over, as well as keeping Ned's small army of plasterers, plumbers and electricians busy at their allotted tasks.

Which meant Ned had time for a shave and a shower and a bite to eat. Which meant he could then start his working day with a clear head. Which went some way to alleviating his guilt over having nursed himself to sleep with whisky and cigarettes the night before.

Releasing the pillow round which his arms had been wrapped all night, Ned rolled over on to his side and propped himself up on one elbow. He blinked and rubbed his eyes, the bedroom still a blur without his glasses. Then he blinked again, more purposefully this time, suddenly aware that he wasn't alone.

The creature at the end of the cast-iron bed stared back at him – *through* him, it felt like. Its eyes were wells of unfathomable blackness. The flesh on its forehead and jaw was streaked with lugubrious lines of congealed blood which, even as Ned watched, appeared to ooze and slide down its face, before settling into a slick of gory and macabre drool on its chin. Yellow warts patterned its cheekbones and stalks of rhubarb branched outwards from its tangled mess of blonde hair.

'Rhubarb?' Ned muttered aloud.

He fumbled for and finally retrieved his round wire-framed glasses from where he'd hooked them over the bedpost the night before. As he slipped them on, the room shifted into focus with a jarring violence, which made his dark-brown eyes ache.

Blinking once, then twice, he leant forward over the crumpled duvet and examined the creature again. But he hadn't been mistaken the first time: the red protrusions – four of them, to be precise – were most definitely plants of a type more likely to be found covered in custard than sprouting from a satanic scalp. And there, come to think of it, didn't those warts bear an uncanny resemblance to Rice Krispies? And wasn't that blood's consistency reminiscent of Heinz tomato ketchup, and those dark bags beneath the eyes the exact same texture as Marmite?

'Boo!' the creature shrieked, before collapsing into a fit of giggles and ducking out of sight.

Ned lay back and gazed up at the skylight in the white ceiling. He smiled. He loved his daughter with all his heart. Even now, when by rights he should be grouching around the place like a bear with a sore head, Clara's very presence warmed him, like a burst of bright sunlight on a cold winter's day.

'Help!' he croaked, his voice reverberating around his skull. 'The Bogeyman's come to get me!'

'Not the Bogeyman, silly,' Clara chastised him, resurfacing at Ned's end of the bed. 'The monster Messooder,' she explained, waggling her head at him so that the rhubarb stalks swayed from side to side, causing the mass of Sellotape holding them there to crackle like static.

'Ah,' Ned said, finally understanding their relevance.

He'd shown his five-year-old daughter a picture of Medusa, the snake-haired monster slain by Perseus, in an illustrated book of Greek mythology the night before. Ned read to Clara every night he could. Lying on the bed beside her, looking at the pictures and slowly turning the pages, he

59

watched her succumbing to the illusion of it all, to the clear story book division between right and wrong, and to the inevitability of a happy ending every time. He watched her and he envied her, but could never feel the same himself.

'Where's Debs?' Ned asked.

'Downstairs,' Clara answered. 'She told me to come and see you. Because she says she can't believe the mess I've made in the kitchen. And because she's gone to have a bath.'

'I see,' said Ned, also seeing that the parental buck stopped here.

Adjusting his pillow behind him, he leant back against the bedhead and picked up the pint glass of water from his bedside table. He was aware of Clara watching him as he drank, her head cocking gradually and subconsciously to one side, as if mimicking the tilt of the glass.

'You look poorly,' she commented suddenly, gazing up at him.

And feel it, too, he thought, retorting aloud instead, 'And you smell of Marmite. Which', he added, putting the empty glass back down, 'is very good news, seeing as I'm going to have to eat you.'

Clara's jaw dropped in surprise. 'Eat me?' she checked.

'Eat you,' Ned confirmed.

Her eyes narrowed. 'But why?'

'Because I'm a dad and any monster I meet, I eat. Otherwise', he explained, 'they might scare my daughter. And I can't have that.'

'But I *am* your daughter,' she declared.

Ned ran his fingers through his short fair hair. 'No,' he said, 'you couldn't possibly be my daughter Clara.'

'But why?'

'Because she's ever so pretty. But you: you're all covered in gunk and goo.'

'But Dad!' Clara wailed. Then an idea struck her. 'What if I go and wash it all off?' she asked.

'What?' he checked. 'Every last bit?'

She nodded her head furiously. 'Yes.'

Ned stroked his chin. 'Well,' he contemplated aloud, 'I suppose that if you did that then, instead of having Messooder for my breakfast, I'd have to have . . . oh, I don't know . . . toast?'

'Brilliant!' Clara exclaimed, kissing her father hard on the cheek to seal the bargain, before spinning on her heels and running for the door.

Ned exhaled as he watched her go, feeling like an inexperienced actor who'd just scraped through a tricky audition. He touched the sticky residue of ketchup she'd smeared across his jaw and sighed.

As with Wobbles, so with Clara: discipline wasn't exactly his speciality. He considered himself better suited to the more collaborative aspects of his daughter's upbringing: like dishing out pocket money, and building sandcastles with her down on the beach, and treating her to fish and chips and ice creams on the way back home – or 'the fun stuff', as Debs liked to call it.

The other stuff – the bad cop stuff, as he still couldn't help thinking of it, in spite of his thirty-six years – he tended to leave to Debs. This included all things confrontational: the regulation and management of table manners, television, bedtimes, bath times, mealtimes, tantrums and sulks. To name but a few.

Ned was determined to remain Clara's friend, not her foe. He wanted to be there for her throughout her life, always available and always accessible. He never wanted her to feel she couldn't talk to him or that when she did he wouldn't listen. The way he saw it, life was too short and too important for it to be any other way.

61

Getting out of bed, Ned stepped over the decapitated head of a furry toy rabbit which Wobbles had deposited in a pool of dog slobber at the foot of the wardrobe. He walked to the window and gazed idly out, watching the slate-grey clouds sweeping across the sky, but picturing in his mind's eye his snug Cheltenham house and the people he knew there.

He thought fleetingly about the personal belongings he'd put into storage when he'd rented out his Cheltenham home and moved here to Shoresby last year: his CDs and his DVDs, his books, his photographs, his paintings and his precious architectural drawings. He hadn't expected the Appleforth House project to take this long (already over a year), but the more it went on, the less Ned missed his possessions and the less he missed his friends.

In two more months, though, three at most, his work up at Appleforth House would be done and he'd be out of this rented cottage, and Clara would be out of her temporary school. They'd return to Cheltenham and then everything would become permanent again, inescapable and smothering. He'd be claimed once more by his old life, swamped by all the reminders of his past, which he'd left behind him without regret.

Ned turned round and faced the room. Paracetamol, that's what he needed now. Paracetamol, a cold shower and some food. And then he could get on with the rest of his day.

Forty-five minutes later – having dropped Clara off at school and Debs down at the shops – Ned stepped off the wind-racked High Street and into the warmth of the Jackpot Café.

Ned had worked on enough properties around the country to know that the Jackpot was nothing special. It could have been anywhere, on any street in any town in England, Ireland, Scotland or Wales. The blackboard menu above the service counter was the same, with the same specials chalked up at the same low prices. The tea was always weak and the coffee always stale, the radio was always loud and the counter always greasy. But it didn't bother Ned. The service was quick, the food freshly cooked and he didn't plan to eat it in here anyway.

'Hi, Ned,' said the twenty-something red-haired girl behind the counter as he walked up to her. Keeping her elbows resting on the tabloid she'd been reading, she cupped her pale, freckled face in her hands and flashed him a smile.

'Hi . . .' Lucy? Katie? Emma? Ned flicked through the possibilities in his mind. She'd told him her name a couple of weeks ago, the same morning she'd asked him what his star sign was and read him his horoscope, and informed him that the two of them were an ideal astrological match. Emma, he thought Emma, but he wasn't sure enough. 'How are you?' he settled for instead.

'Aching,' she said, rolling the sleeve of her grey woollen top up over her elbow to expose her toned forearm. 'Yoga,' she explained. 'How about you?' she asked. 'How's work going up at the old house?'

'OK.' Ned wasn't surprised she knew where he worked, even though he hadn't told her himself. A lot of townspeople, especially the shopkeepers, had an interest in the work Ned was overseeing up at the Appleforth place, what with its history being pivotal to the tourist trade and, of course, the fact that a lot of the workers Ned had employed spent time and money down here in the town.

'Let me guess,' Lucy-Katie-Emma said. 'One scrambled egg and bacon roll and one tea, milk no sugar . . .' Again, she shot him that smile. 'Because you're sweet enough as it is . . .'

Ned nodded, embarrassed by the attention. He knew she liked him, in the same way that he knew she was pretty. But that's all it remained: knowledge, facts. He couldn't seem to engage beyond that. He couldn't even remember the last time he'd met someone new and felt anything even close to desire. He smiled briefly at the girl now before looking away, out of the half-steamed window and on to the deserted street outside. He caught a glimpse of her reflection in the window as she cracked eggs over a bowl and whisked them with a fork, but he didn't turn round.

His phone buzzed and he checked it for messages. There were a couple of work-related texts, which he left for later. Then there was one from his mother, asking him if he wanted to spend the weekend with her and his father at their holiday cottage in West Wales in two weeks' time. He keyed her back that he was too busy, partly because it was true and partly because he'd only just seen them both last month. He'd already agreed to spend Christmas with them as it was (it had been his parents-in-law's turn last year), so it wasn't like they were being deprived of Clara's company or anything. And although he knew they wanted to see him, too, he liked to keep his own life as separate as he could.

It wasn't that he didn't love them; he did. It was just that he found their constant worrying over his, Debs's and Clara's wellbeing undermining. He wasn't a kid any more. He'd rejected that precious only child image a long time ago. All he wanted now was to be left to make his own decisions about his own life.

A few minutes later he was leaning up against the Jackpot's external red-brick wall, tucking into his roll and swigging down his tea from a warm polystyrene cup.

Weather allowing, whenever he visited the café he always ate his food out here. There was something curiously intransigent about it that appealed to him, like he could have been anyone, a traveller passing through, with no particular place to go and no particular responsibilities awaiting him when he got there.

All of which couldn't have been further from the truth, as Ned was actually here in Shoresby because of the largest commission he and the company he owned had ever taken on.

STAR (Spencer & Thomas Architectural Rejuvenation) had been up and running for the best part of a decade now, renovating and restoring architectural oddities from Martello towers to Regency follies, as well as performing interior design make-overs on Belgravia terraced houses and other more common period properties.

But none of these projects had come close in either scale, difficulty or sheer remuneration to the restoration of Appleforth House, which Ned was currently supervising.

The owner of the Appleforth Estate, and the man Ned had flown out to Salem, Massachusetts two years ago to see, was a Mr Jonathan Arthur. He was a fast-food baron in his late sixties, who'd decided to take an interest in his ancestral home, buying back the site and the surrounding land piece by piece, with a view to having the manor house and grounds rebuilt and restored in a faithful historical manner. Jonathan Arthur wanted to retire here to England, a country he'd never lived in, but had every intention of dying in – and he wanted Ned Spencer to make it possible.

Ned couldn't relate to Jonathan Arthur's desire to relocate in this way. He found it sentimental, ridiculous even. But from an architectural point of view, the further Mr Arthur had gone into the problems that would need to be surmounted before the move was possible, the more intrigued Ned had become. Quite simply, Ned had soon suspected, this could prove to be the greatest professional challenge of his life.

Appleforth House, Mr Arthur had explained, had been burnt down in 1871 by his great-uncle, a wealthy tea trader named Alexander Walpole, who'd intentionally incinerated himself in the process.

Overwhelming grief, Jonathan Arthur had put this cataclysmic event down to: earlier in that year, Walpole's daughter, Caroline, had committed suicide by hurling herself off a cliff at the edge of the estate's grounds.

The manor house had been left to ruin over the last century, then, as Ned had discovered on his first visit to the site a few weeks later. Following the fire, what had been left of the property had been boarded up and left to nature. Ivy had snaked through its brickwork and colonised its windows and doorways. Its interior had degenerated into a dank, labyrinthine garden of collapsed staircases and rotted beams, and its gardens had reverted to wilderness. Whole segments of the house's walls had been appropriated by local farmers for use in their outbuildings, and entire garden follies – well documented in the paperwork Jonathan Arthur had provided Ned with – had disappeared altogether.

Ned had been dismissive of the Walpoles' story, left cold by the human drama that had been responsible for Appleforth House's demise. Chances were, in his opinion, it had been a Tourist Board invention anyway, or at the very best an exaggeration of a far less romantic and intriguing truth. But he'd fallen in love with the remains of the Georgian building the moment he'd seen them.

Armed with the house's original plans, as well as a

number of artist's sketches collected by Jonathan Arthur, Ned had visualised Appleforth House as it could be, not how it had become. He'd pictured its Ionic columns restored to their original grandeur, its façade reverted to its white neoclassical glory. He'd imagined its porticoes standing proud once more, its double-pitched roof newly tiled and its wrought-iron verandah slick with fresh paint.

He'd seen all this and so much more, and he'd determined there and then to convert this vision into reality. He'd make it his labour of love and through it he'd carve his mark indelibly upon the landscape. With every ounce of care, skill and determination at his disposal, he'd vowed to restore this Appleforth House to life.

And that's exactly what he'd gone on to do. He'd spent the last eighteen months researching, restoring and rebuilding. He'd buried his head in the past, hunting out skilled labour and master craftsmen, tracking down materials, sifting through architectural salvage and reclamation yards, as well as commissioning reproduction materials wherever the original couldn't be found. He'd loved every second of it.

And now that he'd successfully reconstructed the building's skeleton, he was in the process of reproducing its innards and making the house a fit home for his absurdly wealthy client to retire to.

Licking his lips, Ned chucked the teacup and paper napkin into the bin, then turned up the collar of his brown corduroy jacket – the same article of clothing with leather patches on the elbows which Debs invariably referred to as his English teacher jacket, and which Wobbles liked to think of as an inanimate yet strangely attractive member of his own species.

The dog was sitting at Ned's feet, tied to a lamp-post, and

was cocking his head suggestively across the road at the steps that led down to the beach, and swishing his tail across Ned's scuffed steel-toe-capped Doc Martens work boots.

'Keep that up for an hour,' Ned told the dog, 'and you might even get a shine out of them.'

Wobbles let out a whimper of anticipation at the attention, his eyes flicking beachwards and back, in case Ned still hadn't got the message.

'All right, all right,' Ned told him.

Ned waited for a car to pass before allowing Wobbles to drag him across the road. The dog knew where they were going just as well as Ned and, as they approached the top of the steps to the beach, Ned leant down and unhooked the leash from his collar. 'Off you go,' he said.

But instead of darting for the steps, as he did every morning, the collie took a single step forward, before stopping dead in his tracks and starting to growl.

'What's up?' Ned asked, but the dog's only response was to shift his growl down into an even more menacing key.

In search of an explanation, Ned's eyes followed the line of sight that ran between Wobbles's quivering tail and his outstretched snout: eastwards along the High Street. But there was no one there.

Or, hang on – Ned squinted through his glasses – no, there *was* somebody, maybe forty yards away, just coming out of the Grand Hotel. And there was no doubt about it: it was definitely this person who'd caught Wobbles's one good eye.

Ned couldn't understand it. OK, so Wobbles liked to bark at people. He liked to chase the odd car. But at heart he was a coward. He only ever barked from behind the safety of a glass window. He only chased cars which were already driving away from him. Apart from his pathological penchant for ripping out the fluffy guts of furry toys, he was about as vicious as a gerbil.

Edging towards the animal, with the intention of slipping his leash back on, Ned watched as the figure on the High Street walked towards him, coming increasingly into focus with each step. It was a man, Ned decided. No, he corrected himself, it was a woman . . . a tall woman . . . with short blonde hair . . . a tall woman, with short blonde hair . . . dressed in a . . .

'Oh, shit,' Ned gulped. But even though he'd guessed what Wobbles was about to do a split second before Wobbles actually did it, he still didn't have enough time to prevent it from happening.

As Ned's hand swiped at thin air, Wobbles bolted clear across the road, narrowly avoiding being mown down by a motorbike in the process.

'Come back!' Ned yelled, giving chase. 'Now!'

But it was no use. Wobbles had the woman in his sights. Or, more specifically, the woman's fur coat: for Ned was in no doubt *that* was what the dog was after. Fur . . . be it part of a toy rabbit, or an article of clothing . . . it made no difference to Wobbles. Fur was there for one reason only: to be chewed. And nothing, it seemed, was going to keep Wobbles from his mission. Gone was the cute domestic pet of only seconds before. He'd now transformed into a hunter-gatherer of most singular determination.

Ned looked on with a mixture of growing horror and proprietary admiration as the collie closed on the woman with the speed of a prizewinning greyhound, before hurling himself at her with a final bark of primeval intent, and knocking her back with a thud against the Lloyds Bank cash-dispensing machine.

By the time Ned reached them, Wobbles had sunk his

teeth into the hem of the woman's coat and was standing on his hind legs, flick-flacking from side to side like a great hairy fish on the end of a line.

Ned didn't have time to take in the woman's face. A flash of white teeth, a swish of blonde hair, and then his attention was back on the dog. 'Let go!' he commanded. He dropped to his knees at the woman's feet and made a desperate lunge for Wobbles's collar.

'Get him off!' the woman shouted.

But Wobbles wasn't listening to either his master's voice or hers. Wobbles was a dog obsessed, concerned only with keeping his teeth embedded in the woman's fur coat and snarling for all he was worth.

'Get him off me now!' the woman was shouting down at Ned. 'Or I'll –'

But Ned never did get to hear the woman complete her threat, because she decided to carry it out instead. Clawing her fingers into Ned's hair for support, she kicked out at the dog . . . and promptly missed, overbalancing and bringing both Ned and Wobbles crashing down on top of her.

Wobbles – probably, Ned guessed, because he had more legs to work with – was the first to extricate himself from the scrabbling, growling, swearing tangle of limbs that followed. He signalled his departure from the fray with a growl and a rip.

And it was than that Ned found himself staring into the woman's shining hazel eyes, bewitched. The moment was dreamlike, calm. Ned felt as though his heart had stopped beating, as though – so long as he didn't move or breathe – the moment could and would last for ever.

Then the woman's eyes flickered fractionally and his did the same, taking in her other features: her small, slightly upturned nose, with her nostrils flaring as she continued to

70

get her breath back; her smooth skin, burning with exertion; and her lips, half-parted. . .

'I'm so s—' Ned started to say, but even such a tiny instance of movement as opening his mouth to speak had caused them to touch, his nose brushing against hers.

'You're sorry?' she cut in. 'Good. Now would you mind getting the hell off me?'

He stared at her in confusion.

'Do it!' she snapped.

It was only then that Ned became aware of her body beneath his and realised that they were still lying on the floor. He scrabbled quickly to his feet.

'Here,' he said, reaching down to help her. 'Let me.'

She ignored him. Slowly – and with a considerable amount of elegance, Ned thought, considering the circumstances – she stood. Then she glared down the High Street at Wobbles, who was prancing in delight outside the Postcards From the Edge gift shop, tossing a ripped piece of fur coat triumphantly into the air.

'He's not normally like that,' Ned started to explain, noticing that the woman was as tall as him and that the cut of her blonde hair added a severity to her face that hadn't been there a moment ago.

'That creature should be in a muzzle,' she said.

'He was only playing,' Ned apologised.

The woman stared at him, stupefied. 'He practically skinned me alive.'

'Oh, come on. It's not like he bit you or anything.'

'No?' She tugged at her coat, holding the torn hem out before her like an exhibit in a murder trial. 'What's that, then?'

'It's only a coat,' Ned gently protested. 'It's not you. It's not the same thing at all. Listen, why don't we –' He'd

71

been about to suggest that they go for a coffee to talk this over like rational human beings, since for some reason drinking coffee with her suddenly seemed like the thing to do.

But the woman had other ideas. '*Only* a coat.' She repeated his words slowly, as if she were giving him time to take them back or correct her if she'd misquoted him. 'This isn't *only* a coat, you imbecile,' she then went on. 'This is a *Donna bloody Karan*. Which happens to have cost me over a month's salary. A sum which, I might add, I'm holding you *entirely* responsible for!'

Ned wasn't good at being shouted at. Like his daughter and his dog, he had a problem with authority. But if there was one thing he liked even less than being shouted at, it was being shouted at in public.

He glared back at the woman. What the hell had he been thinking of, nearly asking her out for a coffee? What temporary madness had gripped him there? So she was a looker . . . so what? And as for finding her *bewitching*? Well, he'd got the witch bit right. 'The only reason', he stated, 'that your Donna bloody Karan's bloody ripped at all is because you bloody well fell over when you tried to kick my bloody dog.'

'Don't you try and turn this round on me,' she warned. 'It's your animal that did it and *you*'re to blame.'

'Well, what do you expect?' he snapped back at her. 'Going around dressed up like that in some dead animal's skin? Act like Cruella de Ville and you should expect to be treated like her.'

'It's fake, actually,' she informed him, before pulling a notepad and pen from her pocket. 'Name?' she demanded.

'What?' he jeered. 'So that you can report me to the police and have Wobbles put down? Forget it.'

She didn't even blink. 'You owe me the cost of this coat,' she said.

'So sue me,' he replied, turning his back on her and marching away.

She yelled something after him, but whatever it was, the wind destroyed its sense. Big deal, Ned thought, as he reached Wobbles and slipped him back on to his leash, wrestling the piece of fake fur from the dog's mouth and stuffing it into his coat pocket. She could shout at him as much as she damn well liked, because as far as he was concerned, there was *nothing* she had to say that he wanted to hear.

Chapter V

The William Bentley Hospice in which Jimmy's gran was dying was on the other side of Shoresby from her flat in Carlton Court, and Jimmy biked straight there after his History lesson on Wednesday afternoon.

It was an ugly granite slab of a building, overgrown with ivy and facing out across North Beach, looking like nothing more than what it truly was: a mausoleum, a place people entered when the living world was done with them.

Either side of it, stretching over the brow of the hill, were row upon row of pensioners' bungalows. Jimmy had got stoned here one night with Ryan and they'd counted the squat rectangular buildings in the dark. Jimmy remembered how sad he'd ended up feeling that the ghoulish blue light of a TV set had been flickering on and off in every single one. Depressing, that's how it had struck him, all those people choosing to sit in on their own at night, surrounded by neighbours doing exactly the same thing, none of them wanting to talk.

Ryan, though, he'd just reckoned it made sense to put all the worn-out city folk next to the hospice where, chances were, they'd end up anyhow. 'Saves on ambulance petrol, doesn't it?' he'd pointed out.

Jimmy left his bike out in the car park, beside the frost-pocked flower beds, not bothering to padlock it, knowing that this was no Cuckoo's Nest and that no manic Jack Nicholson would be breaking out of here on the lookout for transport today or any other day. There was no hope here. You entered in a wheelchair and you exited in a box.

Jimmy headed inside, signed in at the desk, passing the time of day with the duty nurse, before setting off on autopilot through the familiar maze of spartan corridors and shining, polished stairs to his gran's room.

Cancer, Jimmy thought as he walked, always cancer. It ran in the family, in the town. Sometimes he wondered if it was something in the water, some heavy metal leak from the nuclear power station down the coast. Mum in 1986, not even a memory for him there, just some old photos and a letter she'd written him the week she'd passed away, telling him she'd always love him and would always be watching over him. Like an angel, she'd said.

Next, of course, had come his gran. Jimmy had been there when Dr Kennedy had explained to her that she had leukaemia. She'd still been in the flat at the time, on familiar ground, but this new thing, this disease that had invaded her blood, it had only confused her. It hadn't even been something she'd been able to pronounce, let alone comprehend.

Jimmy didn't bother knocking on the door, just went inside instead. His gran – snared in a bad dream – was breathing heavily and sounded like she was running for her life. That's how he remembered her: always in motion, never still. Until she'd got sick, he couldn't recall a single morning when she'd slept in past seven, or an evening that she'd spent vegetating in front of the TV.

The unkempt plumes of white hair on her scalp looked exactly the same as on his last visit, as if in all that time she hadn't moved an inch. Only the flowers on her bedside table were different: chrysanthemums, splashes of yellow and purple against the otherwise white canvas of the room.

Rachel had picked them up from the garage the day before, but still they failed to hide the reek of chemicals.

Jimmy kissed his gran on the cheek, before settling himself down on the chair next to the bed and taking her hand in his. She twitched in her sleep at the contact and momentarily opened her rheumy eyes, staring past him at the ceiling, before returning to her dreams. Her breathing became more peaceful and Jimmy hoped she'd seen him and that a snapshot of him now drifted through the fog of her mind, bringing her comfort.

Her skin was drawn tightly now across her cheeks, and the healthy flush vanquished from her once well-rounded face. Her eyes were sunken, no longer sharp. But even these changes couldn't hide the essential kindness of her features.

Jimmy found it so easy to see past her as she was this instant and remember her as she used to be. A late summer afternoon stuck out now, when Jimmy had been eight and his gran had just turned seventy. They'd spent it walking across North Beach together, looking for pretty shells to put in the clear glass jars she'd kept on the bathroom shelf. Then they'd kicked off their shoes and walked into the shallows to skim stones.

Her clothes had always been clean and tidy. She'd been dressed in a blue short-sleeved shirt and pleated lilac trousers. Her hair still had streaks of black in it then, mixed in with the grey, and she'd worn it in a bob. They'd stood there side by side, throwing stone after stone, her with her trousers rolled up and him in shorts, with their sandals and trainers respectively lined up behind them.

'Feels nice, doesn't it?' she'd commented, gazing down at the shimmering water, as a wave had pulled back across their feet, returning to the sea and sucking the sand out from beneath their wriggling toes. 'It makes you feel like you're really part of the planet.'

He'd planted his feet further apart and had crouched down low before unleashing a smooth round pebble across the flat sea surface.

'Seven,' his gran had then announced, counting the bounces. 'Not bad.'

She'd crouched down, too, and had released a stone of her own.

Jimmy had taken his turn in performing the arithmetic. 'Five,' he'd said. It had been the first throw she'd lost.

'Either I'm getting old,' she'd said, 'or you're getting better . . .'

'Probably both, Gran,' he'd replied.

Something about his answer had amused her and she'd turned to him and smiled. 'You could well be right.'

He'd watched her bright grey eyes moving quickly over his face, inspecting every millimetre of his skin. 'Don't, Gran,' he'd said.

'Don't what?'

He'd shrugged at her awkwardly. 'That. Looking . . . you know?'

She'd laughed. 'And why ever not?' she'd asked. 'You're a beautiful boy and you're much too young to be self-conscious.'

'What does that mean?'

Her eyes had narrowed in concentration. 'It means worrying about old women looking at you.'

He'd scrutinised her in return. 'You're not old, Gran,' he'd then decided. 'I mean you are, but you're not, if you know what I mean.'

She'd laughed, a light and airy sound, which had soon been lost in the breeze. 'I'm not altogether sure I do,' she'd said.

'We-ell . . .' – he'd searched for the words to explain – 'you look older than my friends' mums, but you don't act it. Like, you'd never catch them down here skimming stones, because they're all much too boring for that.'

'Perhaps they just don't like skimming stones,' his gran had suggested, before loosing another stone on cue.

'Nine,' Jimmy had scored.

'Or perhaps they're just not as good as I am,' she'd added.

He'd glanced at her and had seen that she was smiling again. 'Why *do* you look at me that way sometimes, Gran?' he'd asked.

Quickly, she'd pulled a face at him. 'Like this?'

He'd pushed her playfully. 'No, like you were a minute ago. Like you're checking I'm all here . . .'

She'd nodded her head, as if to herself. 'Because, Jimmy Jones, you're changing faster than you could ever guess. And I sometimes worry that if I don't watch you carefully, then one day I'll turn round and you'll have grown up and I won't remember how it happened or how you once were.'

'You'll remember, Gran. The same way you remember stories.'

His gran had had a phenomenal memory. She'd known about fifty bedtime stories word perfect. Her and her friend Arnie had always won the pub general knowledge quiz at the Lewis Arms and all Arnie had ever had to do had been to buy the rounds while Jimmy's gran had filled in the answers.

'I know,' she'd said. 'But it's just in case I don't.'

He'd thought about this for a few seconds. 'In that case it's OK,' he'd said.

'What is?' she'd asked.

'You looking at me. If you want to, you can. I won't mind.'

She'd bowed to him. 'Thank you.'

'You know all those other mums I was talking about . . .' Jimmy had then said.

'What about them?'

'None of them are as good as you at anything, including throwing stones.'

His gran had slipped her arm round him then and had squeezed him in close. 'Come on,' she'd said, turning them about and staring across the beach where only a few holidaymakers had still remained. 'Let's make our way home, because I don't think today can get any better.'

Jimmy watched her sleeping now, here in the hospice room, and hoped she could remember it all. He'd give anything to make her well again.

He started to tell her about his day, about getting an 'A' in his *Macbeth* essay, but only scraping a 'C' in his History spot test. He told her about Rachel getting drunk the night before and crying because she was missing Jimmy's dad so much. But it wasn't this he really wanted to tell his gran about at all.

'There's a girl,' he finally admitted, watching the dark gather in around the window like a cloak. 'She's buff,' he began. 'Beautiful,' he hurriedly corrected himself. 'Her hair's . . .'

But hair colour, and height, and all of Verity Driver's other physical attributes . . . none of them came close to summarising how Jimmy actually *felt* about her. Because Verity, to Jimmy, was all about change. She was about dreams and endless possibilities. She was about a limitless future, as wide and as unpredictable as the sea. She was everything his land-locked here and now was not.

He started to tell his gran about his failed attempt to ask Verity out the day before yesterday on the way to school

79

instead. 'I made a right arse of myself,' he confessed, not because he knew she wasn't really listening, but because his gran had never been averse to a bit of swearing herself in her time.

Gran would like Verity, he went on. She'd like the way Verity woke stunned sometimes from her daydreams in class, and stared around like she couldn't quite believe the classroom was real, or like she'd just woken up on an alien planet. 'The same as you do here, Gran,' he said. 'There's a hidden world behind those eyelids that you can't help wanting to explore.'

And Gran would like the sound of Verity's voice, the way people listened to her whenever she read in class or school assembly, and the way people fell silent whenever she sang. 'Her voice is so sweet, Gran,' he told her. 'I could hear it all day long and never get bored.' Jimmy squeezed his gran's hand harder. 'Then I messed it up,' he concluded. 'I chickened out when it counted the most.'

But he didn't get a reply. All he heard was the laboured sound of his gran breathing.

Rage boiled up inside Jimmy as he walked back down to his bike. What was wrong with this world? he wanted to shout. So much shit happened to the wrong people. And now it had happened to his gran. Like it hadn't been enough for her to have been losing her marbles, the way she had been these last two years before the hospice had taken her in. Like it hadn't been sufficient for her to have forgotten who she was and to have been doomed into looping in and out of her past, losing whole days to strange delusions of dementia.

'God bless you, Gran.' That's what he'd told her just now when he'd kissed her goodbye.

'What God?' he now imagined Ryan's voice echoing on

80

the wind as he stepped outside and watched the setting sun throwing the buildings of the town into silhouette. 'The God that took your mum from you? The God that stole your gran's spirit and now wants her body as well? Don't be so daft, Jimmy. You don't believe in God any more than I do. Just us, Jimmy. That's all there is. That's all we need. Just you and me, boy, living our lives the way we want to and living them for ever.'

Jimmy climbed on to his bike and rode through the hospice gates and onwards towards the town.

'For ever!'

That's what Ryan had shouted the night Jimmy's whole world had exploded.

How could you have got it so wrong, Ryan? Jimmy thought now, as a tear stretched from his eye across his cheek, as if being drawn that way by the wind. *How could you? You, who made more sense than anyone I ever knew?*

'For ever!' Jimmy remembered Ryan's face as he'd shouted the words, the way he'd thrown his head back as a challenge to the sky. It had been almost a year ago now and Ryan had been standing outside the George Inn, swaying on his feet like there'd been a breeze, even though the harbour waters had been as flat and motionless as the daguerreotypes of the town's past hung up in the glass cases outside the Community Hall.

'For ever!' Ryan had bellowed up at the heavens. 'I'm gonna live for ever!'

And three hours later, he'd been dead.

Stocktaking was a code word, only it wasn't like a code word that anyone had ever sat down and worked out on a piece of paper. Rather, it was the phrase which Marianna Andrews, Video-2-Go's owner, had always used as an excuse for shutting down the store for half an hour before the evening rush started on the nights Jimmy worked there, so that she and Jimmy could be alone.

Heavy with the smell of floor polish, Video-2-Go's stockroom was separated from the front of the store by a security door for insurance purposes and was lit by a single strip light, which hummed like a fridge and flickered like a candle, throwing up shadows across the shelves of white-stickered videotapes, console games and DVDs.

Marianna Andrews was an obsessively skinny, diminutive thirty-eight-year-old bottle blonde with a thick black wedge of pubic hair and a jagged scar on her right buttock from when she'd slipped off a Spanish pub table during a wet T-shirt contest in 1985, the same year Jimmy had been born, and the same year in which she'd met and married her husband.

Lying here now, on the plain wooden table in the centre of the room, with Marianna perched on top of him, bucking and grunting like a rodeo queen, Jimmy remembered the first time they'd had sex. It had been early last year, a couple of weeks after Jimmy had started working for her.

One minute he'd been helping her to move some boxes from one set of stockroom shelves to another, the next he'd been caught checking out her legs as she'd bent over in front of him to pick up a dropped DVD case from the floor.

She'd stood and stared at him as he'd blushed. But she hadn't been angry. Instead, she'd told him what lovely eyes he had and then she'd made her move. There'd been no romance to it. All it had involved had been a simple question and a statement on her behalf ('Do you want to make love to me, Jimmy? Because I want to make love to you'), and a stunned failure to reply on his.

The rest was history: Jimmy had been working under her ever since. He'd been a virgin before Marianna had got her manicured mitts on him, and would probably be a virgin still if it wasn't for her. But now? Well, now he wasn't so sure that this was what he wanted. Of course, he still enjoyed the physical side of it, but that was just it: the physical side was the only side there was.

Jimmy looked away from her manic flashing eyes, unable to hold her stare, knowing that in ten minutes' time they'd both be back behind the shop counter. By then, Marianna would have secreted her black lace French knickers back inside her workaday jeans, and smoothed down her hardened nipples beneath her demure lambswool sweater. And there'd be nothing so sexual as a sidelong glance between the two of them.

Marianna never spoke during the act itself and never referred to it once it had ended, kind of like it had never happened, kind of like she hadn't been unfaithful to her husband, Bill, at all.

But where, Jimmy wondered, did all that leave him? Was he an exploited member of the working class? Or merely the hapless beneficiary of a not unattractive Mrs Robinson's sexual frustration? *I mean*, he thought, as Marianna clawed her fingernails across his chest, *there had to be more, right? There had to be more to a relationship than this?*

And he knew that, of course, there did. Because nothing about Jimmy's affair with Marianna involved equality, he was only too aware. What had started out as a teenager's wet dream come true – and one that even Ryan had admitted to being jealous of at the time – had become repetitive and little more than an expected, however pleasurable, perk of work.

He felt nothing for Marianna any more, not now that he'd

allowed himself to feel so much for Verity Driver. He recognised that what he'd felt for Marianna had been lust and nothing more, whereas what he felt for Verity Driver was something infinitely more complex than that. He knew that if he had asked Verity Driver out and she had said yes, he wouldn't be here now. Then he'd have had something to shout to the world about, not conceal inside a windowless room.

Jimmy called time out on himself. All this thinking was getting him nowhere.

Because the point was, he hadn't asked Verity out. Which is why all this obsessing about her, he knew, had to end. Whatever might have been between himself and Verity was now never going to happen. It was high time he accepted that and stopped kidding himself that it could ever be otherwise.

So that was what he did, right there and right then. Lying flat on his back as Marianna Andrews clasped tightly at her breasts and built herself up towards a shuddering climax, Jimmy Jones resolved to stop thinking about Verity Driver and move on.

Four hours later, towards the end of his shift, and Jimmy was boxing up and handing over a copy of *Lord of the Rings* to Michael Francis, the beaded, bearded owner of the terminally unfashionable New Age trinket shop on Southcliffe Street.

Slouching casually over the counter – as he liked to slouch, in case any of his friends should walk by or in – Jimmy watched Michael limp out of the store and on to the dark street outside. He glanced across at Marianna, who was perched on the stool next to him, nattering away to her best friend, Melissa, about the skiing holiday they had planned for the New Year. Even the pink in her cheeks had faded away.

Jimmy's phone blipped. There was a text from Tara, reading: 'Beer aw8s don't B L8.'

She'd be down the Sapphire and, twenty minutes from now, he'd be with her. Wednesday night drinks were a tradition for them both, had been since Ryan had declared Wednesday to be the new Friday the year before, arguing that there was less chance of the police nicking them for under-age drinking, and that it was easier to get a seat and a game of pool.

Jimmy picked up a stack of empty display boxes and was about to return them to the racks, when the doorbell chimed and he looked up to see the film guy – Scott – he'd helped down at the cottage on Quayside Row earlier in the week.

Jimmy felt sick. He stared down at his hands. He didn't know what to do with them. He felt like a thief who'd just been caught cold with his fingers in the cash register. One of the display boxes slipped from his grip and clattered to the floor.

Scott smiled at him, but Jimmy ignored the gesture. He stared instead at the wall-mounted widescreen, like he really cared about what the super-tanned MTV VJ was jabbering on about. In truth, though, Jimmy couldn't even focus on the VJ. All he could picture in his mind's eye was Scott and all he kept wishing was that he'd leave.

Go away, Jimmy repeated like a mantra inside his mind, wishing he could disappear. Then, *Remember*, he told himself. *Remember how you'd planned to handle this.*

Because he did have a plan for this eventuality. He'd thought about bumping into Scott and Ellen again. How could he not have, living in a town this size? It had been inevitable and he'd decided he'd ignore them and avoid them, not because he'd wanted to, but because it would be safer that way. There was stuff Jimmy knew about Lost Soul's Point, secrets that he wanted to remain just that. He didn't want to be talking to people who were intent on digging up the past.

'Hi, Jimmy,' Scott said, sliding a DVD case across the counter towards him.

Jimmy kept his eyes on the screen.

'OK . . .' Scott went on. 'Well, maybe you've got a membership form I can fill in?'

'We're shut,' Jimmy told him, his voice cracking as he did, uncomfortable with being aggressive like this.

There was a pause, then, 'It says ten on the door.'

'Whatever,' Jimmy answered, opening a drawer below the counter without looking and slapping a membership form down on the counter. 'You'll need three proofs of ID and –'

'All present and correct,' Scott said, depositing a bundle of papers next to the DVD case.

Conscious of Marianna's proximity, Jimmy finally deigned to look at Scott and, the moment he did, he felt his resolve weakening. It was Scott's smile that did it: open and easygoing. It was impossible to hate a man who seemed to have no malice in him himself. Reluctantly, Jimmy picked up the papers and flipped through them as Scott started filling out the form.

Jimmy watched him for a moment, before glancing at the DVD case Scott had selected. It was *Charade*, a Stanley Donen movie, starring Cary Grant, Audrey Hepburn and Walter Matthau. Jimmy prided himself on the fact that he'd watched every film in Video-2-Go's limited archive. Scott was the first person to take this one off the Classics stand in all the time Jimmy had worked here.

'Fake Hitchcock.' The words had left Jimmy's mouth before he'd been able to stop them.

'What?'

Jimmy was furious with himself. The last thing he'd wanted was a conversation, but he couldn't bail out, not now that he'd started it himself. '*Charade*,' he half said, half mumbled. 'It's a rip-off. It's got all Hitchcock's trademarks in it, but it's not by the man himself.'

Scott handed over the completed form. 'And what's so wrong with that?'

Jimmy turned to the computer and began transcribing the information from the membership form into the system's data fields. 'Nothing. So long as you know. Otherwise when you do find out, you'll end up feeling conned. You know, like when you find out a song you really love in the charts is just a load of samples from other, better tracks.'

Jimmy watched Scott's reflection nodding in the screen as he weighed the *Charade* case thoughtfully in his hand. 'Know a lot about films, do you?' Scott asked.

'Enough. It kind of comes with the turf, working in a place like this.' Jimmy took out a membership card and handed it over for Scott to sign.

Suddenly Marianna was at Jimmy's side. 'He's being modest,' she told the Australian. 'He's going to film school next year, aren't you, Jimmy?'

'Hoping to,' Jimmy admitted.

Scott's brow furrowed and, for a second, Jimmy thought he was going to pursue this line of conversation further. But 'Good for you' was all Scott said as he slipped the membership card into his black canvas wallet.

'And the Donen film?' Jimmy asked.

'You've kind of put me off,' answered Scott, nudging the case aside. 'Perhaps you'd better recommend me something more original that I can watch instead. And something I haven't seen already, mind.' The easygoing smile was back on the Australian's face. 'And that might be harder than you think.'

Jimmy wavered for a moment, thinking that maybe he should just tell Scott no. But it was too late now. He'd messed up on the 'ignore' plan already and switching back to it now would only mark out his behaviour as odd.

And in truth, his dread over seeing Scott again was diminishing by the second. He'd been being paranoid, he decided. Scott hadn't even mentioned the documentary. No, so long as they were just chatting about movies Jimmy had no reason to be afraid of Scott. And anyway, there was nothing that Scott and Ellen could possibly find out about Lost Soul's Point that wasn't already common knowledge.

You're in control, Jimmy reminded himself. *No one can see inside your mind. No one can make you speak about the things you saw or tell about the things you did.*

And it was true. It was true. Everything was still OK. Everything was going to stay OK.

He felt the weight slowly slipping from his shoulders. 'We'll soon see about that,' he told Scott, safe in the knowledge that, no matter what Scott thought, this was one challenge Jimmy was certain to win.

Half an hour later Jimmy was sitting in the snug bar of the Sapphire. He was in a good mood. He'd fulfilled his promise to Scott, having produced a copy of *Election*, an overlooked modern classic, he reckoned, which left the over-hyped *American Beauty* (which had been released in the same year) for dead. Plus, he'd just been paid and had cash to spend and cash to put into the bank tomorrow. Half a crafty spliff down (courtesy of Tara in one of the cubicles

88

in the draughty women's toilet five minutes ago) and with a pint of Stella in hand, he was feeling more relaxed than he had all week.

The bar was small, but then again so was everything about the Sapphire and the other ancient squat buildings here in the centre of the old town. Polaroids of New Year celebrations were pinned across the lengths of the blackened oak beams in the low ceiling, which was bowed itself as if a flood were gathering above, waiting to cascade down. The windows looking out on to White Lion Street were greasy with condensed cigarette smoke and the red lino floor was scuffed and cracked.

Sitting with Jimmy were Mark, Charlie, Toni and Danny, all of them seventeen and all of them wrapped in some hush-hush bitch-off which Jimmy had missed the start of and Tara hadn't seemed interested in when he'd arrived. Skateboards stacked against the wall, Ru and Tim were over at the pool table, all slick stances, crew-cuts and hard-hitting shots. They'd all known each other since primary school, the same as Tara, who was sitting on Jimmy's left, sucking on a cigarette and grinning at him over what he'd just confided in her.

Tara was short and skinny, and this week her hair was dyed red and was combed round her face in such a way that you couldn't see her pointed pixie ears or the tiny black snake tattooed on her neck. She was wearing an oversized So Solid Crew T-shirt and her eyelids flashed silver whenever she blinked, which she hadn't done for whole seconds now. 'But how', she finally asked, 'can something be over when it never even began?'

'Because . . .' Jimmy started to reply, but got no further, because he already knew that Tara was right: everything that had existed between him and Verity had only ever existed in his mind.

'I don't get what you see in her myself,' Tara reflected. 'I took French with her last year and she never so much as spoke to me. So either she's a snob, or she's got nothing to say. Probably both.'

Jimmy's eyes glazed over. He already regretted telling Tara about what had happened with Verity on Monday morning and blamed the spliff for loosening his tongue. 'You've got her figured out pretty well for someone you don't know.'

But Tara hadn't finished. 'And besides,' she went on, 'if you've made a resolution not to think about her, then what are you doing banging on about her now?'

Jimmy said nothing. He blamed the spliff for the weakening of his resolve on that front as well.

'OK, OK,' she answered for him. 'You're male and your brain's in your pants, and Verity Driver's fit, I'll grant you that. But beauty, remember, is only skin deep.'

Jimmy grunted. 'Spare me the clichés, eh?'

'You've got to be practical, that's all,' Tara continued. 'Put things in perspective. Don't just think of her, think of yourself. You're bright and cute enough, I suppose. You'll find other girls to be with. Another year and you'll be out of here, off at film school and making a name for yourself in the big wide world. Trust me, you'll forget all about her.'

Jimmy stubbed out his cigarette. 'Let's talk about something else,' he said.

'Oh, come on, Jim,' she said, hooking her elbow round his neck and pulling him close, 'don't be like that. I'm only trying to help.'

'Well, you're not.'

'OK,' she decided, releasing him, 'there's only one way to deal with this.'

'Go on.'

'Ask her out properly. Don't fart about giving her CDs and crap like that. Just come out and say what you mean: Will. You. Go. Out. With. Me?'

'That easy, eh?'

'At least that way you'll know.'

'And then what?'

'She'll tell you to piss off and we can take your life off pause.'

'Thanks.'

'Or', Tara said, getting to her feet and squeezing past him, her loose black dress trailing over his thighs, 'she'll say yes.' Standing beside him now, Tara looked down her thrice-studded nose at him. 'And you'll get to find out just how dull she really is and you'll dump her and we can take your life off pause again.' Her eyes twinkled. 'Either way, Jimmy, we'll get the real you back.'

'That's why I respect you so much, Tara,' Jimmy called after her as she walked off towards the Ladies, 'you're a born optimist.'

Jimmy took a swig from his beer. She was right, of course, about asking Verity out. And for real this time, not just some feeble attempt like on Monday.

Will. You. Go. Out. With. Me?

How hard could that be? His blood raced at the possibility and no matter how hard he tried to look casual and normal as he sat here waiting for Tara to get back, he just kept picturing Verity's face in the seconds following his question and, for once, all he could see her lips framing was the word 'Yes'.

Only then, his pint halfway to his own lips, he froze. Because there, at the table to his right, where he already knew that Denny Shapland was sitting, he'd just heard somebody speak Verity's name.

Slowly, he moved his pint to his mouth and drank. He looked across at Denny and the man – thickset and suited – he was talking to. Jimmy didn't even taste the lager he swallowed, because all he was doing now was listening.

'Which one's she, then?' the guy in the suit asked Denny. 'Is she part of the Searchlight crowd?'

The Searchlight was the name of one of the town's two late-night bars. It was something of an under-age den, frequented by the town's older-looking teenagers and subsequently the source of the majority of Shoresby's petty gossip and scandal.

'No, you wouldn't know her,' Denny answered with some confidence. 'Clubs aren't really her thing. She's more the quiet type. Shy, you know? She's hot, mind,' he added tantalisingly. 'Long hair, long legs. I mean, if she did ever pitch up at the Searchlight, she'd certainly turn a few heads.'

'How did you meet her?' asked his friend, lighting a cigarette.

'She just walked into the shop the other day and said hello.'

'Christ, I should be so lucky.'

'Must be my good looks and natural charm, mate,' Denny told him with a grin. 'Seriously, though,' he continued, 'I've been giving her the eye all year, every time I've seen her, hoping she might get the hint.'

Please, Jimmy thought. Please let me have misheard her name. Jimmy didn't like Denny Shapland. He didn't like him because of his money and the way he flashed it about, and he didn't like him because girls Jimmy's age fell for guys like Denny over guys like Jimmy all the time.

But he hadn't misheard her name. He'd heard it exactly right.

'So there it is,' Denny concluded, stretching luxuriously.

'This Saturday night, I finally get it together with young Verity. And you know what? I can't bloody wait. I really think this could go somewhere, I really do.'

Jimmy had heard enough. Leaving his drink, he pulled on his leather jacket and stood up.

'Looks like Elvis is leaving the building,' Denny said, glancing up and surveying Jimmy's jacket with obvious distaste.

'Nice combat trousers, though, eh?' Jimmy replied, giving Denny's brain a couple of seconds to make the connection over whose shop they could have been lifted from.

On his way out of the pub, Jimmy paused only for an instant, and then only to tear down a notice pinned to the door. Community concert, it said at the top in a lurid shade of desk-top-published green. But that wasn't why Jimmy scrunched it up in his fist and stuffed it deep into his pocket before stepping out into the night. It was what had been written in the small print beneath that had caught his eye.

It had been Ryan's name and the date of his death.

'Tossers!' Jimmy shouted.

Up on the clifftop, a hundred yards south of Lost Soul's Point, overlooking the shimmering lights of the town, Jimmy glared down at the crinkled piece of paper in his left hand. His right hand held the strings of a luminous green kite, which idled thirty feet above him, drifting in and out of the thermals which rose upwards from the musty earth.

Jimmy stared up: the sky was as ablaze with stars as the screensaver on the PC monitor at Video-2-Go. He turned round. There, twenty yards behind him, loomed the silhouette of the Wreck, the Appleforth Estate family chapel, which had been his and Ryan's home from home as they'd been growing up.

Constructed of great stone blocks and enmeshed by creepers, it stood at the perimeter of the Appleforth Estate. Whatever mason had built it had chiselled his mark on the lintel above the door: 1804. Apart from that, Jimmy didn't know much about it. One thing was for sure, though, nobody else gave a damn about it – not even the builders who'd been fixing up the main house this last year. Until he, Ryan and Tara had first forced the door in 1998 and replaced the rusted old padlock with one of their own, no one had set foot in it for years.

Wintertime, the chapel was freezing and black as a mineshaft. There wasn't enough ventilation to risk a fire, because they'd stuffed up the two-inch-wide arrow slit windows with old cloths to stop the wind. The nights they'd hung out in there, it had been with the aid of torches and storm lamps to begin with, and later a lighting system which Ryan had rigged up with an old ship's battery. But it had been worth it for the privacy and, come the summers, Jimmy had known no better place on earth.

The stuff most kids kept in their bedrooms, Ryan, Jimmy and Tara had kept up here: music, booze, dope, books and magazines. The three of them, sometimes with others, used to come here most days after school, when they'd been too young to drink down the Sapphire.

Jimmy had been inside only minutes ago, not bothering with a match to light his way, feeling with his fingers and his memory through the familiar space and digging out the kite before retreating back outside again.

He wasn't someone given to crying easily, but he was crying now. He couldn't do a thing about the tears flowing freely down his face, the same as he couldn't stop sobbing as he thought of his best friend, dying down there on the outcrop of rocks which bulged up out of the sea.

It had been almost twelve months since Ryan had died, but the way Jimmy felt right now – the way this paper notice made him feel – it could have been tonight.

'Tossers,' Jimmy cursed again.

A community concert to remember Ryan's passing. *Passing*? What the fuck was that? Ryan hadn't *passed* anything. He'd died, mangled in the shrieking metal and poisonous petrol fumes of a stolen convertible car.

So what was this? This concert to bring the community together? This benefit gig to raise funds for a new, improved Youth Centre? This intention to build a place where Shoresby's juvenile population could come together and find friendship and support when they needed it? This centre for channelling people's energy in a positive and creative way?

It was bullshit, that's what it was. It had nothing to do with Ryan at all.

Jimmy shivered. He could feel Ryan near him, drifting up here in the wind like the kite they'd always flown together when they'd been too wasted to speak. What would Ryan make of all this now? Jimmy wondered.

It didn't matter. He wasn't here any more.

Jimmy spat. He wanted to hate this town. He wanted to hate the people in it, the ignorant do-gooders who were organising this concert. All that crap wasn't going to bring Ryan back. He wanted to hate the stupid legend of Lost Soul's Point and the tourist industry built around it. And he wanted to hate Verity as well, for being shallow enough to agree to go out on a date with that prick Denny Shapland.

He wanted to hate them all, but he couldn't. Even as he raged against them now, a part of him refused to let his rage win, because just as a part of Ryan remained behind, so too a part of Jimmy would belong to this town for ever. And there wasn't a thing he could do about it.

Life was so fucking precious. That was all Jimmy really knew. And that was how come Ryan's death still hurt him so much.

'I miss you, man,' Jimmy said. 'I miss you so much.'

Jimmy brought the kite down on the flat ground to his right. He then stood and ripped the concert advertisement into a dozen smaller pieces and clenched them in his fist. He stood and walked forward to where the land gave way to thin air and slowly unfurled his fingers. The wind took the twelve pieces of paper, first rolling them across his upturned palm, and then carrying them out to sea like a flock of tiny birds.

Chapter VI

A flock of pigeons shot up from the tarnished statue of Alexander Walpole as Ellen hurried inside to where the stallholders were starting to pack up the Thursday farmers' market. Checking her watch, she headed to Little's Cleaning and Alterations, one of the small shops surrounding the covered market square.

'I'm afraid there's nothing we can do,' said the young woman a few minutes later, as she carefully laid out Ellen's Donna Karan coat between them across the Formica counter. 'We've all had a look. We could send it away but . . .' She looked at Ellen apologetically, before picking up the ragged hem of the coat and tutting at the damage. 'What a shame,' she said, almost to herself.

'Then would you mind writing me a note to say that it's irreparable?' asked Ellen, realising too late that she sounded terribly bad-tempered.

'Well . . . I . . .' began the woman hesitantly, her hand fluttering to the collar of her white overall.

'It'd make all the difference if you would,' Ellen said, remembering she wasn't in the dry cleaners in Oxford Circus and a softer approach was needed. 'You see it was a birthday present from my partner,' she continued. After all, there was no harm going for the sympathy vote. She would try to claim for the coat on insurance when she got round to it, but she'd already been to that overpriced Wave Cave place and had bought an all-weather Berghaus jacket, which was much more practical. 'I could tell you what to write, if you want,' she added gently. 'It's just that something official might mean that I could get some compensation . . .' *From him*, she thought, feeling a steely knot of anger in her chest. The arrogant, spiteful, horrible . . . In a second, Ellen was back on the Appleforth Estate on Monday afternoon.

Despite her disastrous morning, she'd been quite excited as she'd made her way up there to take her first look around. Having put on a slick of lipstick for luck, she'd parked the Land-Rover next to the other cars and trucks, and stepped into the wind and stared at the impressive Georgian mansion ahead of her.

Seeing the signs for the site office, she walked round the back of one of the wings, picking her way among wheelbarrows, cement mixers and ladders. Walking gingerly across some planks to where a chipboard door was rigged up, she knocked loudly. Then, stepping back to wait for an answer, she turned to look at the incredible view over the coastline, drawing in a deep breath as she surveyed the distant stampede of white horses racing towards the town across the wide expanse of sea.

A few moments later the door opened and she spun round with her brightest smile. Standing above her on the step was a man in a hard yellow hat holding a steaming mug of tea. He was laughing, as if at a joke, his face turned to the men in the room behind, and, for a split-second as Ellen took in his profile, she thought of what Beth, her oldest friend would say: 'Workman! Woof!', with a suitable whistle for his rugged good looks.

But then, as the man turned to face her, Ellen realised she'd made a huge mistake. This wasn't an attractive man at all. It was the man with the mad dog.

'You!' they exclaimed in unison, their smiles simultaneously wiped off their faces.

Ellen stared at the man standing before her, slack-jawed with disbelief at the rotten run of her luck.

'What the hell are you doing here?' he said, looking her up and down.

Ellen hugged her folder to her chest. 'I'm looking for the foreman, or the person in charge,' she said. 'Not that it's any of *your* business.' She looked back at him dismissively, before trying to peer round him to the room behind.

'As it happens, you're wrong,' the dog-man replied, blocking her view. 'I'm Ned Spencer and I *am* in charge.'

To her horror, Ellen felt her cheeks burning and her bravado plummeting like a rock into the pit of her stomach. She knew from Amanda's notes that Ned Spencer was the one person she needed to get onside in order to make the documentary.

'Oh, I get it,' he continued, before she'd had the chance to say anything. 'I suppose you're here to make a complaint about that coat of yours. Haven't you got anything better to do than to stalk me?'

Ellen narrowed her eyes at his arrogant jibe, forcing herself not to sink to his level. 'My coat is a separate issue. For now, I'm here because I'm going to be shooting a documentary about Lost Soul's Point. We're planning to start right away, so if you'll just let me have a look around and sort out where we need to set up –'

Ned Spencer snorted with laughter, before pushing his old-fashioned round glasses up his nose. There was something boyish about his face, like an overgrown Harry Potter. 'Er . . . like *that*'s going to happen,' he said, before taking a sip of tea, his eyes dancing with amusement, as he looked at her over the rim of the mug.

'But surely my colleague, Amanda Pearson, spoke to you several months ago?'

'Nope.'

'Well, we've got permission coming from the American owner, who knows all about the project, if you'd care to check . . .' Ellen said more desperately, riffling through the correspondence in her folder. 'There,' she said triumphantly, pulling out the letter Amanda had written. 'It's addressed to a Jonathan Arthur of Salem, Massachusetts . . . Your boss, I believe?'

Ned Spencer took the letter from her and quickly scanned it, before handing it back. 'All this says is that you're asking for permission.'

'But there've been phone calls. My production secretary –'

'You're wasting your time,' he interrupted. 'Everything here happens through me. Until I see correct documentation and have officially approved the project, you won't be filming anything.'

'But you don't understand –' Ellen protested, but it was obvious that he did and, what's more, he was enjoying this.

'No. *You* don't understand. You're trespassing. I suggest you leave.' And, with a smug smile, he waggled his fingertips at her, with all the sincerity of a department store Santa dismissing a particularly odious child, before going back inside and kicking the door shut behind him with the heel of one of his dirty boots.

That had been four days ago and thanks to Ned Bloody Spencer, as she now referred to him, Ellen hadn't even started yet on the Lost Soul's Point programme.

Instead, she'd ended up getting nothing done on Monday and had then had to spend Tuesday and Wednesday back in London. There, Joy had been increasingly unhelpful. One of

100

the other programmes had problems and it was obvious that Shoresby was way down on her list of priorities. Ellen had been about to chase Jonathan Arthur herself, but Joy had already contacted him and had delivered a stern lecture to Ellen about professional boundaries and treading on toes.

Ellen probably wouldn't have felt quite so helpless and frustrated if she hadn't had to spend several long stints in the dingy Soho editing suite rescuing the Hadrian's Wall footage. By yesterday she'd been crawling up the walls and desperate to get back to Shoresby. She didn't want to be spending all her time improving other people's work. She wanted to be making her own programme. It was only when she'd arrived back at the cottage last night that she'd started to feel more in control.

Now, as Ellen watched the woman in the dry cleaner's painstakingly write out the note she would shortly present to Ned Bloody Spencer, she felt a small moment of triumph in her otherwise bleak week.

She was brought out of the opening act of yet another psychodrama, in which she was about to give Ned Bloody Spencer a rather large piece of her mind, by a blast of cold air, as the door behind her opened and a young boy came in. He was wearing a hooded sweatshirt and an anorak over the top, but even half covered Ellen could still see his cheeks were flushed from the wind.

'All right, Toby, love,' the woman in the dry cleaner's said to the boy, smiling at him affectionately. 'What are you up to?'

'I'm handing out leaflets for Clive. Will you put a few of these up in the window?' asked the boy, digging deep into his pocket and handing over several small sheets of green paper.

''Course I will,' she said, taking them.

'Thanks, Beverly. See ya,' he said, rushing back out of the shop.

Beverly watched the boy go. 'He's pals with my youngest,' she explained.

The woman – Beverly – didn't look old enough to have children, let alone a 'youngest' of at least ten. Now Ellen felt guilty for privately patronising her for writing so slowly. It couldn't be that easy working all day and looking after kids as well.

She smiled and Beverly turned the flyer round so that Ellen could see it, too. 'They're doing a memorial concert for that boy, Ryan.'

'Oh?' said Ellen, her curiosity aroused.

'He was only a teenager,' Beverly said, as Ellen read about the auditions for the planned concert. 'Broke his poor parents' hearts.'

'What happened?'

'He drove himself off Lost Soul's Point in a stolen car last year. They say he was on drugs . . .'

It was getting dark by the time Ellen stepped back on to the High Street, the implications of a recent suicide rushing round her head. It seemed the more she knew about Lost Soul's Point, the more there was to find out. There'd been no mention in Amanda's notes about this local boy killing himself. All the suicide victims Amanda had come up with were from out of town. But using this story was a much more unified and poignant approach, Ellen thought. If she started with this boy Ryan's suicide and then maybe filmed the memorial concert . . .

Her phone rang and she cursed. Why did she always get interrupted? She groped in the bottom of her bag for the mobile, hoping it wasn't Joy on the other end. But then she saw the international number on the display panel, took an excited breath and turned away into a doorway out of the wind. It must be Jason. 'Where've you been?' she asked, not knowing whether to be angry with him, or relieved that he'd finally got in touch.

'I told you it would be difficult to call. Don't be upset, darling. I've got to be quick.'

'Where are you?' Ellen asked, pressing her finger into her other ear, in order to hear better, but the echo down the line meant that she got Jason's question first.

'How's it going in Shoreton?'

'Shoresby,' she corrected.

'I'm in Bogotá,' Jason said, replying to her question. 'Hang on . . .'

The line went muffled and Ellen hunched down into the doorway, desperate to hear more. Nothing happened for almost a minute and Ellen was on the verge of giving up when Jason came back on the line. His voice was clear and the echo had gone.

'What were you saying?' Jason asked.

'Nothing,' said Ellen with a smile, happy to hear his voice again. 'Tell me about your trip. How's it going? Have you started shooting?'

'Chance would be a fine thing,' Jason moaned. 'We've been stuck here all week waiting for some papers.'

'Snap! You wouldn't believe this guy I've had to deal with up at the Appleforth Estate, Jase. You'd loathe him. I can't tell you how much time I've wasted just because of him.'

And as Ellen unloaded all her anger and frustration about Joy, Appleforth House and Ned Bloody Spencer, she started to feel better.

'Do you want me to have a man-to-man chat with him?' Jason offered, as the line crackled once again.

Ellen laughed, appalled. 'I think I can handle him.'

'Oh shit! It looks like I'm going to have to go,' Jason said, and Ellen could hear an engine starting in the background.

'No!' she exclaimed, horrified that she'd wasted this precious phone call talking about that bloody dog-man. 'Don't go. You haven't told me anything –'

'I'll call you again when I can. Love you,' Jason said and then the line went dead before she had a chance to reply.

Ellen switched off her phone, hating these all too familiar emotions. She'd been looking forward to hearing from Jason so much, but now that she had, she felt more dissatisfied than ever. She couldn't shake a mental image of him laughing and swinging into the back of an open-topped jeep and heading off to the jungle, without a care in the world.

It wasn't fair, she thought. He probably didn't feel a bit like she did. And even if she did tell him how rankled and disappointed she felt, he still wouldn't get it. She could even play out their argument in her head. He'd rung when he could, hadn't he? *And* he'd told her that he loved her. What more did she want, for God's sake? She was the one who'd wasted the phone call by talking about her problems. She was the selfish one, not Jason. Then a guilt trip would inevitably follow about Ellen not understanding how important his career was. He was fulfilling his life's dream, etc. etc. And he was right. Of course he was right. And she loved him.

She thrust her phone in her bag and turned away from the doorway. Jason was thousands of miles away. There was no point in beating herself up about international phone calls which, as she knew from plenty of past experience, were invariably a disaster. She must focus on what was important. After all, she had a career too.

'Come on, woman,' she said to herself aloud. 'Let's get this show on the road.'

Michael Francis was an ex-university professor who'd written a booklet that Ellen had found in the local library entitled *The Legends of Shoresby*. Despite the author's clear penchant for the supernatural, it was very well written and Ellen wanted to use the text about Alexander and Caroline Walpole's suicides as source material for the voice-overs she had planned for the documentary. All she had to do was check out the authenticity of the author's claims and, of course, get his permission to quote.

Having consulted Cheryl at the Grand, who was fast becoming her personal oracle, Ellen had found out that Michael Francis ran a shop called Equinox in Southcliffe Street, which was where she headed now.

Apart from Jason, Ellen was the least superstitious person she knew. Admittedly, she wasn't quite on the same level as Jason, who sneeringly dismissed everything from horoscopes to hypnosis, believing more in the law of animals and survival of the fittest. But having lived with him for so many years, Ellen had to admit that some of his scepticism had definitely rubbed off on her. However, as she stood alone in the pool of yellow light cast by the creaking hurricane lamp outside Equinox with the wind whistling past her down the dark cobbled alley and the grey-brown clouds fast-forwarding across the black sky, she couldn't help shivering with something more than the cold.

In front of her, the window was crammed with every sort of occult and supernatural paraphernalia. Voodoo masks, ouija boards and an inflatable fluorescent alien jostled for space next to a large cauldron decorated with tarot cards. Telling herself that it was all a load of hocus-pocus, Ellen

105

pushed open the door and, accompanied by a loud clatter of bamboo wind chimes, made her way inside.

She was met by soft, ambient music and an over-whelming smell of patchouli oil mixed with the curling wisps of smoke from two Byronesque candles, which cast flickering shadows up the wall of books. Glancing over the tickertape labels on the wooden shelves, Ellen could see past *The Celestine Prophesies* and *X Files* books to whole rows of esoteric texts on crop circles and Wicca. Above her the low ceiling was completely covered with a meticulously painted bare-breasted Amazon riding on the neck of a fire-breathing dragon.

At the back of the shop, directly below the forked tongue of the huge beast, Michael Francis sat on a high stool behind a desk, wearing a green Aran jumper with a paisley cravat. Aged around fifty, he was peering intently through the half-moon spectacles on the end of his nose as he painted a miniature Dungeons and Dragons figurine in the light of an anglepoise lamp.

'I'll be with you in a second,' he said, not looking up as he finished a detail with the tip of his brush.

Ellen stood beside the heater, holding her hand in the warmth from the tangerine bars, and looked at the large Arthurian map on the wall.

Michael Francis sighed with satisfaction as he put down the figurine next to an army of goblins on the newspaper-strewn desk and looked up at Ellen. 'You've come to ask me about *The Legends of Shoresby*,' he said, scratching the side of his curly grey beard.

'Don't tell me you're psychic?' Ellen asked, with an incredulous laugh.

Michael Francis smiled, wiping his hands on a cloth. 'Mary, my wife, works at the library and she always tips me off when anyone buys one of my pamphlets. It's pretty rare.'

'More people should,' Ellen replied, smiling back at him. 'I thought it was very good. Fascinating, in fact.'

'Shoresby's a fascinating place. Did you know that this shop marks the exact convergence of ley lines from all over the area? Where you're standing, in fact.'

Startled, Ellen looked down at the floor, noticing she was standing in the middle of an elaborately painted pentagram. 'What's going to happen now? Am I going to go up in a puff of green smoke?' she asked.

'I doubt it. But you should expect the unexpected. Odd things happen to people here.'

'Really?' Ellen said. 'So . . . what's happened to you?'

'It depends how long you've got.'

In the end, it took about forty-five minutes for Michael Francis to tell Ellen some of his background and his interest in Shoresby. As she listened, sipping a glass of his home-made ginger beer, she found herself liking him more and more, especially when she found out that his research relating to Caroline Walpole's suicide at Lost Soul's Point and the subsequent burning of Appleforth House came from a first-hand account.

On the night Caroline's father, Alexander Walpole, had burnt himself and Appleforth House to the ground in remorse, he'd sent all the staff away to the town. Michael Francis's great-uncle had been a young kitchen boy at the house.

This was great, Ellen thought. Her source material was accurate and all that reading she'd done on the train to London and back had been worthwhile.

Michael smiled at her pleasantly. 'If you do have any other questions please feel free to drop in any time.'

'Well, actually,' Ellen began, 'there is something I was wondering about . . .'

Ellen thought about how to phrase her question. Of course she wanted information but she realised, now that she had come to ask it, that the aspect of Caroline's story which most intrigued her was not the tragedy surrounding her death, but rather the ill-fated romance with Leon Jacobson, her father's Jewish secretary, that had led up to it. There was something wonderfully Shakespearean about a beautiful, intelligent young girl meeting her lover in the dead of night to elope, knowing that she was giving up everything, including her family, for love. And it was this all-or-nothing certainty at the heart of Caroline's story that fascinated Ellen. Her love for Leon had been so pure and so intense that she'd been willing to give up her life for it in the blink of an eye.

Ellen knew she was being romantic, but she was fascinated by that level of emotion. After all, what were the chances that anyone she knew had ever felt anything near that level of passion for a lover, even as teenagers? She certainly hadn't.

Even now, she knew that she loved Jason, but it was an altogether different type of love from Caroline's heroic love. It was the type that happened in a modern world dominated by deadlines, commitments and compromises. It was love in the grey area, while Caroline's love was stead-fastly black and white, and Ellen couldn't help wondering what that must feel like. 'So what happened to Caroline's lover, Leon Jacobson?' she asked, after she'd expressed some of these thoughts.

'No one knows. Alexander Walpole paid him off just before he was about to elope with Caroline. Then he disappeared into thin air and no one ever heard of him again. I don't know if he even knew that the poor girl had killed herself when she found out he'd deserted her.'

'How tragic.' Ellen sighed. 'It's so sad. How could she have got it so wrong? Surely it takes two to feel that passionately? It just doesn't make sense.'

'Love very often doesn't make sense,' Michael said wisely and Ellen smiled at him.

They chatted for a while longer and Ellen finished the ginger beer. Then, after he'd agreed to let her use his research, she shrugged on her coat. 'You watch it up there, mind,' he warned, helping her into it. 'I've seen Leon Jacobson's ghost myself and that's not all . . .'

'Oh?'

'There's UFOs. Luminous green ones. Up in the sky at night.'

Ellen smiled, noticing, as he scrunched up the news-paper, that beneath the glass top of the desk was a large display of bongs and marijuana pipes. 'I'll take care to watch out for them,' she said.

The next morning, despite the fact that there was an ominous mass of charcoal-grey storm clouds over the headland, Ellen felt better than she'd done all week. She was in Scott's good books, having lugged down a duvet and a blow-up double mattress from her flat, and in return he'd scrubbed the cottage from top to bottom. Lying in her bed, she felt cosy as she listened to the chink of boat masts in the harbour.

She found Scott downstairs curled up under the duvet on the sofa, engrossed in a DVD on his laptop. 'This is a great movie,' he said, pausing it and removing one of his earpieces. 'Jimmy, that boy we met, works at the video store and recommended it. He's a bit of a film buff himself. And he's bright, too. I was thinking . . . if we haven't got the budget for a decent-sized crew, then the least we could do is make our lives a little easier and give this kid a break into the bargain.'

'Well, you could be on to something. Your Jimmy might be able to help us. Have you seen this flyer about the memorial concert?' Ellen handed over one of the green sheets she'd taken from Beverly.

'What's it all about?' Scott asked, reading it.

'Apparently, this Ryan boy was a local teenager who committed suicide at Lost Soul's Point last year. He must have been about the same age as Jimmy . . .'

She was interrupted by a knock at the door and she shuffled around Scott to answer it.

Outside, battling with an umbrella that had been turned inside out by the wind, Cheryl Driver's face smiled out from the small hole left by the drawstring on the hood of her red pac-a-mac. 'I've got the fax for you!' she shouted triumphantly, starting to pull a long stream of paper from her pocket.

'Fantastic! Come in! Come in!' Ellen urged, taking Cheryl's arm and pulling her through the door.

Scott tucked the duvet more tightly round his chest, disgruntled at the blast of cold air.

'Stay for some tea,' Ellen declared happily, taking the fax from Cheryl, who was already busy untying her hood. Ellen pushed the door shut and walked into the room as she unravelled the fax so that it almost touched the floor.

'Oh, Scott, look. Here's the permission. I take it all back about Joy. She's included all the correspondence. Great!'

'Shall I . . . um . . .' Cheryl began, looking uncertainly between Ellen and Scott. Ellen looked up from the papers and slapped her forehead, realising her rudeness. 'Cheryl.

110

Sorry. The kettle's just . . .' But she was too distracted by the fax, eager to read on.

'Don't worry,' said Cheryl confidently. 'You carry on. I can do it.'

Scott shuffled back into the corner of the sofa as Cheryl walked past him to the kitchen, as if she'd been there a hundred times before.

Ellen held up the long ream of fax paper and grinned at Scott. 'I've got him!' she declared. 'Ned Bloody Spencer won't have a leg to stand on.'

'I'll just use the normal tea, shall I?' Cheryl enquired from the kitchen.

Scott glared at Ellen, obviously displeased at Cheryl's nosy presence, but Ellen regarded her as an ally and she flipped her hand dismissively at Scott's concern. 'Normal's fine,' she shouted back.

'It's a bit shabby in here, if you don't mind me saying,' Cheryl said, poking her head through the bead curtain.

Ellen shrugged. 'Believe it or not, it's all we can afford. We're not planning on being here for very long.'

'It's cheap, but it's freezing,' Scott mumbled. 'It'd be fine if the fire worked, but it smoked us out.'

'You should have said something before,' Cheryl said. 'I'll send Russell over this afternoon. He's a regular Dick Van Dyke when it comes to chimneys.'

'Really, you've been kind enough already,' Ellen said, raising her eyebrows at Scott.

'Consider it done,' Cheryl said, disappearing into the kitchen and Scott poked his thumbs up from under the duvet at Cheryl's offer of salvation.

'We can make a start right away,' Ellen said to Scott, perching on the arm of the sofa by his feet. 'And I meant what I said. I really think this Ryan thing could be our way

111

into the modern slant I wanted to run alongside the historical story. Have a word with your pal Jimmy, would you? See what you can get out of him.'

'I don't know,' Scott said. 'It's a bit recent. They might have been friends.'

'Even better,' said Ellen.

'I'll make a deal,' said Scott, fixing her with a serious look. 'Agree to divert some of our lousy resources Jimmy's way and I'll talk to him. Work experience for him, back-up for us. Everyone's a winner.'

'You're really keen to help this kid out, aren't you? You hardly know him.'

Scott shrugged. 'I know what it's like to grow up in a piss-poor town and want something better for yourself.'

Ellen smiled at Scott. Why weren't there more good guys like him around? 'We're not going to be able to give him much,' she warned.

'If he's up for it, it won't be because of the money anyhow.'

'OK. But he's your responsibility.'

Ellen stood up as the kitchen curtain twitched and Cheryl pushed aside the beads with three mugs of tea.

'We should definitely film the benefit concert,' Ellen said, starting to visualise the footage. 'That could be our intro and tie-up sequence to end the film on an optimistic note.'

'You're filming the concert, Ms Morris?' Cheryl interrupted, placing the mugs on the coffee table in front of Scott.

'Call me Ellen, please,' Ellen reminded her. 'It's just a thought.'

'I know the organisers,' Cheryl said. 'I could have a word. You should definitely go to the auditions tomorrow night. Clive, from the Community Centre, will be there. He's a very approachable man.'

112

'Hey, that's an idea, Scott,' Ellen said. 'We could get some kids for the historical reconstructions from the auditions. It'll save us doing our own.'

'Are you sure you want to do all this right away?' Scott asked, leaning forward to grab a mug of tea.

'Have a bit of imagination, Scott. Now we've got this,' Ellen said, waving the fax, 'we can do anything we want. Now come on, I want to go up there and do a recce.'

'In this weather? You must be bloody mad, woman.'

'That man is not going to waste any more of my time,' Ellen declared.

'I'd better be on my way, then,' said Cheryl, hastily putting down her tea.

'Hang on, Cheryl, we'll finish this while Scott gets dressed. Then I'm sure he won't mind if we give you a lift back to the hotel,' Ellen said, with a big grin at Scott.

'But I'm busy,' Scott protested.

Ellen lifted the laptop away from him, yanking the earphone from his ear. 'That's the beauty of technology. It can wait until later. This is what you're paid for, remember?'

The storm had broken by the time Ellen and Scott drove through the Appleforth Estate gates. Rain lashed against the windscreen as they pulled to a stop in the car park. Ellen turned off the engine, but kept the windscreen wipers flick-flacking across the screen. Even with them on full, it was impossible to see anything other than the shape of the house in front of them and a few of the workmen's vans.

'Ellen, this is ridiculous,' Scott implored. 'Look at it. We're not going to be able to do anything.'

'If we wait for the weather to stop in this place, we'll be waiting all year. You can stay here if you want, but I'm going. It's only rain,' Ellen said, pulling up her hood and zipping up her jacket right under her chin.

Outside, leaning into the wind, Ellen marched towards the house. Thankfully there was no sign of Ned Bloody Spencer and even if he were to find her, she was armed with her fax.

Feeling confident, Ellen walked right round the house, taking in its austere grandeur. It was certainly a dramatic location and Ellen started to think about where she'd be able to put the camera to get the best shot.

As she walked backwards, framing the house in her mind, she found herself in the gardens. They were so wild and beautiful that she decided to walk on, trampling through the overgrown paths that had once been formal gardens, exploring behind the ivy-covered walls until, a while later, she found herself near to the cliffs.

Holding her forearm up against a sudden lashing of rain, she decided to follow the cliff path, to see whether she could get a view of the house from a distance.

To her right, Ellen could hear the waves booming against the rocks far below and she kept looking down at the ground, to make sure of her footing. Before long, the path curved away and Ellen turned head-on into the wind, which whipped her hood back. She gasped as the rain hit her like a bucket-load of water.

It was then she heard something.

Shaking her head, she looked around her, the thought of the Appleforth House ghost flitting through her mind. Then she heard the noise again: a pitiful crying sound, rising and falling in the wind.

She stopped and listened, straining to hear, but when the noise came again, Ellen hurried forward and, a few metres later, saw where it was coming from.

There, crouching on the ground, a little girl was crying loudly, her hands wrapped round her knees as she shivered uncontrollably. Her wet, honey-blonde hair was plastered to her skull and she was wearing pink sparkly boots, a blue skirt and a pink jumper, but she wasn't wearing a coat.

Without hesitating, Ellen leapt forward and squatted down by the little girl. 'There, there,' she said, unzipping her jacket and putting it round the girl. 'It's going to be all right. Hold on to me.'

The little girl allowed Ellen to lift her up.

'You shouldn't be here,' Ellen said. 'It's so dangerous.' Now that she was holding the girl, she could see the sheer drop to the rocks below.

'What's your name, sweetheart?' she asked the girl, rushing away from the edge of the cliff to safety.

'Clara.'

'Where's your mummy, Clara? Is she here?'

Clara shook her head, wiping her nose on the sleeve of Ellen's jacket. Ellen could feel the icy rain seeping through her sweatshirt, but she didn't care.

'What about your daddy?' she asked, trying to sound as calm as possible, although she was starting to feel panicky at this totally unexpected discovery.

Clara pointed back towards the house.

'He's here?' Ellen asked, but she was already running in the direction of Clara's outstretched finger.

By the time they'd reached the house, Ellen was out of breath and Clara was too heavy to carry any longer. Ellen lowered her gently to the ground, watching the hem of her new jacket fold into a muddy puddle as the little girl stood on shaking legs, but Ellen didn't care. Clara's chin wobbled as her teeth chattered and her large eyes stared out from under the dripping hood. Ellen's heart melted. She was

115

unbelievably cute. 'Clara, where's Daddy?' she asked again gently. 'Is he inside the big house?'

'No. He's over there,' Clara said in a small voice and Ellen followed her outstretched arm.

Now Ellen could see a Portakabin set away from the house by some outbuildings. 'Right,' she said, scooping up the little girl and running towards it.

For the third time that week Ellen faced Ned, who opened the door. There was a split-second of shocked silence as his eyes met hers. Then he rushed forward to help.

'Daddy!' Clara yelped, yanking herself away from Ellen and transferring herself into Ned's arms.

Ellen stood back, her brain trying to make sense of all this, but Ned motioned her to come inside and she stepped up and shut the door behind her. She rubbed her hands together, shivering now that the warm air hit her, watching Ned peel her coat away from Clara and fling it over the back of a chair by the desk, as Clara kicked off her boots.

'Darling, darling,' he muttered, kissing his daughter and stroking her hair.

Ellen looked down at her mud-covered feet and folded her arms across her chest. Then, as Clara laid her head against Ned's shoulder, her legs wrapping round his waist, he finally looked at Ellen.

In every scenario she'd imagined Ellen had either been angry and indignant, or coolly indifferent when she'd seen Ned again, but now that she was finally face to face with him she couldn't summon up any anger. Instead, she felt foolishly embarrassed, as if she were an intruder on this intimate scene. She was completely thrown by the fact that he was a father and seeing how tender he was with Clara only confused her more.

'I found her up on the cliff,' said Ellen, wiping the drips away from her face.

Ned drew away from Clara, and held her chin between his thumb and forefinger, forcing Clara to look up at him. 'Is this true? I thought you were reading in the back.' He glanced towards a closed door leading to another section of the cabin.

'I got bored,' Clara said. 'I climbed out through the dog flap. But then it was raining and I got lost.'

'You can't go wandering off when you feel like it. I've told you before. It's dangerous out there. Especially in this weather.'

Ned crouched and put Clara down before he grabbed a towel hanging on a hook by the wall heater. He put it over Clara's head and rubbed her hair, but Clara struggled immediately. Leaving her to it, Ned watched her wrap the towel over her head and hold it closed under her chin, before she looked between Ned and Ellen with a gappy smile.

'It doesn't matter, Daddy,' Clara replied. 'The nice lady found me.'

Ned slapped his hands on his knees. 'Yes, well, the *nice lady* shouldn't have been there in the first place,' he said, standing up.

Ellen's smile at Clara's compliment faded as soon as she heard Ned's tone and saw his stony expression.

'But,' he said, sighing, as if against his will, 'thank you, anyway. I'm very grateful.'

Clara ran behind the desk, jumped up on to Ned's swivel chair and started to spin gently.

Ellen pressed her lips together, trying not to laugh at Clara's cheekiness. Ned watched his daughter and then turned back to face Ellen.

'Look, Mr Spencer,' she said, before she'd had time to think about what she was going to say. 'I know we've got off to a bad start, but maybe we could try again?' It was ridiculous, but why was she feeling this nervous? She had every right to be here and Ned should be the one being nice to her after she'd saved his daughter.

Ned exhaled and smiled kindly, the corners of his eyes crinkling. 'Yes, yes, you're right,' he said. 'Let's start again.'

'I'm Ellen,' she said. 'Ellen Morris.'

She held out her hand, but realising how silly this formal introduction seemed, she laughed and made to drop her hand. But Ned grabbed it. His hand was warm and he squeezed hers gently.

'Well, Ellen Morris, you're freezing,' he said. 'Let's get you warmed up.'

Five minutes later, Ellen had her hair in a towel turban and had swapped her sweatshirt for a baggy woollen jumper of Ned's. As she sat warming herself by the wall heater, she folded up the long sleeves and watched Ned pour two fresh coffees from the jug. He seemed at home in his makeshift office and, she had to admit, there was something cosy about the place, even though it was a complete mess.

The huge desk was covered with ornate architectural plans and an overflowing ashtray sat by a new Mac laptop, along with a half-empty bottle of Tallisker whisky. The coffee machine was perched on a bookcase laden with large, well-thumbed books on interior design and haphazard piles of carpet and wallpaper samples. Behind it, the walls were covered with a jumbled montage of photographs showing the progress of the restoration of Appleforth House, along with several of Clara's childish paintings. In the corner, Ellen was relieved to see, the dog basket was empty.

Ned handed the coffee to Ellen and she accepted it gratefully, before pulling the towel off her head.

'So,' Ned said, perching on the edge of his desk. 'You want to film here?'

He looked so competent and in control that Ellen felt excited about telling him all about the programme. 'I've got the fax from Jonathan Arthur,' she added, leaning forward and digging the soggy papers out of her jacket pocket. 'The correct documentation,' she said light-heartedly, reminding Ned of his words on Monday. He half smiled as he took the fax from her.

Ellen combed her fingers through her hair, as Ned scanned the fax.

After a moment, he put it down on the desk beside him and smiled at her properly. 'What have you got in mind?' he asked.

'I want to tell the original legend of Lost Soul's Point. It's a great story,' she began, going on to explain what she'd learnt so far through Michael Francis. 'I was hoping to use the house to do a bit of reconstructed drama, if that's OK with you. Just . . . you know . . . edgy black-and-white shots with a voice-over. Now that the house is nearly back to its original state, it's going to look fantastic.'

'I've got some papers that Jonathan sent over. There's letters and all sorts. You can have a look some time, if you'd like,' he said.

Ellen nodded enthusiastically. 'That'd be great. Anything like that would be so helpful. Obviously, we can dovetail it with thoughts about the modern victims.'

'How do you mean?' Ned was frowning.

'Well, we're going to look at how the legend lives on, that kind of thing. Link the original story into the modern suicides. There was one just last year. We were going to start off with the memorial concert –'

119

'Hang on,' Ned interrupted, standing up and putting his coffee cup down. 'You're not seriously thinking about including that, are you?'

'Why not?' Ellen asked.

'Because making a programme about suicides that will be shown on the television, when people in the town are still grieving . . . well it's wrong. . .'

'But it's not about right or wrong,' Ellen explained, smoothing a strand of hair behind her ear. 'It's a matter of public record. All we're doing is reporting on what's already happened.'

'And that's entertainment, is it?'

Ellen looked at Ned, feeling herself stiffen as she saw his appalled expression. Where had she gone so wrong? They were getting on so well a moment ago. She carefully replaced her mug on the table. 'It's not entertainment. I'm trying to make a programme of value,' she said, as calmly as she could. 'It's going to be a sympathetic, relevant . . .'

Ned was shaking his head, looking at his shoes. There was a moment before he said anything. Then he glared up at her. 'What you're doing has nothing to do with sympathy or value. You're down here to make money out of other people's misery. It's irresponsible and it's shallow, and if you knew anything about death and how it affects people, you'd know that I'm right.'

Ellen stood up and snatched the fax from the desk. Something about Ned's tone had cut her to the quick and she felt anger shoot through her. 'Who do you think you are to lecture me about people's feelings? What gives you the right to claim some moral high ground? I'm just doing my job, Mr Spencer.'

Ned shook his head. 'People like you disgust me.'

'Daddy!' Clara whimpered, hopping off the chair.

'*I* disgust *you*!' Ellen exhaled, astonished at his arrogance. 'That's rich! Look at you. Letting your daughter run off in a storm. I'd call *that* irresponsible!'

'Ned?'

Ellen turned to see the door open behind her and a tall, beautiful young woman hurriedly stepping into the Portakabin with a coat held over her head. The dog who'd savaged Ellen's coat ran in past the woman and shook his wet fur all over Ellen's legs.

'Is everything all right?' the woman asked, looking between Ellen and Ned as she pulled away the coat. Even frowning, she had a glowing, earthy kind of beauty. She went and stood next to Ned, and Clara immediately ran up and hugged the woman's legs.

Ellen looked at the family unit before her, three pairs of hostile eyes staring at her, accompanied by the low growl of the dog. Grabbing her jacket, she pulled the note from the dry cleaner's out of her pocket and smacked it on the desk next to Ned. 'You owe me,' she said. Then she stormed out of the Portakabin, slamming the door behind her so hard that it bounced in the door frame and swung wide open.

A few moments later Ellen yanked open the door of the Land-Rover and hurled her jacket in the back. 'We're leaving,' she shouted at Scott, as she clambered into the driver's seat. Turning on the ignition, she revved the car hard.

'What's wrong?' asked Scott, turning down the stereo, as the Land-Rover lurched away.

'Of all the lousy, pig-headed –' Ellen began, gripping on to the steering wheel. 'Words just . . . .ugh!'

'Calm down,' said Scott. 'You're soaked. Start at the beginning. What happened?'

'I found his little girl,' Ellen shot back, not calming down at all. 'And that arrogant bastard –'

'Who?'

'Ned Bloody Spencer! Who do you think?'

'You two still aren't seeing eye to eye?'

'He's not a man you can deal with,' Ellen ranted. 'He's beyond belief! Blinkered –'

'Ellen, where are you going?' Scott asked, gripping on to the dashboard.

Ellen ignored him. 'He accused me of being irresponsible. Me! He's obviously got some prejudiced nonsense from somewhere. He didn't even give me a chance to explain about the documentary before he completely attacked me . . .'

'Ellen,' warned Scott again, lurching over and leaning on the steering wheel so that they narrowly avoided a bollard.

'Where's the gate?' she shouted.

'Over there,' said Scott, pointing through the windscreen.

'And that . . . that child bride of his!' Ellen continued, swerving the car round towards it. 'What kind of pervert is he, with a woman that young? It's practically cradle snatching!'

She sped towards the gate.

'Uh!' screamed Ellen, as at that moment she saw Ned in an ancient left-hand-drive Beetle converging on the gate at the same speed. As she got closer, she could see the woman sitting next to him.

'The child bride?' Scott queried, peering through the window. 'She's hardly a child, but she is gorgeous.'

Putting her foot down on the accelerator, Ellen sped towards the gate to beat him to it, but Ned was accelerating, too. Seconds before they hit each other, Ellen and Ned both slammed on the brakes. As the cars stopped – barely inches apart – Ellen leant on the window button, seeing that Ned had opened his window, too. For a split-second, she glared

122

down at him. 'Wanker!' she shouted as loud as she could, before furiously turning the wheel and driving round Ned's Beetle to make it through the gate first. Then, looking in the rear-view mirror, Ellen snorted with satisfaction as she saw that Ned's car had stalled, its windscreen completely obliterated by mud.

'Take that, Ned Bloody Spencer!' she yelled.

Chapter VII

Too stunned to speak, Ned Spencer found himself staring at the Beetle's windscreen. Not through it, he noted, because that was no longer possible. All he saw was mud, weeping brown mud. It was as if a giant cow had crapped on the car. And in a way, Ned considered, one had. And what's more, that cow had a name. And its name was Ellen Morris.

Ned noticed that he was still gripping the ignition key. The skin around his knuckles was blanched and he forced his fingers to relax and let the blood flow back through. 'Is everybody OK?' he finally asked.

Clara's reflection nodded at him in the rear-view mirror; Wobbles continued to lick the door handle obsessively; and Debs – to Ned's right in the passenger seat – nodded too, before staring fixedly at her knee-length black patent boots.

'Good,' Ned said. Then, 'Did you –' he began, before lapsing back into silence again.

Suddenly he became aware that his window was still open. He wound it up and turned to Debs, who was now looking away from him, across the churned-up turning circle where the building materials were always unloaded.

In the distance, the west wing of Appleforth House shimmered spectrally in the rain, as gloomy as a prison. Closer by, a buzzard perched stoically on a fence post like some harbinger of doom. All that was missing, Ned thought, was the Grim Reaper himself, rising up out of the ground with a swish of his scythe to let Ned know that his time was up and things really couldn't get any worse.

'Did you see what that woman did?' he finally uttered.

Debs's shoulders trembled. Probably shock, Ned deduced, beginning to shiver himself now as his adrenalin kicked in, bringing with it a fresh wave of self-righteous indignation.

How *dare* Ellen Morris have done this to them?

How *dare* she have put their lives at risk? How *dare* she have nearly rammed him? If it hadn't been for *his* speedy reactions, they might have . . .

It didn't bear thinking about what might have happened, if he'd failed to stop in time.

'She gave me the finger,' Ned said. 'Me,' he went on in disbelief. 'At my own place of work. In front of a child. In front of – my God – in front of *my daughter*.'

Debs's shoulders were now shaking even more forcibly than before, Ned observed. Her long auburn hair shifted across the surface of her acrylic blue puffer jacket with a hiss as she leant forward. She rested her head in her hands.

'Are you all right?' Ned enquired, placing his hand on her arm in a gesture of reassurance, suddenly concerned that she might have suffered whiplash.

'Mm,' she half said, half whimpered, before finally turning to face him, her hands cupped over her mouth and nose.

It was then that the realisation hit Ned. 'I don't believe it,' he said.

But he had no other choice. Her high, pronounced cheekbones burnt the same healthy red as whenever she got back to the house after her evening run. The tips of her wide smile were plainly visible above her perfectly manicured forefinger and thumb. Her tiny nose wrinkled and her nostrils flared.

Ned spoke slowly, so there could be no mistake: 'You – actually – find – this – funny?'

Debs shook her head furiously, her straight fringe slanting across her wide brow as she dipped her head once more.

'Nn—' he heard her say.

'Good,' he snapped, 'because if you did then you'd leave me with no other option but to –'

But the rest of his warning was drowned out by the great burst of laughter that escaped from Debs's mouth and nose. 'I'm sorry!' she wailed helplessly, the force of her declaration exaggerating her usually understated Edinburgh accent. She rubbed at her shining eyes, smudging her mascara and leaving her looking like she'd been out partying for a week. 'I'm so sorry,' she went on. 'It's just . . .' Gasps punctuated her words. '. . . your face . . .'

'My . . . face?'

Debs rocked back, gripped by a fresh and uncontrollable spasm of mirth. She was pointing at him now as if he were her own personal circus clown who'd just slipped on his fifth banana skin in a row. She writhed in her seat, gasping for air.

Ned twisted the rear-view mirror violently round so that he could see the reflection of his own face. 'Oh, yes, how hilarious,' he growled, making no attempt to wipe the streaks of mud away, 'how terribly bloody amusing for you.'

'No!' Debs gasped again. 'Not the mud . . . You . . . What you were saying . . . it made you look so . . . so . . .'

'So?' Ned prompted. He attempted to glare her back into maturity; he failed.

'Pompous!' she blurted out at him, before curling up in her seat, unable to look at him for a second longer.

Clara slotted herself into the gap between the driver and passenger seat. 'What's a wanker, Daddy?'

Debs snorted with laughter. Ned tried the ignition again. The engine turned over, once, twice, then failed.

Debs cleared her throat and let out a long sigh. 'It's a word used by grown-up people when they're angry,' she interceded on Ned's behalf.

'Like an idiot?' Clara asked.

'Yes,' Debs explained, wiping her eyes with the back of her hand. 'Only a lot ruder than that.'

'Like a prat? Or a berk? Or a greaseball?'

'Greaseball?' Debs asked. 'Where did you get that one from?'

'Tommy Carey called me it when I put salt in his yoghurt at Friday lunch,' Clara began to explain, 'but only because he broke my pencil on purpose by stamping on it,' she added, 'when he thought I wasn't looking . . .' she went on, 'only I was,' she concluded.

'OK, OK,' Debs said, pulling a Kleenex from the box on the dashboard and stretching over to wipe Clara's nose, 'we get the message: Tommy Carey had it coming.'

Ned glared at the windscreen. Ellen Morris had called him a wanker. A wanker . . . him. How could she? He was one of the least wanker-like people he knew. All right, so perhaps he shouldn't have gone off at her like that in the Portakabin. Perhaps that had been a little wanker-*ish*, a tad wanker-*esque*. And, fair enough, he certainly shouldn't have done it in front of Clara. But he hadn't done it on purpose, so much as . . . well, so much as because it had just happened. What Ellen Morris had said, it had . . . it had made him see red, hadn't it? And something inside him had snapped.

But as for what she'd just done in return . . . well, alongside *that* his own behaviour now seemed positively mild.

127

'The only wanker around here is Ellen Morris,' he stated aloud.

'Ned!' Debs said.

'Dad!' Clara gasped.

'Well, it's true,' Ned announced, 'and what's more, I should report her to the police.'

He pictured Ellen Morris's face at the moment of her arrest: the outraged stare; the attempt to justify her psychotic driving. But the police wouldn't listen. On with the handcuffs and into the back of the van – *that*'s what would happen to her. Oh, yes, it was a picture Ned could hang on his wall and never grow tired of looking at.

'But she hasn't done anything illegal,' said Debs.

'I like her,' said Clara. 'I was freezing and wet, and she gave me her coat.'

'All she actually did was beat you to the gate,' Debs pointed out.

'It's not what *did* happen,' Ned said, 'it's what *could* have happened.'

Debs clicked her tongue in stolid disapproval. Clara tut-tutted and Wobbles, bored now of licking the door handle, started to whine, rolling his good eye round and round in its socket, while his blind eye locked on Ned, as lifeless and impenetrable as a glass marble.

With a growl of frustration Ned tried the ignition again. This time the engine fired and kept running. Ned switched on the windscreen wiper, which moved no more than a millimetre before whining to a halt in shuddering protest. He switched the engine off. 'Incredible,' he said, though it was more of a curse than anything else.

He got out of the car, leant over the arched bonnet in the pouring rain and began the messy task of scooping the mud clear from the windscreen with his bare hands.

As he looked through the glass at Debs and Clara talking, and Wobbles repositioning himself on the back seat and starting to chew his paw, however, the anger that had consumed him began to dissipate. Maybe it was the fresh air and the rain on his neck cooling him down, or maybe it was simply that, looking at this scene as an observer from the outside, he suddenly felt incredibly blessed.

Ned turned towards the estate entrance through which Ellen Morris had triumphantly sped not five minutes ago. The ruts left by her car's tyres were already filling with rain and would soon be obliterated. But something else about her remained, something he couldn't see, but could still feel. Life force, that was the only way he could think of to describe it. It was as though all that energy she possessed had stamped its signature on this place and, indeed, on him. 'Incredible,' he repeated, though this time it wasn't a curse at all.

Back in the car, he looked Debs and Clara over. 'Change of plan,' he said. 'It's obviously not going to clear up out there, so the beach trip's off.'

'Oh!' Clara groaned.

'But don't worry,' Ned continued, starting the engine and turning the car round in a wide arc, so that it faced Appleforth House, 'I've got a much better idea.'

The conservatory was a recent addition to the property, insisted upon by Jonathan Arthur, and pushed through the planning permission authorities by Ned on the back of a mountain of paperwork.

Ned had resisted the idea at first, feeling that it went against the spirit of his initial brief: to restore Appleforth House to its original condition. But now, sitting inside it on the polished teak floor, with the rain drumming down on the extravagant pattern of glass panes he'd commissioned from MapleLeaf Conservatories, he felt pleased with the way it had turned out. Thanks to the crisp white paintwork of the wooden frame, the room was light and airy, and would soon, he hoped, produce a perfect harmony between people and plants.

It was unfurnished at the moment, but wouldn't be for long. Plant pots and a wrought-iron dining table and chairs were on order, as well as a rare and intricately ornamented garden seat by Thomas Chippendale, which Ned had secured through Sotheby's, and which currently lay in storage in Park Royal.

This lack of furnishing suited Ned fine, though, because as far as he and Clara and Debs were concerned, this wasn't a conservatory at all right now, but a beach. And it wasn't raining either; it was a sultry summer afternoon.

On the other side of the tartan picnic rug, which Ned had brought in from the car, sat Debs, with her boots off, her trousers rolled up over her knees and her shades perched jauntily on top of her head.

Her toenails were bubblegum pink from where Clara had just finished painting them and glittered under the bare high-wattage bulb which Greg, the chief electrician, had suspended for them from an aluminium stepladder. Debs pulled an apple from the wicker picnic hamper at her side and, biting into it with a loud crunch, picked up a copy of *Heat* and started to read.

Clara was sitting beside Ned, waggling her toes in the warm draught of the fan heater. She held her flattened hand up to her brow and peered beneath it like Robinson Crusoe out to sea. Above the hum of the heater came the occasional clang and shout of the men and women working in the main house.

'But hang on! What's that over there?' Ned cried out in a shabby attempt at a pirate accent. He was pointing beyond the double glass doors at the front of the conservatory, to where piles of timber were stacked beneath blue plastic tarpaulins. 'Sails, by God! It's the rescue fleet sent by the Queen to find us! We're saved!'

'Watch out!' Clara shouted back, pointing to the left, along an avenue of beech trees which terminated at a ha-ha, the sunken ditch of which was overgrown with a glossy barrier of cherry laurel. 'Here comes a massive wave and it's going to knock all the boats over! Whoosh!' she shouted, cackling with laughter. 'All the boats are sinking!'

Just then, Dan the foreman's head came into view, then his shoulders and the rest of his body, as he hurried up the steps leading from the garden on to the stone terrace at the front of the conservatory.

'But look!' Ned retorted, determined to give the story a happy ending, in spite of Clara's aspirations towards naval tragedy. 'One of the sailors has swum all the way to the shore!'

Noticing them sitting inside, Dan hurried over and pressed his blotchy square face up against the outside of the glass. He then roared demonically, sending Clara into a fit of the giggles, before disappearing from sight once more.

'He's a ghost!' Clara shrieked, getting her way after all.

As Clara continued to laugh, Debs peered over the top of her magazine at Ned and rolled her eyes. Ned smiled, then watched as Clara signalled her boredom with their game of shipwreck by rolling on to her stomach and starting to pick at the remains of the potato salad on her plate.

Ned sighed, gripped by a sudden sense of longing. It was easy sometimes to delude himself over what a great family unit the three of them made. It was easy sometimes to forget they weren't a family at all.

'Is everything OK?' Debs asked.

'Yeah,' Ned acknowledged, remembering the first time he'd interviewed Debs after his own mother had – quite unknown to him – placed an advert in *The Lady* three years ago, asking for '*a capable and experienced nanny, prepared to take care of two messy kids: Clara, aged two, and Ned, aged thirty-three*'.

Ned gazed across the room at a delta of water that had formed on one of the glass panes. Mary, Ned's wife of six years and Clara's mum, had died a year before Debs had started working for Ned, just after Clara's first birthday.

That next twelve months of coping on his own had been like being trapped inside a sped-up piece of film for Ned. He'd found himself changing nappies, pitching for new business, pushing prams, cooking meals, waking at six and flaking out at midnight – all at an impossible, incomprehensible speed. It had happened in a blur and he'd done none of it well. And he'd done it all while attempting the impossible task of coming to terms with Mary's death.

Debs's arrival had saved both him and Clara from himself. He was certain of that now and he couldn't imagine life without her. She was a mother to Clara and a good friend to him. Even if it wasn't a family, it was as close as he could manage for Clara at the moment.

'Is it scary here at night?' Clara asked suddenly, threading a breadstick free from its cardboard box and biting off its tip.

'No, darling,' Ned replied. 'What makes you ask?'

'Tommy Carey at school said that ghosts live here.'

'Did he now?' Ned knew all about the stories that circulated around the town below. It was hardly surprising, considering the people who'd killed themselves up here. 'Well, you shouldn't believe everything that Tommy Carey tells you,' he told her.

'I don't. He's a liar and everyone knows it.' Clara traced a snake in the cheese and chive dip with her breadstick. 'What's a ghost?' she asked without looking up. 'I mean, apart from being scary.'

'I don't exactly know,' Ned pondered. 'I don't even know if I believe in them. I suppose it's what some people turn into when they die.'

'What people?

'Well, people who were unhappy when they were alive.'

Clara thought about that for a moment, adding another twist to the snake she was drawing. 'Where do ghosts live?' she then asked.

Ned glanced at Debs, but all she did was shrug and raise her copy of *Heat* up over her face. He looked back at Clara, who'd stopped moving her breadstick and was waiting for a response. 'I'll tell you if I ever see one,' he said.

Clara began to hum. It was a theme tune off the telly, from one of the kids' programmes, but Ned couldn't remember which. The tune stopped.

'What about Mummy?' Clara asked, still without looking up. 'Where does she live?'

Ned had answered this question a thousand times before. 'She lives in heaven,' he said. 'You know that.'

But even as Ned said this, he knew it wasn't the case. Mary didn't live anywhere any more; she was dead.

'Is she a ghost?'

'No, darling. Mummy's an angel.'

'Is that because Mummy was happy when she was alive?'

'Yes, darling. That's right.'

'What about you? Will you be a ghost when you die?' She

133

looked up at him for the first time in the conversation. 'Because you get unhappy sometimes, don't you?'

Ned didn't know what to say. He didn't have an answer.

'Clara,' Debs said, lowering her magazine, 'I think we should start clearing everything up now.'

Ignoring her, Clara shuffled across the floor and snuggled up next to Ned. Putting her arms as far round him as she could manage, she rested her head against his chest. 'Tell me about Mummy,' she said as he'd heard her say a thousand times before. 'Tell me the story about how you and Mummy met and had me.'

And so he did. As Debs set about clearing up the picnic and packing the plates and cutlery away in the hamper, Ned told Clara about Mary.

It was a story full of absolutes, a story which was designed not to raise questions, a story which could – and Ned hoped would – be taken at face value.

Mary Thomas had been beautiful, just as Clara was beautiful now. Mary had been a brilliant landscape artist. Ned had fallen in love with Mary the first time he'd seen her, before he'd even spoken to her. Ned had watched Mary painting at an easel in a graveyard when he'd been a student working in the nearby church tower. Mary and Ned had gone on dates to the movies and to restaurants and to bars. Mary and Ned had grown to love one another with all their hearts. Mary and Ned had set up a business together. Mary and Ned had got married. Mary had given birth to a baby girl and Ned had become Daddy and Mary had become Mummy. And Mummy's and Daddy's baby had been the most beautiful baby they'd ever seen, and so they'd decided to call her Clara, because they'd thought that was the prettiest name they'd ever heard. And both Mummy and Daddy had loved Clara with all their hearts.

'But then, when you were still only a baby,' Ned heard himself concluding the story, running his fingers now through Clara's hair as she listened, 'Mummy became very ill . . . there was something wrong with her brain . . . it was a terrible disease and nobody could help her, not even the doctors.'

'And then she died,' Clara said.

'Yes.' Ned wondered what it meant to Clara, her mother's death. The way she said it made it sound so simple, so much a natural part of life.

'And she went to heaven,' Clara concluded.

Only Ned didn't believe in an afterlife, only in the life Mary had left behind. 'Yes,' he told Clara.

'And that's where she watches us from now.'

'Every day,' he assured his daughter.

'As an angel.'

'Yes.' But Ned didn't believe in angels either.

'And one day we'll see her again.'

'Yes,' Ned said, continuing to stroke her hair, 'one day we will.'

Ned looked away across the lawns. But as he did there was something hard about his eyes that had nothing to do with longing at all.

Chapter VIII

Jimmy's face was set in a scowl, an expression he'd never seen reflected in a mirror and one which would shock him if he ever did. It was Friday afternoon and he was walking through the harbour yard, with two plastic buckets containing four live lobsters swinging in his hands, and he was thinking about his father.

Jimmy's dad, Ben Jones, had failed to call last night, a broken promise from two weeks ago, when Jimmy and Rachel had heard from him last. Jimmy hated thinking about his father. He preferred thinking of himself as strong and missing his father, like he was now contradicted that.

Independence: that was how Jimmy always put it to himself. He was independent of his father. He'd grown that way out of necessity. He'd taught himself to look elsewhere whenever the flickering spectre of his father's face had popped into his mind with its promises and its dreams.

But today was one of those days he couldn't seem to shake his dad at all. Dad. Christ, even the word felt like some sort of cruel joke. The sense of doom and injustice which had eaten into him up on the cliff the night before last chewed at him still, and his scowl remained as he lifted the freshly painted black latch on the gate that divided the harbour from Quayside Row.

It wasn't hard for Jimmy to *excuse* this uncharacteristic lapse in his independent attitude. There was the bitter taste of salt on his lips. There was the itching, stretching feeling on his hands from when he'd been cleaning mackerel and

136

the scales had now started drying in the wind and would soon be flaking off like dead skin. Then there was the dampness of his scalp from when the sea had sprayed over the bow of Arnold Peterson's boat, the *Lucky Susan,* when it had made its run for the harbour entrance half an hour ago. And there was the singing of the ships' rigging all around Jimmy now and the slap-slosh of the buckets as he turned and closed the gate behind him.

They were locked into Jimmy's memory, all of these sensations. From years ago, when he'd sat back there on the warped wooden planks of the quay with his dad, legs long and short dangling beneath them, as they'd fished for crabs and small fish with pieces of luncheon meat on hand-held lines.

He remembered his dad telling him how one day, when Jimmy was bigger and stronger, they'd cross the sea together and make their fortunes. Like Sir Francis Drake, Jimmy's dad had declared. They'd commandeer themselves a galleon and set sail for the Spanish Main. And back they'd come with a cargo full of gold to be knighted by the Queen. And then they'd live happily ever after, like kings.

Jimmy stared across the choppy waters to where the *Susan* was moored. Arnie had bought the motor boat ten years ago, after the European commercial fishing quota system had finally done for his real business. There Arnie was on deck, busying himself with stowing the two carbon rods from which he and Jimmy had trawled their feathers around the bay for mackerel these last two hours, in between hauling up Arnie's pots.

The *Susan* was canary yellow like the Birds custard Jimmy's gran had cooked up every Friday teatime since the year dot, and Arnie's bald brown scalp was as dull as dry terracotta. He waved at Jimmy and grinned, shouting something up which got lost in the wind.

Jimmy wanted to smile back, but he couldn't. Instead, his scowl tightened as he turned his back on the sea and set off up Quayside Row towards the town.

There were no galleons waiting to be commandeered any more. There were no cargoes full of gold to be found across the sea. There was only his dad, full of shit. And for Jimmy, there was only this small town with its small boats left. And bigger and stronger though he now was, he was still stuck within its confines.

He'd never forgive his dad for all these lies, for pretending to be someone he wasn't.

Jimmy heard Scott before he saw him. The sound of knuckles rapidly rapping on glass caused Jimmy to flinch and check his stride. Water slopped from the buckets' rims on to his work jeans. He saw the flash of a face in the window of the cottage next to Arnie's, and then the door was flung open and the Australian stepped out on to the path. 'Hey there, Jimmy,' Scott said, taking a pace forward and blocking Jimmy's way. Scott was wearing a cotton shirt, which ruffled and bucked in the wind as if something live was wriggling up against his chest.

'All right,' Jimmy said, the buckets weighing heavy now in his hands.

'I've been looking for you,' Scott said, glancing down at the buckets' contents. 'You weren't there at the vidi store when I took the movie back this morning.'

'I only work there part-time.'

'I liked it, by the way: the film,' he elaborated. 'Smart recommendation.' Curiosity getting the better of him, Scott leant down and peered inside the buckets. He reached out and touched one of the lobsters' rubber-band-bound claws. 'Tasty,' he said, putting on a Mockney accent, meaning what he said, though, as if in some way he'd absorbed the crustaceans' flavour through his fingertips. 'Runts compared with the ones back home, mind.' He considered, before asking, 'They for sale?'

'Already spoken for by Mrs Driver up at the Grand.'

'Ah,' Scott said, straightening up, 'the illustrious Cheryl.'

Verity's face darted like an assassin into Jimmy's mind. Tomorrow, she was going on her date with Denny Shapland.

Jimmy shivered as a blast of wind sealed his wet jeans against his thighs. He glanced up towards the High Street, to where the façade of the Grand reared up against the speeding sky.

He was dreading dropping the lobsters off there, in case he bumped into Verity. He couldn't handle that, not yet. It had been tough enough sitting through lessons with her at school yesterday and this morning. She hadn't so much as glanced at him, let alone thanked him for the CD he'd given her at the start of the week. He felt bad enough, then, already, without her catching the stench of the mackerel guts on the soles of his boots as well.

Jimmy cleared his throat. 'You know her?' he asked. 'Mrs Driver?'

'Hardly a lady you forget,' Scott said with a sly smile, leaving Jimmy uncertain as to what he meant. 'All these jobs you've got,' he continued, 'the vidi store and the fishing boat . . . you're obviously a very busy fellah, which is a shame . . .'

'Why's that?'

'Just that the reason I was looking for you was because I wanted to offer you some work . . .'

Jimmy's pulse quickened. 'What kind of work?' he asked.

'After chatting to you the other day, you know, and that woman at the vidi store mentioning about how you've got plans to go off to film school . . . I thought that maybe you might be up for giving me and Ellen a helping hand while we're down here.'

Any elation Jimmy might have felt over this offer was crushed beneath his fear over where it might all lead. It was like Scott had pressed a button and a steel wall had snapped down between them.

'I don't think –' Jimmy began to say.

But Scott was already talking, scratching his nose as he cut Jimmy off mid-sentence: 'Of course, I'd understand if you felt you've got enough on your plate as it is, or it's too much responsibility for someone who's still at school, or whatever . . .'

There was a brightness in Scott's eyes the instant he finished speaking, kind of like he was daring Jimmy into something. It reminded Jimmy of Ryan, the way he'd always been when he'd got a plan that he knew Jimmy would get a buzz out of if he'd only give it a try. The Butch and Sundance look, Jimmy had always privately thought of it as, the one Redford and Newman had shared before spurring their horses over the ravine in the film.

Scott was fishing for him. Jimmy could see that clearly enough. The same as with Arnie and the lobster pots, here Scott was laying out his bait and inviting Jimmy to step inside.

'Then again,' Scott went on, 'maybe it *is* something you're keen on. I mean, the pluses are pretty monumental. You get to learn all about how a documentary gets made. You get something solid to take to film school with you, maybe even to help get you in there in the first place, and, well, who knows where it all might lead, eh?'

Jimmy knew he should turn the Australian down flat. Forget about his ambitions for his future. They were far outweighed by the dangers buried in his past. The very fact that Scott and Ellen were here to investigate Lost Soul's Point should have been enough to put him off.

But at the same time Jimmy wanted this. He wanted this because it was the kind of break he'd spent years dreaming of, sitting there in his bedroom in Carlton Court, poring over his movie mags and his spine-cracked volumes of *Halliwell's*. He wanted it because it would make him *someone*. And he wanted it because it would let him prove what he so desperately wanted to believe: that nothing was impossible, not even for him.

You're in control, Jimmy reminded himself again. *No one can see inside your mind. No one can make you speak about the things you saw or tell about the things you did.*

The steel wall inside his mind slowly started to rise. *Forget Dad. Forget failure. Forget the past.*

'What's the score, then?' he asked, finally putting the buckets down on the ground.

'Little of this, little of that. I'll tell you what,' Scott suggested, 'let me go grab a coat, and then I'll walk up to the hotel with you. I've got some stuff that needs doing in the town anyways.'

'Why not?' Jimmy said, hooking his thumbs into his jeans pockets.

As Scott disappeared inside, Jimmy stayed where he was and peered after him through the open door. Jimmy had been in there before, a decade ago now. His gran had used to clean properties for the holiday rental firm that owned this one and Jimmy had often kept her company during the school holidays when there'd been nobody else to look after him.

What could he remember? Her humming all those old jazz tunes she'd liked? Singing songs about Dinah from Carolina and Honeysuckle Rose? Her whipping the linen off the bed like she'd been some great magician making an elephant appear on stage before an audience's disbelieving eyes? Or her simply scrubbing down the kitchen floor, with him – aged what? Four or five? – trailing around after her, or getting under her feet, building dens here in the sitting room, pushing the furniture together and covering it with sheets and towels.

The immediacy of the memory left him feeling jangled over how moments like that could never be again and he turned round. A hundred yards offshore, he could see the lifeboat back on its mooring, dipping in and out of the see-sawing waves.

He hadn't been sleeping too well these last few nights: more nightmares about Ryan, waking him up, scaring him out of switching off the light and going back to sleep. Around four last night – lightning running like cracks across the window-pane – he'd sat in the living room, watching the lifeboat's red port and green starboard lights ploughing out into the storm-tossed sea.

He smiled, glad that it was light now, and glad the night was over and the boat had made it safely back.

Locking the front door of the cottage behind him, Scott joined Jimmy and picked up one of the buckets. He waited until Jimmy had picked up the other and then the two of them set off up the path.

'OK, let me fill you in on what we're doing. It's part of a series on famous landmarks Ellen's company's been commissioned to make,' Scott began, before running the series idea past Jimmy and elaborating on his and Ellen's consequent interest in Lost Soul's Point.

As Scott continued to speak, Jimmy listened and didn't interrupt. That's what people did in job interviews, wasn't it? And they exuded confidence, too . . . wasn't that how it was done?

'We're going to be talking to people in the town . . .' Scott was saying a few minutes later, as they paused for a few seconds' rest and gazed up the length of Crackwell Street. '. . . and doing some location footage which we can then run with whatever commentary Ellen comes up with. Next up, there'll be a few short dramatic reconstructions relating to the legend. Dastardly lover disappearing into the night; distraught Victorian girl chucking herself off the cliff: and – hey presto! – a legend is born. You get the gist, I'm sure.'

'You're going to be using actors for that, then?' Jimmy asked, holding the bucket in both hands now as they walked up the steep road towards the High Street. 'The dramatic reconstructions . . .'

It was the first time Jimmy had spoken since Scott had started his pitch. Hearing his own voice sounding so normal in this weird situation gave Jimmy the confidence to say more. He even decided to risk a joke. 'Let me guess,' he said, 'Kate and Leonardo are flying in for the job.'

'Cute.' Scott laughed. 'No, Jimmy, mate, we're going to be looking a lot closer to home for our talent.' He inclined his head towards the front door. 'You know they're doing that memorial concert thingy to raise funds?'

Jimmy felt his guts clenching, but he managed to keep his voice neutral. 'I saw one of their flyers,' was all he said.

'Right you are. Well, we're going to be there doing a spot of casting ourselves. Non-speaking roles, of course, or we'd be in a pile of union strife.' Scott chuckled to himself.

'What?' Jimmy asked.

'Ah, nothing,' Scott said with a sigh, 'just that Cheryl Driver's apparently got some all-singing all-dancing daughter and Cheryl reckons she'd be perfect for us. For playing the Victorian girl who died. Now *her* I can't wait to meet. Chip off the old block, I should imagine.'

143

Jimmy looked down at his boots. Possibilities flooded his mind. He saw Scott, Ellen and him on a shoot, and there beside him, he saw Verity too . . . But then he remembered Verity's date with Denny and wondered if she'd be turning up to tomorrow's auditions at all.

'But back to business,' Scott hurried on. 'The thing is, Jimmy, we're on a crappy budget. No full-time sound man . . . no production assistant at all. Even me and Ellen are only working down here part-time. We're going to be working in tandem, news team-style, you know?' Scott glanced across at Jimmy.

'Sure,' Jimmy bluffed, not really knowing at all.

'And what we're gonna need is someone who'll be able to muck in on an ad hoc basis, if you catch my drift, to get on and do the camera marking for editing, that kind of thing,' he went on, his breath becoming laboured as they approached the top of the street. 'A bit of techie stuff, then, but you'll pick it up quick enough, no worries. And then there's general runner stuff. Gofer work: me and Ellen shout for something and you go find it.'

'And that's all?' Jimmy asked, as they finally drew level with the High Street.

Scott laughed. 'If you call that *all*, then you really have got a whole stack to learn before going off to film college.'

Scott put his bucket down on the pavement and turned to face Jimmy. He cleared his throat. 'There's something Ellen wanted me to ask you,' he said, putting his hands on his hips. 'Only I want you to know that it's got nothing to do with me offering you the work. Because you can take my word for it: it hasn't.'

'What?' Jimmy asked.

'This kid they're doing the benefit for: the one who was messed up on drugs and committed suicide in the stolen car,' Scott began.

'Ryan,' Jimmy said.

The name sounded like a bell tolling in Jimmy's mind. He couldn't remember the last time he'd said it aloud. None of Jimmy's friends talked about Ryan any more. And Jimmy knew he was no better. He hadn't even been to see Ryan's parents since the funeral, in spite of his promises to Ryan's mum and sister at the time, and in spite of the fact that they only lived on the other side of town. But he hadn't known what to say to them. What did you say to someone about their dead son?

'Ryan,' Jimmy repeated, almost as a penance. 'His name was Ryan.'

'He was a mate of yours, then?'

Jimmy had walked past there once, past Ryan's parents' short-fronted stone-clad terraced house, a month after the funeral. But he hadn't gone in. All he'd been able to do had been to picture them the way they'd been that day at the Stanfield Crematorium. Jimmy would never forget the lack of comprehension he'd witnessed in their eyes, or their blank stares as they'd moved – drifted, it had seemed – up the aisle to their seats in the front pew. Sleepwalkers, Jimmy had thought at the time, like none of this had been real; not for any of them.

'He was my best friend,' Jimmy told Scott.

After the funeral, at the Church Hall on St Mary's Street, as Ryan's friends and family had nibbled at biscuits and curling sandwiches, and sipped at cups of weak tea, Jimmy had seen the change that had overtaken Ryan's father. And it was that – the fire behind his weeping eyes – that had stayed with Jimmy most of all. Because Jimmy had known with absolute certainty what it had meant. It hadn't been anger. It hadn't been sorrow. It had been shame that had started Ryan's father's tears and shame that hadn't let them stop. He'd been ashamed of what his son had done and he'd been ashamed that he hadn't been able to stop him from doing it.

That was when Jimmy had got up and slipped out of the Church Hall and into the street. That was when he'd started running. And that was when he hadn't stopped running till he'd reached the Wreck and had huddled up in a corner and dragged a blanket round his heaving shoulders.

But mainly that was when he hadn't stayed to stop Ryan's father's tears, even though he'd known something that could have made a difference, something he hadn't had the courage to say then; and didn't have the courage to say now.

'I'm sorry,' Jimmy heard Scott telling him. 'About what happened to him. There's nothing worse than losing someone you care about. Sounds lame, I know, but I mean it.'

Jimmy felt his face tightening, like it was a mask he'd worn too long and was starting to crack. He couldn't bring himself to speak. He felt the same shame as Ryan's father's bearing down on him. He could have stopped Ryan. He knew he could have. If he'd acted differently towards him . . . if he'd only stood up to him and saved him from himself . . . then Ryan might still be alive.

'The reason I brought it up. Ryan,' Scott swiftly corrected himself. 'The reason I brought *Ryan* up is that Ellen wanted me to ask you about him. Because you're the same age and she guessed – rightly, as it turns out – that you might have known him and therefore might know what made him do it.'

'Something nice and juicy for your story,' Jimmy said, bitterness rising in his throat.

'No, Jimmy. Not because of that. Because Ellen wants what we do here to be accurate. Because we are going to be making enquiries about people who've committed suicide up there and because we don't want to end up saying things about them that aren't true.'

Jimmy covered his eyes with his hand as a vision zoomed into focus: the night-time sea as seen from Lost Soul's Point, slithering hungrily over the rocks below, as black and as viscous as oil. It was the same vision that filled his night-mares: the great black mouth of the sea opening up to swallow him whole, the waves striking out for him like cold wet fingers and tongues, stretching up to tear him down. His breath came shallow in his ears.

'Are you all right?' he heard Scott ask.

Jimmy blinked heavily and when he opened his eyes the vision had receded. 'They got it wrong,' he said simply; he'd said it before he could stop himself. 'About what happened to Ryan . . .'

'How?' Scott asked. 'That he wasn't a drug addict?'

Jimmy looked down at the gutter. 'He wasn't depressed,' he said. 'He wasn't depressed because he was on drugs. That wasn't why he died.'

'Then why did he do it?' Scott asked.

'I don't know. Nobody does. That's why what everyone's been saying about him is such shit.'

Jimmy leant forward and picked up the bucket Scott had been carrying. He knew there was nothing more to talk about and that the interview was at an end. He'd messed it up good and proper. He hadn't given Scott anything useful and the Aussie probably couldn't wait to see the back of him after the way he'd just been about Ryan. Still, he thought, at least he wouldn't have to talk to Scott or Ellen about Ryan again.

But Scott hadn't finished yet. 'In which case', Scott said, 'there's no need to say any more about it, is there? I'll tell

Ellen what you've told me. And that's what we'll use: that it's a mystery as to why Ryan did it, and all that we do know is that he did.'

Jimmy shook his head. 'I'd best be off,' he said, taking a step forward.

'And the work?' Scott asked.

Jimmy stopped. 'What about it?'

'Are you still up for it?'

Jimmy tried to read Scott's face, to see if he was joking. 'Are you serious?' he finally asked.

'So long as you are,' Scott answered.

It was back again: the Butch and Sundance look: that connection again between Scott and Ryan.

'And it would be good to have your decision soon, so as you can tag along at the auditions tomorrow and get a better idea of what we're going to be up to.'

Jimmy stared down at the lobsters trapped in their buckets, knowing that in his heart the decision had already been made.

Chapter IX

'She's a beauty!' Russell Driver exclaimed, holding up one of the large lobsters that Jimmy had delivered to the kitchen earlier, as Verity pushed through the back door of the hotel, laden with packages.

Verity's Friday post-school shopping spree with Treza had been an exercise in spending most of her savings account in order to find *the* outfit that would impress Denny tomorrow. Thanks to Treza, she had several bulging carrier bags which now cut into her fingers.

'Looks like someone's got a hot date,' her father commented, manipulating the lobster in a tasteless attempt at ventriloquism. Rudi, the chef and Goran, the other kitchen porter, neither of whom spoke a word of English, chuckled loudly.

'Stop it, Russell!' Cheryl reprimanded with a sideways scowl, as if teasing Verity were cruel.

Verity put down her bags and looked between her parents, feeling a foreboding sense of embarrassment. How was she ever going to be able to introduce her parents to Denny? He'd think they were awful. And he'd be right.

Ever since she'd seen him the day before yesterday, thoughts like these had been keeping Verity awake at night. What if she just wasn't good enough for Denny? What if she couldn't match up to his expectations. Already, things seemed to be going so fast.

She'd been outside the chemist on Wednesday afternoon, on her way to her piano teacher's house, when she'd seen

Denny whizz past on his motorbike. She'd waved and called out his name, but still she'd hardly been able to believe it when he'd done an abrupt U-turn in the street, brought the bike to a stop next to where she was standing and quickly eased off his helmet.

He hadn't even said hello, before he'd reached out and pulled her towards him. 'I'll pick you up at seven on Saturday,' he'd said huskily, kissing her cheek, as if they'd been going out together for ages. 'Dress up, if you want. I've got somewhere special lined up.'

She'd been so shocked that she'd only been able to nod, touching her face where he'd kissed her. 'I can't wait,' she'd managed.

'Me neither.' Then he'd winked and smiled, and she'd felt as if she'd been lit up inside. 'See you soon, beautiful,' he'd said.

Then he'd replaced his helmet and driven off again, holding up one hand as he'd sped away from her. Verity had looked around her, stunned that everyone was behaving normally, as if nothing amazing had just happened.

And, at that moment, she'd started to believe what her heart had only dared to hope: that Denny Shapland was going to be her first true love.

Now, she looked at her parents with despair as her father carried on pretending to converse with the lobster, while her mother hovered uncomfortably at the counter, where she was hastily finishing a bowl of pasta and salad, eating unnaturally loudly.

Verity hadn't said anything about Denny before, but now she decided this might as well be the moment to break the news. 'Actually, I am going on a date,' she said.

The corners of Russell's mouth turned down in an

150

impressed look at Cheryl, who in turn dabbed at the corners of her mouth with a paper napkin.

'Tomorrow night. Just so you know.'

Not waiting for an answer, she picked up her bags and made for the stairs.

'Stop right there,' Cheryl said and Verity froze, her hackles rising along the back of her neck. She was all too familiar with this particular note of disapproval in her mother's voice. What was it going to be this time? A Spanish inquisition about the suitability of her date? Her mother had done exactly that when Verity had first gone out with Stephen Blacks when she was sixteen.

Not content with quizzing Verity, she'd bombarded Verity's first boyfriend with a firing line of questions. As a result, Verity had been dumped and Stephen had spread it about in school that Verity's mother was worse than the Gestapo and any right-minded boy should avoid going out with Verity at all costs.

Well, that was never going to happen again. Especially not with Denny.

Slowly, Verity turned.

'You can't go on a date,' Cheryl said, folding her napkin and flattening her hand on top of it decisively. 'You're going to the auditions for the benefit concert.'

'What?'

Cheryl hooked a finger into her mouth and dislodged some food from her back teeth. 'I've already told Clive you'll be there.'

'Clive? You hate Clive.'

'No I don't,' Cheryl said, standing up and putting on her blazer which was hanging over the corner of an open cupboard. 'He's very community-spirited. He agrees that it will be a perfect showcase for you.'

Verity couldn't believe what she was hearing. 'Mum,' she said incredulously. 'Please tell me you're not serious.'

'Of course I'm serious. It's important that you represent the town,' said Cheryl, straightening out her blazer.

'But you said that the benefit concert was a waste of time,' Verity argued, aghast at her mother's double standards. 'You said that no amount of free table tennis would stop junkies like Ryan from killing themselves.'

'Yes, well that was before it was going to be on television. I happen to know that Ellen Morris is filming it,' Cheryl countered smugly. 'And she'll be choosing people to appear in her documentary tomorrow night. If you're not there, she won't choose you.'

'What makes you think I want to be chosen?'

'Don't take that tone with me. It would be a travesty for anyone else to do it. After all your father and I have given up so that you can do your music and drama, and here's a free ticket on to national television and you're taking that tone.'

Verity could feel the anger bubbling up in her. It was the sheer level of her mother's presumptuousness that got her. 'You're such a hypocrite,' she said, hating the fact that her voice was catching in her throat. She was determined not to cry in front of her mother. If she showed any emotion her mother would have won. 'You hated Ryan and everything he stood for. You were *glad* when he died. You even said he deserved it.'

Cheryl gasped and Verity saw that she'd scored a bull's-eye.

'I did not,' Cheryl said in her most outraged voice, but her cheeks were red. Verity stared at her mother and raised her eyebrows in a challenge, but Cheryl pointed her index finger defiantly at her daughter. 'Verity Driver, you are going to do this concert,' she continued. 'You are going to represent this family and this town, and show just how we feel about that poor boy –'

'You're so full of –' Verity sneered.

'What?' her mother interrupted. 'What did you say?'

'You can't make me,' Verity said, snatching up her bags.

'Ladies, ladies,' Russell interjected, waving the lobster like a red card between his wife and his daughter.

'Shut up, Russell!' Cheryl snarled, her head twitching with such a force of suppressed anger that Verity took a step backwards, just in case her mother finally snapped and lashed out. 'While you live under this roof, I can make you and I will,' she said, glaring at Verity with icy control. 'You will do this concert whether you like it or not. Because if you don't do it . . .' Cheryl thrust her hand in front of Verity's face and, with the other, pointed to her fingers as she spoke. 'There will be no driving lessons, no allowance and you can forget going on any more dates, now or in the future. Is that understood?'

Upstairs, in her room, Verity flung her bags into the corner and threw herself like a skydiver on to her king-sized bed. Burying her face in the mound of pale-blue checked pillows and soft toys, she screamed until her lungs were burning for air.

Then, wiping her mouth on the back of her hand, her cheeks as sore as if she had blown up a hundred balloons, she pointed the remote control at the music system, holding her finger down on the volume button until the windows shook with her favourite song on the CD Jimmy had given her. Ever since Treza had made a copy, declaring it to be a neat mix and given the CD back, Verity had listened to it non-stop. Jimmy might be a weirdo, but at least he was a weirdo with good taste.

She sat on the edge of her bed, her hands tucked under her thighs, and glared at the oblivious seagulls sitting on the window ledge, their feathers ruffling in the wind. She knew she was being childish, but she didn't care. She knew that with the music on this loud, it was only a matter of minutes before someone came up and told her to turn it down. But until then, she wanted to shut everything out.

How could this have happened? Of all the things to scupper her date, the stupid benefit concert was the last thing she'd ever have expected. But she already knew that there was no point in trying to defy her mother. She had past experience of just how unpleasant Cheryl could be when she didn't get her way.

But how was she going to tell Denny? How was she going to blow out their first date together, without him thinking she was a total baby? She closed her eyes, feeling hatred for her mother wash over her like a giant wave.

There was no solution. If she told the truth, Denny would think she was pathetic. If she lied, she was bound to get found out. Someone would tell Denny that she'd been at the audition and she'd look even more of a fool.

Slowly, she walked into the bathroom, shut the door and slumped on to the window seat, pulling the blanket round her. Outside, it was getting dark and over on the high cliff she could see the shape of the fluorescent green kite she'd often seen before. She let her eyes follow it, finding herself mesmerised as it dipped and curved in the wind above the cliff. She wondered who it was who flew it there. The view from up there must be spectacular. Perhaps she should go up there herself, she thought, and let the wind clear her head. That's what she'd do: she'd walk up there right now.

When she opened the bathroom door, she nearly jumped

154

out of her skin. Her father filled her vision. 'I knocked, but you didn't hear,' he shouted.

Verity furiously pushed past him and picked up the remote, zapping the sound system into silence. How dare he invade her space like this.

'You OK?' her father asked.

'I'm fine,' she snapped, ignoring his sympathetic scrutiny. The last thing she wanted was a heart-to-heart.

'Will you come down the bottle bank, then?' he asked hopefully. 'Before the evening rush.'

The new out-of-town supermarket lay just off the recently completed ring road. Its sprawling car park was only half full as Russell Driver drove the white van he kept for such purposes to the large steel bottle skips at the far end.

Verity sat miserably next to her father. From up here, the new road stretched away like a string of yellow fairy lights. Beyond, the town lay in a twilit glow, before a wedge of dark sea cut the lights abruptly. Way in the distance, a ship hovered in the darkness, transient as a star.

Russell, always eager to smooth things over after a row, was acting like a dog trying to get attention. He whistled cheerfully as he humped the boxes out of the van and laid them out in a line. Then he opened the passenger door and smiled at Verity. 'You do the reds and I'll start on the whites, eh?' he suggested, gesturing to the box.

Verity got out of the van. She loved her dad and always would, but he hadn't turned out to be much of a role model for her, she thought dismally. It would be OK if he stood up to her mother once in a while, but the fact that he let himself be bossed around annoyed her. But then, who was she to judge? She didn't stand up to her mother either, so she could hardly blame her father for opting for an easy life.

'Nice evening, isn't it?' said her father, as she picked up the first empty bottle.

Verity posted the bottle into the rubber-lined hole in the side of the skip, twisting the bottle bottom with extra force, so that it smashed deep inside. She could tell her father was watching her closely, but still she kept silent.

Eventually, Russell coughed loudly and Verity looked over at him. He was standing looking at the label of an empty bottle of champagne. 'You know, your mother and I were young when we met,' he said, glancing up at her.

Oh God, please don't, thought Verity, wishing that he would just leave it alone.

'There were plenty of setbacks for us at first, you know. Our parents never *stopped* interfering.' Russell emitted a small, nervous laugh and in that instant Verity knew that her mother had put him up to this. She could imagine her mother nagging him: 'Have a little chat with her, Russell. *You* can get through to her. Make her see that we're not so bad . . .'

As if *that* was going to work! Verity twisted another bottle into the hole with added vigour.

He didn't say anything, waiting for the echo of the smash to subside. Then he stepped towards her. 'This boy . . .' her father said tentatively.

'He's not a *boy*, Dad,' Verity said.

'Well, you know what I mean,' he stumbled. 'He'll understand, you know, if you tell him the truth.'

'No, he won't,' Verity snapped, angry that her father had the gall to interfere, but at the same time she felt relieved that he'd hit upon the one thing that had been obsessing her.

'Don't you see, though?' her father blundered on. 'He'll think you're playing hard to get. It'll make him even more keen, believe me.'

156

Verity knew that her father was doing his best, but all the same, what would he know about Denny? Hadn't her father sussed that he was the last person in the whole universe whom she would ever take relationship advice from?

But it was obvious he hadn't. Interpreting her silence as a sign that he was getting somewhere, she watched as he hunched up his large frame and laughed conspiratorially. 'Your mum!' He chuckled. 'It took months for me to actually take her out. She was full of excuses, but it never put me off. And now look at us. After all we've been through. We're not perfect, but here we are.' He sighed with the fatalistic happiness of the willingly henpecked and it struck Verity that if it had been anyone other than her father, she would have wanted to throw up with the corniness of his show of sentiment. But as it was, it just made her feel an uncomfortable mix of love and pity.

'What I'm trying to say', her father continued, 'is that things will turn out all right in the end, if they're meant to be.'

Verity had to turn away to hide her face. Because after what she'd seen two months ago, she'd never believe anything her parents said, ever again.

Of course, after she'd found out, everything had slotted into place: the mobile phone she'd found hidden in the office desk, her mother's sudden change of hairstyle, the erratic 'charity work' that had come up, but until Verity had seen her mother kissing another man in the front seat of a green Vauxhall Astra outside the UCI multiplex, she'd never imagined that her mother was capable of anything sexual – towards her father, let alone anyone else.

It still baffled Verity that someone would actually want to have an affair with her mother. As far as Verity was concerned, her mother was wholly unappealing. For starters,

157

she was an appalling snob and had the worst clothes taste going. Add to that the fact that she was blunt to the point of rudeness and her mother came rock bottom on Verity's scale of romantic heroines.

But then, it took two to tango. So what was her mother's motivation? Cheryl Driver, the woman who actively sniped at any unmarried couples who dared to check into her hotel, had, for whatever reason, taken the risk of having an affair in the one place where everyone knew everyone else's business.

It didn't make sense. How many times had her mother told Verity that she'd given up everything for the Grand? So why would she risk losing it, as she would if she split up with Russell? Why would she put everything she cared about in jeopardy? Didn't she care?

And what about her long-suffering husband, the man she shared a bed with every night? Granted he was no Russell Crowe, but surely the Driver variety wasn't *that* bad? So what had tempted her mother away?

Verity hadn't got a clear view of the man who was currently cuckolding her father, but she knew he was older and not very attractive. Verity had been so shocked when she'd seen them together that she'd run away almost instantly and had not wanted to know anything more about the mystery man. When she thought about it, it made her feel physical revulsion.

At first, she'd wanted to confront her mother about it, but when her mother had covered her tracks that evening with such a seamless lie, Verity had realised the depths of her mother's deception. She'd been so dismayed that she'd lost her nerve and missed her moment.

Afterwards she'd been glad that she had. And she was glad, too, that she hadn't told anyone else, not even Treza.

The longer she left it, the more sordid and embarrassing the facts were to put into words.

So she kept silent. Sometimes it made her feel more powerful to have such potentially explosive information. But knowing that she could shoot her mother to pieces at any moment, ruin her career and her marriage in a sentence, didn't help, because most of the time and especially at times like this when she faced her father, it just made her miserable.

Getting back into the van, Verity glanced at him as he turned the key in the ignition. She wanted to cry. Couldn't he see that everything was a lie? His whole marriage was a sham and he couldn't see what was right underneath his nose. She loved her dad and hated to think of him being deceived like this.

Well, one thing was for sure: when she had a relationship – and she hoped to God it would still be with Denny – everything would be different. It would be real and it would be true, for ever.

It was cold in the Community Hall when Verity arrived at seven o'clock on Saturday night. She shivered and folded her long brown cardigan more tightly round her as she walked forward along the aisle between the rows of linked orange plastic chairs to where Mr Peters, her music teacher from school, was handing out photocopied sheets from the top of the battered upright piano. Today, he was wearing his usual uniform of tight-fitting black polo-neck and black jeans that were belted too tightly and pulled high up on his stomach.

But despite his quirky appearance, with his blond floppy fringe and ginger-flecked moustache, Verity admired him. He was an unbelievably talented jazz pianist. He had more records in his house than Verity had ever seen and he had an encyclopaedic memory about blues singers. He was also a good teacher and had always encouraged Verity. She liked him and he waved to her as she came forward.

A dozen or so people she recognised, mostly from school, were scraping chairs across the stage to form a semicircle around the upright piano. Verity winced as Clive Cox, the benefit concert organiser and manager of the Youth Centre, rewound a tape in an ancient recorder that screeched. He was short, stocky and gruff-looking, with a constant three-day beard. He always wore a long black leather jacket that had once been fashionable in the early Eighties and never would be again, and he chain-smoked, like a TV detective, looking at each cigarette as if it were going to be his last.

Over by the kitchen, beneath the flickering lights in the multicoloured ceiling panels, a couple of the women whom Verity didn't recognise fussed about, providing plastic cups of orange juice through the hatch. So much for her Saturday night on the razzle, Verity thought as she pushed her way to the front.

'A word, Verity,' said Mr Peters and Verity followed him as he drew away, refolding the collar of his polo-neck jumper. 'It's going to be a review, but you'll be singing all the solos. We can't trust any of this lot,' he said, flicking his head to indicate the kids behind them. 'But you know how Clive is a stickler for fairness. So be a darling and go through the motions, would you?' he asked, patting her wrist. 'I know I can rely on you.'

Then he turned and clapped his hands loudly. 'Let's begin, people,' he bellowed.

Verity withdrew. If the auditions were rigged, what was the point of being here at all?

She slunk away to the back of the hall and shuffled into a row of empty seats. She glanced at the badly photocopied sheet of paper with the lyrics from the musical *Chicago*. She already knew the number backwards and she tossed the paper on the seat beside her and pulled her diary out of her bag. Then, putting her feet on the seat in front, she hunkered down and opened up the pages.

What she would do to be with Denny now, she thought, fingering the pages. Just the thought of him stopped her feeling so alone. Flipping back through her diary, she took in the pages of dense handwriting. There seemed to be so much to reflect on since she'd met Denny and she hadn't even been out on a proper date with him yet.

She read back over her diary entry from last night and smiled to herself. *The shame. Saw D, but had worst fashion accessory in the world with me: Dad!*

They'd popped into the supermarket after her father's lecture at the bottle bank. Verity had been feeling so depressed that she hadn't been able to believe it when she'd seen Denny in the queue, unloading his basket on to the conveyer belt. He'd waved and beckoned her to come over.

It had been her absolutely worst nightmare to see Denny in this kind of situation and she'd felt herself go weak with nerves. She hadn't been ready to introduce her father, especially since he'd been looking dreadful in an old sweatshirt, cheap trainers and white socks.

'Hi, Denny. This . . . this is my dad,' Verity had mumbled, unable to avoid their inevitable encounter.

'Russell Driver.' Her father had extended his hand.

'Hey, Russell.' Denny had switched his motorbike helmet from one wrist to the other, enabling him to shake Russell's hand. His hair had been swept back, showing off his tanned face, and he'd been wearing a blue shirt, unbuttoned so that

Verity had been able to see the hair on his chest. His soft leather trousers had made his lean legs look unbelievably sexy.

Verity had felt something flickering in her stomach, like a trapped canary. She hadn't been able to take her eyes off Denny. She'd spent so long obsessing about him that it had come as a shock to see him somewhere so ordinary as a supermarket. Everything she'd been planning on saying to him had vanished from her head.

An awkward moment of silence had followed. It'd been obvious that Russell had been waiting for some sort of explanation as to how Denny fitted into Verity's social life, but she hadn't been able to find any words.

'I'm just doing some shopping,' Denny had said eventually, breaking the tension and moving through to pack up his stuff.

'Us too,' Verity had mumbled gratefully, smoothing her hair behind her ear and darting a warning look at her father.

Thankfully, Russell had taken the hint. 'I'll see you in the . . .' He'd flapped his hand in the direction of the dairy section.

Verity had blushed to the soles of her trainers beneath her flared jeans, as she'd followed Denny through the checkout. 'Don't say anything,' she'd implored. 'I can't help my dad.'

'He seems OK to me,' Denny had replied, his eyes locking with hers.

She'd helped him pack up his shopping, passing him a block of butter and a loaf of bread, wishing with all her heart that Denny would somehow take her away with him, too. Inside, she'd counted to five, then had taken a deep breath. 'I can't make it tomorrow, Denny.' She'd felt sick, as she'd said the words. 'I'm so sorry.'

162

Denny had looked serious. 'But you still want to go out, right?' he'd checked.

'Of course I do!' Verity had exclaimed too loudly, before lowering her voice. 'I've been thinking about it all week.' She'd stopped, mortified by how eager she'd sounded. 'I mean, I –'

'Then we'll go out next week instead,' Denny had interrupted calmly. 'You can meet me after work on Monday and we'll make plans.'

Verity sighed as she looked at the three pages she'd written about how sensitive Denny had been. He'd even kissed her again on the cheek, once he'd paid for his shopping and had been about to leave. But it was the way he'd spoken to her that had stuck with her. It was as if being with each other had been all that had mattered to them both and everything else had been just mere detail. *Plans. He wants to make plans*, she read. *More than one!*

She was just about to start her entry for today when she glanced up and saw Jimmy Jones coming in through a side door, with that TV woman, Ellen Morris, who her mother was always going on about, and another man. Jimmy was laughing with him and, her train of thought interrupted, Verity sat up in her seat to get a better view.

She couldn't work Jimmy out. He'd been on her mind since he'd talked to her on the way to school at the beginning of the week and she'd wanted to thank him for the CD. But every time she'd looked at him in class he'd looked away as if he'd been deliberately avoiding her gaze. It was as if one minute he'd wanted to talk to her and the next he hadn't even wanted her to exist.

As if somehow being aware that she was thinking about him, Jimmy glanced over at her and, even more perplexingly, smiled as if they were long-lost friends. She saw him say something to the man. Then he climbed over the backs of several rows of chairs and slipped down into the seat next to her. 'How's it going?' he asked.

Verity nodded and they both looked ahead. Up on the stage, a girl whom Verity recognised from the class two years below her was murdering a Britney song.

'You're not auditioning, are you?' Verity asked, as she closed her diary and hugged it to her chest.

The girl on stage was struggling for the high notes and Verity and Jimmy both grimaced and then giggled.

'Not with such tough competition,' Jimmy joked. 'I'm just keeping an eye out for Ryan's sake.'

They fell silent as the girl gave up and fled the stage.

Verity smoothed her lips together, tasting the melon-flavoured lip salve she'd applied earlier. She was aware of Jimmy's shoulder pressed lightly against hers and she thought about moving away, but instead, she shifted in her seat to look at him more clearly. 'I know I haven't said anything before. But I want you to know that I'm sorry about Ryan, Jimmy,' she said. 'Really. It must have been terrible for you, being so close to him.'

Jimmy glanced at her and looked down at his hands.

'It was such a waste,' Verity continued, 'I didn't really know him, but when they told us in assembly what had happened, I felt bad, you know?'

'He was a good guy. The best.'

Verity wanted to touch him, to make Jimmy see that she was sincere, but instead, his attention was caught by the guy with Ellen Morris, who was waving over in their direction.

'Do you know them?' Verity asked.

'Yeah. That's Scott. He's a cameraman.'

Scott was walking down the aisle towards them and Verity thought how easygoing and friendly he looked.

When he reached them, he smiled and put one foot up on the row of seats in front.

'This is Verity,' Jimmy said, glancing at Verity. 'Verity . . . Scott.'

Scott stared at her for a long moment, and Verity was tempted to ask him whether she had ketchup on her nose or something.

Then Scott's gaze abruptly left her and he leant forward and clapped Jimmy on the shoulder. 'Whenever you're ready, mate,' he said, his Australian accent surprising Verity.

When Scott had turned to leave, Verity stared at Jimmy. 'What's all that about?' she asked.

'I'm doing a bit of work for them,' Jimmy replied, getting up to leave.

'You? Working for them? But how?'

'Oh, you know, contacts . . .'

'So you're doing this thing up at Lost Soul's Point, then?' Verity asked, her curiosity aroused. 'The documentary they're doing auditions for?'

'Well, it's not every day you get a film crew on your doorstep, so it'd be a shame not to see what it was all about while they're here.'

Verity tilted her head and looked at Jimmy. She had never thought he'd get involved in anything like this, but seeing him here had put him in an altogether different light.

'You interested in a part?' he asked.

Verity shrugged. 'I don't know much about it.'

'Leave it with me,' he said. 'I'll see if I can put in a good word for you.'

Verity didn't reply. She was still angry with her mother for forcing her to be here, but already she was thinking that maybe Jimmy was on to something. Maybe it might be kind of fun. And he was right. Nothing ever happened in Shoresby.

Jimmy climbed over her and she smiled at him. As he walked away, laughing with Scott, Verity noticed how good Jimmy looked in his jeans. Feeling momentarily shaken by this guilty thought, she picked up the pencil lying in the pages of her diary and dreamily wrote Denny's name surrounded by a garland of daisies, then, below it, the lines from a Shakespeare love sonnet she'd learnt off by heart.

Chapter X

In the same way that Ned didn't believe in angels, he didn't believe in ghosts. Death, as he saw it, was the end of everything and the beginning of nothing. And yet, sitting here on the windowsill in what he now knew had once been Caroline Walpole's bedroom, on this unseasonably hot Tuesday afternoon, he was at least hopeful of extracting some information from the dead.

An hour ago Stan, one of the craftsmen from Coalbrook Marbles, had come and knocked on Ned's Portakabin door. Stan had been engaged in the intricate task of re-creating the fluted pilasters on either side of the Robert Adam fireplace in one of the upstairs bedrooms. He'd told Ned that he'd got something to show him, but had refused to say what it was.

Once he'd led Ned up here, Stan had guided him past the fireplace and pointed at the base of the bare brick wall to its left. 'Look,' he'd said.

A single red brick, dry and split in two, had lain on the new oak floor.

'Mac's out working on the kitchen garden wall,' Ned had told him, peeved that Stan hadn't gone and found the bricklayer himself. Ned had been busy swotting up on the original designs for the ballroom ceiling and Stan's interruption had wrecked his concentration. 'I'll get him to pop up and take a look at it before he goes home.'

'No,' Stan had said, 'it's not the brick that's bothering me. That fell out when I chucked my toolbox up against it this morning. I mean the hole. Look inside.' He'd shot Ned a sardonic smile at this point. 'I thought that if someone was going to disturb it and maybe wreck it in the process, it should probably be the boss, eh?'

Ned had stepped forward and knelt down, first peering inside the dark and musty recess which the brick had once half filled, then reaching inside and gently removing what had been hidden there.

It was remarkable that it had survived at all, Ned considered now, as he turned another page of Caroline Walpole's private diary. The diary's fine red morocco covers had lost their flexibility and were brittle and scorched. Its gold clasp had been tarnished by the heat of the blaze and the smoke. Damp had seeped across the bottom half of each page, leaving the handwriting there illegible.

But even so, enough had been preserved of Caroline's words for Ned to have bothered skimming through her sentimental scribbling in the hope that she'd have recorded some period detail – observations regarding her room, or any other part of the house or grounds – which he'd have found of use in his work. But now, as he finally reached the last page, he accepted that his hope had been in vain. 'What a waste,' he said aloud.

'Say what?' asked Stan, looking up from the fireplace.

'It doesn't matter.'

Ned weighed the diary in his hand, annoyed over his wasted effort and half tempted to have it bricked up again. It was of no practical use to him. All it contained were the foolish notions of a naïve girl who'd read too many romantic poems and novels. Other than giving him a glimpse into Caroline's private world – a place where love reigned supreme – the diary had told him nothing he hadn't already known.

The events leading up to and surrounding Caroline's death had been recorded by the local magistrate during the inquiry that had followed her suicide. The recorded facts of the case were that Caroline's bigoted father, Alexander Walpole, had learnt of his daughter's plans to elope with Leon Jacobson. On the night of the elopement, Alexander had intercepted Leon on his way to their clifftop rendezvous and had negotiated a fee for him to leave and never return. With Leon safely on his way to Southampton docks, then, Alexander had gone to the clifftop himself to bring his daughter home. Only when he'd told her how easy her lover had been to buy off, instead of having been cured of her infatuation (as her father had assumed), Caroline had thrown herself off the cliff, broken-hearted and betrayed.

Jonathan Arthur had Fedexed Ned copies of the inquiry's records some months ago, in case they might have been of interest to him. But they hadn't been. Ned was more interested in bricks and mortar than flesh and blood. The records were buried now in some drawer or other in the Portakabin. Ned neither knew nor cared where.

He snapped the diary shut and refastened its clasp. Fortunately, he hadn't had to rely on Caroline's help in renovating the room. As well as having obtained all the legal documents relating to the house and its former occupants, Jonathan Arthur had secured for Ned the original plans and specifications for the house and gardens. Physically, then, the room as it now stood was how it would have appeared when first built.

As for the way in which the bedroom would have been furnished and decorated, Ned was spoilt for choice. The style of the period during which the house had been destroyed had been one of great eclecticism, and Ned had already sent Mr Arthur a variety of schemes to consider, any one of which Ned would be happy to implement.

The sound of a woman's laughter reached Ned and he walked over to the window and looked out. Down on the lawn stood Ellen Morris and the short, dark-haired man who'd been with her in the car on Friday. Disconcertingly, Ned felt a dart of happiness run through him. He was glad to see her, though he couldn't immediately comprehend why.

He thought back to how she'd nearly rammed his beloved Beetle. He remembered how he'd reacted to her plans for her documentary. Or *over*reacted, as he now felt. Because, even though he'd meant every word he'd said about making money out of other people's misery . . . well, he *hadn't known* that that was Ellen's only motive, had he? Maybe – and this was the bottom line – she *was* a sympathetic journalist. In which case, maybe she'd deserved the benefit of the doubt.

Ellen and the man were standing next to the honeysuckle arbour by the newly pointed kitchen garden wall and Ned watched in fascination as they bowed formally to one another, before bursting into laughter at some comment made by Mac, who was working on the wall a few yards away from them.

With her blonde hair glistening in the sunlight, Ellen cut quite a figure, even from where Ned was standing. She was dressed in a white, open-necked shirt and dark denim jeans, which stretched down her long legs and terminated in a pair of glitzy silver trainers. A chunky brown leather belt hung loosely round her waist and, as she cocked her hip now and pointed at the arbour, the belt draped down lower still across her thigh, giving her the appearance of a gunslinger itching to draw. As she broke into another laugh, throwing back her head so that he could see her face, subconsciously the corners of Ned's mouth twitched into a smile.

There'd been a time when Ned would have been hopelessly attracted towards a woman who looked like Ellen, when he would have walked straight up to her – no matter where she'd been, or whom she'd been with – looked her directly in the eyes and asked her out. There'd been a time when he would have sent her flowers at home, posted letters to her at work and left restaurant addresses on her answerphone, and a time when he would have bought aeroplane tickets in his and her name, and shown her places he loved but she'd never seen.

And there'd been a time when Ned would have been hopelessly attracted towards a woman who acted like Ellen, too. He'd been thinking a lot about their argument in the Portakabin four days ago. It had left him exhilarated. And not because – as he'd thought at the time – he'd been justified. (How, he now understood, could he know whether he'd been justified or not, when he'd hardly let her speak?) No, the buzz he'd got from their encounter had been something far less self-righteous than that.

He'd been left exhilarated because she'd stood up to him, because she'd acted as his equal – his better, in fact – and had seen fit to challenge him. She'd demanded his respect. And Ned couldn't recall the last time that had happened, in either his business or personal life. In both he was king. No one at the site ever questioned his wishes and no one (with the obvious exception of Wobbles) at home did either.

What Ellen had made Ned remember was that he *liked* being challenged, *liked* being forced to think on the spot, *liked* the feeling of adrenalin racing through his blood.

Oh, yes, he thought, looking deliberately beyond her now, at the elms and alders and half-restored walls, there'd been a time when he'd have been drawn to a woman like Ellen all right. But that time had long since past and all thoughts of her now were nothing other than idle speculation. Ned wasn't looking for someone to share his life with any more. He'd done that with Mary and he couldn't face that kind of pain again.

'OK, Scott,' Ned heard Ellen telling her companion a few minutes later, as he walked unobserved towards them across the dry grass, 'let's forget about filming the first formal meeting and go for something more intimate instead.'

'Sounds good,' Scott agreed.

Scott . . . Ned stared at him for a moment, wondering who the stocky young Australian was. Probably a work colleague, he deduced, stopping a few yards away from them. He turned his attention back to Ellen, enjoying the rarity of not finding himself shouting at her and not being shouted back at in turn.

He felt strangely nervous, now that he was no longer observing her from afar. He could see the subtle make-up on her face, the designer squiggle on her jeans pocket, and the labels and insignia on her trainers and shirt, which he'd never encountered before. She was from a different world, one he'd lived in but had now left. She was city. She was media. She was what he plainly was not.

'OK, Scott. I've got it,' she said, sitting down on the bench beneath the arbour. 'How about we go for something more romantic . . . maybe Leon reading a Tennyson poem to Caroline. And then we could film them kissing. We can shoot it after the section with them inside the house. Yes, that would be perfect: their first kiss.'

Ellen leant back against the bench and, with a giggle,

closed her eyes and began to feign kissing an imaginary Leon, hamming it up for all she was worth.

'Nine,' Ned said, stepping smartly into her line of sight.

Ellen sprang to her feet. Her eyes flashed in the sunlight as she turned to face him. 'What?' she demanded.

'Out of ten,' Ned explained, smiling now. 'For your kissing technique,' he elaborated.

There was a pause as the penny dropped, then: 'For your information, I was actually planning out how to shoot a scene,' Ellen answered, clearly embarrassed, her cheeks beginning to smart.

'Well, your technique certainly looked very professional,' Ned joked.

But Ellen clearly wasn't in the mood for his attempts at humour. 'How about you keep your opinions to yourself?' she suggested. 'You shouldn't be snooping around here anyway, not when we're trying to work.'

'It might have escaped your notice yet again,' Ned said, the anger in her voice filtering through into his own, 'but this happens to be my site and I can therefore snoop wherever the hell I want.'

'Jesus,' Scott implored. 'Will you guys just give it a rest, yeah? I'm sorry, mate,' he said, turning to Ned. 'I've never met you and I don't want to go offending you, right? But all these bad vibes you two keep throwing up, they make me want to dig my way back home, I swear to God.'

Ned stared at him. Seconds passed. He had to admit that the Australian did have a point. Finally, he turned back to Ellen.

'So why are you here?' she asked evenly.

'Glasnost,' he replied.

'What?'

'You know, the dissemination of information.'

'You're talking in riddles,' she said with an impatient tap of her foot. 'Nothing's ever easy with you, is it? Everything always has to be a struggle.'

'Fine,' he told her, turning his back on her and starting to walk back towards the house. 'In which case you probably won't be interested in this.' He held the diary up above his shoulder where she'd be able to see it. 'Caroline Walpole's diary,' he shouted back. 'You know, the girl you're making the film about, the girl who used to kiss so well . . .'

Ned started to count to ten.

'Wait!' Ellen shouted.

Ned smiled. He hadn't even got to two.

It was ten minutes later, and the spirit of glasnost engendered by the handing over to Ellen of the diary had developed into a somewhat cagey *entente cordiale*, which had in turn resulted in Ned, Ellen and Scott leaning against the bonnet of Ellen's car, basking in the sunshine while they drank from bottles of Diet Coke provided by Scott's cool box.

'You're lucky working here,' Ellen was saying.

'On days like today,' Ned agreed, assuming she was referring to the weather.

'No,' Ellen went on, 'I mean being in charge of a project of this size, being able to have a vision and follow it through.'

'It's no different from you two and your film,' Ned said, trying to hook Scott in, still curious about what his part in the documentary was. But the Australian had his eyes shut and his face to the sun.

'No,' Ellen answered, 'there's a world of difference in scope between us. I mean, just look at the size of that house. And from the photos I've seen of what it was like a year and a half ago, the way it looks now is all down to you.'

Ned felt a swell of pride in his chest when he heard this. Jonathan Arthur hadn't been over for an inspection for six months now and the opinions of the artisans working here on how progress was going were as subjective as Ned's own. It felt good, getting a compliment from Ellen, though. It felt earned, because he knew from recent experience that if she'd thought that what he'd done to the house was rubbish, she'd have had no hesitation in telling him that, too.

'Maybe you'd like a tour,' he said, before he'd had time to think about it. 'I mean, you haven't had a chance to look around yet, have you?'

'No.'

'I could introduce you to my foreman, Dan, and a few other people, so they can help you out with whatever you need if I'm not around.'

They both glanced up at the sound of a car horn.

Ned's Beetle trundled over the drying mud towards them and creaked to a halt. Debs grinned out through the open window, pushing her sunglasses back on to the top of her head. 'Oh, good,' she said with a deliberate lack of tact, 'we're all speaking now, are we?'

'So it seems,' said Scott.

Debs ran her eyes up and down the Australian with obvious interest, before turning back to Ned. 'I'm off to collect Clara from school,' she said, 'and wanted to know if you needed anything picking up.'

'No thanks, and don't worry about coming to collect me later,' Ned told her. 'I'm in the mood for a walk.'

'Right you are.' Debs flipped open the glove compartment and took out an envelope. 'This came for you and I opened it by mistake. Sorry,' she said, handing the envelope over to Ned.

'Er, hang on,' Scott said, quickly stepping forward as Debs ground the car into gear. He turned to Ellen. 'Um, are we done here for today? Only I've . . . there's something I've forgotten . . . that I need to pick up from . . . and I could . . .' He shot Ellen a look of appeal.

Ellen shrugged and Scott turned to Debs.

'Hop in,' Debs told him, stretching across the passenger seat and pushing open the door.

Ned opened the envelope. It was a wedding invitation from Gareth Riley, one of Ned's old student friends, but Ned didn't even bother checking the date, knowing he'd RSVP in the negative, the same as he always did these days. What with work, he hardly had enough time for Clara, let alone old friends from way back when. Pushing the invite into his pocket, he watched the Beetle disappearing through the gates.

'You're pretty laid-back, aren't you, letting her give a lift to a strange man like that?' Ellen said.

'He seems harmless enough.'

'Oh, he has his moments . . .'

Neither of them spoke for a minute. Ned examined his watch, feeling suddenly awkward at being left on his own with her, as though he might say the wrong thing if he opened his mouth. It reminded him of how he'd been in his early teens, when he'd always run out of things to say to girls. It baffled him that he felt this way, that even though this was his place of work and Ellen was now here at his suggestion, he no longer felt completely in charge. It was with relief, then, that he heard her clearing her throat.

'Have –' she began, before stopping.

'What?' he asked.

'Nothing. It's none of my business.'

'No, go on, what?'

'I was just wondering how long you two have been together,' Ellen said.

'Who two?'

'You and her.' With a nod of her head, Ellen indicated the gate through which Debs had driven. 'Clara's mother . . .'

Ned smiled, amused by the assumption. 'Ah, you mean Debs,' he said, 'although she's not Clara's mother.'

'Oh?'

'Yeah, we've been' – he repeated her choice of word carefully – '*together* for about three years now.'

'She's very pretty.'

'I suppose so,' Ned concurred, deciding to let the ruse run a little longer, 'but you know how it is with people: you don't notice their faces after a while.'

There was a satisfyingly long pause after he'd said this and it was all Ned could do not to laugh.

Ellen looked at him curiously. 'Er, no, Ned, actually I don't,' she said.

'Still,' Ned went on, 'ours is a good, solid and, above all, practical arrangement. So I mustn't grumble.'

'Practical?' Ellen's question came out half garbled in disbelief.

'Oh, sure,' Ned answered. 'Clara was such a handful by the time she reached two that I thought I'd better sort myself out with someone to take some of the strain off me . . . and Debs, well, financially it made sense for her . . .'

'But that's so . . . so clinical,' Ellen protested. 'How can you . . . and, my God' – she'd noticed the grin sliding across Ned's face – 'you actually think it's funny . . .'

Ned stepped away from the car and wolf-whistled at Wobbles, whom he'd just spotted racing around a chugging cement mixer in the distance. 'I'll tell you what,' he suggested to Ellen, 'why don't we start that tour of the

177

house I promised you, and I'll tell you the truth about my oh-so-clinical relationship with Debs on the way?'

With the tour over and Ellen having driven Ned and Wobbles into town, the three of them were now sitting in the Hope and Anchor's beer garden on the Esplanade, overlooking South Beach.

'Cheers,' Ned said, clinking his pint glass of bitter against her glass of gin and tonic. He took a deep, sweet swig. 'I never thanked you properly,' he said.

'For what?'

'For bringing Clara back.'

'You did,' Ellen said. 'You may not remember it, but you did.' She narrowed her eyes. 'A few sentences before you told me that I disgusted you, if my memory serves me right.'

Ned grimaced, embarrassed now. 'I overreacted,' he said. 'And I'm sorry.'

But Ellen was smiling. 'It's in the past,' she said. 'Forget it.'

Ellen looked down at Wobbles, basking in the late-afternoon sun. 'Hard to think of him as a savage killer when he's like that, isn't it?'

Ned laughed. 'You're not still going to sue me, then?'

'Not so long as you carry on being as nice to me as you have been today.'

'I guess I don't have a choice, then, do I?'

The stare between them became awkward and Ned broke it off. He reached into his pocket, got out his tin of tobacco and started to roll a cigarette.

'So . . . Scott and Debs . . .' Ellen said.

Ned snorted. 'You've got a real mischievous streak to you, you know,' he commented.

'Well, they're both single, aren't they?'

178

'Yep, and aren't we both a bit old for matchmaking?' he asked in return.

'Nah,' she scoffed, 'you're never too old to dabble in romance.'

'I think it's for kids. You grow out of it. Life teaches you to.'

He became aware she was scrutinising him. 'You're winding me up again, right?' she checked. 'I mean, everyone's romantic at heart, aren't they?'

Ned lit his cigarette. 'You want the truth?'

'The truth.'

'The truth is I think romance is bullshit.'

He wasn't sure why he'd told her this, when lying and simply agreeing with her would have been so much easier. Was it because her optimism in relation to affairs of the heart grated against his own experience? Or was it that he already felt closer to her than he wanted to be? Was that why he had this sudden urge to push her away?

'What about this, then?' Ellen said, weighing the diary he'd lent her in her hand. She'd been scanning through it on and off since they'd arrived. 'What about what Caroline Walpole wrote and what she did because of love? You can't tell me that this isn't true romance, because it is. To be so in love with someone that you want to spend every waking hour with them . . . to . . . to . . .' – Ellen flicked to the last page of the diary with writing on it – 'listen,' she told Ned, before quoting, '. . . *I shall not be without my Leon a moment longer, however, for if kept apart from him I know that I shall die . . .*' Ellen looked up, her eyes shining with conviction. 'Well?' she asked Ned.

'Well, what?'

'Well,' Ellen said, gently closing the diary. 'That entry was dated 21st April 1871.'

179

'The same night that Leon betrayed Caroline and she killed herself,' Ned worked out for himself.

'Exactly,' Ellen said. 'Those were probably the last words Caroline Walpole ever wrote . . .'

'And?'

Ellen growled with frustration over Ned's lack of reaction. 'And they're exceptional, of course!' she exclaimed. 'The emotions in this diary are enriching and real. To want to die if you can't have someone . . . I mean, it's incredible. It's romantic to its core. Admit it.'

But Ned wasn't being drawn. It was as if the more she tried to convince him of the life-enhancing qualities of love and romance, the more he wanted to prove her wrong and show it up for the delusion it was. 'What's so worthy about throwing yourself off a cliff and dashing your brains out on the rocks below?' he asked. 'And what about the people Caroline left behind, the people who had to live with the consequences of what she'd done? Look what she made her father do to the house. Not to mention to himself . . .'

'Forget the house,' Ellen insisted. 'What she did was pure, because she did it for love.'

Ned dismissed the idea. 'Leon Jacobson?' he said. 'Some love his turned out to be, that her father could buy it off for a few pounds.'

'So she was wrong about Leon,' Ellen protested. 'But so what? That doesn't cheapen what she felt, does it? It doesn't make the power or nobility of her love for him any less.'

'Not nobility, stupidity,' Ned retorted. 'She put her faith in love and she got burnt. The same way everyone always gets burnt. The same as her father did. And that, Ellen, is why romance is bullshit. Because it never works out. Not for real.' There, he thought. He'd told her now. He'd shown her who he was and now she would leave.

'What about you, then?' she asked instead. 'You're telling me you've never been in love?'

'I was once,' he admitted. 'A long time ago.'

'And?'

'And the same as Caroline, I was young enough and dumb enough to think it would last for ever.'

'But it didn't,' Ellen surmised.

'That's right.'

'Who was she?' Ellen asked after a few seconds' silence. 'Clara's mother?' she guessed.

'Her name was Mary,' Ned said. 'She was my wife and now she's dead.'

Ellen nodded. 'What happened?' she asked.

The directness of the question took Ned by surprise. People didn't do that. Whenever people found out his wife had died, they changed the subject, or at best said they were sorry and nothing else. Despite the seriousness of the conversation, Ned allowed himself a rueful smile.

'What?' Ellen asked.

'Nothing.'

'No, go on, what?'

What he wanted to tell her was that most people were afraid of talking about death. What he wanted to tell her was that her asking him about Mary the way she had done just now made him suddenly realise how much everyone else in his life had been tiptoeing around him since Mary's death. What he wanted to do was to repay Ellen for her openness, by telling her the truth about how Mary died.

'Do you really want to know?' he asked her.

'Only if you really want to tell me,' she said.

What he wanted to do more than anything else was to trust her and to believe that she wouldn't either judge or pity him. But something inside him prevented him. It was as

181

though all the barriers he'd put up these last three years had rusted together and now they wouldn't budge. And so, instead of the truth, he told her the lies. He told her the same story he'd told Clara when they'd picnicked in the conservatory, all about how Mary had got sick after Clara had been born, and about how she'd died. Because of a brain disease, he told Ellen, a brain disease that had eventually killed her.

Four pints later (three after Ellen had left, called back to the cottage by Scott to help deal with some queries from their London office) Ned was over on South Beach. Black clouds had started to scud across the previously blue sky. Wobbles's lead hung uselessly in Ned's hand, but Wobbles himself was nowhere to be seen. Giant clumps of grass protruded from the dunes like desert islands in a yellow sea, and the same heron that Wobbles had set off after in hot pursuit was now nimbly picking its way across the shallows of the thin estuary which split the beach in two.

'Wobbles!' Ned shouted for the fifteenth time – up towards the links course beyond the dunes – but still he got no answer. 'Stupid bugger,' Ned muttered, only this time it was to himself.

He cursed again, rubbing furiously at his brow with the palm of his hand. He had a venomous migraine on board. It was slicing through his head every ten seconds like a piece of shrapnel. Served him right, he knew. Getting half drunk, as he was now, well, the migraine came with the territory, didn't it? He should have gone straight home, not hung around the pub like that on his own after Ellen had left. He should have known better.

But that was him and booze all over, wasn't it? He never did know better. He never could have just the one drink. He always had to have more. Either don't go to the pub at all, or go and get so drunk he couldn't even remember being there: that was Ned's modus vivendi all right.

Because that was the other thing, wasn't it? It wasn't as if he had fun when he got drunk. Sure, the first drink was nice. It gave him a buzz. It made him feel lighter and brighter and happier. But after that it was all downhill, always. Maudlin, that's what he became. A wall gazer. A frowner. The bloke on his own at the table with a full ashtray and an empty glass.

He looked at his watch. There was probably about another hour of daylight remaining. He'd give Wobbles twenty minutes more to find his way back, before searching further inland for him. He rolled a cigarette, sat down on the cool sand and looked out across the darkening horizon, and smoked. It gave him a sense of perspective, staring out to sea. He liked the feeling of being dwarfed by its vastness. It made him feel insignificant, as though none of the mistakes he'd made in his life mattered.

Then, unaware he'd even slipped it from his wrist, he found himself staring at the inscription on the back of his watch. It had been a Christmas present from his wife, Mary, given to him in the last happy year they'd spent together, the year before she'd got pregnant with Clara. He should have got rid of it, he knew. He should have chucked it out to sea, lobbed it into a canal – stamped on it, pawned it, smashed it, anything – because all it did was remind him of how things had once been between them and how they would be still if she hadn't done what she had.

The inscription read: *To my Darling Edward, With my Love, Today and Always.* Always, Ned thought with an automatic shake of his head. She couldn't have been more wrong if she'd tried.

The story Ned had always told Clara about her mother's death was a lie. But when she'd first started asking about Mary, he hadn't known how to tell her the truth. And he didn't still.

Or perhaps it wasn't a lie. Perhaps it just wasn't the whole truth. Perhaps it was simply a sanitised version of events, a story without the details – the details that made the fact of Mary's death so much worse than it already was.

Today he'd told that same half-truth to Ellen. And now he felt bad about it, bad about lying to yet another new person who'd entered his life, but bad about lying to Ellen in particular, too. What if he hadn't needed to lie this time? This was the question which plagued him now. What if – as Ellen had given every indication so far – she was more than capable of handling anything he or anyone else had to throw at her?

The whole truth – the one which Ned could spare Clara, but never himself – was this. Mary had got ill after Clara had been born, as Ned had always told Clara. The details were that she'd sunk into a post-natal chemical depression so deep he hadn't been able to reach her. She hadn't wanted him and she hadn't wanted Clara. And nobody else had been able to help. Not the doctors and not their drugs, which had sent Mary dashing out on manic credit-card sprees one week, only to rip the ground from under her feet the next.

Mary had died as Ned had always told Clara. Only she hadn't gone to heaven, because according to the Catholic Church into which Mary had been born, the circumstances of her death had made that impossible.

And the circumstances – the details, which Ned hadn't told Clara or Ellen – were that Mary had killed herself. It cramped Ned's stomach in pain to think about it, to remember how he'd come home from work to find Clara lying helpless on her back in the middle of the kitchen floor, exhausted and fast asleep. He'd known there and then what had happened, hadn't needed to go upstairs to see for himself. But still he'd gone, step by step, first sighting and then following the white electric extension cord which had led from the bedroom into the bathroom.

The whole truth was that Ned had found Mary Thomas – the same quick-witted, dark-haired beauty he'd fallen in love with, had set up a business with and had wanted to spend the rest of his life with – scorched and dead in the bath, with an electric hairdryer still gripped tightly in her dead hand. There'd been a piece of paper on the bathroom chair, with the single word 'SORRY' scrawled across it in Mary's handwriting.

'Hey, mate!'

Ned looked round, the beach sliding back into focus, the memory of Mary fading from the space it had occupied in the waves. He watched the lighthouse over on St Catherine's Island flash and realised it was getting dark.

'Look out!'

But whoever it was who'd shouted out the warning, it was too late. Just as Ned was starting to stand, he was knocked flat on his back. His head hit the sand with a thud.

'What the –' he started to say, but there was no point: he already knew what the warning had been about.

Wobbles stared down at him, his paws on Ned's shoulders, dribbling slobber on to his chin before licking the entire length of Ned's face.

'Are you all right?'

Ned peered up. A teenage boy stood over him, peering down. The hood of his parka was up, but his face was plainly visible. Something about him looked familiar to Ned, but he couldn't quite place him.

'Get off,' Ned told the dog, pushing him aside and scrabbling to his feet.

Wobbles hurtled across the beach into the shallows and started to bark at the waves, and Ned stood up. The boy was roughly the same height as him and they stared into each other's eyes.

'He was over in the car park, trying to get at the bins,' the teenager told him. 'I saw you lying here and guessed he was yours, so I chased him over.'

'Thanks.'

The teenager studied his face. 'You're the bloke in charge of the refit up at the old Appleforth place, aren't you?'

Ned smiled at the use of the word refit, like he'd been doing nothing more complicated than changing the spark plugs on a car all these months. 'That's right,' he said, still trying to work out where he knew the teenager's face from. 'I'm Ned Spencer.'

'Yeah, I thought so. I go walking up there sometimes.'

Ned pinched his brow, suddenly feeling faint. He was confused, disjointed, as if the completed jigsaw of his day had been stamped on and scattered. He pictured Ellen standing by the arbour; he heard her questioning him in the pub; and then he saw Mary again, floating face upwards in the bath.

The teenager pulled the hood of his coat further down over his face. 'You're going catch one hell of a cold if you stay out in this, you know.'

'In what?' Ned asked.

But the teenager had already started walking back along the beach towards the town.

Ned touched his clothes, uncomprehendingly at first, as he felt the cold water which had soaked them through. And it was only then that he looked up at the sky and understood what the teenager had been talking about: it was tipping down with rain.

And that was when Ned remembered where he knew the kid's face from: he was the one he'd seen hanging around the cliff-side chapel up on the Appleforth Estate, the one he'd been meaning to catch up with and talk to.

But it was too late now. The boy was twenty yards away already, fading like a ghost into the rain.

Chapter XI

They were standing in the drawing room of Appleforth House and Ellen was biting down on the same apologetic smile she'd been wearing since she'd got off the phone to Thomas Stirling's mother a minute ago.

'You're kidding, right?' Jimmy asked her.

Ellen looked from the black top hat in her right hand to the absurdly long grey coat and the heavy flannel breeches in her left. She shook her head.

The clothes Ellen was wearing – high-heeled black leather boots, a brown suede skirt with a slit up one side and a cream T-shirt and a loose cardigan, patterned with plastic amber beads – looked strikingly modern in comparison. And this was a fact which Jimmy, wearing worn, torn jeans and a cotton hoodie, was tempted to point out right now.

Instead, he glanced at Scott, who was over in the corner, setting up a big overhead lamp, which Jimmy now recognised and was able to name as a chimera. As well as its name, he knew how powerful it was, just as he now knew the names and wattage of the smaller lamps, which he'd seen Scott using before for lighting indoor shots: the red-head (eight hundred watts) and the blonde-head (two kilowatts).

It was Thursday and, earlier in the week, Jimmy had helped Ellen and Scott on two interviews they'd done, one with Michael Francis over in his freak shop on Southcliffe Street and the other with the enthusiastic new vicar in the vestry of St Mary's church. Jimmy had got up to speed on working as part of a team, but even so, surely what he was being asked to do now was going above and beyond the call of duty. 'Tell me she's joking,' he begged Scott.

But all Scott could muster was a helpless shrug. 'She's the boss,' he said. 'And, hey, it could be worse,' he pointed out, 'at least she's not asking you to play the female lead.' Shooting him an amused grin, he turned his back on Jimmy and called over his shoulder, 'Mind you, Jimmy, you never know . . . that little feathery hat that Verity's gonna be wearing might kinda suit you.'

Jimmy groaned.

'What's that about my hat?' Verity called out on hearing her name.

She poked her head around the side of the dust sheet, which Scott had rigged up for her to get changed behind. Jimmy stared at her. Her neck was bare, dappled and golden in the early afternoon sunlight which stretched through the wide window and slanted across the room. Her brown hair was piled up in tight ringlets on the top of her head and, as her eyes met Jimmy's, she cocked her head to one side in expectation.

Jimmy blinked for the first time since she'd appeared. *You're the most beautiful person I've ever seen*, he wanted to tell her. She was like an angel, he thought, like the stained-glass one that looked out from the round church window over on Tudor Square.

'Well?' she prompted him.

Jimmy cleared his throat. 'Tom Stirling's mum just rang Ellen,' he answered.

Tom, or Stirling as Jimmy had always known him, was a guy in the same year at school as Jimmy. Stirling was captain of the school soccer side and had himself down as something of a superman. He'd given Jimmy a kicking in the school car park three years ago. For no other reason than the hell of it, Jimmy had found out later, after Ryan had gone behind Jimmy's back and knocked Stirling flat on his behalf.

But even though Jimmy hated Stirling's guts and could picture – as clear as if it had happened this morning – Stirling's boot swinging into his ribs, he'd give anything for that very leg not to be broken now. Because it was Tom who was meant to be dressing up and playing the part of Caroline Walpole's treacherous lover, Leon Jacobson, today.

'He bust his ankle this morning in soccer practice,' Jimmy finished off explaining.

A look of consternation spread across Verity's face and she made to step forward, before suddenly stopping. 'Hang on,' she called, vanishing from view, then reappearing a moment later with a rich green full-length skirt pressed up against her body, covering her from the bottom of her neck to the tops of her thighs. 'Does that mean the filming's off?' she asked.

Jimmy turned to Ellen in desperation. 'There's got to be someone else. From the auditions, right?' he suggested. 'I mean, you must have had a second choice . . .' But already Jimmy was doubtful, because only a handful of guys had turned up to try out for doing numbers at the memorial concert – unlike the girls, where half the town's female teen population had rocked up like a coach party of groupies off to see *Fame*.

'Ye-es,' Ellen, admitted. 'But they're not here now, are they? And you are, and so's Verity and so's Roy,' she continued, indicating the sound man, who'd travelled down from Bristol for the day and was currently typing something into an electronic organiser.

'And Roy can't make tomorrow, can you, Roy?' Scott said, walking past him.

'Afraid not,' Roy answered, 'I've got to be up in Manchester by midday.'

'And I'm on holiday tomorrow and heading off sight-seeing for the weekend,' Scott said.

'And I can't get another afternoon off lessons till next Thursday,' Verity added.

'So it's got to be today,' Ellen concluded.

Jimmy glared at the clothes which Ellen was holding in her hands. 'But I can't wear . . . those –'

'Why not?' she asked.

'Because for one thing,' replied Jimmy, 'I'll look like a complete nob in them. And . . . and for another, because . . . because I can't act,' he protested. 'How's that? The last time I went on stage was dressed as the back end of a donkey for the primary school nativity play. And I even managed to mess that up,' he added, remembering the sinking feeling that had swamped him as Mary – carrying a plastic baby Jesus wrapped in nylon swaddling clothes – had slipped off his back into the orchestra pit after he'd stumbled over his own shoelace.

Verity gasped. 'You were the hind legs?' she asked.

'See,' Jimmy told Ellen. 'I totally trashed everyone's night.'

'Particularly Mary's,' Verity confirmed, raising her eyebrows in mock reproach. 'I had bruises for a week.'

Jimmy had forgotten she'd played Mary, it had been so long ago. But he found himself smiling back at her all of sudden, enjoying the fact she felt she could tease him like this, grateful that they had enough common ground between them for that to be possible.

Seeing this crack open in Jimmy's armour, Ellen strode

quickly forward to take advantage of it. 'But what you're going to be doing today is easy,' she soothed. 'And you're not even going to have to set foot on a stage. We're going to film you standing next to the window, looking out over the terrace together. And then we'll do another brief scene with you being greeted by Verity at the main entrance to the house. Neither of you is even going to be heard speaking. Once we're back in London, we'll get a professional actor to read a few lines from Caroline's diary as a voice-over to explain what's going on.'

'It's a cinch, Jimmy. Don't be such a wimp,' Scott shouted over.

'Yeah, come on: it'll be fun,' Verity added.

Jimmy snorted. 'Like the last time we worked together?'

'Well,' Verity said, a less than sincere twinkle in her eyes, 'I'll just have to remember not to climb on your back this time, won't I?'

'But –'

But Jimmy's arguments seemed to fade from his mind as he continued to look at Verity – or more specifically, as she continued to smile at him. At *him*, he thought. Verity Driver was smiling at him, Jimmy Jones. Suddenly Tara's words came back at him: *Will. You. Go. Out. With. Me?* They didn't seem at all ridiculous right now and the fact that Verity had something going on with Denny Shapland was also no longer the end of the world. If a girl's smile could make Jimmy feel this way – light-headed, almost high – then he couldn't help thinking that surely it had to mean something to her, too? And if it did, then not wanting to hang out with her – even if he would have to be dressed up like an undertaker while he did – would be the act of a madman.

'And it's not like you're going to be looking any more

silly than me,' she told him, rolling her eyes upwards for a second, indicating her hair.

'But *you* don't look sill—' Jimmy started to point out.

But Ellen obviously felt they'd wasted enough time already. She jerked the top hat firmly down on Jimmy's brow. Then, without giving him time to protest, she knelt down before him and held the breeches up against his legs. 'Just as I thought,' she said with satisfaction. 'They're going to be a perfect fit.'

'Fit up, more like,' Jimmy muttered, as Verity disappeared back behind the screen again.

Even as he said it, though, it was all he could do to stop himself from whispering Verity's name, just the same as he'd been doing every time he'd thought of her since he'd chatted to her during Saturday's auditions.

It had thrown him, to be honest, seeing her there at all, after what he'd heard Denny Shapland saying in the Sapphire on the Wednesday before about them going out together. But then Jimmy had guessed that they'd probably be hooking up in a pub after the auditions had ended.

Still, Jimmy hadn't let that put him off going over and sitting down next to her and saying hello. And he was glad he'd taken advantage of Denny's absence like that. It made him proud of himself for a number of reasons. Firstly, for having pulled up the courage to go and talk to her in such a public place, when he'd wimped out every time at school. Secondly, for having succeeded in acting significantly cooler than when he'd given Verity the CD. (Although, let's face it, he thought, that hadn't exactly been difficult.) And thirdly, and most importantly, for putting all that negative stuff he'd felt last week on the cliffs – about Verity and the rest of the town – to the back of his mind.

OK, so Verity had agreed to go on a date with Denny and

Denny was a dick. But it wasn't like Verity had *chosen* Denny over Jimmy, see, because it wasn't like Jimmy had even asked her out yet. And as for the auditions, well, Jimmy had changed his mind about them, too. He'd enjoyed watching Verity do her piece, and watching Ellen and Scott exchange the kind of glance that made it clear they'd just found their Caroline Walpole.

Fair enough, so he still thought the idea of the concert sucked and smacked of self-righteousness. But he hadn't felt guilty or complicit about attending, the same as he hadn't felt like he'd been letting Ryan down or anything. He'd gone there looking out for himself, for his future and for his career. And he'd gone there looking out for Verity, hoping she'd be there. And he couldn't think of many better reasons for doing anything than these.

He walked over to the corner of the room and started to get changed.

Jimmy got back from Scott's and Ellen's Land-Rover with the cool box and walked over to Scott, who was standing with his back against the left side of the main entrance of Appleforth House. It was nearing the end of their afternoon break and, in spite of the cool air, the Australian had his shirtsleeves rolled up over his hairy arms, his wraparound ski shades on and his face to the sun, which hung low, yet brightly on the horizon.

'Working on your tan?' Jimmy asked.

'In a country like this, you've got to worship the sun every chance you get.'

'Here,' Jimmy said, chucking Scott the car keys.

Scott snatched the keys from the air and slipped them into his shirt pocket in a single fluid motion. His head didn't move so much as an inch, though, as if his body were on autopilot while his mind was somewhere else entirely.

'So, let me guess,' Jimmy said, 'you're fantasising about slobbing out on some beach in Sydney, or off skiing some place?'

Scott chuckled. 'Not even close. Though the word fantasising does just about sum it up . . .'

Jimmy knelt down and opened up the cool box – or Esky, as Scott called it. 'Thirsty?' he asked, proffering a can of Diet Coke to Scott.

'Nice one.' Again without looking at Jimmy, Scott took the can from him, opened it and took a swig. 'She's quite a stunner, isn't she?' he then commented, wiping his mouth on the back of his hand.

Jimmy pictured Verity upstairs an hour ago, when they'd stood side by side at the window for the camera and Ellen had directed them to hold hands. 'She's perfect,' he said, almost as a reflex. 'Even holding hands with her was . . .'

But Jimmy couldn't find a way to describe what he'd felt as Verity's fingers had entwined with his. There'd been heat. The touch of her skin had warmed him like a fire. Or had it been cold? Because it had caused him to shiver as well, hadn't it? But there'd been more to it than these purely physical reactions, too. What had stayed with him most had been what her touch had made him think of: excitement, hope, security, trust, a sense of arrival and belonging all rolled into one. And it had been what her touch had made him want to do: to kiss her gently and wrap his arms round her and pull her close into his body; to walk with her hand in hand away from this town and to another place which they could make their own.

'Yeah,' he concluded. 'She's perfect all right.'

In the silence that followed, Jimmy became aware of Scott

repositioning himself for the first time since Jimmy's arrival with the drinks. He watched as the cameraman raised his mirrored sunglasses on to his brow and looked Jimmy over with amusement.

'What?' Jimmy asked.

'I wasn't talking about Verity, mate,' Scott then explained with delight. He pointed to Jimmy's right. 'When I said she was stunning, I was talking about *her*.'

Craning his neck, Jimmy followed Scott's stare. There was a tall, red-haired woman in her twenties ten yards along the path that bordered the house. She was walking slowly towards them and a little girl was hopping alongside her.

Jimmy groaned with embarrassment, realising his mistake.

'But thanks for sharing your feelings with me about our leading lady anyway,' Scott said, before cracking up laughing and slapping Jimmy on the shoulder.

Jimmy felt like finding the nearest bucket of sand and sticking his head into it. He said nothing, though, not wanting to make the matter any worse. Instead, he continued to watch the woman. She wore a short blue plastic mac and her long – less red, more auburn, he now saw – hair hung down over her chest in thick bunches. Scott was right: she was stunning, even from this distance.

The woman smiled and waved, and Jimmy looked up to see Scott waving back.

'Er, you know her, then?' Jimmy enquired, hoping to keep the subject away from Verity.

Scott shrugged. 'Not as much as I plan to, but a little, yeah,' he said. 'She gave me a lift home the other day.' He paused for a second, before continuing, 'But it's not serious. It's not like we've held hands or anything yet . . . not like you and Verity, eh?'

196

Jimmy grimaced up at the cameraman who'd broken out into a grin again.

'You won't say anything to her, will you? Verity, I mean,' Jimmy elaborated in case there was any more confusion.

'What?' Scott teased. 'Not even the bit about how perfect you think she is?'

'Ple-ase,' Jimmy begged.

The Australian scratched his chin pensively. Then he winked. 'Forgotten it already,' he said.

Jimmy sighed with relief, knowing that Scott meant it. He trusted the Australian and respected him, too. Scott had been true to his word about the job, teaching Jimmy stacks already. He'd kept Jimmy busy, having him fill out shot lists and record time codes from the camera's monitor, as well as doing more mundane tasks, such as lugging around everyone's gear and sorting out refreshments. More importantly, he'd kept his promise about not making a gratuitous fiction out of Ryan's death. His and Ellen's only interest had been in working out the best way to shoot the upcoming memorial gig, and letting the facts speak for themselves.

'What are you two talking about?'

Jimmy flinched at the sound of Verity's voice, but promptly recovered and set about rearranging the Esky's contents in as casual a manner as was humanly possible – for someone who'd just confessed to having been thrown into raptures on the back of holding his co-star's hand, that is.

'Our love lives,' Scott answered. He gently nudged Jimmy's ankle with the tip of his Timberland boot. 'Isn't that right, Jimmy?'

Ignoring him, Jimmy hurriedly got up and handed over a can of Diet Sprite to Verity, who – on the back of Scott's comment – was now looking at Jimmy with polite expectation.

'Er, yeah,' was all Jimmy could think of to say, itching at the gross starched shirt collar he'd been forced into wearing. Pure Clark Gable, he thought to himself as soon as the words had left his mouth. A yawn would have been as charming.

Verity looked between the two of them as she folded her magenta costume coat over her arm. She cracked open her drink, slurping at it as it foamed out of the can. Jimmy concentrated first on it and then on the flat, rounded pork-pie hat she was wearing, which had three green feathers sticking up on its side – anything to avoid having to look into her eyes and to have Scott scrutinise that moment's contact.

'Who are the lucky girls, then, boys?' Verity asked.

Cocking his thumbs into his waistcoat pockets, Jimmy flashed Scott a warning look. But Scott's sunglasses were back in place over his eyes and he gave no clue as to whether he'd seen, let alone understood, Jimmy's signal.

'Well, she's mine over there,' was all Scott said, pointing with his drink towards the woman on the path, who was now in profile and had started walking away from the house along one of the gravel paths that led into the gardens. 'Only she doesn't know it yet,' he added with a smile.

'She walks like a model,' Verity remarked, smoothing down the front of her pale-green dress so that it lay flat against her stomach.

'Yeah,' Scott agreed, 'now that you mention it, I guess she does.'

'What's her name?' Verity asked.

'Debs.'

'But doesn't the fact that she's got a little girl –' Verity started to say, before cutting herself off.

'What?'

'Nothing.'

'No,' Scott insisted pleasantly, 'if you've got something to say, then say it.'

Verity looked Scott up and down, as if trying to work him out. 'Well, wouldn't it bother you, having someone else's kid around all the time?' she asked. 'I'd have thought it would make most blokes run a mile . . .'

Scott's face scrunched up in mock-concentration. 'Nah,' he then replied, 'not a bit of it.'

The scent of coffee drifted towards them from some-where near. Verity gazed after Debs and, in the few seconds' silence that followed, Jimmy found himself thinking about Rachel. She was probably back home in Carlton Court with baby Kieran, watching TV, or showing him pictures in a book. Either that or she'd be down at the playground at the South Beach end of town.

Jimmy had watched Rachel there at the playground one time from a distance, as she'd stared out to sea and pushed Kieran up into the sky on the swing time and time again. It had nearly torn his heart in two, he'd felt so sorry for her, being on her own the way she was. It had worried him sick, thinking about what she'd do if his dad let her down. And even though he'd only been going there to ask her if she'd needed him to pick anything up from the market, he hadn't been able to take another step.

'And even if Debs *was* that little girl's mother,' Scott was saying, as Debs and the girl disappeared from sight behind the smooth grey-brown trunk of a giant sycamore tree, 'which she isn't, by the way . . .'

Verity turned back to face him, a look of confusion on her face.

'Because Debs is just her nanny,' he explained, before going on, 'then it *still* wouldn't bother me. Kid or no kid,

199

what's the difference? I reckon you should be into people for who they are inside, not because of what family or other commitments they've got. It's character that counts, not circumstance. If you only look at surface, then the chances are surface is all you'll get.'

'Yeah,' Jimmy said. 'I agree.' He glanced into Verity's eyes, then gazed down instead at the tight stitching on her quaint black leather shoes.

'Why?' she asked him.

'Because, otherwise,' he said, his eyes no longer wavering from hers, 'you might as well just go out with people because of their image, say because they wear expensive clothes, or because they've got a fast' – he'd been about to say motorbike, but managed to stop himself just in time – 'car, or a stack of cash, or whatever. . .'

Denny. Even though he'd said car, he still might as well have been spelling it out for her. But that's what he wanted her to know, that if she never looked past possessions and status symbols, then she'd never see him, Jimmy Jones, because he couldn't afford a single one. Because even though he'd give her all he had, all he really had to give her was himself.

'I suppose,' Verity said, but she seemed noncommittal.

Jimmy turned away. He wondered what restaurant or bar Denny had taken her to after the audition. He wondered if he'd taken her out since.

'What about you, Jimmy?' Verity asked. 'Who are you going out with at the moment?'

Jimmy felt torn, flattered by Verity's assumption what he was the kind of guy who did have a girlfriend, but unsure how to set her right without making himself look like a loser. He needn't have worried, though, as Scott stepped in to save him his blushes.

200

'Anyways,' Scott interrupted, peeling himself off the wall and slipping his sunglasses into his shirt pocket, 'that's enough idle chit-chat from you two lazy buggers. Here comes the boss, so let's look lively, eh?'

Across the lawn, in the distance, Jimmy saw Ellen walking towards them with a man at her side. Jimmy hurried over to the doorway and picked up his top hat and coat from where he'd left them.

'Jimmy!' Ellen called over to him.

Quickly, Jimmy brushed the brick dust off the coat, hoping that Ellen hadn't noticed. When he turned, he saw that she was still walking towards him, but her companion had held back and now stood stationary on the lawn.

'Ned wants a quick word,' she informed him as she reached him.

'Eh?'

Without any further explanation, she pointed across the lawn, before walking over to talk to Roy, who was lying on a low wall nearby, fast asleep.

As Jimmy crossed the lawn and the distance between himself and Ned diminished, the name and face slotted clearly into place. 'All right, again,' Jimmy said, remembering how messed up Ned had seemed when he'd seen him the day before yesterday. 'Ellen said you wanted to talk to me.'

Up close, Ned looked younger than he had done on South Beach in the rain. The nuttiness had gone from his eyes, as well. There was a confidence to his stance, a relaxed way of standing here on his own turf, which caused Jimmy to decide straight away that it was probably best not to mention the beach episode at all.

But Ned thought otherwise. 'Thanks for yesterday,' he

began. His smile made him appear younger still. 'For bringing my dog back,' Ned went on. 'And' – he cleared his throat, embarrassed – 'of course, for informing me of the local meteorological conditions.'

'No problem,' Jimmy assured him.

Ned nodded in gratitude and then removed his spectacles, before starting to clean their lenses on one of the loose tails of his shirt. He looked at his hands and not Jimmy as he spoke. 'The family chapel over on the cliff-side,' he said. 'I know you and some of your mates hang out there. And there's a lock on it, so I suppose you probably keep stuff in there, too,' Ned continued, still polishing. 'Which is fine. And has been fine. Up until now, that is,' he added, finally looking up and putting his glasses back on.

Jimmy didn't answer. From the businesslike tone which Ned's voice had transposed into, it didn't sound like one was required. Jimmy found himself checking out the older man's clothes: the worn jeans, mid-range Adidas trainers, untucked, nothing-special shirt and the dodgy brown corduroy jacket. Scott sure was right about surface and everything. This guy dressed like a gardener, but he was the boss.

Ned frowned and Jimmy looked down at his shoes, waiting for the pay-off. 'I hate to be the one to break it to you, but you're going to have to clear out of there. And soon. We're starting work there two weeks on Monday. That's two days after the concert that Ellen's just been telling me you're all going to be filming.'

A silence followed, which Jimmy knew he was meant to fill. He'd been dreading this moment since he'd first watched the builders arrive. He'd been wondering every day how long it would take them to come and invade that small part of the world he and Ryan had made their own.

'I'm sorry,' Ned was saying, 'but that's just the way it is.'

Jimmy stared evenly into Ned's eyes. 'To tell the truth,' he told him, 'I'd kind of been expecting it.'

And to tell the truth, now that it had finally happened, he felt nothing but relief.

Chapter XII

'Where has this week gone?' Ellen asked Scott, as they packed up the equipment on Castle Hill. They'd taken advantage of the afternoon sun to film the ruins of Shoresby Castle and the panoramic view that Castle Hill afforded over the town and along the coastline.

Now, in the late afternoon, the light was gradually fading. There wouldn't be a sunset tonight, but the overcast light-grey sky was getting darker by degrees, like some giant swathe of blotting paper, soaking up ink.

'We're getting there,' Scott said, fastening the metal clips on the camera case and hauling it towards the car.

Ellen smiled at him. She knew he'd put himself out again, staying to complete the shots, when she knew he was keen to get going on a trip down to Cornwall to see the Eden Project.

'At least we've got Michael Francis, the vicar and Clive in the can,' Ellen said, following him and consulting the thick pile of notes on her clipboard. 'And there's three more interviews planned for next week already, so don't get too wrecked this weekend.'

Ellen's phone beeped with a text message as Scott rolled his eyes at her fussing.

'That's good,' she said, reading it. 'Roy's confirmed that he's coming down again next Thursday to do sound, so we'll be able to do the bower scene we planned out and two of the interviews. God! There's so much to do.'

'You can't do very much more this weekend,' Scott said,

fixing her with a calming stare. 'Why don't you come with me? It'll be fun.'

'Thanks for the offer, but I'll leave all that tourist thing to you. I think I'll just hang around here.'

'But won't you be bored?' Scott asked. 'Why don't you go home and catch up with some friends or something?'

Ellen groaned. 'I haven't got the energy,' she said, meaning it. She'd already been back and forth to London yesterday and she was exhausted. 'Besides, I hate being in the flat when Jason is away,' she added, thinking that if she went back there now just for the comfort of sleeping in a double bed, she knew she'd end up losing her whole weekend to a dozen household chores. She might as well make life simple for herself and go to the launderette in Shoresby. She followed Scott to her car, which she was lending him for the weekend.

'I'll drop the camera back at the cottage and then I'm going straight off. Do you want a lift?'

'No, I think I'll walk.'

'Are you sure you'll be OK?' Scott checked again. 'What are you going to do?'

Ellen smiled affectionately at him, appreciating his concern. 'Sleep, probably. I'll be fine. Just promise me you'll come back safely on Sunday?' she said, resting her hand on the open window ledge of the driver's door.

'Yes, Mum,' Scott said, before starting the engine and revving it, so that Ellen stepped back, laughing.

'Have a good time,' she called, as she waved.

Ellen hadn't been at a loose end on a Friday night for as long as she could recall. Last Friday, after she'd rescued Clara and had argued with Ned, she'd been out with Scott who had calmed her down by getting her drunk in the curry house. Since then she hadn't had a moment to herself. As she opened the door of the Sapphire's saloon bar, a few hours later, it occurred to her that it had been even longer since she'd been to a pub on her own. But, having soaked for an hour in the bath and seen the pitiful choice on the television, she'd felt like a change of scene. And since her mobile phone didn't work in the cottage, it also gave her the chance to sit in a quiet corner and finally make a few calls.

'Hello, stranger,' Beth said, when Ellen called her oldest friend. 'I thought you'd dropped off the planet. Where have you been?'

'Sorry,' Ellen said, feeling guilty. 'I've been meaning to call and I was going to come back this weekend and pop round, but things have been so hectic, I've decided to stay here.'

'How's it going? You must be going crazy, mixing with all the yokels. Are you dying without shops?'

'No,' Ellen said, surprising herself with how defensive she felt. 'I'm enjoying myself. Shoresby's not what I expected, but I like it here.'

'Can we come down for a weekend?' asked Beth, enthusiastically.

'Well . . . .' Ellen began, feeling put on the spot. She'd known Beth since she'd shared a room with her when they'd been studying at Oxford Poly. She'd been a bridesmaid at her wedding when Beth had married Sim and was godmother to their five year olds, George and Harry. 'I'd love to see you, but –'

'That's a no, then.'

Ellen tried to laugh off her friend's disappointment. 'There's not much space in the cottage and I'm afraid my schedule is very tight, and what with all the bloody driving up and down to London . . .'

'Oh, yes, the busy schedule ruse,' Beth teased, not taking her seriously. 'What are you hiding down there?'

'Nothing!'

'Divine Jason? How's he?'

'Away again. South America.'

'Ellen!' Beth berated her. 'How are you two ever going to have kids and stuff when you're never in the same continent?'

'I know, I know,' Ellen said, exasperated.

It was the same ear-bashing she got from all her friends, most of whom were married and breeding like crazy. But Ellen had always been secretly proud of her unconventional relationship with Jason and she was glad she was with someone who travelled the world and had incredible stories to tell, rather than a stuffy nine-to-five bloke. That was part of Jason's attraction, Ellen had always argued. It just meant that when they did spend time together it was amazing.

But this last trip, Ellen had been running out of reasons to justify what it was about her and Jason's lifestyle that was so great. The truth was that the time they did spend together wasn't *amazing* any more. She couldn't just drop everything and spend long days in bed with him, ordering in their favourite food and giggling together into the small hours, as she once had. She had a career now, and if she was honest, she resented the fact that she had to take all the responsibility for paying the bills and keeping the flat together, while Jason came and went as he pleased. She couldn't put her finger on when it had started to change, but more often than not, when Jason came home these days, rather than bouncing in with presents and kisses, he was tired and irritable, and always making preparations to go away again. So when he was around, Ellen spent most of the time being annoyed with him because he was about to go again.

But Ellen couldn't share any of this with Beth. She knew that Beth wouldn't hear a word spoken against Jason, whom she regularly declared to be one of the most attractive men in the world. And she was too proud to admit to her friend that things between her and Jason were anything other than perfect. Beth wouldn't understand. She would interpret it as some sort of crisis, when it wasn't at all. It was just circumstantial and Ellen was sure it would all change in time.

Five minutes later, Ellen switched her phone off, poured the rest of the little bottle of tonic into her glass and flicked through the local paper. She'd been planning on calling some of her other friends, but speaking to Beth had exhausted her. She couldn't face explaining to anyone else why she was apart from Jason and alone on a Friday night in a pub in the middle of nowhere.

Well, she might as well make the most of it, she thought, standing up to go to the bar. She smiled at the huge landlord, who was polishing glasses, his sleeves rolled up.

'Stood you up, has he?' he joked, nodding at her phone on the table.

'Yep. Looks like it,' Ellen replied, not bothering to explain.

'Can't understand it. Pretty girl like you,' the landlord continued. 'Same again, then?'

She laughed, embarrassed and flattered at being described as a girl. She leant on the bar as the landlord squeezed a clean glass against the optic of gin and she glanced through the bar to the other part of the pub. The pool table was surrounded by scruffy teenagers and the games machines bleeped incessantly above the crackle of the log fire. Yet there was still something unique and quaint about it, not like the soulless chain pubs she was used to in town.

Suddenly, just out of sight by the slot machine, a glass smashed and there were raised voices, and, startled, Ellen strained to get a better view. Then she saw Ned. He looked dishevelled. His cheeks were flushed and his hair was messy, and Ellen could tell at a glance that he was drunk. She watched him walk towards the door.

'You're drunk,' she said, a moment later, catching up with him outside.

'So sue me!' Ned laughed. 'Oh,' he continued, 'you already are.' Then he pulled out his car keys from his pocket and strode off into the road. 'So long,' he called, throwing his jacket over his shoulder.

'You're not thinking of driving?' she asked, horrified. 'Give me those,' Ellen said, catching up with him and trying to snatch the keys.

'Ah, ah,' Ned said, shaking his head. 'I've seen your driving. You're not coming in my precious car,' he warned, reaching the Beetle and putting his hand on the curved wing.

Ellen lunged for the keys and, finally wrestling them from Ned's grip, opened the driver's door. Then, unlocking the passenger door from inside, she pushed it open. 'Just get in,' she said.

She had no idea why Ned was still driving around in this ancient student contraption, when he was obviously quite successful and could afford a grown-up car. It was almost as if he were stuck in time, she thought, as she looked around the cold dark interior.

Ned got into the passenger seat. Ellen put the clutch down, but something was obstructing it and, leaning down in the cramped space, she unearthed a dog chew, which she threw into Ned's lap. Even worse, an old sandwich was lodged under the handbrake and Ellen turned up her nose, having second thoughts about her mercy mission. 'Where do you live?' she asked.

'Ah . . . first, I want to know where *you* live.'

'I'm staying over there, in the harbour cottages,' Ellen said calmly, pointing down towards Quayside Row. 'The one with the blue door. Satisfied?'

Ned peered out of the window to try to see her cottage, but she could see he wasn't really focusing.

'Now you,' Ellen prompted.

Ned waved his hand up towards the top of the town. 'Up there. I'll show you,' he said. He leant forward to open the glove compartment, grabbing ancient tapes one by one and throwing them over his shoulder into the back, until he found one he was looking for. Ellen laughed, despite herself.

'Ah, this is it. Pulp!' Ned declared, holding up a tape triumphantly. 'Last album I bought.'

'But this was out in 1995,' Ellen said, recognising the label. 'Haven't you bought anything since?' Ellen had to help him line up the tape, to get it into the cranky player.

'Nope.'

'Why not?'

'Don't know. I just got old.'

Ned turned the music up and Ellen winced.

'Definitely a time warp,' she said, although Ned didn't hear her. Then she added to herself, 'I must be crazy.'

It took ages for her to elicit directions out of Ned and even longer for her to find his house. Ned was singing along at the top of his voice and, although Ellen hadn't heard the album for years, she was too nervous to think about joining in. She wasn't used to manoeuvring in a left-hand-drive car and, after the Land-Rover, she felt as if she were driving a baked-bean can. With her concentration divided between the road and Ned, who kept showing off into an imaginary microphone and making Ellen laugh, the journey was somewhat haphazard. Eventually, however, Ned pointed out of the windscreen and, with relief, Ellen parked by a row of Victorian cottages.

Once the clatter of the engine and the tape player had cut to silence, Ned sighed heavily. Then he looked at her with bloodshot eyes and she remembered how he'd looked when she'd left him on Tuesday in that pub near the beach.

'How much did you drink?' she asked him gently.

'Enough.'

He leant back against the seat, then covered his face with his hands, as if he were about to wash something away.

'Why?' she asked.

'Don't you ever need to lose control?' he said wearily, sitting up and staring out of the window ahead. 'To forget everything?' he asked, his eyes seeming to glaze with sadness. 'Just for a bit?' He turned to Ellen then. 'Or is that terribly, terribly wrong?'

'I'm not judging you, Ned,' she said, but before she could say anything more, Ned had lurched forward to get out of the car.

Ellen stepped out of the driver's seat and locked the door, before handing the keys back to Ned. He didn't look at her as he took them in his hand.

'You're a good woman, Ellen Morris,' he said quietly. 'Too good to be wasting your time looking after a bad man like me.' He stared at her with an intensity that filled her with panic, as if he'd seen something deep inside her which made him want to cry. But then it was gone and he shook his head. 'Do you want to know what the worst thing about life is?' He didn't wait for her to answer. 'Timing,' he told her. 'Sometimes its timing is shit.'

211

*

The next day Ellen couldn't get Ned out of her head. Something about their encounter had deeply unsettled her and despite trying to analyse it, she couldn't pin down her feelings. As she mooched around the stalls in the covered market by the old railway station, she told herself to stop being ridiculous, but no matter how hard she tried, she couldn't stop trying to make sense of it.

Why had she behaved the way she had? Why had she taken him home? What had compelled her to look after a man she barely knew, as if it were the most natural thing in the world? Why hadn't she just called a taxi for him? She would have done for any of her friends in London. What was it about Ned Spencer, of all people, that made her feel this strange mixture of empathy and intrigue? Not to mention anger and frustration? She'd never been volatile or impulsive like this, ever. Not even with Jason. OK, so she moaned at him occasionally, but he was so easygoing that they hardly ever rowed.

Just forget it, she told herself. Ned was drunk. He was talking nonsense. The best thing to do would be to pretend last night never happened. But still, his comment about timing nagged at her. What had he meant? And that look! There'd been something so primeval in his eyes, a kind of longing that made her heart beat faster just thinking about it.

Loaded up with an old-fashioned eiderdown and some candles, and still pondering these questions, Ellen walked through the town to the front and stopped at the esplanade overlooking South Beach. Behind her, there was a row of lifeless holiday bungalows, next to a closed-down teashop, its curved Thirties windows decorated with faded bunting. Now, out of season, the wide stretch of tarmac overlooking the front was empty. Ellen looked along the rows of empty cast-iron benches and fixed telescopes pointing out at nothing in particular, imagining the sound of ice cream vans and the rush of tourists in the summer.

Way below her, down the steep zigzagging concrete steps, the tide was out. The sweep of beach was festooned with a tidemark of seaweed and, behind it, some kids were drawing in the sand with a stick. A dog was running around them in circles, splashing in the shallow ripples. Ellen felt a pang of loneliness. She thought about her conversation with Beth last night and how Beth's twins would love it here. Maybe she should invite them down, after all, she thought. She could just see Harry and George running around in their little red wellies.

How had these years passed so quickly? she thought, leaving her shopping on a bench and walking towards the front. How did she get to have five-year-old godchildren and none of her own?

Dropping a coin into the slot of one of the telescopes, she looked through the viewfinder and out over the flat grey sea. She hadn't looked through one of these things for years, she thought, focusing in on a distant flock of seagulls, bobbing on the waves, before finding a yacht on the horizon. If only she could look to the other side of the world, she pondered. If only she could see Jason right now, then maybe she wouldn't feel so alone . . .

Ellen stood back, wrenching her gaze away from the telescope, the horizon springing back to its original perspective and the seagulls disappearing into the grey swell of the sea. Of course she couldn't see Jason. But she had the next best thing, she thought, reaching into her pocket.

She stared at the phone in her hand, daring herself to dial

the number. She had the emergency number for Jason's satellite phone, but she never used it. She'd called him once before, a few years ago and he'd gone nuts as the ring tone had disturbed a flock of wild birds that he'd been camping out to film for days. Since then they'd had a strict agreement that he would call her and not the other way around.

Well, she didn't care. Not today. Jason didn't make the rules. She needed to speak to him. And she needed to speak to him right now.

'What's wrong? What's happened?' Jason panicked as he came on the line.

'Nothing,' Ellen said, feeling foolish. He'd seemed such a long way away in her head, but hearing his voice made him real again. Jason was on the other side of the planet and it was probably the middle of the night. What was she thinking of?

'I just –' she began.

'What?'

Ellen took a deep breath. She knew he was annoyed, but she had to say what was on her mind. She pressed the phone against her ear, listening to the echo on the line. This was ludicrous, she thought, that she could only communicate with Jason via space. Suddenly, he seemed impossibly far away: nothing more than a disembodied voice in a phone. Well, it wasn't good enough. She needed him here. She needed to see him in person, to be able to talk to him. But most of all she needed a hug. She needed to touch him and to be touched back in return.

'When are we ever going to be together?' she blurted, feeling tears rising in her voice as she leant against the telescope. 'Why are we always apart? I can't stand it.'

'What?'

'I'm sorry,' Ellen said, amazed that she felt so churned up.

'I know I shouldn't call on this line, but I had to hear your voice.'

'I thought it was something important.'

'It is important!'

Jason sighed, and she could imagine him rubbing his forehead, in the way he always did when she got emotional. 'Ellen, baby, look. Do we have to talk about our future right this minute?'

'If we're not going to talk about it now, when are we?' This was going all wrong. She hadn't meant to have a meltdown at all. Ellen looked down at the kids on the beach. 'I mean . . . I don't even know if you want a future with me,' she continued.

'Jesus Christ, Ellen!' Jason exploded in a frustrated whisper. 'What on earth's got into you? Of course I want a future with you. What a ridiculous thing to say!'

There was a pause. Ellen stared at the puddles rippling in the pitted tarmac.

'Are you OK?' Jason asked, sounding concerned.

'Yes,' she said. 'I don't know. . .' She ran her hand through her hair, feeling more at a loss than ever. 'This just feels worse than the other times you've been away. I'm really missing you.'

'Are you sure that's all?'

Ellen bit her lip. That was it, wasn't it? 'Yes,' she said. 'I'm fine. I'm sorry, I –'

'Oh, darling,' Jason sighed gently. 'I'm sorry I haven't been around much, but it doesn't mean I don't care. I love you, baby. You know that, don't you?'

'Yes,' she said, swiping away a tear.

'I promise we'll talk when I get back.'

'You promise?'

'I promise. Now I've got to go, OK?'

Ellen switched off the phone, put her hands in her pockets and stared out to the horizon. The phone call hadn't given her the feeling of relief she needed, but at least it had helped a little. Jason was hers, she reminded herself. And she loved him.

Looking out at the sea, she tried to picture Jason's face, but the details eluded her. Concentrating hard, she searched her memories, scanning across events to find suitable footage that she could replay for a sentimental fix. But she could only think of times when she was alone and missing him, like now.

Picking up her bags and walking slowly in the direction of the cottage, she thought back to the beginning of their relationship. She could remember times when they were on holiday together, but still she couldn't animate Jason in her mind and her recollections remained static and impersonal, like flipping through old postcards in a second-hand store.

The facts were the facts, she said, being stern with herself. Jason had promised they would talk when he got back and that wouldn't be long now. She would just have to wait.

Later, Ellen felt much more calm, as she lit the fire in the cottage and set about cooking a batch of Bolognese sauce, which would hopefully last the week and appease Scott's ferocious appetite. Humming along to the radio as she cooked, she thought about the kitchen in her flat in London, about how much the slate floor tiles had cost and how long it had taken the temperamental builders to fit the teak units and five-ring hob. How odd, she thought, that here, in the tiniest kitchen in the world, she felt just as much at home.

Maybe she should remortgage the flat and buy a little cottage by the sea, she thought, as she poked the logs on the fire. Maybe that would solve her quality time issues with

Jason. They could get somewhere where they could hide away at weekends together, like they used to. Maybe she should suggest it when he came home.

One thing was certain; after today's conversation, she was going to make a special effort when he came back. She would prove to him that her meltdown had been a one-off. She knew how much Jason hated needy people. He always told her he liked the fact that she was independent and didn't lean on him emotionally. But on the other hand, perhaps it was a good thing, she mused. Perhaps that phone call was what they needed to get things back on track between them.

She had just fitted her new candles into the china holders she'd found on the dresser, when there was a knock on the door. When she opened it, still wiping her hands with a tea towel, she was shocked to find Ned outside with Clara.

She looked at Ned, feeling a blush rising to her cheeks, as if she'd been caught out. Was it possible that he could somehow know how much she'd been thinking about him? He looked tired, but sober, she thought, seeing that he was clean-shaven with an ironed shirt. He even looked as if he'd had his hair cut.

'Ellen,' he said simply, thrusting a bottle of wine, wrapped in white tissue paper, towards her. 'I came to apologise. About last night –'

'There's no need for this, really,' she said gently, taking the bottle and smiling at Ned. He smiled back and shrugged, looking relieved. There was a moment of silence between them, until Ellen became aware that Clara was gazing up between her and Ned. Embarrassed, she looked down. 'Hello, again,' she said to Clara.

'I made you a painting,' Clara said matter-of-factly, stepping forward to hand Ellen a thick piece of warped paper.

'You did?' Ellen flipped the tea towel over her shoulder and leant down to take the painting from Clara's outstretched hand.

'It's you in a dress,' Clara said, before her face wrinkled into confusion and she leant her head to one side. 'Do you have a dress?'

Ellen looked at the crude picture of a woman in a huge dress decorated with brightly coloured bows and then down at the black trousers she practically lived in, along with the grey cashmere jumper. She looked terribly drab in comparison with Clara's painting. 'I do have dresses,' she said to Clara, 'and if I look this good, I'll have to wear them more often. Thank you. I think your picture is lovely.' She smiled and looked at the painting again. 'I'll tell you what . . . maybe we should have a tea party some time and we could both dress up. What do you say?'

'Can we have it now? I'm hungry.'

'Clara, no!' Ned said, putting his hand on her shoulder. 'We just popped round and we're on our way home for supper.'

Ellen watched as Ned started to steer Clara away, and impulsively found herself saying, 'Why don't you stay?'

As soon as the words were out of her mouth, Ned stopped and turned. As Ellen's eyes met his, she caught her breath guiltily, remembering her phone call with Jason. But she wasn't doing this for Ned, she thought, deliberately lowering her gaze to Clara. 'Do you like spaghetti?' Ellen asked her with a smile.

Clara nodded vigorously. 'Can we, Daddy, can we?'

'No, really, thanks for the offer, but you've done enough . . .' Ned began.

Ellen batted away his polite refusal. 'If you really want to make it up to me for last night, you can come in and keep me

218

company,' she said, challenging him. 'I hate eating on my own.'

Clara was more fun than Ellen could ever have imagined. In Ned's company she behaved like a small adult and constantly made Ellen laugh with her observations and natural instinct to play games. She insisted on a competition to make each of them suck strands of spaghetti until their faces were covered with splashes of sauce and they were all laughing. Eventually, when Clara started yawning, Ellen realised how late it was. 'Why don't you come upstairs with me?' she asked Clara, raising her eyebrows at Ned for approval. 'I bought a new quilt today in the market. I'll show you, if you like.'

Following Clara, Ellen smiled at the giant steps she took up the wonky stairs.

'It smells nice in here,' Clara remarked, as Ellen unlatched the bedroom door and turned on the small lamp she'd bought in town. Its red and gold glass shade cast a soft glow in the room.

'Oh, I had an accident with my perfume, so everything's a bit smelly,' Ellen explained. 'Here, look at this.' Ellen took the quilt out of the bag and laid it out on the bed.

'It's pretty,' Clara said, her small hand running over the pattern of pink flowers.

'I think so, too,' said Ellen. 'And it looks so cosy. I haven't tried it yet, though.'

Then Ellen crouched down and looked at Clara. 'I've got an idea. Will you test it out for me?'

Clara nodded and Ellen gently wrapped Clara in the quilt and then, lifting her up, laid her on the bed. 'Why don't you see how warm you get? I'll be downstairs with Daddy, so you can come and tell me how it is in a while, OK?'

Clara snuggled down more deeply, closing her eyes.

Ellen leant towards her, instinctively wanting to smooth her hair, but she stopped herself and tiptoed out of the room.

Downstairs, Ned had cleared the plates. 'If you've got the knack to get Clara to go to sleep, you're a genius,' he said.

'There's no trick. There was almost half a bottle of red in that sauce,' Ellen replied, putting her hands in the back pockets of her trousers. Now that she was alone with Ned, she didn't know what to say. Something about this situation made her feel guilty. As if she were doing something illicit and wrong.

Ned's a colleague, she told herself. There was no harm in them being alone together, surely. Especially with a child upstairs. Jason is thousands of miles away, she reasoned. If he were here, he'd be with them right now and it would be the three of them drinking wine. But something about the mere thought of that situation felt like trying to press two magnets together in her mind; as if Ned and Jason repelled each other.

Ellen forced herself to think about Jason. 'I love you,' Jason had said just a few hours ago. 'You know that, don't you?' Of course she knew it and she loved him, too. She wasn't doing anything wrong being with Ned, surely?

Ned came and stood opposite her, by his chair. He took off his glasses and laid them on the table. 'Look, Ellen, about last night . . .' he began, speaking in a rush, as if he'd been holding his breath. His face was caught in the light from the candles on the table and she thought how handsome he looked without his glasses, especially now, as he narrowed his eyes in embarrassment. 'Trying to drive home. What must you think?'

Ellen shrugged, not able to look at him. She hadn't thought of him as handsome before, so why had she thought that just now? 'I guess we all need to let go

220

'sometimes,' she said, deliberately echoing his sentiment from last night.

'It's just that . . . I don't know,' Ned continued. 'Sometimes I get so angry about what happened.'

'I suppose I would, too, if I were you.'

'I'm not an alcoholic, if that's what you're thinking.'

'Good. Then we can have some more wine,' she said, deliberately turning the conversation on to a light-hearted note and pushing the bottle towards him. He smiled and topped up their glasses.

There, she told herself. You can do it. You can keep everything professional. There's no need to get close to him . . .

Ellen took a sip of wine and glanced at Ned. Who was she kidding? she thought. Ned was simply too fascinating. And anyway, there was no way she could put her whole life on hold until Jason came back. Jason was a world away and Ned was right here. If a friendly relationship between her and Ned was developing, then why was she trying to stop it? She could be friends with someone of the opposite sex. After all, there were probably loads of women out in South America with Jason. And what did they talk about round the campfires late at night? She doubted they would only be talking about work.

Besides, she liked the fact that she was able to get Ned to open up to her. She liked the feeling that maybe he trusted her and that he cared enough to come round and apologise for last night.

Ellen thought back to Ned in the car and how he'd looked so weary when he'd asked her if there was anything wrong in trying to forget everything. There were so many questions she wanted to ask him. She wanted to know how Ned had felt when his wife had died, how he'd mourned,

221

how he'd coped with Clara and, most importantly, how he felt now. But there was something so matter-of-fact about the way he'd recounted the facts the other day that warned her that if she rushed him now he'd only clam up. And she didn't want that. Now that Ned had let her in a little, she wanted more.

'Tell me about her. Tell me about Mary,' Ellen said, relaxing back into her seat. 'What was she like?'

'Before she became ill, you mean?'

Ellen nodded.

'She was, just . . . just Mary,' he said, seemingly at a loss.

'So what was it about her that first attracted you?' Ellen persisted.

Ned rubbed the back of his neck. 'Her smile, I guess. She had a beautiful smile. And she was talented. She was a truly gifted artist.'

Ellen leant forward, resting her elbows on the table. 'Go on.'

'She had a unique way of seeing things. She could paint life into everything.'

'What about you?' Ellen asked. 'How did she make you feel?'

Ned frowned. 'What an odd question.'

'Not really,' Ellen said. 'I mean . . . did you get on?'

'Of course we got on. She was my best friend more than anything. We set up the business together, but she was always the one with the inspiration. She would come out with mad plans and then challenge me into doing them. It's down to her that the business ever became successful in the first place.'

Ned walked to the fireplace, resting his glass on the mantelpiece. Ellen couldn't see his face, but she could tell he was smiling as he spoke. 'She had a wicked sense of humour. In the early days we always seemed to be laughing.' For a while, Ned was silent, as if he was caught up in memories. Then he half laughed and looked into the fire. 'She had so much energy. She wanted to go everywhere. She was always surprising me with tickets to places she'd read about . . .'

Ellen slid her elbows down the table and rested her head on her hands, as she listened to Ned talk about trips to Paris, Venice and Rome. She stayed silent, too frightened to interrupt unless he stopped. Some instinct told her that it was good for him to be remembering Mary like this.

Besides, it was fascinating. The way Ned described things, she could almost imagine herself seeing those views and experiencing those faraway cities. Enraptured, she listened, amazed that Ned was made up of such romantic memories. Surely if he used to be like this, Ellen thought, then it was still possible that he wasn't really the cynical person he made himself out to be.

'Sorry. I'm boring you,' he said after a while, turning round to face her. His eyes were glistening.

'No, no. Not at all.'

'I never usually . . .' he went on, as if he'd surprised himself.

'It sounds like you were very happy,' Ellen said gently.

Ned nodded. Then he straightened up and, as if locking his memories away, walked back breezily to the table, as if he'd just been talking about some small practical matter, instead of the love of his life. 'What about you, Ellen?' he enquired, pouring some more wine into his glass. 'Are you happy?'

'What? Generally?' Ellen asked, startled by his sudden change of mood.

'No, I mean, are you happy . . . with someone?'

223

It struck Ellen as odd that she could feel so close to Ned and yet he hardly knew anything about her. How had she managed to avoid talking about Jason? 'I'm with someone, yes,' she replied, then corrected herself. She'd made it sound so casual. 'I mean, I have a partner. Jason,' she added, not knowing how to elaborate further. Despite Ned's openness about Mary, she now felt awkward about talking about Jason. How could she describe her own relationship? It seemed so shallow and one-dimensional compared with what Ned had had with Mary.

Ned nodded. 'Jason,' he said, as if trying out his name. 'So is it . . . serious?'

Ellen smiled ruefully. 'Yes, although sometimes I think it's as serious as it's ever going to get.'

'And that's not serious enough?' Ned surmised from her tone.

'What we've got is as serious as Jason can be. Put it that way.'

'I'm not really following you.'

'We've been together for nearly a decade and we live together. It's all great on paper, I suppose. But to be honest with you, I'm not Jason's first love,' she confessed, surprising herself. She'd never told anyone this secret doubt.

'Oh?'

'His work is.'

'Ah,' said Ned slowly, nodding understandingly and replacing his glasses.

'Don't get me wrong,' Ellen said, keen not to portray Jason in too much of a damaging light. 'Jason is wonderful. I mean, he's a truly fabulous person . . .' Ellen glanced at Ned and knew she couldn't tell anything but the truth. 'Except that he's always somewhere *else* being fabulous.'

'Idiot,' Ned stated and Ellen laughed, suddenly feeling relieved to have shared this with Ned.

'That's what I think, too,' she agreed.

'No, I mean it,' Ned said seriously. 'He is an idiot. I should know. If there's one thing I regret it was spending too much time on the business and not being with Mary when she needed me. It was a mistake I paid too high a price for. If I had my time again, that's the one thing I'd do differently. I'd be there no matter what.'

'Maybe you'll get a second chance one day . . . with someone else.'

'No,' Ned said decisively. 'There's no such thing as second chances. I'm done with all that. Once was enough.'

Ellen was surprised by the severity of his tone. Instinctively, she wanted to challenge him, as she had when they'd argued about romance in the pub on Tuesday. But there was something in his eyes that warned her not to. Whatever shutters had been opened enough for him to talk about Mary were now firmly shut again.

'Tell me how you're getting on with the documentary.' Ned changed the subject abruptly.

Ellen felt guilty about Jason. She felt as if she'd told Ned too little. She hadn't had a chance to explain all the good things about their relationship and had only told him the bad things. But it was too late. The moment had passed. 'It's going well,' she said. 'Too well, probably. I could make a whole film about this place. Amanda, the series producer, is on maternity leave and she's going to kill me when she finds out how much stuff I've done, but I'm enjoying it. To be honest, it's my first real break.'

'You don't act like it.'

'Don't I?' Ellen laughed. 'It's all bluff. I was scared shitless on my first day.'

225

'You look like you're doing a great job to me. Why don't you make a feature-length documentary if you've got enough material? You know, aim high. You could do it.'

And there it was again, Ellen thought, that look he'd given her when she'd gone up to the Portakabin the day she'd found Clara. The look that challenged her and made her want to tell him everything.

She smiled. 'I don't think I can. I mean, I haven't got enough resources. And it's hard enough ordering all the material I do have.'

'Anything I can help with?' he offered.

'If you promise not to start shouting at me,' she teased, 'you can help me with the voice-over scripts if you like.'

Three hours and nearly another bottle of wine later Ellen had covered the floor with typed sheets showing the running order she had planned and the different sections of voice-over scripts. Ned, it turned out, had been more helpful than she possibly could have imagined. His logical approach had helped her order her thoughts and make more sense of the material than she ever would have been able to on her own. Now, as the fire crackled, she thought how wonderful it was to have someone interested in what she was doing.

She'd completely lost track of time, as she and Ned knelt in front of the fire, gathering up the pages. Her head was fuzzy with wine and they were laughing as Ned reached out and grabbed the last piece of paper to put it in the pile with the others. 'So that's it.'

'No, no,' said Ellen, taking the paper from Ned's hand, but he didn't let go.

She froze. Her hand was on Ned's. Her skin tingled, as if connected to electricity. Ned stared down at her hand. He didn't move. Neither of them seemed to be breathing as they knelt next to each other, their thighs almost touching.

Ellen looked at her hand, willing herself to move it from Ned's. Every sensible instinct told her to break the moment, to apologise, laugh it off . . . But still she did nothing. Not thinking, not daring to think, Ellen turned to face Ned, her hand still touching his. Their faces were just inches apart.

Nothing happened, but in that moment everything happened. Ned's face filled her vision. Ellen couldn't breathe, his dark gaze stripping her naked, as he had last night. She knew then what it meant. That in Ned's eyes she'd unwittingly found the answer to a question she didn't dare to ask.

Forgetting everything . . . everyone . . . her face moved imperceptibly towards Ned's. . .

A split-second before their lips touched Ned pulled away, shattering the moment. 'I should . . . er . . . I should be going,' he said, falling back away from her, as if he'd been burnt. He got to his feet, scratching behind his ear, to avoid looking at her as he pointed at the door with his other hand.

'Absolutely. Sure,' Ellen said, stung. She stumbled to her feet. Her brain was reeling with what had almost happened.

'I'll get Clara,' Ned mumbled.

Ellen nodded and hugged herself, shivering with shock as Ned bounded up the stairs.

She wiped her hand over her mouth, not knowing how to feel. Adrenalin rushed through her. 'Jesus!' she muttered in shock, as she paced back and forth on the carpet. What the hell had she been thinking?

A minute later Ned came down the stairs holding Clara in his arms. At the bottom, he started to unwrap the quilt from around her, but Ellen rushed towards him. 'No, no, keep it,' she whispered, leaning over to have one last

227

glimpse of Clara. 'Don't wake her up.' She looked heart-breakingly young asleep in Ned's arms.

Ned didn't look at her, taking a step towards the door, almost as if he was going to walk through it. Ellen rushed to open it and he eased past her, careful not to touch her. 'Well . . . goodnight,' he said, stepping on to the cobbles.

Ellen swallowed hard. He still didn't look at her. 'Yep. Um . . . thanks for your help,' she managed, but Ned didn't respond. He was already walking away.

Hastily, Ellen closed the door and put her back against it. 'Shit!' she whispered, before covering her face with her hands.

Chapter XIII

What a Saturday night! Verity closed her eyes. This was it, she thought. Denny Shapland was going to kiss her for the very first time. So what if it was the first date? So what if Denny thought she was an easy conquest? She was conquering him, too, wasn't she? Wasn't that what this was about?

Inside the car, she leant forward towards him, her heart pounding in her chest. But Denny had other ideas. He leant forward too and planted the smallest, most tantalising of kisses on the side of her mouth. And that was it.

Her eyes blinked open as she heard him pull away and lift the handle on his door. Her cheeks reddening with dashed hopes, Verity watched as her best date ever walked around the bonnet of the red car, before opening her door and offering her his hand.

On the pavement, Verity smoothed down the wrinkles in her skirt and hooked her bag over her shoulder. As she looked at her feet, questions crashed into her mind. Why didn't he want to kiss her? Had she said something wrong? Didn't he fancy her at all?

But a moment later she felt Denny take her hand. As he raised it to his lips, his eyes locked with hers. Verity held her breath as Denny kissed the back of her hand, pressing his lips into her flesh, like a rubber stamp. 'Ciao, bella,' he whispered, smiling at her.

Then, with a wink, he threw his car keys up in the air, snatched them back and sauntered round to the driver's door. In a second he was gone.

Verity stood, rooted to the pavement, her hand on her chest as she watched the car until it was out of sight.

It was perfect, she thought, looking up at the moon. He was perfect. It had been the most wonderful evening of her life. Letting a grin spread over her face, she unleashed the pent-up excitement she'd been feeling for the past few hours, until her whole body was tingling with excitement. Then, clenching up her eyes and her fists, she jogged on the spot victoriously.

'Are you OK?'

Verity stopped abruptly, mortified that she'd been caught.

She turned to see Ned Spencer walking towards her, carrying what looked like a small child in a bulky pink quilt. Verity had seen Ned up at the Appleforth site the day before yesterday and he often drank at the hotel bar, although she hadn't seen him there much recently. She liked him, although he seemed like a bit of a loner. He was about the last person she wanted to explain herself to right now, though. Quickly, Verity let her hair fall over her cheeks to hide her embarrassment and, without saying a word, she darted towards the hotel steps.

Inside, in her bedroom, Verity put on Jimmy's CD. Then, flopping on to her bed, she looked up at the moonlit shadows flickering on the ceiling and replayed the evening in her mind, polishing and editing her memories, so that she'd remember them.

Of course, she'd eaten in lots of restaurants before, especially on holiday in Spain, but she'd only ever been for pub meals and to the Indian restaurant in Shoresby. So when Denny had driven her out of town, along the coast and wordlessly escorted her through the doors of the Oyster, Verity had been completely overwhelmed.

This had been it, she'd thought, as she'd taken in the fairy lights draped among the ornamental fisherman's nets. This had been her first proper date. Like a proper date should be, like they'd been in the movies.

Even her parents hadn't been to the famous seafood restaurant and when Verity had thought about the potential bill, she'd wanted to cry. But Denny had made her feel completely at ease, ordering her food for her and making her feel sophisticated, in a way that she'd never felt before.

At first she'd wanted to pinch herself and call Treza to tell her where she was, her mind reeling with how impressed she'd be, since Treza had been trying to get Will to take her there for ages. But instead, she'd taken a few hurried sips of wine and had concentrated on impressing Denny.

The problem had been that everything she'd thought about saying had seemed silly or juvenile. She hadn't wanted Denny to think she was childish by telling him about school. And her impending piano exam – which was the only other thing she'd been able to think of – had seemed pointless and ridiculous next to the business decisions and responsibilities that Denny faced on a daily basis.

There'd been a tense moment, as Denny had stared at her expectantly. 'So,' he'd said, smiling at her. 'Did I tell you yet how beautiful you look?'

Verity had flushed and wriggled in her seat at Denny's compliment, glad that she'd got ready at Treza's house and had let herself be persuaded into wearing the stretch lace top. She'd protested at the time that it was too revealing, but Treza had insisted, saying that if she was saving Verity from Cheryl's scrutiny by letting Denny pick up Verity from her house, then the least Verity could do to make up for her friend's generosity was to obey a few fashion rules.

And there, in the restaurant, Verity had been grateful. Even though she'd also found herself wondering that if Denny ate in swanky restaurants all the time, then who else had he brought here to keep him company?

'Do you come here often?' Even Verity had grimaced at her corny line. She'd taken a slug of wine, trying to cover her embarrassment, but Denny had laughed.

'No. Not often,' he'd said, eyeing her cheekily through the tall candlesticks.

'Sorry,' she'd blustered. 'I didn't mean ... It's just that there's so much I want to know.'

'Like what?'

'Everything, I guess.'

After that, conversation hadn't been a problem. She'd only had to ask Denny a question and he'd been happy to talk. As she'd listened to him telling her about his flat and the shop and his various surfing accolades, she'd almost lost track of what he'd been saying, engrossed as she'd been in memorising him: the way his eyebrows stopped in neat wedges, his long curling eyelashes and the small beauty spot just under his left eye. She'd hardly said a word, but by the time she'd left the restaurant at ten o'clock, she'd felt as if Denny Shapland had seen into her soul.

On the way back, everything had seemed magical. Above them, the full moon had cast an indigo light on the fields and spilt a sheen of glitter over the sea beyond. Ahead of them the trees had cast criss-crossed shadows over the silvery tarmac of the empty road. As Denny had driven fast along it, Verity had watched his face flicker like that of a hero in an old black-and-white movie.

Then, just to complete the moment of perfection, Denny had flicked a button on the CD and Verity had immediately recognised the introduction to Lauretta's aria 'O mio babbino caro', which she had performed in last year's sixth form review.

'Puccini.' Denny had sighed. 'I love it.'

'I've sung this,' Verity had gushed, looking between the sound system's flickering graphic equaliser and Denny. She had been astonished that Denny had similar taste to hers. She'd never met anyone who loved Puccini before. 'It's my favourite,' she had said with a happy sigh.

'No shit!' Denny had sounded impressed as he turned up the volume.

Now, Verity clasped her hands against her chest and rolled across the bed, curling on to her side, wishing she'd said more before he'd dropped her off. She was aching all over with excited confusion. What did it all mean? Did he like her? Did he want to see her again? Was she sophisticated enough? For the first time that she could remember, she didn't have the upper hand. She didn't feel like she usually did – like an overprivileged girl, taking compliments from a boy she wasn't interested in. This time she was in a completely new league. And she was loving every minute of it.

By Monday Verity's agony had only increased. She hadn't been able to sleep, eat, or even think. It was as if Denny were a liquid and her brain had absorbed him like a sponge, until it was full.

At lunchtime she came home to do some piano practice. She hated playing in the hotel lounge, apart from in the very early mornings, but the music room at school had been taken and she had no choice. Her exam was in a week, so she closed the large doors into the reception area of the hotel and sat on the piano stool by the bay window. Opening her bag, she took out the familiar Debussy, Beethoven and

Brahms music books along with her diary and, picking up her pencil, wrote her thoughts.

It's love. I'm sure of it. He's better than I ever could have dreamt.

Verity sucked the end of her pencil and looked down at the words she'd just written. Then she wedged the diary in the music stand in front of her on the piano, before scooping up her hair into a knot at the back of her head and securing it with the pencil. Flipping the music open, she started her practice, her fingers finding the tender cadences of the Beethoven sonata with ease.

Yet as she played the familiar notes, her eyes were drawn from the music to the words she'd written. Somehow they seemed so inadequate compared with how she felt. She'd never been in love before, but she knew already that the word love didn't cover it. It was so much bigger than that.

She'd had feelings for one or two boys, but she'd been a child then. Denny was different. He was grown up and he was mature, and her feelings were stronger and truer than anything she'd ever felt. All she wanted to do was to skip forward to the day when she could tell Denny that she loved him.

Finding the romance of the music, Verity swayed slightly on the long piano stool, realising that the notes had finally lodged in her subconscious and she knew it by heart. Then, closing her eyes, she transported herself to Denny's arms as she played the soundtrack to her most romantic fantasies.

'What are you doing?'

Verity swivelled round to see her mother, a set of freshly ironed tablecloths draped over her arm.

'I thought you were supposed to be practising. You stopped about five minutes ago.'

234

Verity picked up her diary and closed it. 'I didn't know you were listening.'

'Only if you're going to waste your time daydreaming, you can help me instead. I've got a hundred things to do –'

Verity drowned her mother out by starting a scale, belting out the notes as fast and evenly as she could.

But her mother wasn't finished. She came and stood by the piano. 'There was a phone call earlier for you,' she shouted.

Verity stopped playing immediately, just before the scale reached its conclusion at the top of the piano. The sudden silence left an urgent atmosphere in the air.

'I think it was . . . Daniel? Darren?'

'Denny,' Verity gasped, furious with herself for not having given him her mobile number. How could she have made such a stupid mistake? 'When? When did he ring?' she asked desperately.

'Some time this morning.'

'You could have said!' Verity exclaimed, hastily shutting the piano lid.

'I'm telling you now.'

Verity took a deep breath, forcing herself to keep her anger inside.

'Who is this Denny character, anyway?' her mother persisted. 'Are you at school with him?'

'No,' said Verity, standing and gathering up her music.

'How do you know him?'

'I just do, OK?'

'Where's he from?'

'Mum!'

'I don't see why you're being so secretive. Is there something wrong with him? He's not into drugs, is he? Verity, answer me. He's not a rough type, because –'

'He has his own shop,' Verity interrupted.

235

'What kind of shop?'

'Does it matter?'

'Why are you being so defensive?'

'I'm not being defensive. I just don't see why I should have to give you every single detail.'

'What he does for a living is hardly intimate information, Verity.'

'OK, OK. If you must know, he owns Wave Cave. Satisfied?'

Verity got up with her diary and, with a fake smile, passed her mother and left the room before she had a chance to say anything. Since her mother knew just about everyone in Shoresby, she was bound to have some sort of received opinion of Denny and Verity didn't want to hear it.

Upstairs, Verity looked up the number for Wave Cave in the phone book, then with her finger just below the number, she took a deep breath. This would be the first time that she'd ever spoken to Denny on the phone. Her nerve almost deserted her. What if he didn't want to speak to her? What if he'd called to say he didn't want to see her again? But her fingers seemed to ignore her doubts, dialling the number.

'Wave Cave. Can I help you?' Denny asked, on answering the phone.

'Hi, Denny, it's me,' Verity said, her hand making the phone tremble against her ear.

'You,' Denny said, pausing dramatically. 'Wow. You have got the sexiest telephone voice I have *ever* heard. People must have told you that before, right?'

'Denny, stop it.' Verity giggled, hugging her knees against her.

'I hoped it would be you,' he said. 'What are you doing right now?'

'Nothing.'

'Then come and see me.'

'What? Now?'

'Yes. Just stroll on down the road and I'll meet you at the shop. It's quiet, so how about we shut the shop up and spend the rest of the afternoon at my place?'

'Denny, I can't!' Verity cried, as she paced across the carpet of her bedroom. 'I'd love to, but I've got stuff to do. Work and stuff.'

She felt so feeble saying it, but Denny just laughed.

'OK, Miss Conscientious. I won't lead you astray this time. You do your work and meet me later. How does that sound?'

Verity thought of the piano lesson she would have to blow out. But what the hell, she thought. Missing one wouldn't hurt and she could use it as an excuse to get out of telling her mother where she was going. 'Perfect.'

'I'll see you later, then.'

'OK.' Verity giggled.

'But I warn you,' Denny said. 'I'll be counting the minutes . . .'

Verity smiled uncontrollably as she rang off, a squeal of joy escaping her.

By Wednesday Verity had skipped another piano lesson, two study periods and had elaborated a complex web of lies in order to be with Denny. She knew she should be working for her mocks, or practising for her piano exam, but Denny insisted that he wanted to see her and she couldn't turn him down. After all, she wanted to see him too.

Just hanging out with Denny in his shop made her feel special. He talked to her and looked at her the whole time, making it clear that he was deliberately tearing his eyes away when she caught his eye.

'He's just *so* romantic,' she gasped to Treza, as they packed up their books by the lockers in school.

'Come to the café, I'm dying to hear all about it,' Treza said. 'You've hardly told me anything.'

Verity looked at her friend, realising guiltily that for the first time she hadn't even thought about Treza for the past few days. Now, as Treza looked up at her, she saw the same expectant look in her eyes that Verity knew so well. But even so, Verity didn't want to share all the intimate details of her relationship just yet. It was too new and too exciting. If she told Treza everything she was feeling, it would just be like all the other times they'd talked about boys. And Denny wasn't the same at all. Not even in the same league. 'I'm sorry, Treze. Not tonight. I've got to dash. We're going to the cinema later.'

'Wow!' Treza said, smiling, but Verity knew her well enough to tell she was disappointed. 'You're not wasting any time, are you? Are you sure this isn't going too fast?'

'It doesn't feel like it. And anyway, Denny hasn't been pushy at all. I feel like I've known him for ever.'

'It's only been a week or so. Don't you think you should . . . you know . . . stretch it out a bit?'

'You sound like my mother,' Verity laughed. 'Talking of which, if she calls, I'm with you, OK?'

In the cinema, Verity could hardly concentrate as she sat with the box of popcorn on her lap. She surreptitiously glanced at Denny, looking at the shape of his legs beneath his jeans and, once again, she couldn't help wondering what he'd look like naked. She wouldn't mind betting he would be incredible. She felt a flush of excitement run through her just thinking about it. The more she saw of Denny, the more she fancied him and every cell of her body yearned for physical contact.

The only problem was that Denny still hadn't made a move. Part of the reason Verity hadn't wanted to talk to Treza had been that there weren't very many intimate details to share.

Before their date, when Denny had kissed her on the cheek in the street and in the supermarket, Verity had been convinced that Denny would want things to happen quickly between them, as soon as they were properly dating. But then, on Saturday, when he'd driven her back from the restaurant he'd hardly even kissed her.

Now, enough time had passed for Verity to get paranoid. The longer they didn't kiss, the more she wanted to, but never having made a move on a man before, Verity was clueless about what to do. She knew Denny fancied her – well, she *hoped* he did – but what if he was waiting for some sort of signal from her?

Verity couldn't help feeling hopelessly inadequate and out of her depth. Maybe other girls Denny had been with had been more comfortable physically with him. But just the thought of Denny's sexual experience compared with the complete lack of her own made her feel even more nervous.

As if sensing her troubled thoughts, Denny looked at her and smiled. 'Come here,' he said, putting his arm round her.

Verity smiled happily as she leant into his embrace. Even though the arm of the seat dug into her ribs, she didn't care. She closed her eyes, breathing in the scent of Denny's aftershave and nuzzling into his neck, taking no notice of the film at all. All she wanted was for everyone she knew to see her right now, just for a second. Just so they would know she was Denny Shapland's girlfriend.

Later, Verity was still glowing as she walked back along the Esplanade hand in hand with Denny. She was in no particular hurry to get back to the hotel and, since it was a clear night, she'd jumped at his offer of a stroll along the seafront.

Verity had never thought of Shoresby as being remotely romantic, but now, as she walked along with Denny, she realised she'd been wrong. Above them, the white lights along the Esplanade shone across their path and cast silver fingers into the dark water that gently lapped against the sea wall. 'Isn't it amazing that we've hardly known each other any time, and yet I feel like it's been ages,' she ventured, noticing the soft glow from the old street lamps for the first time.

Denny shrugged. 'People always tell me that I rush into relationships, but I guess I'm just in touch with my feelings.'

'Well, I like you that way,' said Verity, putting her other hand on top of Denny's and smiling up at him.

'So, what are you doing tomorrow?' Denny asked.

'More of the film thing up at Lost Soul's Point.'

'Oh, yeah?' said Denny. 'What have they got you doing this time? Are they getting you dressed up as that dead girl again?'

Verity nodded. 'I'm doing some sort of romantic scene with Jimmy Jones. He's playing Caroline Walpole's lover.'

'Romantic?' Denny asked. 'What do you mean?'

Verity was surprised at his tone. 'Just looking-into-each-other's-eyes romantic,' she reassured him. 'Boring stuff. Nothing more.'

Denny nodded. 'Jimmy Jones,' he said. 'I know him. I reckon he nicked some trousers from the shop a couple of weeks ago. Not that I can prove it. I'd have thought he was a bit of a loser anyway to be playing a role like that. Couldn't they find anyone better?'

Verity looked at the ground, her loyalties torn. Jimmy had seemed so nice last Thursday that she didn't want to say bad things about him. She'd really enjoyed the filming, but now Denny's reaction wrong-footed her. She assumed the fact that she was being filmed at all would make her seem sophisticated and interesting, but Denny's low opinion of Jimmy meant she now felt foolish. 'I guess Jimmy can be a bit weird,' she mumbled.

'Yeah, well,' Denny said, a warning tone in his voice. 'So long as it's all hands-off between you on camera as well as off, then I don't mind. I don't want you doing anything that we haven't . . .'

Verity gasped and stopped. 'With Jimmy? No way!' Then she smiled reassuringly at Denny. 'I've just got to pretend to be in love with him. It's nothing, really.'

'If we're together, I've got to be able to trust you,' Denny said seriously, turning towards her and holding her shoulders. 'I'm a very jealous guy. I can't help it. If I'm with a girl, then she's mine.'

Verity felt as if she'd been sprinkled with fairy dust. She was Denny's. And she wanted him to know it, completely. 'You can trust me. I'd never do anything like that. With anyone. I promise, Denny. I'm all yours.'

Denny lifted her up then, as if overtaken with passion and when her face came level with his, he kissed her for the first time, his tongue parting her lips. Verity squeezed her eyes shut, feeling his teeth bump with hers and she thanked God with everything she had that she'd had her braces removed in time for this, the best kiss of her life.

After a while, she tried to pull away, but Denny slid his hand into her hair and cupped the back of her head, drawing her closer and kissing her more and more deeply. Verity tensed as his tongue darted further into her mouth.

At last, as his grip slackened and her feet finally touched the ground, Denny groaned. Verity's lips were stinging

241

from where his stubble had grazed them. She could feel his penis through his jeans, pressing against her thigh. She let him fold her into his embrace, her eyes open, as her nose pressed against the soft wool of his jumper. Inside, her heart raced with panic and excitement. What was she meant to do now? Did Denny expect her to touch him? What if she did it wrong? Too frightened to move, she heard Denny's low groan.

'God, Verity,' he said. 'I want you so badly. It's killing me, I want you so much.'

The next day, up at Appleforth House for the Thursday filming session, Verity knew that it was only a matter of time before things got really serious with Denny, but after last night something had changed. She was ready for him. It was as if in his declaration of desire he'd finally turned her into the woman she was meant to be.

In one of the downstairs storerooms near the back kitchen, Verity sat on a low stool, in front of a mirror, as Edith from Shoresby Styles curled her hair into ringlets with hot tongs. Verity looked at the dress hanging from the back of the door that she would soon put on in order for her to be transformed once more into Caroline Walpole. She knew, now, how the dead girl must have felt: desperate with love, determined to be with her lover at any cost, despite her father's disapproval. Despite everyone.

It was unusually sunny outside, and Ellen and Scott seemed anxious to get on and make the most of the light, beckoning to Verity to hurry up as she finally emerged through the back kitchen door in her costume. She picked up her skirt and hurried along the old stone path to where Scott, Ellen, Roy and Jimmy were waiting for her underneath the arbour. Various lights were set up around the bench against the stone wall where Jimmy was sitting, already in costume.

Ellen squeezed the top of Verity's arm as she sat down next to him. 'Just hold on one minute, you two,' she said and Verity smiled at her, envying Ellen's trendy designer glasses with large brown lenses. She was wearing a frilly white shirt tucked into hipster jeans, with an expensive-looking blue jumper slung casually round her shoulders. As she walked back to where Scott was standing near the monitor, Verity couldn't help thinking how elegant Ellen was. How lovely it must be, she thought, to be like her. She looked so in charge and in control.

'You look happy today,' Jimmy said to her, as Verity arranged her skirts over the bench.

'Do I?' she replied. She knew she sounded haughty and offhand, but after what Denny had said, she didn't really want to get too friendly with Jimmy.

But Jimmy didn't pick up on her tone and wasn't letting her off the hook. 'Yeah, you do.'

'Well, it's nothing to do with this costume. I feel ridiculous.'

'I wish my gran could see you,' Jimmy said almost to himself, sighing wistfully.

What did Jimmy's gran have to do with anything? 'Your *gran*?' Verity asked, surprised.

'It doesn't matter,' Jimmy said.

But Verity couldn't help being intrigued by his sad look. She realised she didn't know anything about his family background. 'Tell me about her,' she said.

She listened, amazed at Jimmy's connection with his paternal grandmother. As he told Verity about how his gran had bought him up, she could hear the regret in his voice that she wouldn't be coming out of the hospice. She'd

243

always assumed that Jimmy was detached and didn't really care about anything, but this small insight into his personal life made her realise that her opinion was entirely wrong. The way Jimmy spoke about his gran – with real love and compassion – took Verity by surprise. It made it clear to her how sensitive Jimmy was. She'd assumed he was typical of the other guys of their age, who took the piss out of the town pensioners and poured scorn on the old people who made a fuss about graffiti and litter. But she couldn't have been further off the mark.

Now she felt ashamed that Jimmy had all these responsibilities in his life and yet he never complained, while she sat in her hotel suite every night thinking about how difficult her life was. 'Do you think your gran will see us on TV, though?' she asked.

'I don't think she'll make it,' Jimmy said. 'It's such a shame. I'd love for her to see me like this. To give her a laugh. And to see you, of course. You'll look great on TV.'

Verity winced. 'Don't. I don't even want to think about it.'

'You're kidding?'

'I'm not. I'm terrified about it. There's no way I'm going to watch it. I'm just going to hide away when it's on.'

'I don't understand. I thought you liked the filming.'

'It's not the filming that bothers me, it's what it's going to look like on screen. Everyone says that you look really different on television and I bet I'll look awful. I'll look ugly.' Verity gestured to her hair and what she considered to be her ghoulish make-up.

'You could never look ugly,' Jimmy said.

Verity snorted with denial.

'I can get Scott to show you the rushes on the monitor if you like,' he offered.

'No, it's not the same. His screen is tiny. I mean on a big

244

screen. I guess I'm just being stupid, but the whole thought scares the hell out of me. I'm going to die of embarrassment. I know it.'

'Right,' said Ellen, interrupting Jimmy's quizzical look and saving Verity from explaining herself further. Scott came to adjust one of the large lights and then stood back by the camera, his legs wide apart, as he looked through the viewfinder. Roy stood next to him, holding a big fluffy grey microphone on the end of a large boom. He adjusted his headphones and nodded at Scott.

Verity looked deliberately at Ellen, pouring all her concentration into what she was saying.

'Jimmy, I want you to be reading Verity a Tennyson poem from this book,' Ellen said, handing over a worn leather-bound volume. 'Don't worry about getting the enunciation to a point of RADA excellence, as you're not Equity cleared, so we're going to have to drop it down in the sound mix anyway. But the point to remember is that Caroline and Leon are meeting in secret and they are desperately in love, so Verity, I want you to watch Jimmy as he reads. Then, I want you to clasp hands as if you're parting. Shall we give it a go?'

Verity brushed off a leaf from her dress and shuffled upright on the seat, as Jimmy gently opened the book.

'Here goes,' Jimmy said, lifting it up.

As Jimmy started reading the poem, he glanced at her as if he already knew the words and Verity found herself listening intently. Despite what Ellen had said about enunciation, the way Jimmy read it he could be on stage. It was beautiful, like he'd written it himself. Perhaps she should learn the poem off by heart herself and recite it to Denny, Verity thought dreamily. If he loved opera, he was bound to be into poetry, too.

245

'Brilliant,' Ellen said, chipping in and stopping Jimmy mid-sentence. 'You two are naturals. Jimmy, keep doing what you're doing. Verity, try if you can to look a bit more dreamily *at* Jimmy, rather than the book. We'll go for the shot.'

'You look great together,' Scott chipped in, winking at Jimmy, who pulled a face at him.

Verity couldn't help giggling. It was sweet that Jimmy was finding this so embarrassing. She was the one who ought to feel embarrassed, but seeing him so nervous made her feel more calm.

As the camera started to roll, Verity smoothed her lips together and stared at Jimmy. He looked so different dressed up as Leon. His face had completely changed with the make-up. He looked older and more sophisticated, and there was something more alive about him than usual. She was used to seeing him slouching around, as if he were half asleep. But now, with his hair tied back away from his face, she could almost pretend he was a different person altogether. She let herself look into his eyes as he read, marvelling at what a good actor he was and wondering how many other things he could be good at if he gave them a try.

When Ellen called 'cut', Verity averted her eyes.

Ellen nodded at Scott and Roy, the sound man, who fiddled with some knobs on a square box he was carrying on a strap round his neck.

'I'm going in for a close-up,' Scott said to Ellen, moving the camera forward on its tripod. Then he looked up over his shoulder at the sky. 'We'd better do this quickly, before the light changes.'

'Right, just one more shot,' Ellen said, consulting her clipboard, as Scott adjusted the legs on the tripod.

She picked up a red leather-bound book from the top of

one of the camera boxes and came towards Jimmy and Verity. 'Look guys, I've been reading Caroline's diary,' she said, flipping it open. 'She wrote a lot about her stolen kisses with Leon under the arbour.'

'You want us to . . .?' Verity asked, swallowing. She hadn't been expecting this.

'Do you mind?' Ellen asked, looking as if she were perplexed that there was a problem.

Jimmy shrugged and looked away, and Verity could see that his cheeks were pink.

'It's no big deal if you don't want to,' Ellen continued. 'But it would make it so much more authentic. I'm not talking about a gigantic snog. Pretend this is their first kiss.'

Ellen smiled, then, at them both and Verity smiled back nervously, wanting to please her. She thought about Denny, briefly. But this had nothing to do with Denny. Ellen, Scott and Roy were here. It was only acting, after all.

'Let's just give it a go,' Ellen continued casually, folding her arms and standing next to Scott. 'See what happens. Just do what feels natural. Take it from where they're holding hands. OK . . . and camera.'

Verity counted down in her head, silently, as Ellen had taught her. She took a deep breath and looked at Jimmy. He looked back at her, his blue eyes intense as they met hers. Despite herself, Verity could feel her knees trembling with nerves. Why were they wobbling? There was nothing to feel nervous about, surely? This was just pretend. Verity concentrated hard on forgetting the black lens of the camera, as Jimmy's hands found hers. She wondered whether he could tell that her hands were sweating and wished that they weren't.

Then he was gently pulling her towards him. Verity looked at him, concentrating hard. *Forget the camera, look natural*, she thought, drumming it into her head. But Jimmy was getting closer and closer.

Then he was filling her vision and Verity could feel his breath on her cheek. Up close, he smelt of make-up and sunshine, and she breathed in the unfamiliar, yet strangely intoxicating smell of him. Jimmy tilted his head, his lips only millimetres away from hers. Feeling terrified and excited all at once, Verity held her breath. *He's Leon*, she thought, *Leon, Leon* . . . But then Jimmy's lips were on hers and Verity couldn't move. Her whole being zoomed into focus on the sensation of their sealed lips.

She closed her eyes, every nerve ending in her body on red alert. It felt like hours that Jimmy stayed there, connected with her, but it could only have been seconds. It was as if she'd been sucked into another dimension of their own. She felt almost dizzy as Jimmy moved, his lips tentatively opening. Feeling as if she were floating, her stomach flipping over, she felt Jimmy come closer still, pressing himself against her, his hands tenderly holding her face. It was then that she had no choice but to give in and, having forgotten everything – including the camera – Verity kissed him back.

With a jerk Jimmy roughly pulled away from her, being wrenched out of the seat. Verity gasped with shock as she saw Denny grip Jimmy by the collar of his frock coat, draw back his fist and punch him in the face.

'Stop it, Denny, stop it!' Verity screamed, as Jimmy staggered backwards and crashed against the arbour wall, falling on to his knees.

Denny rushed forward to grab Jimmy again and Verity lunged at him, trying to hold his arm, but he shrugged her off.

'You . . . you . . .' Denny growled at Jimmy, yanking him up again.

248

'Get off him,' Scott yelled, pulling Denny away, grabbing him under the arms.

Jimmy struggled to his feet holding his face. Verity could see blood trickling from one of his nostrils.

'What the hell's going on?' Ellen shouted, standing between Jimmy and Denny, and holding out her arms to keep them at a distance.

Denny pointed at Verity. 'You promised,' he snarled, shrugging Scott off. 'You promised me.'

'Denny,' Verity sobbed, going to him, but he wouldn't let her touch him. 'It was just pretend. I wasn't really –'

But Denny just shook his head, his face pinched with scorn as he pushed her away.

'Denny! Denny! Come back!' Verity cried, but it was too late.

Chapter XIV

'Wasn't that the guy from the surf shop?' Ellen demanded. 'What the hell did he think he was doing?'

'He's my . . . my boyfriend,' Verity whimpered, staring after Denny, who was striding away from the set, kicking one of Scott's boxes out of the way.

'Best to leave him to cool down, don't you think?' Ellen suggested, eyeballing Scott and putting a restraining arm on Verity.

Roy had kindly donated his handkerchief to Jimmy, who now stood staring at Verity, dabbing the blood away from the end of his nose.

'Would someone mind telling me what this is all about?' Ellen asked, staring between Jimmy and Verity. She couldn't believe what had just happened. How the hell had that nutter appeared without anyone noticing?

'I'm so sorry, Jimmy. I'm so sorry,' Verity sobbed. 'It's all my fault.'

'You're too good for him,' Jimmy replied, looking at the blood on the handkerchief and back at Verity.

'You don't understand,' Verity cried, her tears doubling at the unmistakable roar of a motorbike starting by the house.

From the look of desolation on Verity's face, Ellen guessed that the wheels churning up the drive undoubtedly belonged to Denny. Verity covered her face, full of shame. 'I promised him that I'd . . . that I'd never be unfaithful.'

'Come on, Verity,' Ellen soothed. 'Stop being so hard on

yourself. That guy – Denny – well, he was way out of order. I *asked* you and Jimmy to kiss. It's hardly being unfaithful.' She put her arm round Verity, looking over her bowed head towards Scott who, thankfully, picked up on her baffled expression.

'You're OK, though, mate, aren't you?' Scott asked Jimmy.

Jimmy was staring at Verity. 'I'll be fine,' he answered.

'Because if you're not, and you feel like getting the law on him, I've got the whole thing on film.'

Verity stared up at Scott, aghast. 'But –' she gasped.

Her and Jimmy's eyes connected.

Jimmy then turned to Scott. 'Like I said,' he reiterated. 'I'll be fine.'

'I've ruined everything. You don't understand,' Verity said, looking up at Ellen and then at Scott, her eyes brimming with tears.

'Understand what?' Ellen asked, exasperated.

'I kissed him back,' Verity choked, darting a look at Jimmy. Then she was off, running down the kitchen garden path in a mass of billowing skirts and bobbing ringlets.

'I guess that's it, then, for today,' Roy said, unplugging the boom mike.

Ellen sighed loudly and slapped her thighs. 'I guess so. What a disaster.'

'I'm sorry, Ellen,' Jimmy said sheepishly.

'Jimmy, don't apologise! It's not your fault. Why don't you go and get yourself cleaned up, eh?'

Ellen watched him go. She felt sorry for the kid. He hadn't stood a chance against that idiot, Denny. She'd grown to like Jimmy since he'd been helping them out and now she wished there were something she could do to help him. She thought about calling out to him, to thank him for playing Leon so well, but it probably wouldn't help the situation, she thought, and turned away.

She could have done with another take, but she had to admit that the parting kiss between Caroline and Leon had been just about as perfect as she could wish for. She'd been so absorbed watching it that Denny's appearance had completely taken her by surprise.

'I think I've got enough. You can cut away before the punch,' Scott said, starting to unscrew the bolt under the camera tripod.

'Teenagers,' Ellen said, shaking her head. Listening to Verity talk in such black and white terms about right and wrong had only made Ellen realise how complex and blurred her own emotional life had become.

'My kids are all like that,' Roy said, looping cable round his arm. 'Drama this, drama that. All in love one minute and breaking up the next.'

'I just don't get it.' Ellen put her hands on her hips and looked at Jimmy's departing figure. 'It was acting! Jimmy wasn't really kissing Verity.'

Scott smiled.

'Well, I suppose he was, technically,' Ellen said, picking up on Scott's look, 'but there's nothing going on –'

Scott gave her an even wider smirk. 'You heard the lady yourself. She kissed him back.'

Ellen stared at him, letting his words sink in. So there was something going on between Jimmy and Verity? Ellen threw her hands up, exasperated. 'Great. 'I'm supposed to be the director and I can't even spot what's going on right in front of me!'

Scott laughed and although Ellen tried to smile, inside her sense of panic clicked up a notch. It was as if everything were spinning out of control – even the small things, like the filming, which should have been so easy.

She'd been feeling like this since Ned had left on Saturday night. No matter how hard she tried to tell herself that nothing happened, she couldn't get round the fact that something almost had. They had almost kissed. That was the truth. Some sort of romantic chemistry had happened between her and Ned, making Ellen take leave of her senses. She couldn't even blame the alcohol. She'd been drunk with plenty of men before, but she'd never been tempted to kiss them. The seriousness of her near fall into the abyss of infidelity had frightened her right to her core, challenging everything she held dear.

At first she'd blamed Ned. He'd come to her house. He was the one trying to seduce her – telling her romantic stories and staying up into the small hours helping her.

Then she'd blamed Jason. It was Jason's fault for being away. It was because of him that she was left vulnerable to another man's advances.

But in the end, she'd reached the conclusion that she was just trying to deceive herself. She'd let Ned into her life and had let herself be weak. There was no one to blame but herself and that knowledge made her feel sick. If she couldn't trust herself, how could she expect Jason to trust her?

But it *hadn't* happened, she reminded herself. It wasn't like Verity and Jimmy – she and Ned hadn't actually touched lips. So why was she feeling as if she'd been unfaithful to Jason? Worse, perhaps, than if she and Ned *had* kissed each other?

She knew the answer. The unassailable fact about the near kiss was that Ned had stopped it happening. She hadn't. Ned had broken whatever spell she'd been under and had run away as fast as he could. And now, as well as the guilt that plagued her every waking thought, there was also the shame.

It didn't happen, she repeated to herself. Yet it seemed that the harder she tried to forget it, the more life threw it back in her face as a taunt – even now with Jimmy, Denny and Verity. It was almost as if they'd been playing out her very own fears.

She'd spent most of the week deliberately avoiding Ned. She hadn't come up to Appleforth House until today, so that she wouldn't have to see him. She'd also avoided going out too much in the town, in case they bumped into each other. But now, Ellen knew she'd run out of excuses. She would have to see Ned and clear the air.

The only way she'd be able to function and finish the shoot was if she told Ned the truth about Jason. And the truth was that she'd been upset after an unsatisfactory conversation, which had led her to play down their relationship, which, in turn, had given Ned completely the wrong impression. She would explain that she'd been feeling lonely and, helped by the wine, had temporarily taken leave of her senses. The fact was that Jason and she were, in all likelihood, going to be together for ever. There was absolutely no way she had ever, or would ever, consider being unfaithful, now or in the future.

There, she thought, having rehearsed these lines in her head a few times, that would set the record straight and make sure there was no atmosphere between her and Ned. She would be strong and honest. She owed it to Ned and to herself.

Inside Appleforth House, Ellen stood at the foot of the grand main staircase, trying to attract the attention of the workman who was fixing the new mahogany banister. 'Have you seen Ned?' she shouted above the whine of the drill.

'In the ballroom,' he replied, pointing down one of the corridors leading off the hall. Ellen made her way across to it, sidestepping ladders and treading softly over the dust sheets draped over the new floor.

Decorators were everywhere. The hall was filled with dust and the loud tinkle of the chandelier crystals as several workmen tried to attach the vast light to the ceiling, shouting strained commands to each other from the top of their ladders as they balanced it between them.

As she walked down the long corridor towards the large panelled doors at the end, the noise of the workmen began to fade. She could see the wires where the light fittings would go along the walls, but it was dark as she approached the doors and she could hear her trainers squeaking on the tiles. Taking a deep breath, Ellen twisted the porcelain handle and, opening the large door slightly, quietly slipped inside.

The tranquil sight that greeted her was totally different from the noisy hallway and gloomy corridor. In the ball-room it was calm, the huge empty space filled with shafts of sunlight, which spilt in from the full-length, arch-topped windows along one side, making the inlaid marble floor sparkle. Thousands of mosaic tiles spun away from Ellen in an intricate pattern of flowers and swirls to a central floral design beneath the dome in the ceiling. The effect was breathtaking and, as she stepped on to it, she immediately felt the urge to twirl across the vast expanse of the sun-filled room.

'Stop!' It was Ned's voice that boomed out the harsh command.

Ellen froze, looking up to see Ned standing on the far wall against the door frame, fifty feet away.

'It's just been laid,' he said more gently. 'I don't want anyone on it for twenty-four hours.'

Ellen tentatively retracted her foot as if from thin ice. 'It's beautiful,' she said, her gaze running across the floor and up to where Ned was standing, his hands in the pockets of dark-grey moleskin trousers. She'd thought about him so much in the last few days, about how his face looked when they'd been kneeling side by side, that it seemed strange to see him from a distance. He was wearing his glasses and his hair was dishevelled, but still, he was undeniably attractive. She felt her cheeks burning. 'What's it made of?' she asked, looking back at the floor.

'Purbeck marble.'

When Ned didn't elaborate, there was an awkward silence. She felt ridiculous standing so far away from him, but Ned wasn't moving. She cleared her throat, ready to start her speech about Jason. But now all the things she'd been planning to say seemed too embarrassing or presumptuous.

Nothing happened, she reminded herself. Why was she trying to turn this into a big emotional event? Surely, if she did that, Ned would think even more badly of her?

But then, did Ned really think badly of her? Did she know that for sure? What did Ned really think? It was impossible to say anything, until he gave her some indication of how he felt. Was he going to acknowledge that what *didn't* happen actually *did*? Or was he going to ignore what *did* happen and pretend that it *didn't*?

Ellen felt as if she were sinking in emotional quicksand. Time was running out and she had to say something, even if Ned wasn't going to. 'I came to tell you that we've

256

finished filming for the day,' she said hopefully, her voice echoing in the vast room.

'Mm-hm,' Ned mumbled, concentrating on the floor.

Ellen tapped Caroline Walpole's diary in her hand, wishing he'd look at her. If he wouldn't look at her, how could she start a conversation with him?

She thought about telling him about the drama with Denny, Jimmy and Verity, but when Ned didn't say anything, she lost heart. 'I brought back the diary,' she said, holding it up. 'I thought you might want to keep it with the other papers.'

Ned looked at her then, his face neither unfriendly, or friendly, just terrifyingly neutral. As their eyes connected across the sun-filled room, Ellen's heart seemed to jump, but Ned betrayed no emotion. 'Thanks. You can leave it there by the door.'

This is intolerable, thought Ellen, tempted to run across the tiles and shake Ned until he listened to her. But she knew that would be hopeless. Slowly, she crouched and put the diary down, stroking the leather cover. She couldn't stand this atmosphere between them. She had to say something. 'Ned,' she began as she stood up. 'About the other night –'

'I must remember to give you back the quilt. Clara's quite taken with it.'

'No, not that,' Ellen implored. 'About –'

'I don't want you to get the wrong impression, Ellen,' he said quietly, looking at his shoes. 'I meant what I said about there being no second chances for me.'

When he looked at her, Ellen felt as if he'd punched her, just like Denny had punched Jimmy. He'd already run away from her once; he wasn't supposed to push her away again! How dare he think she was coming on to him, she thought

257

indignantly, when she'd come to tell him just the opposite.

'I'm with Jason,' she said, almost spitting the words out at him. 'And I intend to be with him for ever.'

'Good. I hope you'll be very happy,' Ned said.

The note of finality in his voice made her nose sting with tears. 'Thanks,' she mumbled. When she looked up, Ned had disappeared through the door and she was alone.

Ellen was still smarting from her meeting with Ned when she and Scott drove back down into town and, at Scott's suggestion, stopped by the Mr Chips near the arcade for some late lunch.

'Yes, you can borrow the car,' Ellen said to Scott with a sigh, as she pushed against the shop door. Immediately she walked into the steamy interior, her nostrils were assaulted by the delicious smell of fresh chips and she realised that Scott's idea to come here had been a good one.

'I won't if you don't want me to,' said Scott, following her inside, but Ellen knew that he didn't mean it. Ever since Scott had finally been out on a date with Debs last night, he'd been plotting where to take her next. Tonight's venture involved a moonlit drive by the sound of it.

Ellen knew she was being mean, but the truth was that she was a little jealous that Scott was so happy about Debs. And she was worried that things were about to change. She liked it when he was around at the cottage, and, even though it was she who'd suggested that he combine the filming with a holiday, she hadn't expected him to spend his time going out on dates.

'It's OK. I'll go back on the train,' Ellen said, looking up at the chalk board menu on the wall behind the counter, but inwardly groaning about the journey back to London. 'I think there's one in an hour.'

'You're making me feel bad. I'll buy you chips to make it up to you for being such a fabulous boss.'

Ellen glanced at Scott, who was grinning at her. 'Creep,' she said. 'You don't feel bad. You're too loved-up for that. It makes me sick.'

'You've got to admit she's incredible.'

'Enough already!' Ellen exclaimed, having heard nothing from Scott apart from Debs's virtues all day. She was beginning to regret her ideas of matchmaking him and Debs, even though she hadn't had to do anything. Ellen had only dropped a few hints and before she'd known what was happening, Scott had already asked her out. She had to admire his forthright attitude. 'I admit that Debs is very pretty and, from what I've seen of her, she seems . . . nice,' Ellen conceded.

'Nice!' Scott scoffed. 'She's more than nice!'

'Yes, well, pity she works for such a pig,' Ellen grumbled.

'I thought you and Ned were getting on.' Scott said, looking confused, before ordering chips from the girl behind the counter.

'We were,' Ellen said with a sigh as they waited. She was tempted to tell Scott what had almost happened between her and Ned, but she was too embarrassed. Now that he and Debs were an item, she couldn't guarantee that Scott wouldn't say something that would get back to Ned. 'Forget it, it's a long story. Let's just put our differences down to emotional baggage.'

'It sounds like Ned's got a carousel full of it.'

'Is that what Debs says?' Ellen asked despite herself. She was determined to forget Ned and that anything had ever happened between them. After what he'd said in the ball-room earlier, Ellen was convinced that her initial impression of Ned Spencer had been the correct one: he was conceited and arrogant. He always had been and he always would be.

'Debs says he doesn't talk about things much. Especially not her.'

'Who? Mary?'

Scott nodded his head. 'Poor guy. He's been through a hell of a lot. Fancy finding your wife like that . . .'

Scott accepted the two cones of chips from the woman behind the counter and handed one to Ellen. Then he started to move towards the door.

'What do you mean?' Ellen asked, stopping him.

Scott munched on a chip. 'Ned's wife. Mary. He found her electrocuted in the bath,' he explained. 'She did it with a hairdryer. I guess you don't get over that in a hurry.'

Ellen dropped the small wooden fork she was holding. Her mouth fell open, as Scott opened the door and she was hit by a blast of cold air. But that was nothing compared with the physical sensation that was going on inside her. She felt her stomach lurch, as if she'd driven fast over a very large bump in the road.

'I thought you said Ned talked to you,' Scott said, frowning at her.

'He said . . . he said . . . she died of a brain disease,' Ellen mumbled. 'He didn't say that she'd . . .'

Ellen's confusion over Scott's revelation had only increased as the train sped through the countryside into the dark outskirts of the city. She snuggled down in her seat and tried to read her book, but she'd read the same passage over and over again without concentrating. Beside her, the aisles filled up with commuters, men and women in suits with tired expressions, and the air became muggy and soporific with bad moods and condensation from dozens of damp umbrellas.

By the time the train pulled into Paddington, Ellen felt

260

weary and dirty. After nearly three hours of travelling, all she wanted was a hot shower and to go to bed. She'd only been sitting on a train, but she felt as if she'd crossed a continent and her day in Shoresby now seemed like a memory from a different planet.

As she walked along the platform, Ellen felt unnerved by the number of people purposefully striding past her, their faces set with determination. It's so unfriendly, she thought, as a woman shoved past her to get on to the escalator down into the tube. Ellen could feel the hairs on the back of her neck prickling, as she was sandwiched between two people, her bag pressed against her, so that she could hardly breathe.

On the tube, Ellen held on to the overhead rail, trying not to look at two drunk city boys who were telling crude jokes in the seats below her. She'd always been able to glide around the city, ignoring the ugly facts about it, making it her own. But now she noticed the filth and the dirt, and it made her want to run away.

Even when she made it off the tube and walked the familiar route to the flat, she felt uneasy. Usually, she was so sure of her home and her roots, but now she felt slightly unstuck, as if part of her was adrift.

The heating hadn't come on, so it was cold in the flat when Ellen got inside. She could see the answerphone blinking with messages, but she couldn't face any of them. Flicking through the mail, she walked into the kitchen to the fridge, but she already knew before opening it that there would be nothing edible in it. She chucked the unopened letters on the side, grabbed the corkscrew and pulled out a bottle of wine from the rack.

In the living room, Ellen shoved all the papers and magazines off the sofa on to the floor, then, flopping down, she flicked on the widescreen TV. Yet still, after a few more glasses of wine, she couldn't relax. She'd thought that coming back to the flat would help her focus. She'd thought that being in the space she shared with Jason would make everything better. But it only made her feel more alone.

From her vantage point on the sofa she looked around her, taking in the tastefully framed prints and large glass lamps. She'd decorated it. This was all her work. There wasn't one thing visible of Jason's to remind her of him. Even the books were hers.

In the bedroom she opened her bag, letting the contents spill out on the bed. It was then that she saw she'd brought Ned's jumper, the one that he'd lent her the day she'd rescued Clara. It must have been in the bottom of her bag, and she stared at it, unable to believe that she'd subconsciously brought a piece of Ned back here into her home.

As the jumper lay across her and Jason's bed like a flattened-out hug, all the times she'd shared with Ned, all the conversations they'd had, filled her head.

Why hadn't Ned told her? Why hadn't he trusted her with the truth? Ellen sat down on the bed and picked up the jumper. It all finally slotted into place – Ned's anger at her documentary, his need to get blind drunk. It was all because he was still grieving over Mary's suicide.

And that was why he'd pushed her away. That was why he didn't want any second chances.

Ellen closed her eyes, sadness and confusion overwhelming her. This wasn't fair, she thought. All she was trying to do was her job. She hadn't expected her whole life to be turned upside down. She hadn't done anything physically, but everything had changed. Everything she'd always taken for granted in her life now seemed to be slipping away from her.

Ellen felt tears welling up in her eyes and a dull ache

spreading inside her chest. What was wrong with her? Why did she feel so sad? Was she sad for Jason or for Ned? Was she missing the man who loved her, or the one who never would? Hugging Ned's jumper to her, she curled up on her bed and silently wept.

Chapter XV

'The big one's a sapphire,' Marianna Andrews answered Jimmy. 'And the little ones clustered around the edge are diamonds.'

It was Saturday morning, two days after Jimmy Jones had been punched in the face by Denny Shapland and half an hour before Video-2-Go was due to open. Marianna stepped out of her black lace knickers and walked over to where Jimmy was sitting on the edge of the wooden table in the middle of the stockroom. He was swinging his legs and letting the soles of his trainers scuff along the concrete floor like a kid, and it was only when she reached him that he stopped. She pressed her left hand down on his thigh and splayed her fingers over the denim of his jeans.

'Do you *really* like it?' she asked, leaning forward in such a fashion that the only way in which he was able to examine her engagement ring was by staring directly down between her breasts. The citrus scent of her perfume filled his nostrils and the sapphire sparkled intermittently under the flickering strip light.

'I wouldn't have said it otherwise,' he confirmed, although really and truly, of course, he didn't either like it or hate it.

Really and truly, her engagement ring struck him as incongruous and fake – particularly when, like now, it was the only thing she was wearing. Really and truly, it made Jimmy feel guilty, the same as the framed photo of Marianna's husband, Bill, who grinned stupidly down at them from the stockroom wall with a fishing rod in one hand and a dead conger eel in the other. And really and truly, the only reason Jimmy had commented on the ring in the first place had been in an attempt to induce these feelings in Marianna as well.

But Marianna was proving more impervious to Jimmy's powers of suggestion than he could have ever imagined. Flexing her left hand like a spider, she slowly began to claw her blood-red nails up over Jimmy's thigh towards his groin. 'And this?' she whispered, leaning further forward, so that Jimmy could feel her breath on his lips. 'Do you *really like* this, too?'

Jimmy cleared his throat. 'Listen, Marianna,' he began, 'there's something I think we need to –'

'Ah-ah,' she cut him off, pressing her forefinger against his lips. 'You know the rules.'

But Jimmy didn't want to play by them right now. 'No,' he said, shifting sideways across the table's edge. 'Not today. Today I want to' – he knew she wasn't going to like this, but he knew he had to say it anyway – 'talk,' he stated.

Marianna's eyes flashed wide as if he'd just asked her to bend him over and give him a good spanking. Strike that, he thought. She was looking at him as though he'd just asked her to do something that she *wouldn't* enjoy.

'Talk? What on earth about?' She clicked her tongue in disapproval. 'We didn't come back here to talk, Jimmy,' she pointed out. 'Come on: time's precious. We can talk in the shop whenever we want.'

'I know,' Jimmy replied, 'but . . .'

'But *what*?' She tapped her bare foot on the concrete.

For some reason the action conjured up an absurd image in Jimmy's mind of Marianna as a snorting bull getting ready to charge and himself as a hopelessly inadequate matador. With an effort of will, however, he dismissed the thought. He was determined not to let Marianna dominate the situation. He wasn't going to chicken out now, no matter how awkward she made him feel. He had to forget the fact that she was his boss. He had to forget the fact that she was twice his age. He slid off the table and stood facing her. 'This has got to stop,' he announced.

There, Jimmy thought, *that wasn't that hard, was it?*

Only Marianna wasn't going to make it that easy. 'Stop what?' she protested. 'We haven't even started yet.'

'Us,' Jimmy insisted. 'All this . . . what we've been doing . . . it's over. It's time for it to end.'

Marianna's whole body stiffened. 'Says who? Says you? *You* say it's over? *You* say it's time? *You* are saying *that* to *me*?'

'Listen,' Jimmy tried to explain, 'there are some things that . . . things in my life,' he went on, 'that have changed . . .'

Marianna's expression relaxed. 'Oh, that,' she said.

'What?'

'Your grandmother. How ill she's become.'

Jimmy was confused. 'I don't think –'

'It's OK,' said Marianna. She folded her arms and leant up against the table, exactly the same as she did against the shop counter whenever she was chatting to a customer – only there, of course, she did wear clothes. 'I know all about it,' Marianna explained. 'I bumped into Rachel yesterday afternoon and I asked her if you were feeling any better . . .'

Jimmy reddened. He'd called in sick yesterday morning, leaving messages for Marianna at Video-2-Go when he'd known damn well that she'd be out, telling her that he'd got food poisoning. He'd been putting off coming here, putting off the very conversation he was having now.

'And after she'd told me that there was actually nothing

wrong with you,' Marianna continued, 'the two of us sat down and had a chat. And she told me all about your grandmother and about how much stress you've been under lately. Not to mention your accident the day before yesterday . . .' Marianna stared knowingly at Jimmy's eye, still swollen from when Denny had smacked him.

Jimmy had assumed that the wound would have proved an asset in busting up with Marianna, what with it making him look as much like Quasimodo as it did, but she hadn't even mentioned it up until now.

'Debs told me about that, too, about how you fell off your bike and hit your face on a beer can that someone had dropped on the street.'

'Yeah, sure,' Jimmy said, his lie sounding even less convincing when repeated by someone else.

'So it's hardly surprising if your libido's taken a bit of a battering, is it, love?' Marianna continued. 'Stress and trauma do that, don't they? And if you want us to take a break for a week, then of course I'll fully understand . . . but let's not overreact. When you're feeling better, we can pick up where we left off. There,' she concluded. 'I can't say fairer than that.' She smiled at Jimmy coolly, before turning her back on him and walking towards where her clothes lay in a pile.

Watching the jagged scar on her right buttock stretch and straighten as she bent down and picked up her bra, Jimmy considered leaving the issue there. He could act complicit, take the break she'd offered him and just extend it every week. He could let her down softly over time and avoid a full-on conflict altogether.

Her back arched as she started to fasten her bra.

But he didn't want to string her along like that. He didn't want to leave her with the false impression that he still belonged to her. Because he didn't. He belonged to someone else now: Verity. Even if Verity didn't know it yet. Even if she didn't yet care. Because that was what this was really about. It was about *honouring* the way he'd felt during that brief, brief moment he'd kissed Verity. This was about wanting to be with her and no one else.

'I'm in love with Verity Driver,' Jimmy said. 'And that's why I don't want to have sex with you any more.'

Marianna slowly turned and stared at Jimmy for what must have been five whole seconds. He thought that perhaps she'd stopped breathing, or was contemplating such a lengthy verbal assault that it was taking her this long just to prime her lungs. She wore the same look that his stepbrother Kieran did when he was about to launch himself into a screaming fit.

However, what Marianna actually asked was, 'The girl from the hotel? She's the same age as you, isn't she?'

Jimmy nodded.

Marianna considered this for a moment. 'Well, that's something at least,' she eventually said.

'I'm sorry,' Jimmy said.

'So you should be. But I suppose it had to happen sooner or later.' Marianna frowned at him, then smiled. 'I'll tell you what,' she told him. 'You put the kettle on and I'll put my knickers on and we'll have that talk you mentioned after all.'

'So there you have it,' Marianna was telling Jimmy ten minutes later, as she sat with him at the shop counter, sipping her tea from a chipped Cagney and Lacey mug (Sharon Gless was a personal heroine of Marianna's, who still had all the series episodes available for rent). 'If you think you're on to a good thing, go after it for all you're

268

worth. Don't do what I did and end up settling for OK, and then spend the rest of your life regretting it.'

The subject of her regret, Jimmy knew, was obviously her husband, Bill, who ran a fishing tackle shop on Queens Parade. 'But how?' he asked. 'Verity's got a boyfriend.'

'Fight for her.'

Jimmy pointed at his black eye. 'But he's the one who did this.'

'Then fight with your brain . . .' Marianna said, '. . . your heart . . . show her who you are . . . what you like . . . what you do . . . Show her who she'll be missing out on if she stays with him . . .'

'But what if I'm wrong about her?'

'I already told you,' Marianna said with conviction, 'you're not.'

'But how do you know? How can you be so sure?'

'It takes two people to kiss the way you described it, Jimmy. And if she hadn't felt something for you, she would have stopped herself from doing it. It would never have happened.'

There was the sound of a key in the door and both Jimmy and Marianna looked up to see Marianna's husband – a plump man with a satanic-looking black goatee beard – opening the shop door and stepping inside. Bill was accompanied by a mild smell of fish and he looked up and acknowledged them with a nod, before turning his back on them and continuing to talk loudly and querulously into a mobile phone about an order of live maggots for his shop, which had obviously failed to materialise. Marianna glanced at her watch. 'Just as well we did end it when we did, eh?' she whispered into Jimmy's ear.

'Too right,' Jimmy whispered back, before walking over to the PC and starting to boot it up.

Jimmy smiled, watching the screen come to life. He believed what Marianna had just said. Verity *wouldn't* have kissed him if she hadn't felt something for him. Which meant he had reason to hope. And reason to fight. And reason to think of ways to show Verity who he was. He believed Marianna, because all she'd actually just done had been to provide him with confirmation of what he'd intuitively already known.

He thought back to yesterday morning, to when Verity had caught up with him in the crowded school corridor after their English lesson. The whole meeting had lasted only seconds. She'd apologised and asked if he was OK, and whether there was anything she could do. Then she'd told him how upset she'd been by what had happened and, looking into her eyes, in an instant all the anger he'd felt since he'd been hit by Denny had dissolved. In an instant he'd forgiven her for running off on him like that. Because, in an instant, he'd glimpsed something buried there in her expression, and he'd recognised it as something far more intense, and far more secret, and far more rare, than mere friendship or concern. That look had stayed with him long after Verity had gone, pulled off into the crowd by a passing friend.

Here, in the shop, taking up his customary slouched position, he waited for the afternoon's first customer to arrive. He gazed out of the window on to the rainy street, amazed at how optimistic he now felt, and amazed, as well, at how much his mood could have altered from late last night, when all he'd been capable of wishing was that he'd never been born.

Late last night, they'd been round at Jimmy's room, Jimmy and Tara, squatting there side by side on his box bed. Jimmy had been feeling queasy and his eyes had been aching, partly because of the joint they'd shared down on the beach before coming up here, partly because of the black eye Denny had given him the previous afternoon, and partly because of the fact that they'd been playing Metal Gear Solid 2 on Tara's PS2 for upwards of two hours now instead of completing their History assignment for their Monday morning test paper.

'Out-fragged again!' Tara exclaimed as Jimmy bit the dust once more on the screen before them. She pulled a pack of gum from her ripped denim top and popped a piece between her black-painted lips.

'You're just jammy.'

'Just jammy nothing. You're just super-skanky.' She laughed, rattling her recently beaded black hair extensions at him, before falling suddenly silent.

'What?' Jimmy asked.

'Check it out.' Tara giggled.

Tara reached for the sound system and turned down The Streets' *Original Pirate Material* album she'd insisted on playing five times in a row now. The sweet scent of apple bubble bath had been drifting through Jimmy's open bedroom door for the last ten minutes, while Rachel had been giving little Kieran a bath next door.

A sound came, soft and mournful, through the wall. It was Rachel singing to Kieran.

'Bless,' said Tara.

But the word 'Summertime' was as much as Jimmy caught of Rachel's rendition before the shrill and strictly trashy analogue ring of the flat's telephone cut through.

'Can you get that for me?' Rachel called out.

Jimmy rolled his eyes at Tara.

She knew all about his reluctance over answering the flat's landline. 'Go on. It'll be fine.'

'We'll see,' he muttered, getting up and slipping out of the room.

Jimmy glared at the phone as he walked across the living-room floor towards its resting place on the small glass table next to the metal-legged leatherette sofa. Jimmy hated answering the flat phone. For one thing, it was never for him, what with most of his friends not bothering with landlines at all these days. Mainly, though, it was because of who he dreaded it might be: one of the nurses from the William Bentley Hospice, telling him that something else bad had happened to his gran; or his dad, being flaky about when he was going to be coming back from Portugal on a visit, or hooking up with Rachel over there.

'Jimmy!' Rachel shouted again from the bathroom, panicking now as the phone rang for the fifth time.

'I've got it,' he called back, picking the phone up and answering, 'Yep?'

'Jimmy!' his father's voice came down the line. 'How you doing?'

The words sounded as overblown and fake to Jimmy as the 'Enjoy your meal' you got whenever you bought a burger over at the FunBurger franchise on George Street. Jimmy let the silence hang there for a couple of seconds, and when he did speak he made his voice sound as flat and unenthusiastic as possible. Undermining his dad's lame attempts at father–son camaraderie was one of the only powers Jimmy had over him. 'I'm doing OK,' Jimmy said.

'Wicked.'

Jimmy felt a shiver run through him. His dad was forty going on fourteen, and was in the habit of using words that were way too young for him. Words like 'wicked' and 'dumb-ass' and 'minging' and 'sound', words that he'd picked up from hanging out in bars and clubs with kids

Jimmy's own age and younger, words which he was clueless as to what American show they'd been lifted from in the first place.

'So what have you been up to?' Jimmy's dad asked.

'Cotchin'.'

'Eh?'

Jimmy smiled. Gotcha, he thought. 'It means hanging out, Dad,' he told him. 'It's a youth culture thing. You wouldn't understand.'

Jimmy didn't ask his dad what he'd been up to in return, but his dad started telling him anyway. The words sounded rehearsed, like he'd practised them in a mirror before dialling. 'Things are coming on good here. I got a rise and I'm still working on Alfie and his property mates to maybe bankroll me enough to get me started on that theme bar idea I had. I told you about it, yeah?'

Jimmy wasn't in the mood for humouring him today. 'So you're not planning on coming home any time soon,' he stated. 'Not planning on seeing Rachel or me or Kieran.'

'Hey, look. I'm working on it, OK?' his father answered, coming over all hurt. 'But it's a matter of money. I can't just produce plane tickets out of thin air . . .'

His dad's words started washing over Jimmy and he found himself listening instead to the dull throb of a bass line playing in the background. His dad was probably outside a club, about to go in and meet up with someone who wasn't Rachel. He was probably just putting in a call to make himself feel better about what he was about to do. 'Hey, listen,' he was saying to Jimmy. 'What do you think about maybe coming out here for Christmas? You and Rachel and Kieran,' he went on when Jimmy failed to respond. 'We could make it a real family event.'

'What about Gran?' Jimmy asked. 'Or doesn't she count any more?'

'But she's ill. She wouldn't know.'

'No, Dad, I don't think so,' Jimmy told his father, watching Rachel come out of the bathroom and walk towards him with baby Kieran wrapped in a towel in her arms.

Bubblebath foam patterned Rachel's Wrangler sweatshirt and the humid air in the tiny bathroom had caused her blue eyeliner to run down her cheeks, making her look as if she'd been caught out in the rain. Kieran's sparse dark hair stood up in a Mohawk and he completed the seminal punk image by burping loudly and making himself laugh.

Jimmy's dad sighed down the phone, long and loud. 'You're obviously not in a good mood, Jimmy,' he said. 'So maybe we should chat another time and I'll speak to Rachel now.'

'Sure, Dad. That's crovey with me,' Jimmy said.

'What?'

'Go ask one of your friends,' Jimmy suggested, handing the phone over to Rachel, pleased to have left his father perplexed and pleased, too, at not having to listen to any more of his bullshit.

'Ben!' Jimmy heard Rachel admonish his father as he walked back to his room. 'Where've you been? I've been trying to get hold of you all week.'

Inside his bedroom, Jimmy found Tara leaning over the framed photo of herself, him and Ryan taken on the afternoon they'd driven down the coast to Lyme Regis. 'Was he cool, or what?' she said.

Jimmy smiled. Ryan did look cool in the photo. He had a purple headscarf on, tied with a gangsta-style knot on his forehead and his lips were parted as if he'd been about to say something. His arms were folded across his black sleeveless vest and his middle finger was raised for the benefit of the camera. Jimmy was standing beside him, taller than Ryan, but less powerful-looking. He had on his baseball cap, pulled down low on his brow, so that his features from his nose up lay buried in shadow. On Ryan's other side was Tara, in a white-striped blue tracksuit and a red woollen hat, looking so much younger than she did now. She was poking her tongue out and pulling her mouth wide with her fingers.

All three of them had shades on and you would have had to have been there to be able to identify them as individuals at all. They were leaning against the bonnet of the stolen Alfa Romeo they'd driven to Lyme Regis in. And behind them was the beach in Lyme Regis, where they'd sat down later on and watched the sun go down.

Jimmy remembered that day with incredible clarity. He remembered the breeze ruffling his baggy jeans against his thighs as he'd set his pocket camera up on a parking ticket machine in the car park, and then stood on tiptoe to get the car in the shot.

'Hurry it up,' Ryan had said, leaning further back on the car's blue bonnet and pulling Tara in close to him. 'If I've got to stay this close to this gorgeous woman any longer, then I'm not going to be held responsible for myself . . .'

'Dream on,' Tara had told him, but without making any attempt to move away.

'What d'you reckon, Jimmo? Me and Tara. We're made for each other, right? Why shouldn't we just surrender to our base desires and get it over with?'

'Because you're friends,' Jimmy had answered. 'And you never stay friends with people you have sex with. You told me that yourself.'

275

Ryan had nodded his head, smiling. 'Ah, such wisdom in one so young,' he'd reflected. 'Well, it would be crazy for me to ignore my own advice, so I'm sorry, Tara, I think I'm going to have to pass on you after all.'

'Yeah, well enough talking about me like I'm a piece of meat, anyway, you dick-heads, OK?' Tara had piped up, punching Ryan hard on the arm. 'I wouldn't touch either of yours with a bargepole anyway.'

'All right,' Jimmy had announced, gently pressing the camera's self-timer button and running round the ticket machine to join the others, planting himself on the bonnet next to Ryan.

'Shades on,' Ryan had instructed, and all three of them had pulled their shades from their pockets and put them on.

'This guy's going to go nuts,' Tara had said, yanking her hat down on her head.

'We're just spreading a little intrigue into an otherwise dull existence,' Ryan had said.

The 'guy' to whom Tara had been referring had been the owner of the Alfa Romeo, the same person for whom they'd been taking this photograph and several others over the course of the day. The idea had been that they'd get them developed at a one-hour photo shop. They'd then ditch the car back in the Royal Inn's car park (from where they'd borrowed it that morning), leaving the best photos tucked in beneath the driver's seat, for the owner to find, hopefully weeks from now.

'But how about we don't take the car back after all?' Tara had suggested. 'How about we just keep going, to France, to wherever?'

'Because –' Ryan had started to reply.

But then: flash. The camera's self-timer had frozen them there for posterity. Ryan had got up then, Jimmy remembered. He'd walked away from the car and had stood on his own and gazed across the beach. Then he'd turned round to face them and had answered, 'Because we'd only run out of petrol if we tried.'

Here, in Jimmy's bedroom, Tara picked the photo up and kissed Ryan's face. 'I was completely in love with him that day, you know,' she admitted. 'All that stuff he said about me, I know he was only teasing and being sarcastic and everything, but I wanted it to be true.'

'I sort of guessed,' Jimmy told her.

'He never said anything to you in private, did he?' she checked. 'I mean about me? About me and him?'

'No,' Jimmy lied. The day Ryan had died, he'd told Jimmy that if he had been into going out with girls for the long haul, then Tara was the only girl he reckoned he knew whom he wouldn't grow bored of. But Jimmy knew there was no point in telling Tara that now; all it would do was open up old wounds.

'Good.'

'What is it?' Jimmy asked, spotting the frown she was failing to conceal.

'I still think we should fuck him up,' she said.

She meant Denny Shapland. Ever since Tara had first laid eyes on Jimmy's black eye this morning at school, she'd been itching to go round to Denny's shop and graffiti his shop door.

'No way,' Jimmy said. 'He's not worth it. And anyway,' he added honestly, 'it's too risky. He'd probably catch us doing it and beat the shit out of me all over again.'

'What about his scrambler, then?' she demanded. 'I bet it's a piece of piss to hot-wire.' She had a malevolent glint in her eyes. 'We could ditch it in the harbour at high tide.'

'No.'

'Jesus, Jimmy!' Tara snapped, suddenly angry, up on her feet. 'Where's your spirit gone? You used to take risks all the time, remember?'

Jimmy said nothing. He didn't care about Denny, or the fact that he'd been punched by him. 'I kissed him back.' That's what Verity had said. And that's what Jimmy still believed she'd meant, no matter how quickly she'd run off afterwards. No, Jimmy didn't want to hurt Denny Shapland, Jimmy wanted Verity to realise how much better he was than Denny. Jimmy wanted Verity to know that he was the one she should be with. And for that, Jimmy knew – and he was thinking about his relationship with Marianna in particular now – he needed to clean up his act, not dumb it down.

But Tara was still goading him. 'No?' she demanded. 'Well, let me remind you.'

She marched past him and opened the window.

'Pack it in,' Jimmy said, a cold blast of air reaching him.

But Tara ignored him. Instead, she pushed the window wide.

'Why are you doing that?' he asked

'You know why,' she said softly, before clambering up on to the windowsill, and swinging outside and out of sight.

Jimmy stomach turned over. This time, though, it had nothing to do with the game or the joint. He hurried across the room and stuck his head out of the window, staring up. 'Don't be stupid,' he called after her, but Tara was already well on her way. He watched her feet disappearing up the last couple of steps of the fire escape that led on to the flat roof of Carlton Court above.

Jimmy didn't move for a second, two seconds, three. He was still staring up into the grey, moonlit sky. He shouldn't go up there, he knew. He shouldn't follow Tara up that ladder the way she wanted him to. It was crazy, the same as it had been crazy the first time he and Tara had followed Ryan up there.

'What's the matter?' Ryan had asked them both. 'You chicken?'

It had been down to a movie they'd been watching, there in Jimmy's room, on the same TV screen that the PS2 game was paused on now. Jimmy couldn't even remember who'd been in the movie. It had been some late-night straight-to-TV effort about a bunch of American kids their age.

The only reason they'd been watching it at all had been because they'd managed to get themselves trashed on some vodka, which Ryan had lifted from his old man's drinks cupboard. But then the gang initiation sequence had begun on the TV and Ryan had stopped talking and started watching.

'Come on,' Jimmy heard Tara calling out to him now, her voice whittled down by the wind.

But he was already on his way. He was hauling himself through the open window, the same as Ryan and Tara had cajoled him into doing back then after the movie had finished.

The fact that the kids they'd watched on TV hanging one another off the side of a building had probably had safety nets below them, and probably hadn't been kids at all, but stunt men shot from weird and unfamiliar angles, hadn't seemed to bother Ryan one bit.

'Remember this?' Tara was asking Jimmy now as he pulled himself up the last few rungs of the fire escape and walked across the roof towards her.

It was cold up here and silent as an empty stage. Tara was standing at the edge of the flat roof, looking down over the hundred-foot drop on the other side. A gust of wind nudged at her as Jimmy reached her. She teetered forward momentarily, and Jimmy snatched at her denim sleeve and held her steady. Standing beside her, he looked down with her at the car park below.

'Well, do you?' Tara asked him again.

'Of course,' he replied.

Because, of course, there was no way that he couldn't remember something like that, was there? How did you forget the sensation of your two best friends gripping on to your arms and slowly lowering you over the side of a ten-storey building? How did you forget the feeling of every cell in your body shrinking away from the ground, willing itself to crawl upwards against the force of gravity? Or the knowledge that it was only your friends who held you back from the abyss? How did you forget the strength in their eyes as they hauled you back up? And how did you forget the responsibility when they asked you to do the same for them? Or the sense of absolute trust, bonding and love that such an act engendered? You didn't. That was the simple answer. It stayed with you for always.

'I wish we could do it again,' Tara said.

'We can't. I'm not strong enough to hold you on my own,' Jimmy told her. 'And you couldn't hold me either. It would need all three of us together.'

'I know.' Tara slipped her hand into his and squeezed it hard. 'That's why it's only a wish.'

Without speaking, they stepped back together and walked to the centre of the roof. Tara sat down and Jimmy followed her lead.

'Smoke?' she asked, cupping her hands and lighting them both one without waiting for him to reply.

'We shouldn't be here,' Jimmy said.

'I thought that what he – what *we*', she corrected herself, 'were doing up here that night, dangling each other over the edge like that . . . I thought it was about adrenalin . . . getting a buzz . . . taking a risk . . . about proving what roughnecks we all were . . .'

'Wasn't it?' Jimmy asked, unsure what she was driving at.

Tara looked inland, away from the cliffs. 'No,' she said, 'I don't think so; not any more. Ryan wasn't up here for kicks. Ryan was up here because he wanted to get close to death. He wanted to know what it felt like.' She turned to Jimmy, her eyes suddenly darker than the night. 'He was always going to do it, you know, Jimmy . . . kill himself . . . I can see that now.'

'No.'

But she wasn't listening. This was what she wanted to believe, that what Ryan had done had been in some way predetermined and had had nothing to do with them at all. She wanted to believe it was what he'd wanted, as if that somehow let them off the hook as far as responsibility went and made it all OK.

She stubbed out her cigarette and stood. 'Come on,' she said, smiling at Jimmy now. 'Let's go back inside. I'm freezing.'

'You go,' Jimmy said after a second. 'I'll be down in a minute.'

Jimmy watched Tara walk across the roof, back to the fire escape and disappear down it, over the side of the building, like a diver walking backwards into a sea of black.

Then he closed his eyes, remembering again that night the three of them had come up here, remembering when Ryan had taken his turn and allowed them to lower him over the side.

'Better than drugs,' Ryan had declared, staring up at Jimmy with madness-packed eyes.

Only here and now, huddled on the asphalt roof with his eyes closed, Jimmy's memory of the event shifted. Suddenly, Tara wasn't there at all holding Ryan's other arm. Suddenly it was just Jimmy holding on to him and his grip was starting to slip.

'Hold tight,' he imagined Ryan saying. 'Can I trust you, Jimmy? Can I trust you to do that?'

But Jimmy's strength was gone. He couldn't hold on any –

Jimmy opened his eyes, but still he saw Ryan's dream-body falling, screaming up at him before smashing through a car windscreen below.

Jimmy rocked forward, hugging himself, wishing that he'd never been born and wishing again that Ryan hadn't died.

Chapter XVI

Treza wasn't helping. Worse, she was starting to irritate Verity. It was forty-eight hours since the fracas up at Appleforth House and Verity had summoned Treza for an emergency meeting in the Jackpot Café on Saturday afternoon. Much to Verity's dismay, Treza had appeared with a new hairstyle – her jet-back tightly coiled mane twisted and beaded into various elaborate knots on her head. Not only had this change of appearance taken place without Verity's consultation or knowledge, but Treza was wearing a new denim dress, with long boots that accentuated the curves of her small body and made Verity feel childish in her flared jeans and scruffy trainers.

It seemed, too, that Treza's usual gentle and understanding nature had been replaced by a callous and uncompromising side, which Verity had never seen before. 'Denny shouldn't have hit Jimmy and that's the end of it. If anything, Denny Shapland should be apologising to you,' Treza declared, swiping the straw around the inside of the milkshake cup and fixing Verity with a stern brown-eyed stare.

Verity said nothing. She didn't want to argue with Treza when she was in this kind of mood. And anyway, she'd only get herself into more hot water if she allowed Treza to cross-examine her. She knew Treza well enough to know that her friend would soon suss that Verity hadn't been telling the whole truth about the situation with Jimmy and Denny.

She hadn't, for example, told her the facts about the kiss with Jimmy and that she had, in fact, been just as unfaithful as Denny had suspected. Instead, she'd told Treza that she'd accidentally over-responded to Jimmy only because she'd been in front of the camera and had been carried away by her performance. She hadn't mentioned that the kiss had left her feeling unsettled and guilty, and that when she tried to think about Denny, it was the memory of Jimmy's lips that blocked all her thoughts.

No matter how hard she tried to stop herself, she couldn't help comparing her first kisses with these two men, whom three weeks ago she wouldn't have even considered talking to, let alone kissing. On the one hand Denny's kiss had been sexual and overpowering, but then her kiss with Jimmy had been so sensual that Verity found herself wishing Jimmy's kiss had, in fact, been Denny's.

But she couldn't bring herself to say these guilty thoughts, so secret that she couldn't even write them in her diary.

'Well, at least you haven't grovelled to Denny,' Treza continued.

Verity shrank down in her seat. She'd also failed to mention to Treza that she'd called Denny at least a dozen times in the last few days and had even delivered a heartfelt letter to Wave Cave at the crack of dawn this morning.

'You haven't grovelled, have you?' Treza repeated, more sternly this time.

Verity wouldn't meet her friend's eyes, but eventually Treza's silence demanded that she say something. When she looked up, Treza was looking at her, unconvinced.

'I love him,' Verity said, leaning forward across the table. 'I've got to make him understand.'

Treza banged her empty cup down on the table. 'Oh, God! I'm not getting through to you, am I?' she said with an exasperated growl.

'Don't be angry. I want to be with Denny.'

'OK, OK,' Treza said, putting her hands up in surrender. 'You say that Denny isn't a bit like his reputation and all I've heard is about how sensitive he is. So if he's that bloody marvellous, you should have no problem getting him back, should you?' Treza threw a sarcastic smile at Verity and stood to leave.

Verity stared at her friend, stung by her attitude. 'Treze,' she begged. 'Don't be like this.'

'I've got to go, I'm meeting Will. I'll see you . . .'

Left alone, Verity paid the bill for the two milkshakes and tried to make sense of her encounter with Treza. What was wrong with everyone? First Ellen and now Treza – why didn't they get that she and Denny were meant to be? Why was everyone so negative? And now she came to think of it, who did Treza think she was to lecture her? Will worked as a mechanic in some stupid garage. Denny was twice the man he was. So what if he'd overreacted a little. That's what red-blooded men did, wasn't it?

Outside, Verity started the long dawdle back to the hotel. She knew that everyone had relationship glitches, but she hadn't expected to have one so soon with Denny, especially one that had been her fault. She was amazed that in such a short space of time she'd become so addicted to him. It was as if her life was split into before and after Denny, and she couldn't ever go back to the way she'd been before she had him in her life. With him, she felt alive, vibrant and purposeful. He gave her whole existence meaning. Without him, on days like today, with only the prospect of piano practice and homework, her life seemed unutterably bleak and pointless.

It was with these thoughts in her head that she found herself loitering aimlessly in the rain, staring intently at

Wave Cave across the street, indecision and longing battling inside her.

There was nothing for it, she resolved. She couldn't go on without him. Surely Denny couldn't still be angry with her? Not if he'd received her letter. She had to find out where she stood. Steeling herself, she crossed the road.

Denny was busy, but he stopped, staring at Verity, as she pretended to browse through the sweatshirts in the corner of the shop. As their eyes connected, Verity felt as if she could faint with longing.

Standing beneath the speakers blaring out music, Verity wondered how she'd ever got into this situation. Denny was far too good for her. Why did she ever think he wanted her in the first place? But then Jimmy flashed into her head. 'You're too good for him,' he'd said, but that couldn't be right, could it?

Before she had time to deliberate any further, Denny flicked his head, motioning to the storeroom behind the desk, and she scurried to follow him.

'You got my letter?' Verity asked nervously.

Denny nodded and sat down on the edge of a large cardboard box. Behind him, a row of wetsuits hung like rubber cadavers, and the bass of the shop music throbbed in the insulated room. Verity could see a small television above the door behind her, showing the hazy black-and-white images of the customers in the shop. Denny glanced at it, before nodding at her to continue.

'It's probably a bit . . . ?'

'No one has ever written me a poem before,' Denny said, glancing again at the TV screen above her head, his mouth clicking as he chewed gum.

Verity smiled nervously. 'I didn't write it,' she said. 'I copied it out of a book. It's Carol Ann Duffy.'

'Right, right.'

Verity wished now that she'd had the nerve to include one of her own poems, but she'd changed her mind at the last minute. 'I meant what I said, though,' Verity said, taking a step towards where he was perched. 'I mean about being sorry. About the other day. I was only doing what Ellen told me, but I can see how it must have looked . . .'

Denny shrugged.

Verity felt a hitch in her breath. How could she make Denny see that he was the last person in the world that she'd ever hurt? 'Oh, Denny, please,' she begged.

'I told you I was a jealous kind of guy,' he said. 'It just killed me seeing you with someone else. Especially some schoolkid.'

'But I'm a schoolkid, too, Denny,' Verity said, confused. 'Jimmy and I are the same age.'

Denny rolled his eyes. 'Whatever.'

'I don't know what else to say,' Verity implored. 'All I want is for us to be together. That's all that matters to me. It'll never happen again. Anything like that. I'll do anything to make it up to you. Please . . .'

As she started to cry, he took her into his arms and she leant against him, weak with relief.

'I've got to go now, sweetheart,' he said eventually. 'Why don't you come to my place later? We'll have some dinner and chill out and put all this behind us. What do you say?'

In all the times that Verity had prepared to sing in front of an audience, she'd never felt as nervous, or as if so much was riding on something, as on her date with Denny later that night. She knew he'd forgiven her, but she still didn't really know why, or how Denny truly felt. Tonight was the night she'd find out once and for all.

By eight o'clock she'd changed outfits a dozen times, had made up her face and rubbed it all off. She had no idea what to wear to chill out with Denny in his flat. In the end she'd taken a leaf out of Treza's book and gone for a denim skirt and boots, which was still probably too dressy, but she didn't care.

She had just checked her reflection in the full-length mirror at the top of the first flight of stairs when she heard her mother. 'Are you up there?' Cheryl called from the reception area. 'Verity, I know you're there. Can you come down?'

Verity mimicked her mother silently in the mirror. How did she always know her whereabouts in the hotel? Sometimes Verity wondered whether they should rename the Grand Hotel the Grand Gaol, since her mother must have secret surveillance cameras everywhere.

Verity slowly thumped down the stairs to deliberately wind her mother up.

'In the office. In your own time, Verity,' her mother said with a scowl, before disappearing through the office door.

Sulkily, Verity followed. In the office, indeed. Who did her mother think she was? Her headmistress?

Russell Driver was wearing his smart front-of-house blazer and he sat completely still in the office chair as Verity entered. For a horrible moment, Verity thought he must have found out about her mother's affair. Then she looked at his face and when she saw its usual harassed expression she relaxed. He'd clearly been summoned here, too. Maybe they'd found out that she'd missed her music lessons last week. Maybe Ellen had said something to her mother about Denny on Thursday. She prepared to defend herself.

'Your father and I have been doing some investigating,' her mother began.

Forget headmistress, the kids in school were right: she *was* the Gestapo, Verity thought bitterly.

'We're just concerned,' Russell intercepted. 'We –'

'Remember what we agreed,' Cheryl hissed, silencing her husband with a look.

'The point is that Denny Shapland is nearly ten years older than you,' her mother said pointedly.

'So?'

'So . . . he's too old.'

'What's that supposed to mean? He's twenty-five, not sixty.'

'Yes, well, boys of his age have certain . . . expectations.'

Verity couldn't tell whether she was more embarrassed for her parents or for herself.

'The point is that your father and I feel that it would be better if you went out with someone more your own age.'

'And you think it's up to you to decide that for me?' Verity said, astounded. 'You're so two-faced. Dad's met Denny. And his exact word were, "Denny seems like a good bloke," weren't they, Dad?'

'Russell?'

Verity and her mother both stared defiantly at Russell Driver, who shrugged ineffectually.

'If you had objections, why didn't you say something then?'

'Come on, love,' he said. 'I didn't realise it was serious . . .'

'You can't stop me seeing him, you know. You can't.'

And as Verity looked between her parents, any nerves she felt about Denny disappeared. Too old for her, was he? She was too much of a little girl to be with Denny Shapland, was she? Well, she'd soon change that. She was going to lose her virginity to him. There! It was decided. And the sooner the better.

Denny's flat was in a modern complex on the outskirts of town. From the moment Verity stepped out of the stairwell and along the brightly lit corridor to Denny's front door, she was filled with illicit excitement. This was all Denny's. And it was totally private. There were no parents who could interrupt at any minute, no annoying siblings, no demanding guests.

The moment Denny opened the door to her, Verity felt every nerve jangling with anticipation. He looked more relaxed than she'd expected him to. His feet were bare and he was wearing three-quarter-length black karate trousers, with a grey T-shirt. She felt immediately overdressed, as she leant forward and kissed him awkwardly on the cheek.

'Welcome,' he said, drawing back and opening his arm out so that she could see his apartment. The space wasn't huge, but the open living area looked like a picture from a stylish catalogue, with shiny wooden floorboards, two large boxy leather sofas and a low glass table. The walls were white, with two doors leading off the main room.

'Bathroom, bedroom,' Denny said, pointing to them, as Verity followed him to the small open-plan kitchen at the end.

'It's a bit messy,' Denny continued, tidying up some magazines and post from the grey marble-effect counter. 'Sorry.'

'It's not messy at all,' Verity scoffed, laughing. 'You should see my room!'

As soon as she'd said it, she immediately realised that the last place she would ever want Denny to see was her bedroom at the Grand. He would think it was so shabby and childish compared with this.

She smiled and turned away, looking at the framed

photos along the kitchen wall, above the wooden shelf, which housed a pub ashtray, a tree mug and a pristine-looking Jamie Oliver cookbook. She wanted to ask him everything – about the identity of every person in every one of the photos. She wanted to know where the poster-sized picture of Denny surfing on some foreign beach, which hung on the wall above the sofa, was taken. She was about to remark on the naked women calendar, which hung by the fridge, when the door buzzer went.

'You arrived just in time. Pizza!' Denny explained. Verity nodded, feeling a mixture of relief and disappointment. She'd been expecting Denny to cook, but now they were having pizza she felt more relaxed. Maybe this wasn't a big test, after all.

She watched Denny pay the pizza delivery boy and kick the door shut, carrying the two large boxes to the low table between the sofa and huge widescreen television. 'Make yourself at home,' he said. 'Take your coat off. Come and eat.' He knelt down on a sheepskin rug by the table and opened the pizza boxes. Verity laid her coat over the back of the sofa and knelt down next to Denny, looking at the expensive-looking stacked sound system, at which Denny now pointed a remote control. The room was filled with a low indie track Verity recognised.

Denny handed her a beer and flipped open the pizza box. 'I'm starving,' he said, as if he'd been with her all day. 'Tuck in.'

Verity wasn't very hungry, but she couldn't refuse. And anyway, it felt good sitting next to Denny, as if they always did this on a Saturday night. It felt intimate and, after a while, Verity started to relax.

They chatted for some time about Denny's day at the shop, but neither of them mentioned the filming, or what had happened with Jimmy. It wasn't long before Verity had forgotten it and she found herself chatting as they used to, not about important things, but just easily about any old subject, as if they could go on talking all night and not run out of things to say.

By the time they'd eaten the pizzas and drunk a few beers, Verity knew that Denny had forgiven her. She laughed as he slid up on to the leather sofa. 'This is so great,' she said, sighing as she sat next to him.

'So?' he asked, licking his fingertips. 'Are you busy next week?'

Verity stretched luxuriously like a cat. 'I am,' she said coyly, 'but I'm always available for you. I'm just rehearsing and stuff. It's the memorial concert coming up. Do you want to come? It's next Saturday night. I can get you a ticket.' She smiled up at him hopefully, but Denny didn't look as enthusiastic as she expected. 'I'm singing,' she added, trying to tempt him.

'I'm not sure I'll be back in time,' Denny said.

'Back?' Verity asked, alarmed.

'Didn't I tell you? I'm going away on business. I'm going on a buying trip. I'll probably be about a week.'

'You can't leave now,' she whispered, desolation washing over her at the thought of the world without Denny in it. Not seeing him for two days had nearly killed her. How was she going to manage a week?

'Don't look like that.' Denny laughed. 'It's not the end of the world.'

'It is to me,' she said, then looked down at her lap, furious that she'd said something so pathetic.

'You're serious about us, aren't you?' Denny asked.

'I wish I could prove it to you,' she whispered.

There was a small pause.

'Well, there is one way . . .' Denny said softly.

She looked up immediately. When she saw that he was staring straight into her eyes, she had no doubt that they were talking about the same thing. Despite all her intentions for this exact moment to happen, she was shocked by Denny's bluntness. Somehow, she'd imagined that they'd get on to the subject of sex in a more roundabout sort of way. But then, maybe she was just being naïve.

Denny pushed her hair away from her face and held it behind her head. Some of it was caught on his watch strap and pulled, but it was such an intimate moment that Verity felt she couldn't say anything.

'Is it . . . ?' Denny began, but his question fizzled out. He shook his head.

'What?' Verity asked. 'What is it? You can ask me anything.'

'No, no, it's none of my business.'

'No, go on. I haven't got anything to hide.'

'Is it? Well, I guess I was wondering whether it's your first time. Not that you have to tell me. It's none of my business, but . . .'

Verity knew she was blushing. She didn't know what to say. What if she said 'yes' and Denny was too much of a gentleman to relieve her of her virginity? What if she lied and said 'no' and he then expected her to know what she was doing? She felt trapped, unable to breathe. Tentatively, she moved her head and tried to unhook her hair, but it was no use, she was caught.

'If it's your first time, then maybe we should –'

'I want you to,' Verity said, almost throwing herself on to Denny's lap. 'It's OK. I'm not a virgin,' she lied. 'I want to be with you, Denny. Please.'

Denny seemed taken aback by her forcefulness. He

looked into her face. 'Oh, well,' he said with a smile. 'If you really insist . . .'

Verity gasped, realising he was teasing her.

'I'll be gentle,' he reassured her with a cheeky wink. 'Why don't you get into bed?'

Verity nodded mutely as she stood up. Was this normal? she wondered. Was her consent to have sex supposed to be this matter-of-fact? Weren't they supposed to get into the bedroom by stumbling against the walls, kissing in a desperate frenzy?

Denny's bedroom was small. There was only room for the double bed, and a small lamp glowed low down on the bedside unit. On the wall by the door was a fitted wardrobe with a tinted full-length mirror. Ignoring her reflection, Verity took off her clothes and folded them carefully. Then she stood in the pretty pink embroidered bra and knickers she'd chosen especially for this occasion and leant across to switch off the light. As she slipped into Denny's bed and pulled the grey duvet up to her chin, she was trembling all over.

She lay rigid, looking up at the ceiling in the darkness. What if Denny didn't find her attractive? What if it hurt? What if he didn't want to use birth control? What if she wasn't good enough?

She could hear Denny moving about in the living room and, a second later, low ambient music through the wall. She jumped as Denny came through the door, but he didn't seem to notice.

'Bit dark, isn't it?' he said, flicking on the light switch by the door. Verity winced as the overhead light above the bed shone down harshly. She should have kept the bedside light on. 'We want to see what we're doing,' he said, taking a swig of beer from his bottle.

Denny was only wearing a pair of boxer shorts. Verity held her breath as he came towards her, instinctively clutching on to the top of the duvet. It smelt musky.

'You OK?' he asked, putting a bottle of beer down on the bedside unit.

Verity nodded her affirmation, fascinated by Denny's body. She'd seen hundreds of guys before in just shorts down on the beach, but she'd never looked at them, knowing, like now, that the shorts were about to go.

Then Denny pulled back the duvet in one flamboyant gesture and Verity yelped, pulling her knees up and huddling on her side. Denny laughed at her.

'Don't be shy. I just want to look at you,' he said, placing his hand on her hip. Then he let out a slow wolf-whistle of appreciation and Verity started to relax. She lay back on the bed, wondering what to do with her arms.

Denny's hands felt hot on her skin and his breath smelt of beer. He pulled one of her bra cups aside, exposing her breast and she trembled. She hadn't expected his examination to be so . . . clinical. But she'd never been naked with a man before. Maybe this was what it was always like.

'Perfect,' he said, before he leant across her. Her nose crinkled at the heavy scent of his body spray. He opened the drawer in the bedside unit and pulled out a box of condoms, lifting the cardboard flap to check if there were any inside.

'Good,' said Denny, emptying two out on to the pillow next to Verity. She looked at them and then back at Denny as he threw the empty box on the floor. She was just wondering where the others in the box had gone when Denny lay down on top of her. There was no point in thinking about other girls, she reprimanded herself. There were no other girls. Not here. Not now.

Verity closed her eyes, expecting him to kiss her, but instead, he flipped her, so that she was lying on top of him.

Startled, she opened her eyes and looked down at him beneath her.

'Wow,' he said. He traced the outline of her lips with his finger and Verity started to feel better. He might have been much more experienced than her and she might not have been up to speed on Denny's sexual acrobatics, but at least he was being sensitive. 'Verity Driver, you've got perfect lips,' he whispered softly.

Verity smiled. It was going to be fine after all –

'Now then, let's see what you can do with them . . .'

Verity felt his hands on her shoulders, pushing her down.

Afterwards, Verity lay totally still next to Denny, her head pressed against the downy hair on his chest. She listened to the sound of Denny's heart racing below her ear. Gradually the beat slowed, until it was accompanied by the sound of Denny softly snoring.

But Verity had never felt more awake in her life. She was overwhelmed by the unfamiliar scent surrounding her and the reality of being in Denny's bedroom. Without knowing why, the image of Jimmy reading her the poem in the arbour at Appleforth House came to her. She'd thought at the time that she would learn the words that he'd spoken so beautifully and repeat them to Denny at just such a moment as this, but she now knew how ridiculous her romantic notions had been.

Now, as Jimmy's face filled her mind, a tear slid from her eye across the bridge of her nose.

She should have told Denny the truth. She should have told him that it was her first time and that she wasn't ready to do all the things he'd expected. But now it was too late. All the way through, as Denny's thrusts had rocked her body, she'd stared over his shoulder at the paper lampshade, wondering how she was meant to enjoy it. It had been over so fast and now Denny probably thought she was rubbish.

Verity wished now that she hadn't pushed Treza away. She wished they'd talked properly and that she'd shared her feelings with her friend. She'd thought that involving Treza would somehow dilute the intimacy she had with Denny, but now she realised she was just being vain. Treza would have happily given her advice and Treza would be there for her to go to now, but Verity had subtly changed the rules. Without even realising what she'd done, Verity had made Treza's love life and her own love life out of bounds to each other.

Now, more than ever before, Verity felt totally inadequate and totally alone. She'd expected to feel more in love than ever when she lost her virginity to Denny. She'd expected to feel completely emotionally connected to him, but now she just felt cold and sore.

Rousing herself, she tried to slip away from him, but he woke up.

'What's the matter?' he asked.

'I'm going to have to go,' she said, backing out of bed.

'Can't you stay the night?'

Verity shook her head.

'Shit. I hadn't thought. I've drunk too much to drive. I'll have to call you a cab.'

'OK.'

Verity covered herself with the corner of the duvet. It hadn't occurred to her to make up a lie to stay the night. She watched Denny take a slug of beer before he got out of bed and walked to the cupboard. He pulled out a stripy robe and, without looking at her, walked out of the bedroom.

How could he walk in, have sex and then walk out again, as if nothing had happened? How was it possible that he'd done something to change her life and didn't even seem to notice? Shouldn't they be cuddled up naked? That was what was supposed to happen, wasn't it? Verity shook her head in disbelief at the door through which Denny had just walked, before roughly pulling on her clothes.

In the living room she felt strangely awkward being fully dressed. It was as if she'd somehow acknowledged that her naked self hadn't been good enough. As she listened to Denny making the phone call to the cab company, she felt cheap. This was what prostitutes did, she thought.

Denny sat on the sofa and flicked on the television, patting the seat next to him for her to sit down. Nervously, she slipped down on to the black leather cushion, listening to Denny laugh at the comedy programme. He reached out and took her hand, holding it almost subconsciously, as if they'd been going out for ever. Or, worse, as if they were just old friends.

Verity concentrated on the sensation of her hand in Denny's and, even though she knew he wasn't concentrating on the same thing, took solace in the connection. She longed for him to talk to her and tell her how he was feeling, but she knew she couldn't say anything. Why should he be feeling anything? Maybe all the clichés she'd read about men not wanting to hug and talk after sex were true after all.

Verity watched the television, hardly seeing what Denny was laughing at, wishing that everything had been different. It felt like only moments later that the door buzzer sounded.

'I'll call you,' Denny said, kissing her nose at the front door.

Verity felt her chin wobbling and willed it to stop.

'Hey, hey, hey,' Denny said. 'What's all this?'

'I don't want you to go,' Verity blurted out. 'I'll miss you so much.'

'I'll be back.'

'You promise?' Verity begged, holding on to him.

'Of course.'

The cab beeped from outside. Questions crowded into Verity's head, but she couldn't bring herself to voice any of them, and the reassurance she so desperately needed and the promises of commitment were left unsaid.

'I'll see you,' Denny said. 'Now go. He won't wait much longer.'

Verity ran down the stairs and out into the night.

When she looked up at Denny's window, she saw that he was laughing as he talked on the phone. He looked down at the cab and raised his beer can to her, and then he flipped the curtain closed and was out of sight.

Chapter XVII

Her blonde hair had fallen like a curtain across his eyes. He was panting, his lips pressed up against the smooth nape of her neck. Lying on their sides now, spooned together, she wriggled further back against him, forcing him deeper inside her. Each breath she took came out as a moan. Their feet were wrapped in a tangle of sheets. The camomile scent of her hair conditioner filled his nostrils as she clamped her hand down on his, squeezing it tighter against her breast.

Then she was rolling away, repositioning herself flat on her back. She reached out to him, pulling him on top of her, guiding him back inside. Her hands gripped his shoulders now, moving them gently back and forth until he achieved the rhythm she desired. She began moaning again. Her eyes closed and she ran her fingers down the length of his back. He could feel her thighs tightening, clamping against his hips. Her nails dug into his back. Her groaning grew louder, irregular. Then she cried out, shuddering, grinding her pelvis against him. Whatever it was she was feeling came out now in one long groan. He carried on moving against her as her shuddering began to subside and a wide, luxurious smile spread across her face. And finally, as her eyes opened and stared directly into his, he gasped and he came.

The moment it was over, it felt to him like it had happened to two other people, a different man and a different woman – anybody, in fact, but them.

Unable to hold her stare, he looked away, withdrawing from her and flopping over on to his back beside her. They both stared up at the ceiling. Her skin burnt against his: her thigh against his thigh, her hip against his hip, and her shoulder against his.

But a limitless energy still coursed through him. He wanted to jump up, dance across the room, stand on his head, streak through the house . . . Every cell in his body was tingling, craving motion. It was almost unbearable, this stillness, after the explosion of physicality he'd just been through. But he did stay still. Because he knew he couldn't face doing what strangers did every day. He couldn't bring himself to look at her, or even to speak.

Ned Spencer was in shock. How could this have happened? What was he doing here in bed, naked and covered in sweat? And what was Ellen Morris doing lying naked at his side?

It had all been so intense, the release of endorphins so cataclysmic, that he now seemed to be suffering some kind of localised amnesia. Already, he felt that the whole sequence of events might have been fantasised and not real at all. Already, he was wondering whether, if he were to reach out his hand to where he thought Ellen was, all he'd actually find there was his scrunched-up duvet.

But slowly, surely, as his panting became shallower, everything began to slot into place.

Images flickered through his mind of how it had all started in the kitchen downstairs: the two of them leaning over the sideboard where he'd laid out the leather-bound folder containing the various designs used in Appleforth House for her to see; then both of them reaching forward to turn the page and both freezing as their hands had brushed together; turning to face one another, their lips almost touching, as they had done that time on the High Street and again later on in her cottage; him then looking into her eyes, seeing suggestion and agreement simultaneously reached without so much as a blink; then suddenly taut limbs wrapping hungrily around each other; her mouth pressing hard against his; the strength of her tongue twisting inside his mouth; the inexplicable combination of pleasure and pain as she'd bitten down on his bottom lip, and pinned him back against the cooker; the insistent tic-tic-tic of the stove's flint firing behind him, as its ignition button had dug deeper and deeper into his back; him fumbling with her shirt buttons, then giving up and sliding his hand up under the rough cotton of her shirt, tracing the contours of her breasts; her wrestling with his belt as he unfastened her bra strap; her nipples hardening against his fingertips; then her fingers, cold, squeezing down on his cock; he and Ellen shuffling then as if to some awkward staccato beat, away from the cooker, three stumbled steps over to the kitchen table; he'd laid her down there on her back, her legs hanging over the side; pulling her boots and trousers off, dropping them on to the floor, before kneeling on top of them and pulling her knickers aside; then leaning forward, *on to* her, breathing her in, intoxicated by her scent and her taste . . .

And all of this – *all* of it, and all that had followed – without a single word having been spoken between them.

What the hell had he been *thinking* of? That's what he wanted to know now.

Or had he even been thinking at all? Had he just done instead?

There was certainly plenty of evidence. His cock twitched, charged, raring to go again, in spite of the marathon it had just been through. Because there was something about this woman that made him feel like a hormonal teenager – not to mention *act* like one . . . Because, by God, that's what he'd just done, wasn't it? He'd allowed testosterone to get the better of him, packed his brain off on holiday and allowed his penis to run the show for a while.

He'd forgotten himself. *She*'d somehow made him forget. He'd forgotten he didn't do this sort of thing any more. He'd forgotten he was a grown-up who lived in a world of responsibilities and balanced decisions. He'd forgotten he was a father – Christ, it suddenly occurred to him that Clara could have woken up and walked downstairs into the kitchen while he and Ellen had been . . .

Ned groaned softly. Up above him, a neat rectangle of starry sky filled the glass of the dormer window, looking like a paused image on a TV set, as if he could press a button on a remote control and set it into motion. But life wasn't like that. You couldn't just stop it or start it whenever you felt like it, any more than you could rewind it and make something that had happened not so.

The last time he'd rampantly dived into bed with someone he'd still been an Architectural History student at De Montfort University. It had been a disaster, he now recalled, and one he'd easily been able to walk away from.

But this hadn't been a disaster, had it? Quite the opposite. Because it hadn't been this way for Ned even with Mary; he'd known her for months before anything had happened, and even then the sex had taken months more still to get this good. Whereas with Ellen, he'd met her – what? – seven times, maybe eight? And he'd known her for how long? Three weeks?

Should they talk about it? He didn't know. Is that what people did after sex? He couldn't remember. Because the truth was he hadn't had sex with anyone since before Clara had been born. And then it had been with Mary. And then,

303

before she'd become ill, sex had been something they'd done all the time, so they hadn't needed to talk about it, just do it whenever and however they'd wanted.

Ned glanced across at Ellen, searching for a clue. She didn't look as though she wanted to speak about anything just now. Her eyes were closed and her face was expressionless, merely beautiful.

Ned stared back up at the night sky and considered that even if he did attempt to speak about *it* – this thing that they'd done – and even if she did agree, then what would they say? Because there was certainly no point in discussing the pros and cons of whether or not it was a good idea, because the dirty deed had already been done. So would they merely thank each other? Would they compliment one another on their various skills? Might they even offer suggestions for improved techniques and increased future enjoyment?

'You've gone quiet on me,' she said.

'You're not so loud yourself.'

'Are you thinking what I'm thinking?'

He didn't want to know what she was thinking. 'I'm thinking about getting a glass of water,' he said. 'Do you want one?'

'OK.'

'OK.'

He rolled across the mattress and sat on the side of the bed. Behind him, he could hear Ellen breathing evenly and he hoped she was falling asleep. He grabbed some trousers from the bedside chest of drawers, pulled them on, and walked out of the room and down the corridor into the bathroom.

He locked the door behind him. Once privacy was attained, relief swamped him and he opened the bathroom cabinet and reached up to the top shelf, the one which Clara couldn't reach – even when she stood on tiptoes in the washbasin, as he'd once caught her doing. He pulled down the old tobacco tin – his 'hash stash', as he always referred to it – and rolled himself a joint. Then he opened the bathroom window and stood leaning out of it and smoked.

There'd been a time in his life when he would have done this in the bedroom, when he would have done this in bed, a time before Clara had been born, when he and Mary had often seen themselves off to sleep at night with a soothing J. But he didn't want to share this with Ellen. It was oblivion and isolation he was after now, not talk or a sense of communion. All he wanted was to be able to get back into bed and close his eyes and disappear into the dark.

It wasn't that he *couldn't* feel. He felt so much right now. He felt the last traces of sexual exhilaration still dancing like tiny electric charges through his veins. He felt the ghost of Ellen's body still pressed up tight against his. He felt the accumulated sadness of the years he'd spent without physical contact. He felt – and resisted – the urge to follow his instincts: to go back into the bedroom and lie down next to Ellen and cradle her in his arms until dawn, as he'd cradled his duvet every night for years now, wishing it had been someone he loved. But above all this, he felt what he knew to be true: that he *shouldn't* feel; that where relationships were concerned, he was a burnt-out case.

He liked Ellen all right. She was strong, intelligent, challenging and beautiful, and maybe in a parallel world – a world where Ned had never met Mary – the two of them might have stood a chance. But not in this world. In this world, Ned *had* met Mary. And in this world, Mary *had* killed herself. And in this world, Ned was frightened of what love had done to his life. And so in this world, he and

Ellen had no future. She would return to her boyfriend in London and he would return to Cheltenham. And soon it would be as if none of this had ever happened.

Beneath the bathroom window, Ned could see the cottage's back garden, illuminated by the kitchen lights. It was the size of two tennis courts laid end to end, and was enclosed by a mossy stone wall, which was in need of repair and would collapse, Ned had guessed, if not this winter then the next. At the end of the garden, next to a gnarled old pear tree, was a dilapidated wooden-framed greenhouse and, beyond that, away down the lane, the windows of the town houses glowed like torch beams in the night.

Somewhere among those streets and houses and late-night TV shows were Scott and Debs. That's why Ellen had called here in the first place this evening, because she'd lost her keys to her cottage and had wanted to catch Scott and Debs before they'd headed out on their date. And that was why Ned was giving Ellen time to fall asleep, because he knew he couldn't ask her to go home and that he couldn't cope with the conversation about whether it was OK if she stayed and what that might or might not mean to them both.

What had happened here tonight had been wonderful. Ned knew that. But he also knew to his core that tomorrow it would seem no more real than a dream. Because only the kind of people who still hadn't found a reason not to fall in love could sustain the kind of passion he'd felt with Ellen earlier. Only people like Debs and Scott, and anyone else out there who still believed in the omnipotence of love.

Chapter XVIII

Ellen was still in a state of euphoric shock when she returned to the cottage on Sunday morning.

'Where were you last night?' Scott asked with a yawn, as he opened the door.

Ellen didn't answer. She couldn't even look at him. It must be so obvious, she thought, as she stepped inside the cottage. She felt as if she had a neon sign above her head, pulsing with the facts about what had happened. 'Oh, I . . . er . . . left my keys. I was locked out.' Absently, Ellen threw her coat over the chair and turned her back on Scott to avoid a further explanation. 'I think I'll take a bath.'

In the bathroom, Ellen twisted the hot-water tap and watched the water gush into the dark-blue plastic bath. Still fully clothed, she leant back against the door and slowly inhaled the rising steam.

So, she'd slept with Ned. But how she was feeling wasn't about the sex. It was more than that. Much more. Her infidelity had been far greater. It had been total. It was an infidelity of the heart. Slowly, she sank down against the door, until she was sitting. She hugged her knees, the steam swirling around her. It had been wordless, passionate, wild beyond even her wildest dreams. She hadn't known before last night that it was even *possible* for human beings to feel like that. She'd thought that she'd already known what sex could be about, but now she realised she hadn't had a clue.

Ned had felt it too. He must have. Surely it was

impossible to connect with someone that deeply and not be equally rocked?

In the night, Ellen had woken in his bed and watched him sleeping for hours. Even in deep repose, she'd been drawn to him, this damaged, intelligent, beautiful man. Ellen had absorbed him, feasting her eyes on him, staring at him so intensely, as if she might have somehow poured herself into his dreams.

But still she hadn't woken him. She hadn't wanted to break the spell, because in the peace of the night she'd realised that everything was possible. In that starlit bed, Ellen had dared to believe in a magical future where she could be the person she was with Ned all the time.

Ellen stood up as the water level rose in the bath. For a long moment, she watched as it settled and the drips from the taps subsided.

She couldn't wash Ned away. Not yet. She needed him on her body. She couldn't let the essence of him dissolve in the water.

Ellen stared at her reflection in the water. She thought about Ned's wife, Mary, and how she'd died. Looking into the deep bathwater, she thought of the despair that must have filled Mary's heart and the hope that now filled her own. Ned's past was so complicated. Could she really make his future simple?

Outside, Ellen walked slowly along North Beach near the shoreline, her footprints dissolving in the sand behind her. Hugging her arms across her and staring at the harbour entrance, she took a deep breath, thinking of how much she'd grown to love this place.

She stopped, watching the lifeboat bob on the waves. She'd been feeling so confused yesterday, but now, in the light of day, she was calm. She watched the spray, as the lifeboat hit the waves. She'd been rescued, too. She'd been rescued by Ned.

When she'd woken up in her flat in London yesterday morning, still hugging Ned's jumper, she'd abandoned her plans to go into the Soho editing suite and, instead, had shoved everything back in her bag and had caught the train to Shoresby.

She hadn't even known what she was going to do. All she'd known was that she were acting on impulse, as if a force other than her own will power was operating and dictating her every move. Then, when she'd gone to Ned's house, she'd known why she was there. She'd told Ned that she'd lost her keys, but they'd been in her pocket the whole time. She'd been there because she was meant to be with him.

Ellen's phone bleeped with a text message, wrenching her back to the present. Nothing can matter, she told herself as she retrieved the phone from her pocket.

But she couldn't have been more wrong.

Ellen slunk back away from the crowd waiting in the noisy Arrivals Hall at Heathrow. The wide gangway was lined with people. Families bustled around the barriers, crying babies and excited kids, old people, teenagers. Bored cab drivers stood stoically with name boards. Anxious tourists and airport staff all jostled for position – everyone watching the electric double doors at the far end of the gangway, as the tannoy announcements boomed out around them.

Since Jason's text message earlier asking her to pick him up at the airport, Ellen had been suffering from a sustained anxiety attack. She'd known that Jason was planning on being back some time in the next few weeks, but his early arrival had completely thrown her. Since she'd found

309

herself on Ned's doorstep last night, Ellen had known in her heart that there would inevitably come a time when she would have to confess her feelings for Ned to Jason. But it had seemed so far off in the distance. Not now. She wasn't prepared for it *now*, not even remotely. To make matters worse, she hadn't been able to get hold of Ned to tell him she was on her way back up to London to meet Jason, and his lack of response to her text message had thrown her into her current state of panic.

She thought back to this morning, when she'd woken up in bed with Ned. They'd been cuddling so tightly that Ellen hadn't known where she was for a minute. But in that split-second before she'd moved and Ned had woken up, she'd felt happier and safer than ever before in her life.

Of course, after that, it had all been awkward. Ned had been nervous about Clara finding them, so much so that Ellen hadn't felt able to broach the subject of what had happened between them. She'd sensed that with Ned, as with her, the line they'd crossed would take some time to come to terms with.

She'd been longing to say something, desperate to validate their night of passion, but she'd known how fragile Ned was, and if she'd pushed him into some sort of verbal commitment he'd only have run away. Besides, what they'd experienced together had been greater than words, surely?

Ellen's stomach flickered with nerves, as a stream of weary travellers started to move down the arrivals gangway, pushing trolleys laden with luggage. She hadn't planned out what she was going to say to Jason. She was hoping that somehow the words and the moment would present themselves at the right time.

Then she saw him and her sense of fate deserted her, replaced only by dread. There were no words for what she'd done. There was no way she could articulate what had happened. Every instinct told her to flee. But it was too late.

Jason waved as he saw her, his eyes lighting up in his tanned face as he rushed towards her, but Ellen stayed rooted to the spot watching him. She felt sick. Here was Jason. Her rock. Her life. The man who had been her future for as long as she could remember. As she watched him racing towards her, all her resolve disintegrated. He was so real and solid and happy. And he was hers. There was no baggage, no children, no dark secrets. Only the promise that he would love her always.

In that moment Ellen realised the horrible truth. She couldn't tell Jason about Ned. She would have to keep it a secret. She felt guilt slithering around, as tangible as a snake, threatening to crush her.

'You're here,' Jason said, dumping his rucksack and racing forward to hold her in a tight hug.

Ellen's senses had been filled up with Ned, but now they were totally overshadowed by the familiarity of Jason. His smell, his tall, lean frame, the way she slotted into his tight hug as if she were the last piece of his jigsaw.

Panic gripped her and she could feel her knees trembling beneath her skirt, as Jason squeezed her tighter and then let her go.

'You're back early,' she said, her voice husky. She couldn't look him in the eye. Instead, she looked at the pendant he wore round his neck. She leant forward to touch it, feeling the small piece of ebony, as if it were her own. Her heart ached with fear and sadness.

Jason smiled. 'I was so worried about you after you rang, I decided to cut things short.'

'Worried?' she said, remembering the phone call. It was only a week ago, but it felt like a lifetime. As if the person who'd called Jason in desperation was someone else entirely.

'You sounded so low,' he continued. 'I felt so desperate. All I kept thinking about was what you said. That we should be together.'

'You did?'

Ellen felt her throat constricting, but Jason didn't seem to notice.

'Oh Christ,' he said, trying to smother a grin. 'I thought I'd wait. But, hell, there's no point!' He laughed, before opening a small pouch in the combat jacket he was wearing.

'Jase,' Ellen implored. 'There's something I've got to tell you . . .'

But Jason wasn't listening. 'Wait, wait,' he said excitedly. 'Here.' He handed her a small black pouch.

'What is it?' she asked.

'Take it, take it,' Jason urged.

Ellen pulled open the string on the pouch. Inside there were three small diamonds. She tipped them out on to her palm and looked at the stones sparkling against her skin. This can't be happening, she thought. This can't be happening.

'I thought we could design a ring together,' Jason said, grabbing her hand, so that her fist closed round the stones. 'What do you say?' He looked like an excited child as he grinned at her, his eyebrows raised in happy expectation.

'What?' Ellen managed, hardly able to comprehend what he was saying.

'I had some time to think,' Jason said, his words tumbling out. 'And you're right. I've been so wrapped up with work that I didn't realise how unhappy you were until you asked me whether I wanted a future with you. Then it hit me that I'd be lost without you. Oh, Ellen, baby. That's why I came

312

home early. I wanted to tell you . . . to tell you straight away that I want it all. With you. Everything. I always have, but I want the future to start right now.'

Ellen hadn't even realised that she'd started crying, but now she felt sobs racking her.

Jason drew her to him, cupping her cheek with this hand. 'Oh, Ellen, my love,' he said, smoothing her hair. 'It's OK. I'm here now. I'm here.'

From far away, Ellen remembered the words that Ned had spoken in the moonlight. 'Do you want to know what the worst thing about life is?' he'd said. 'Timing,' he'd told her. 'Sometimes its timing is shit.'

It was nearly lunchtime on Monday, by the time Ellen drove up to Appleforth House and parked next to the vans and cars. Now that the house was very nearly complete, all the furniture was being delivered this week, she knew, and there seemed to be people everywhere.

Ellen flipped down the sun visor and checked her face in the mirror for the third time, and combed her hair with her fingers. She remembered doing the same thing on the first day she'd come to check out Appleforth House and had discovered Ned in the site office. Could that really only be three weeks ago?

Opening her handbag, she took out her small bag of make-up and delved inside for the tube of Touche Éclat cover-up. Looking again at the dark lines under her eyes, she skilfully applied the make-up and puffed her face with more powder. She had hardly slept in the last forty-eight hours and she felt almost giddy with exhaustion. But no one was going to suspect. Especially not Ned.

Ellen got out of the car and walked towards the house. She knew that Ned was probably going to be busy, but she

313

had to see him. There was no way she could spend a minute longer without knowing how he felt and where she stood.

She still hadn't spoken to him since she'd left his house yesterday morning. Since then, she'd been on the biggest emotional roller coaster of her life. Only Ned would be able to make her feel steady again.

As she rounded the far wing of the house, she saw Ned and her heart lurched. He was over by a large lorry and several workmen were backing down its ramp, carrying what looked like a billiard table. He was wearing old jeans, boots, a faded red sweatshirt and a hard yellow hat. Ellen watched his profile, seeing how he smiled and talked to the men inside the van, co-ordinating them as they backed down the ramp. She felt a shudder of relief run through her.

Ellen stood, smiling at Ned and holding her hand up to greet him. She'd been so consumed by this man that she almost expected him to be telepathic and look up at her. How could he look so normal, so unaffected?

She moved towards him, but he still didn't see her. He couldn't have seen her, otherwise he would have smiled, or waved back, wouldn't he? Ellen stepped closer, not stopping until she was right behind him.

'Hi,' she said, tapping him on the shoulder.

Ned was holding a delivery note in his hand. He glanced over his shoulder at Ellen. 'Oh, hi,' he said, as if they were still just colleagues and he'd seen her a few minutes before.

Ellen cleared her throat. She followed Ned's gaze to where the workmen were carrying the large table between them towards the house. Ned continued to watch them, paying no attention to Ellen.

'Ned?' Ellen asked, confused.

'Yep. Go on. I'm listening,' he said, but he didn't turn round.

'Um, well . . . ?'

Why didn't he look at her?

'Well . . . don't you think we should, you know . . . er . . . talk . . . ?' she tried, but Ned had darted forward to remove a post in the ground, before one of the workmen tripped over it.

Ellen trailed off as she watched him. Why should she force this? This was the wrong place and the wrong time. He was busy. What was she doing here?

'Sorry,' Ned said, with a brief smile at her, but he still didn't look at her fully. 'You were saying . . . ?'

Ellen prickled. Why was he treating her so . . . so *normally*? There was nothing *normal* about what had happened between them. She waited until the workmen had moved out of earshot. 'Well, I . . . I didn't want you to get the wrong impression,' she tried again.

As soon as she said it, she knew it sounded all wrong. It sounded as if she were being defensive, or dismissive. But if she didn't want him to get the wrong impression, what was the right impression? What did she mean? Should she tell him what had happened since she'd last seen him? Did she have the courage to admit to him how she really felt? 'We . . . we –' she tried, her voice rising in desperation.

'We had sex,' Ned said decisively, smiling over his shoulder at her briefly. 'There! It's not so difficult to say.'

Ellen stared at him. How could he be so matter-of-fact? 'Just sex?' she managed.

'No, actually, it wasn't just sex,' he said, turning to her, his tone terrifyingly friendly. 'It was good sex. Well, I think it was great sex. I hope you did, too?' Ned smiled, as if he were stating the obvious, as if he were asking her opinion about a takeaway they'd eaten together.

And then Ellen realised that he meant it. It was sex. Not

raw passion. Not a meeting of two kindred souls. It was just sex. Impersonal and easy.

Sex.

Ellen felt a blush start right in her heart and spread all over her skin. It wasn't only embarrassment, though. It was a healthy dose of humiliation, too.

'Hold up, fellas!' Ned yelled after the workmen, before hurrying towards them.

Ellen stared after him, dumbfounded. She watched as he followed the workmen inside the house. She realised then that he had no intention of coming back out to her to finish their conversation. That was it. That had been all Ned had to say to her.

Ellen ran to the car and once she'd shut the door, let out a strangled yelp, before covering her mouth. For a moment, she thought she was going to be sick.

How could he? How could he have done this to her?

She rested her forehead on the leather steering wheel, too mortified to cry. It would have been better if Ned had shouted, or been cold. It would have been better if he'd hit her.

Of course it was just sex to him!

Livid, she turned the ignition, not even able to look at the house, but putting her arm over the empty passenger seat and reversing out of the drive. She had to get away.

How could she have thought it would be any different? She'd slept with the man who didn't believe in romance, or love. This was the man who thought Caroline Walpole deserved her fate. What was it he'd said? 'She put her faith in love and she got burnt . . . romance is bullshit. Because it never works out. Not for real.'

And now he'd proved it to her.

*

316

Back at Quayside Row, Ellen parked the Land-Rover and walked past the cottage to the semicircle of concrete at the end of the harbour wall. Hoisting herself up so that she could sit on it, she looked out to sea, listening to the waves slap against the stones below her. She felt like a zombie. She could hardly believe this was happening to her. She could hardly believe what she'd done. Feeling a wave of desolation swoop over her, her mind snapped back to the Arrivals Hall the night before, reliving the torment of her conversation with Jason.

'It's too late,' Ellen whispered, wiping her tears on her sleeve and gently pushing Jason away. There were people all around them, jostling their bags and greeting each other, but Ellen could only see Jason's look of anguish and confusion.

'What on earth do you mean?' he asked, staring down at her. 'I thought . . . I thought –'

'I've met someone else,' she said quickly, her heart seeming to leap into her throat as she spoke.

Jason stared at her for what seemed like an age. She watched his expression turn from confusion, to disbelief, to anger. Every trace of softness left his eyes and, as they hardened and narrowed, Ellen felt the force of what she'd just said hit her like a bullet. As he stepped back a few paces from her, she realised the magnitude of what had happened.

'You've got to be joking, right?' Jason demanded, his voice raised, so that other passengers turned to face them. He paced away from her, clutching his hair, and then back to her.

Ellen stared at the floor, hardly able to believe this was happening. She squeezed the diamonds in her hand hard, pressing them into her flesh to keep herself focused. She shook her head. 'No. I'm not.'

'I don't fucking believe this!' Jason exploded.

'Please,' Ellen begged. She'd never seen Jason angry before and the force of his fury terrified her. 'Please let me explain. Can't we go somewhere where we can talk?'

Jason's face contorted with suppressed rage. 'Who is he?'

'You don't know him.'

'Tell me.'

'It's just . . . His name is Ned Spencer. I met him in Shoresby.'

Again, Jason stepped back, as if he found her physically repulsive.

'So that's why you called me? Because you were feeling guilty?' Jason said. 'Is that it? You were having some sordid, shitty little seaside affair and –'

'Jason, please,' she implored him, holding on to his arm. 'I didn't mean for anything to happen between us. I tried and tried to fight it –'

'Oh, bully for you,' Jason spat.

'Jase, please,' Ellen implored.

'I've never been unfaithful to you. Never. Not once! The only thing I've done wrong is to have a job I give a shit about. And I've even put that on the line for you.'

'I'm sorry. I'm so so sorry,' Ellen said. She watched as Jason covered his face with his hands.

When he looked up, his eyes were filled with tears. 'Do you love this guy?' he asked, his voice no more than a whisper.

'I suppose so.' She was crying now, as well.

'You suppose so! You suppose so! What the hell does that mean?'

'I do, but . . . but . . .'

Jason picked up his rucksack. Then he wrenched open her hand and snatched back the diamonds. 'You know

318

what, Ellen? Fuck you! Fuck you and your stupid games! I don't want to hear it.'

'Jason!' Ellen cried, holding on to his sleeve, but he shrugged her off. He didn't look back as he pushed past the crowd of people and out of her life.

Now, sitting on the harbour wall looking out at the uncompromising sea, Ellen felt the full impact of the mistake she'd made. It was all her fault. She knew that, but it didn't make it any better knowing that she didn't have anyone else to blame. She could see now what she hadn't seen before. That she'd believed in the romance of Caroline Walpole and her story. That she'd become hooked on the heightened emotions of a legend that wasn't real.

What was real was pain. The pain that would always prevent Ned from being able to see what he could have. The pain she'd caused Jason. And the pain she felt now. That was real. She'd detonated her life on a whim – on the strength of a feeling that was nothing more than a fantasy. And now it was too late ever to get back what she'd lost.

Ellen wept, her heart breaking as her tears splashed on to the wall where they would eventually merge with the sea. She wept for the life she had given up and the even lonelier one she would now have to face. She wept for her foolishness and she wept for herself. And yet, all the way through her grief, a childish part of her longed for Ned to find her, for her to fall back into his embrace. But she knew now that it was never going to happen.

'It's useless,' she yelled angrily, digging a tissue out of her pocket. 'It's bloody useless.'

Chapter XIX

Jimmy was hanging around outside the main entrance to Appleforth House, making a show of tying his trainer laces, the same as he'd been doing for the last five minutes. His back was starting to ache, and his neck, too, but he didn't care. He didn't care about anything right now, other than putting his plan into action.

It was Thursday afternoon and nearly a week of careful preparation had gone into his plan, and this casualness he was feigning now, this accidental meeting with Verity Driver he was attempting to engineer, was the key to its success. He wanted the sequence of events that happened to Verity next, the sequence he'd *planned* to happen to her, to come to her as a complete surprise. It was only afterwards that Jimmy wanted her to realise how much care and thought had gone into everything. Because that was what Jimmy wanted most of all: for Verity to be surprised by *him*, by who he was and by what he was capable of.

'Fight with your brain . . .' Marianna had said, '. . . your heart . . . show her who you are . . . what you like . . . what you do . . . Show her who she'll be missing out on if she stays with him . . .'

Well, Jimmy had followed that advice to the letter. If he failed to impress Verity today – a fresh pulse of adrenalin tore through him – then he wouldn't know where to turn next, because he'd already have given it his best shot. But he wouldn't fail. He wouldn't. Ignoring the pain in his back, he stayed kneeling there in the dry dirt, like an athlete primed in starting blocks, ready to run the race of his life.

And then – without warning – Jimmy's race began. The front door of Appleforth House swung open and Verity Driver stepped outside.

'Hi,' he said, slowly standing upright, smiling at her with a confidence he didn't feel. He smoothed down the thighs of his freshly laundered jeans and cocked his thumbs behind his new black leather belt.

'I thought you'd already left,' she said.

He couldn't tell whether she was pleased he was still here or not. Be patient, he urged himself. You'll find out soon enough. 'It's too nice an evening to be rushing about,' he said.

Verity looked past Jimmy, across the gardens, as if checking out whether what he was telling her was true. He found himself studying her, the way he always did when she wasn't looking directly at him.

She was wearing black Reeboks with red laces, a full-length flared denim skirt and a buttoned-up fox-brown coat with its collar turned up. She'd tucked her curled hair up under a brown and cream knitted ski hat, which she'd pulled down low at a rakish angle over her brow, so that only one of her curved fawn eyebrows showed. Her cheeks were flushed after spending so much of the day outside and her lips – well, Jimmy still found it difficult to think about her lips at all without blushing.

He watched as she closed her eyes for a second, breathing in the earthy scent of the lawns and flower beds around them. The grounds were still wet from the afternoon's series of showers, which had now given way to a crisp, clear evening. Water dripped from the wide bent branches of a nearby Scots pine, and Jimmy watched as a grey squirrel darted up the blood-red bark of its trunk.

They'd been filming on the Appleforth Estate since noon. First Ellen and Scott had got Jimmy to act out Leon Jacobson's betrayal of Caroline Walpole, with a local am-dram actor called Seamus standing in for Caroline Walpole's father. Then they'd filmed Verity over on the cliff-side near Lost Soul's Point, waiting hopelessly for the man who'd already betrayed her. And finally they'd done a sequence of Verity running towards the cliff, after having been confronted by Seamus, before ending with a shot of Seamus picking up Verity's glove and staring forlornly out to sea.

Verity scrutinised Jimmy's face and smiled kindly. 'You look as tired as I feel,' she told him.

But if he looked it, he certainly didn't feel it. Even though he'd been up half the night – worrying about today, and running various scenarios and potential conversations through his mind – now that he was actually alone with Verity, he felt more alert than he had done in his entire life.

Reaching out tentatively, she brushed her finger tenderly across his eyebrow where the swelling still showed. 'Does it still hurt?' she asked.

'No.' And it didn't. Right now, it felt amazing. The touch of her finger had seen to that.

'I'm glad you're here,' she said. 'I've been trying to speak to you in private all day, but what with us not doing our scenes together and –'

Jimmy had been avoiding being alone with her today, the same as he'd been avoiding her all week at school. He'd been saving up whatever intimacy lay between them for now, for when it really mattered, for when it was just the two of them. He'd wanted to preserve the tension that had existed between them when she'd briefly apologised to him last Friday in the corridor at school. He'd been desperate for

Verity not to think that everything they had to say to one another had already been said.

'What was it you wanted to talk to me about?' he now asked.

'About what happened, of course, about what Denny did . . . about why he did it . . .'

A part of Jimmy didn't want to talk to her about Denny and wanted Denny to be the furthest thing from her mind. But another part of him – a weaker, more insecure side – needed to know if they were still together or whether what Denny had done to him had been enough to break them apart. He put it bluntly, because he wanted it over with quickly: 'Are you still going out with him?'

'Yes, but . . .' She looked into his eyes. She looked as though she wanted to say more about Denny, as though there *was* more that Jimmy should hear. But her sentence died on her tongue.

Jimmy looked away in an attempt to conceal from her the chasm of disappointment he suddenly felt himself teetering towards. He stared hard at the ground, telling himself that it wasn't over yet, and reminding himself that he still had a plan and therefore every reason left to fight on. He forced himself to look up and he forced himself to smile. And as Verity smiled back at him, he felt the chasm seal up once more and disappear.

Then her expression wavered. 'I should get going,' she said, putting her shiny silver mailbag down and taking her fingerless woollen gloves from her pocket and pulling them on. 'I've got this essay I need to hand in tomorrow, and –'

'"Discuss the nature of ambition in *The Great Gatsby* . . ."' Jimmy said, having the same essay left to do himself. 'Riveting stuff, eh? Personally, I can't wait.'

She looked him over with curiosity. 'I thought you liked that kind of thing,' she said.

'I like reading it, not writing about it.'

'You still get good marks,' she pointed out.

'That doesn't mean anything.'

There was a pause between them, as if she were waiting for him to elaborate. But Jimmy didn't want to talk about school, or books. None of that stuff seemed important to him right now.

Verity swung her bag up over her shoulder. 'Well . . .' she said, looking down the long, curved driveway that led to the estate gates.

'Beautiful, isn't it?' he remarked quickly, gazing inland to where the sun hung low on the horizon, determined to keep the conversation going.

And it was beautiful. The sky was iridescent, beginning to bruise into purples and mauves and blacks, and the stone of Appleforth House glowed like lamplight in the dying day. The three-quarter moon was already visible. Jimmy's heart beat faster as he waited for Verity to reply.

'Incredible,' she half said, half sighed. 'I always used to look over in this direction from the hotel and think how pretty the coast looked,' she went on, 'but it wasn't until we started doing the filming that I realised how much more you could see from up here.'

When Jimmy spoke next, he tried not to make the words sound rehearsed, although they were. Instead, he tried to make them sound as if they'd come from his heart, which they had. 'The view of the sunset's much better from over by the cliffs,' he said, keeping his eyes fixed on the sky, like he wasn't really talking to her at all, like he was simply telling it how it was. 'There aren't any buildings in the way there. Not like here or down in the town. In the last few seconds before the sun goes down, you can look out to sea and watch the darkness sweep towards you across the bay.'

He still couldn't bring himself to look at her. He couldn't bear the thought of carrying her expression around with him for the rest of his life if she were to turn him down on the offer he was about to make. He picked up his gym bag and threaded his arms through its straps, so that it hung squarely on his back. 'I could show you,' he finally plucked up the courage to say, 'if you like . . .'

His whole body stilled.

'Why not?' she said.

Jimmy could have kissed her then, as he turned towards her. But then he could have kissed her always.

Verity was kneeling on Ryan's old black leather jacket and Jimmy was lying flat on his stomach on the thick spongy turf at her side. It didn't bother him, the dampness of the ground or the chill of his skin beneath his Placebo sweatshirt. He was glad he'd been able to do something for her, the same as he was glad that she'd teased him about being a lot more gallant in real life than when he'd been dressed up as Leon Jacobson and acting the villain earlier on.

This is our cinema moment, Jimmy was thinking now, happy to run with the idea that this was their first date, rather than what he most feared: that it could equally be their last.

Here they were, the two of them, side by side, staring at the greatest widescreen of them all. They were mere feet from the edge of the cliff and they were overlooking a view that had never failed to affect him. This is how kings must have once felt, looking down from their castle walls over their kingdoms. That's what Jimmy had always thought

325

whenever he'd been up here before. Only today the thought didn't stop there. Because today, he had a queen with him and that made him a king.

He breathed in deep, as if by so doing he could capture the very essence of the moment and make it all a permanent part of himself. But the salty air hit heavy against the back of his throat like a rebuke. And so he settled instead for enjoying the moment as it was now.

He let his eyes wander the bay below. Over in the steep stone-walled harbour, the tide was on its way in but had yet to reach the fishing boats and sailing school dinghies, which remained slumped on their sides with their keels and hulls exposed to the air, glistening like sharks.

'Watch now,' Jimmy said as, unseen behind them, the sunlight melted away on the western horizon and darkness spread slowly towards them across the sea from the east.

Verity opened her mouth, but no words came out. The darkness continued to sweep forwards, snuffing out the silver light on the crest of each wave as it went. It was like watching a giant blackout blind being drawn across the bay. Jimmy watched as Verity's own features grew pale like a statue. She turned her head to track the darkness as it reached them and flowed inland, like a great grey wave, slowly draining the colour from everything it touched.

He loved her for her reaction. He loved her for her awed expression, because it meant that she felt the magic of this place, too. He loved sharing this with her, second by second, because it allowed their heartbeats to synchronise and allowed them, for a fleeting moment, to become one.

'It gets so cold so quick,' Verity said a few minutes later, placing the back of her hand against Jimmy's neck as proof.

She was shivering in the fading twilight and he realised he was, too.

326

They both stared up at the lilac moon and watched as the first of the night's stars became visible. Jimmy looked at Verity's face, the way it was tilted upwards as if in prayer. He felt something so intimate between them that he almost leant forward to kiss her. But he held back. 'Come on,' he said, standing and picking up his gym bag, pulling out a torch and clicking its wide beam on, 'there's somewhere else I think you might like.'

He'd been half dreading her to say that she should be heading back home, or that it was too dark now to be this close to the cliffs, but she didn't.

Instead, she got up and brushed off his jacket before handing it back to him. 'Which way?' she asked, looking around.

'Are you sure?' he checked, not wanting her to feel he'd pressured her into this.

She raised her arms above her head and let out a low groan, waggling her fingers in a half-hearted spectral fashion. 'Well, I'm not afraid of the ghost of Leon Jacobson, if that's what you mean,' she said with a laugh.

The sound filled Jimmy with happiness. He felt suddenly light, as though the merest of breezes could lift him up into the sky like a kite. 'Well, OK, then,' he said, 'let's go.'

They walked a hundred and fifty yards south along the cliff-side path, to the clearing in the gorse at the end of the tractor lane where they'd re-enacted Caroline Walpole's suicide.

Jimmy didn't want to stop here again. He'd found it tough enough that afternoon, watching Verity walking across the clearing to where it terminated at Lost Soul's Point, the same place Ryan had driven the stolen Mazda convertible over the edge. The place weakened Jimmy. He could feel it draining his energy, as if an aspect of him belonged here.

327

'This is where it happened, isn't it?' he heard Verity asking.

Jimmy pressed on, upping his pace.

'Ryan,' she continued, as he failed to reply, 'this is where he did it, isn't it?'

It was only once Jimmy had turned a corner in the path and knew that Lost Soul's Point was out of sight that he finally slowed. 'Yeah,' he told her, 'that's where he died.'

He swept the surrounding land with the torch. It grew wilder here, with walls of bracken taller than them both rearing upwards on either side. Using the hardened sleeve of his leather jacket, he drew back several strands of bramble, which hung across the path like a barbed curtain. His and Verity's eyes met for a second as she passed him, but he didn't speak. There was no more to say. Not about Ryan. He hadn't brought her here because of Ryan. He'd bought her here because of life – because of how happy she made him when she was near – not because of death, which was what she made him forget.

'Keep going,' Jimmy said, walking behind her now as the path became thinner, shining the torch ahead of them both. 'We're nearly there.'

But Verity wasn't taking a hint. 'What do you think about the memorial concert on Saturday?' she asked.

'What's there to think about?' he replied. 'It's got nothing to do with me.'

'But it has with Ryan.' Her voice was earnest and for some reason he was glad he couldn't see her face. 'Them deciding to hold it on the anniversary of his death,' she said. 'In a way it's for him, isn't it?'

'Is that what you think?' he asked.

'That's what Clive told us all at rehearsal the other night.'

Jimmy grunted noncommittally. He'd come to the

conclusion that people trying to bring something positive out of Ryan's death wasn't so bad. And Clive was all right. He'd lent Jimmy the Youth Centre's camcorder again only that morning.

'Ryan wouldn't give a shit,' he said. 'But it's all right by me.'

'Are you going to come and watch?' Verity asked.

They'd reached a fork in the path and Verity stopped.

Do you want me to? he wanted to ask her. *Are you asking me because you care?* 'I'll be there helping Scott,' he answered instead. 'But even if I wasn't,' he admitted, stepping past her and taking the path to the left, 'I'd come and watch you anyway.'

Jimmy wondered what Ryan would think about Verity singing to commemorate his death. Would he really, he wondered, not give a shit? Jimmy hoped he'd like it. He couldn't picture Ryan's ghost as being sad or mean or vindictive. And if Ryan's ghost did exist, Jimmy hoped the sound of Verity's voice would rise up here on the wind, and each and every note she sang would touch him and soothe him and bring him closer to peace.

Leaving the tourist trail beneath them now, they climbed a second path, which sloped upwards and curved inwards from the cliff. The undergrowth on either side of them grew as thick as a jungle, forcing them once more to walk in single file.

But then they reached another clearing and Jimmy stepped aside and shone the torch there in a broad sweep so that Verity could see.

'Wow.'

She stared at the Wreck. It was still beautiful, shimmering in the torchlight and moonlight as though it were a mirage.

'I must have walked that other path a thousand times,'

Verity said, 'and I never even knew this place existed.' She gazed around, baffled, as if trying to get her bearings. 'It must be the gorse, I suppose,' she deduced.

She was right: all around the flat, rocky clearing, which stretched from the front of the chapel to the cliff's edge, thick brambles, bracken and dense colonies of gorse and heather shut out the rest of the world, keeping this place secret from anyone who didn't already know it was here.

'Some of the branches,' Jimmy confessed, pointing the torch beam over to the edge of the clearing at the cliff-side, where the bracken appeared thickest of all. 'Me and Ryan dragged them there to stop other people coming in. Come on,' he hurried on. 'I'll show you inside.'

He started off round the splintered and hollow grey stump of a cedar of Lebanon tree that had been felled by lightning two years ago. Its giant trunk stretched away to the south, half rotted now into the ground. It reminded Jimmy of an archaeological dig he'd once visited on a school trip, where a Viking chief had been buried inside his boat.

'This is where we always used to hang out,' Jimmy explained, as he struggled to get the key into the padlock, 'me and Ryan and Tara.' His hands were shaking, on edge again. 'Ned Spencer says we've got to clear out, though,' he went on, finally slotting the key home and twisting it round so the lock popped. 'He's sending the builders in on Monday.'

Jimmy pushed open the door of the Wreck and stepped inside. Slipping the padlock and key into his jeans pocket, he walked over to the old ship's battery, which Ryan had hooked up and Jimmy had charged up on the quayside last night.

Four bare bulbs lit up in series around the chapel walls,

illuminating the posters of Howard Marks, Britney and Che Guevara like modern-day saints.

That morning, Jimmy had swept the flagstone floor for the first time in years, creating a sandstorm of dust in the process. It had all settled now, though, he was relieved to see. Verity's silence lent a serenity to the room, a peacefulness that had never existed during the times Jimmy had spent here with Ryan.

As Verity joined him in the centre of the room, she turned, pirouetting in slow motion, as she took everything in: the old leather armchair and the mattress on the floor; the sticker-covered ghetto blaster at the foot of the small marble altar; the posters; and finally the pile of junk and other items in the corner, ranging from punctured footballs to –

Verity froze, her eyes locking on something there. Apprehension swelled in Jimmy as she hurried over to the corner and bent down to examine whatever it was that had caught her attention.

'It's you . . .' she said quietly. When she turned back to face Jimmy, she was holding the luminous green kite. 'I always wanted to know who it was.' She glanced at the ceiling. 'I've seen it flying out there, up against the stars at night,' she said, caressing the silky material of the kite's wings between her fingers and thumbs. 'It always looked so beautiful. I nearly came up here a few weeks ago to see. And if I had done, I would have found you.'

She was looking at him as though up until this very instant he'd been wearing a mask, and it was only now that she was beginning to recognise him for who he really was.

'Take a seat,' he requested, indicating the armchair with a wave of his hand.

'What?'

'Please . . .'

Still holding on to the kite, Verity walked past him and sat down.

Jimmy shuffled his gym bag off his back and stood behind her.

'Don't turn round,' he said, seeing that she was starting to crane her neck, 'or you'll ruin the surprise.'

He crouched down and unzipped his bag, removing the camcorder he'd borrowed from Clive. He pressed the eject button and waited for the mechanism to kick in and give him access to the tape inside. Then, with the tape in his hand, he walked to the table and lifted off the black bin liner he'd covered the film projector with that morning.

'OK,' Jimmy said, 'close your eyes.' He gave her a couple of seconds, before checking, 'Are they closed?'

'Yes.'

The light bulbs dimmed as Jimmy adjusted the ship's battery connections the way Scott had shown him at lunchtime when he'd helped Jimmy rig all this up. Jimmy then switched on the projector that Scott had helped him hire and put the tape in. A rectangle of pale light appeared on the opposite wall of the chapel, approximately six feet by three. Jimmy made a minute adjustment to the projector's focus until the rectangle's edges became sharp. Finally, he disconnected the ship's battery from the Wreck's lighting system and the rectangle burnt brighter and brighter as each of the four light bulbs faltered and died.

Jimmy swallowed. Doubt. He wondered what Verity would think. He wondered whether he was crazy or not. And, right now, he didn't know either way.

'You can open them now,' he told Verity and, as he did so, reached out and pressed 'Play' on the projector.

Verity said nothing as the silent colour images flickered across the wall. First came her face in close-up. She was

332

smiling, trying not to laugh. Light played on her eyes like sunlight on the surface of a brook. A single shining curl of hair quivered against her forehead in the breeze and her lips rolled momentarily inwards as she fought to remain composed. Then the image pulled back to a long shot and the reason for her amusement became clear: Ellen was there, holding up a mirror to Verity's face after she'd applied her make-up. They were standing next to Ellen's Land-Rover at the end of the track by Lost Soul's Point and Verity was laughing now, pulling her costume hat down on her head.

The film stopped abruptly and the rectangle switched back to white.

Jimmy said nothing.

Verity stood and faced him. Her features were bright in the projector's light and her shadow magnified against the wall. She shielded her eyes. 'I don't understand,' she said. She stared at him with hopeless concern.

'You told me last week how nervous you were about seeing yourself on screen,' he said.

'Oh.' Verity turned towards the rectangle of uniform light, as if some further explanation for Jimmy's actions might be hidden there.

'And I wanted you to know how beautiful you are,' he said. 'I wanted you to see yourself the way I see you.'

In the silence that followed, it felt to Jimmy like the room's temperature had plummeted. He felt crushed. She didn't understand. She'd just said so herself. He suddenly knew with absolute certainty that this had been a terrible mistake.

'But we don't know each other Jimmy . . .' she said, her eyes fixed on the wall, '. . . not properly . . .'

'I know enough to want to know more,' he said.

All Jimmy could think of was the smell of her perfume. It

suddenly seemed like the room was full of spring flowers. The heady smell seemed to flow through him, hitting him like a drug, leaving him woozy and numb.

'But you know I'm seeing Denny,' she told him.

He swallowed hard and it hurt. His throat felt dry and cracked. 'I know,' he said, praying that Marianna and he hadn't together got this wrong. 'But I also know that you kissed me because you wanted to.'

'It's not that simple. It's –' she began, her eyes still focused on the screen.

But Jimmy had changed these last few weeks. He wasn't the same person who'd slunk off after giving Verity that CD. If she didn't understand then he'd explain. He'd spent too much time with her and too much had happened between them for him to give up now. Jimmy had spent his whole life missing the boat, doubting himself and not telling people what he felt. But not today and never again with her. 'No,' he said, so firmly that she finally looked back at him. 'Either deny it or admit it, Verity. Because I've got to know.'

Chapter XX

Ned Spencer was sitting on one of the tables outside the – mercifully 'Shut Till Xmas' – funfair on the Esplanade. It was late on Friday afternoon and he was feeling like a complete idiot.

It wasn't his proximity to the concrete and reinforced-glass bunker crammed full of robotic rides and one-armed bandits that was making him feel this way – although, truthfully, he did hate funfairs, finding them neither fun nor fair, but instead unfailingly dull and a rip-off to boot. No, the immediate reason behind Ned's discomfort was, in fact, what was immediately behind his behind: namely the seat he was sitting on, which was positioned inside a plastic moulded elephant and was designed for a child of no more than ten years old and five feet in height. That, of course, and the fact that a child matching that exact description had just that very second cycled past him shouting, 'Oi, mate! You look like a right tit!'

'Piss off!' Ned shouted back now as the kid disappeared into the driving rain, which had forced Ned into taking refuge inside this plastic pachyderm in the first place.

The wind continued to howl and Ned growled, actually *growled*. He could kill Debs right now. Because it was her fault that he was sitting here in the first place. And he didn't want to be here. He wanted to be in the Hope and Anchor pub two hundred yards further along the road. Which is where he'd been heading when his phone had rung and he'd foolishly pulled it from his trouser pocket and answered it. He wanted to be finishing off his first pint while watching his second being poured. Which is what he'd have been doing this very second – in there by the fire, as dry as a bone – if he hadn't agreed to Debs's request of meeting up.

She had something she needed to ask him about before she picked Clara up from school, she'd said. And Dan, the foreman, had told her that Ned had gone into town to get some accounts photocopied (Ned's excuse for sneaking off early for a drink). 'So why not meet up now?' she'd requested, because she'd already been in town, too.

And so Ned had suggested here – 'on the Esplanade, next to the funfair' – because (as with Dan) Ned hadn't wanted Debs to discover that he'd been about to start his Friday night out at four in the afternoon.

Only as he'd been waiting for her, it had started to rain. And now Ned wished he hadn't agreed to the meeting at all. He pulled his phone from his now soaked jeans and stabbed Debs's number into it.

'Where are you?' he practically barked into the phone as soon as she answered.

'Here,' she whispered into his ear, appearing at his side and snapping her phone shut and then her umbrella, before sitting down (with considerably more grace than he'd managed) on the seat opposite him in the other half of the elephant's abdomen.

Ned glared across the tiny grey plastic table that separated them. Debs turned up the dry collar on her dry denim jacket and began to fidget with its dry French Connection buttons. The rain drummed down on the elephant's back and Ned's corduroy jacket hung damp and heavy against his chest.

'What took you so long?' he demanded. 'You've been fifteen minutes.'

Debs ignored the reprimand, taking a bunch of tissues from her bag and putting them on the table between them.

Picking up the tissues, Ned wiped the cold water from his brow and neck. It was a token gesture, though; everything he wore, right down to his paint-spattered canvas trainers and cotton socks, was drenched. He squeezed the tissues into a soggy ball and placed it in the centre of the table.

'I always had you down as more of a T-Rex fan,' Debs commented, gazing across the picnic area towards the dismally unrealistic plastic dinosaur to their left. She absent-mindedly traced her fingers over the smooth convex moulding of the elephant's right bum cheek, then caught Ned's eye.

He found it impossible to ignore the contagious mixture of excitement and apprehension on her face and, despite himself, he smiled. 'Come on, then,' he said, rubbing his hands together, ignoring the ache in his back from being forced to crouch this low. 'What's so important that it couldn't wait until I got home?'

'I want to go to Argentina.'

'With Scott . . .'

'How did you know?'

How could he *not* have known would have been a harder question to answer. Debs had been spending every spare second she had either with Scott, or talking to Scott on the phone, or talking about Scott to her friends. On Scott's days off over the last week or so, when Ellen had been up in London, he'd occupied his time by taking Debs out on trips around the nearby coastal attractions during her free time. Their nights out together had grown longer, too, with Debs staying over with Scott at the cottage whenever Ellen had been away.

'Let's just call it an educated guess,' Ned said.

A cold blast of wind sprayed rain across them and Debs folded her arms, hugging herself to keep warm. 'It's for a month,' she said. 'In January. Scott's got a gig there – a football tournament – and he wants me to go with him.'

'It's a great opportunity.'

'You mean you don't mind?'

Ned smiled. 'That depends if you're asking me for a month off to go on holiday, or if you're handing in your notice. If it's the first, I'll cope,' he said, 'but if it's the second, both Clara and I are going to be gutted. Either way, though,' he reassured her, 'it's your life and you're a friend and I'll do everything I can to help you to do what you want.'

She reached across the table and briefly squeezed his hand. 'Thank you,' she said.

They looked at each other in silence.

'So are you going to put me out of my misery?' he asked.

Her face creased up in consternation. 'What? Oh!' she laughed, realising what he meant. 'It's the first: holiday. Don't worry,' she hurriedly added, 'I've got not intention of quitting.'

'Phew,' Ned said with an exaggerated sigh.

'If it goes well in Argentina,' she told him, 'then Scott was saying that there's this small production company a friend of his runs in Cheltenham . . . and he's been asking Scott to join up with him for ages and . . .'

'I get the picture,' Ned interrupted to save her from justifying herself any further. 'You two have got a chance of a future together.'

'Hence Argentina.'

'Scott's a good guy,' Ned said, meaning it. Anybody who could make someone's eyes sparkle with happiness as Debs's were now doing was all right by him. 'I hope it all works out for you.'

'What about you?' Debs asked.

'Like I said, I'll cope.'

'No, I mean you and Ellen . . .'

The name came at Ned like an accusation, simultaneously angering him and putting him on the defensive. He'd wanted to make what had happened between them a part of his past. Each one of the four days that had gone by since Ellen had come up to the site and seen him, Ned had wished into years. He'd wanted to be able to remember her as someone distant, faded, a voice at the end of a phone line, or a snapshot in a photograph album forgotten in a drawer. What he hadn't wanted was for her to have remained immediate and vivid, as she had. He hadn't wanted to have been blindsided by her time and time again.

It had been as if the harder he'd tried to dismiss what had happened between them – and not just the sex, but the way she'd made him *feel* during the sex – the more undeniable it had become. He'd kept on imagining her reappearing at the front door of his cottage on Saturday night. And he'd kept on remembering how she'd looked when he'd woken up the next morning to find he'd wrapped his arms round her as they'd slept.

'How did you –' he started to ask Debs.

But he already knew. She and Scott must have put two and two together about where Ellen had stayed on Saturday night when she'd lost her keys. Or maybe Ellen had even confided in Scott and he, in turn, had confided in Debs.

Not that it mattered either way, Ned reminded himself. Nothing *was* going on between them and nothing *would*. He'd certainly made that clear enough to Ellen on Monday. And it was still clear enough to him, wasn't it? They had no future. He felt things for Ellen, all right. Oh, yes, he knew there was no way he could deny that. He felt desire, and fear, and sadness, and joy. He wanted to be with her and to hide from her, to run towards her and to push her away. All these conflicting emotions were knotted together inside him, but all they did was confuse him more.

She would return to London and he would return to Cheltenham. And soon it would be as if none of this had ever happened.

'Let's just call it an educated guess,' Debs joked.

'Or an entirely misinformed one,' Ned answered flatly.

The smile faded from Debs's face. 'Oh,' she said, 'but I thought –'

'Well, you thought wrong.'

Her mouth opened slightly, as if she were about to say something, but Ned had already heard enough. 'This rain doesn't look like it's going to stop,' he told her, 'and it's time I got going.' He stood up and promptly cracked the back of his head on the hard plastic above. 'Fuck!' he snapped, scrambling outside and kicking the elephant's flank as hard as he could.

Ned didn't say goodbye to Debs. He turned his back on her and trudged across the playground and on to the road. With the wind and the rain buffeting against him, it was like walking into a waterfall, but he was determined: he could already see the Hope and Anchor shimmering like a mirage in the distance, the warming glow of its windows visible, by now, in the fading light.

But the further Ned walked, the more his anger switched focus. It became less about the stupid elephant and less about Debs trying to play at happy couples with him. The truth was, Ned was genuinely happy that Debs had found someone she wanted to be with and he could understand that she wanted the same to be true for him. No, Ned wasn't angry at the elephant or Debs. Ned was angry at himself. He was angry because, like Debs, he realised that his heart had been snagged by hope. And he was angry at himself for not giving it up, even though he knew that what he hoped for could never be.

Aside from the silent and scrawny barman, who didn't so much as raise an eyebrow at Ned's apocalyptic appearance as he stepped in out of the rising storm, the Hope and Anchor was empty. The bar stank of last night's cigarette smoke and spilt lager, and Ned dripped on the scuffed floorboards as the barman slowly pulled him a pint. In the background some frenetic and dated early-Nineties house tune played on the jukebox, fleetingly reminding Ned of the five-year period he'd spent in London after graduation.

Ned paid for his drink and carried it over to a table beside the giant porthole-shaped window, which offered a panoramic view of the bay. He sat down on the bench and tried shuffling along it towards the open fire, only to find that something had caught on his jeans. As he stood, he saw a grey-as-gristle sinew of chewing gum stretching from his thigh to the edge of the bench. He shifted sideways, snapping the gum, and sat motionless for a moment, gazing into the fire's flickering flames, luxuriating in the blast of its heat. Then he lifted his pint glass to his mouth.

But the moment he'd been savouring wasn't to be: something caused him to recoil, to put the glass back down on the table instead of pressing it against his lips.

He stared at his pint for a moment, trying to work out why he'd just done what he had. It made no sense to him at first, whatever instinct had driven him, but then, here in this gloomy off-season tourist pub, it suddenly became incredibly clear. The same as the couple of nights each week he went out to binge-drink himself stupid, he'd come

341

here to find oblivion. But it hadn't been that knowledge which had stopped him drinking just now. What had stopped him had been the realisation that, for the first time, it hadn't been the unanswerable questions about Mary he'd come here to forget, the questions that snapped at his heels like a pack of famished wolves, demanding his blood each and every day.

Where had he been when Mary had needed him? Why had he buried his head in the sand and pretended that the doctors had been making everything right, when it had been plain to see that the happy, optimistic girl he'd married had all but disappeared? Why had he been at work that day, that hour and that exact minute when everything had finally become too much for her?

No, the realisation which had so shaken Ned just now was that he'd been attempting to flee the thought of Ellen, not Mary. It had been Ellen he'd been aiming to erase from his mind with a bellyful of beer, just the same as he'd tried doing with the joint he'd smoked in the bathroom after they'd had sex last Saturday night.

The sex. He'd thought about it all right, each night since, lying there in bed at night, wanting to pick up the phone and call her, wondering if she was in London or Shoresby, wondering if she'd ever forgive him for the way he'd treated her, wondering if she was with her boyfriend and was no longer thinking about him at all.

He loathed thinking about it, the complacency he'd callously dished out to her at the site on Monday, the way he'd acted as though what had happened on Saturday night had been just sex. It filled him with shame. He was ashamed because he'd hurt her. He knew he had. He'd witnessed it in her eyes. He'd seen the same pain she would have seen in his eyes the moment he'd turned his back on her and his casual and disinterested front had shattered. But he hadn't allowed her to see that, had he? He'd hidden it from her instead. And that filled him with shame, too. He'd lied to her about something fundamental: that he *did* care about what had happened and he *did* care about her.

Just sex . . . good sex . . . Ned sighed and shook his head. If she only knew the truth. What had happened between them on Saturday night had been nothing less than monumental for him. When he'd woken the morning after, and felt her skin against his and smelt her perfume and listened to her softly moan as she'd closed her fingers round his forearm, he'd suddenly – crazily – seen a way forward for them both.

He'd imagined a distant Sunday in the back garden of an immaculately white house. There he'd been, in the heat of noon, walking across the green and sun-drenched lawn, casting barely a shadow. He'd stopped, stretching out and snipping free a perfect yellow rose, before walking on past a child's trampoline and swing, to the terraced dining area at the end of the garden. He'd sat down on a bench and poured himself a cup of hot coffee from the china pot before him. The coffee's aroma had mixed with that of the freshly cut grass and he'd turned to see Ellen beside him, shaded beneath a wide-brimmed straw hat and wearing a blue cotton dress. He'd placed the rose on the newspaper she'd been reading and she'd turned to him and smiled. He'd heard the sound of laughter and had looked up to see two girls rushing through the french doors at the back of the house. He'd immediately recognised the older of the two as Clara. She'd grown taller, yet her face and her smile had remained the same. The younger child he'd never seen before, but in her features he'd seen both Ellen's and his own and, immediately, he'd understood.

But then the vision had dissolved, running away from

343

him like a drawing made of sand, which someone had lifted up to scrutinise.

Ned stared into the embers of the fire. The vision of perfection was one he knew he'd only destroy. Because – the opposite of his professional life – that's what he did in his private life, wasn't it? He built something perfect and then he sat back and watched it collapse into ruin. That's what he'd done with his life with Mary. He wasn't to be trusted. He didn't have what it took to take care of someone else. He was no good. He'd failed to give Mary a reason to live. And he had no right to drip the slow poison of his inability into another person's life again.

Ned stood up and walked to the bar. 'Call me a cab, will you?'

'Something wrong with your drink?' the barman asked, picking up the wall phone's receiver and glancing over at Ned's full pint on the table.

'No,' said Ned, 'just the drinker.'

He dug down into his jacket pocket for some change, scooping the coins out in his fingers, along with the piece of Ellen Morris's fake fur coat that Wobbles had torn off nearly a month ago.

Ned counted out the cash on the bar top. He stared at the piece of fur, before dropping it into the ashtray for the barman to clear.

He went over to the window to keep a lookout for the cab. He needed to see Clara now. He needed to be back at the cottage with her, watching her trace the raindrops down the window-panes and asking her what shapes she could see. He wanted to hug her and prove to himself that his heart wasn't half empty, but was overflowing with love. He wanted to know once more what he no longer did: that his life was complete and enough.

Chapter XXI

The Community Hall was nearly full by the time Verity finally caught a glimpse of Jimmy. He was coming in at the back and Verity put her hand up to try to catch his attention. But Jimmy didn't look in her direction. Instead, he shuffled forward and Verity could see that there was something subdued and sad about him, as he wrapped the leather jacket round himself. Even from this distance he looked dishevelled, as if he hadn't slept for days.

She longed to yell out to him, but with so many people between where she was standing by the stage and the back of the hall, it was impossible. She stood up on the step to the stage, shielding her eyes against the overhead spotlight, in order to see him, but he was lost in the crowd. Verity was desperate to talk to him. After the film Jimmy had shown her the day before yesterday, she hadn't been able to sleep. Yesterday morning she'd been up early, eager to see him, as she'd made her way into their Friday morning English class, but Jimmy hadn't turned up. Since then, she'd been worried sick. She needed to tell him what was on her mind, and she had a horrible feeling that if she didn't tell him soon it would be too late.

Verity had even gone to Carlton Court to find him yesterday afternoon, but there'd been no names on any of the door buzzers and she hadn't been able to find anyone who could tell her which flat Jimmy lived in. She'd been so distracted that it was only when she'd returned home that she'd realised she'd missed her piano exam. Her mother had reacted with typical fury, berating Verity for letting her herself and her mother down. But Verity didn't care any more. She hadn't deliberately missed the piano exam, in some mad act of rebellion, as her mother had suggested. But missing it had made her realise that there were much, much more important things in life.

Verity had tried all day to find a moment to slip away and find Jimmy, but there'd been a dress rehearsal and then, at home, she'd had to get dressed and the time had completely vanished. Now the concert was nearly starting and Verity only had precious minutes to talk.

The straps of her high-heeled black shoes dug into her ankles and the waistband on her Fifties-style black dress hurt her ribs, as she strained to get a better view of Jimmy. She was wearing pink-tinted lip gloss and her hair was piled high on her head, the pins sticking into her scalp. She'd never felt more uncomfortable, and wished she were in her jeans and trainers, and could run to the back of the hall and escape with Jimmy.

Mr Peters pulled her back down, saving her from teetering over the edge of the steps. He was wearing a multi-coloured bow tie and a pink evening jacket, and he had a sheen of sweat over his cheeks. He was carrying a bundle of music, his conducting baton on top. 'You know the running order.' He sounded panicky over the noise of the school orchestra tuning up at the back of the stage. His green eyes looked concerned as he stared out from under his greasy blond fringe. 'You start, then Clive will make the speech and we'll run straight to the interval.'

Verity nodded, hardly listening, as she tried to look over Mr Peters's shoulder, but it was no use. It seemed as if the whole town had turned up for the event, probably because Ellen was filming part of it and they wanted to get their faces on the television. She could see all sorts of familiar people, including most of her teachers from school.

'Good luck,' said Toby, one of the young boys in the choir, as he trooped past her up the steps to sit in the semi-circle of chairs around the piano.

Verity smiled and ruffled his fluffy blond hair. 'You too.'

'I've never been on telly before,' he said.

'Verity, you've got your microphone on, haven't you?' Ellen asked as she approached her, and Verity fiddled with the small black dome that was clipped on to the front of her dress. There was something stern and businesslike about Ellen and she felt hurt that Ellen's warmth and friendliness towards her on the shoot had, for some reason, stopped. She'd been so lovely last week, but ever since the dress rehearsal today, Ellen had been offhand, as if she no longer really cared. She looked different, too. Her usually bright complexion seemed haggard and tired. She must be stressed, thought Verity. It was probably the strain of all the filming she'd been doing. She tried smiling, but Ellen didn't smile back at her.

'You can use the main mike as normal, but the radio mike will pick up everything that Scott needs. He'll be filming from the back now, where we've set up. We've scrapped the plans for a close-up during the concert as it'll be too disruptive.'

'Do you need some more lipstick?' Verity's mother asked. 'You don't want to look plain.' She now peered around Ellen's shoulder at her daughter, as if she were some professional lackey of Ellen's.

'Mum, stop fussing!'

'Two minutes to go,' Mr Peters shouted, as the house lights went down and people finally took their seats. 'Will everyone sit down!' Then he hurried over to Verity. 'I'm

347

counting on you, darling. If you get us off to a good start, then they won't notice how dreadful it'll be.' He nodded to the audience. 'Don't let me down.' Then he was away up the steps past her.

Verity saw Jimmy then. He was at the back of the hall, dodging past people as he hurried down the edge of the aisle towards her. She waved and he smiled at her, and she felt her heart jump with the knowledge that he was here at last. She smiled eagerly at him, as he eased past an old lady in a wheelchair.

Verity started down the steps towards him, but at that moment, almost out of nowhere, Denny arrived at the front of the central aisle, walking towards Verity with his arms outstretched.

He looked smarter than she'd ever seen him looking, with a black jacket on, a mauve shirt and black trousers. He'd trimmed his goatee beard, so that she could see more of his mouth, and he smiled at her, revealing his perfect white teeth. She'd always imagined being in public with Denny, but now she felt nothing. No tummy flips, no heart palpitations. Nothing.

'I made it,' he said, as if expecting Verity to applaud, before folding her into a tight hug. Verity tried to pull away and see Jimmy, but Denny cut her off, planting his lips on hers and darting his tongue into her mouth. 'I missed you,' he said, pulling away, his breath hot in her ear.

Verity wriggled away from him, putting her hands on his chest to push him off.

'Leave it!' Clive said gruffly, appearing from the other side aisle in his long leather coat and raising his eyebrows at Denny. 'You're on, Verity,' he announced, grabbing her arm and pushing her on stage, as Mr Peters, impatient to start, struck up with the piano introduction to 'Bridge over Troubled Water'.

'Break a leg,' Denny called after her and Verity glanced back, watching as he took a place in the front row. Desperately, she looked around for Jimmy, but he'd vanished.

There was almost complete silence from the audience by the time Verity had made it to the front of the stage. She glanced over to the side aisle where Jimmy had been, but the lights were in her eyes and she couldn't see anything but darkness.

She was smarting with humiliation, hardly able to believe that Denny had had the nerve to kiss her in front of everyone. She could sense his gaze on her, making her feel vulnerable, as if she were naked in harsh midday sun.

She thought back to the last time she'd seen Denny a week ago, as he'd stood at his window watching her leave in a taxi. He had no idea how much that night had changed her for ever. He had no idea how much he'd hurt her and how ordinary he'd made her feel.

Now, she could hardly stand seeing him again, or bear the obvious smugness with which he carried around the knowledge of their physical contact. She felt something shrivel up inside her when she thought about what had happened between them.

Ever since she'd locked herself in the bathroom on Saturday night on her return from Denny's she'd been feeling soiled. She'd written the bare, horrible facts in her diary, almost as a punishment to herself for being such a fool. All week she'd waited for Denny to call, to give her back some shred of dignity. But he hadn't. And now here he was, staring up at her from the front row as if she were his property.

What am I doing this for? she thought, catching a glimpse of her mother, who looked at her anxiously. Maybe it was the presence of Denny and her mother and just about everyone else she knew in Shoresby, but Verity felt cheap, as if she were some kind of performing monkey. She didn't even want to be here in the first place and what's more she hated this song.

Mr Peters struck a chord on the piano. It was her cue to start singing, but Verity was frozen. Didn't these people realise she was a fake and a fraud? She was aware of all the expectant faces ahead of her, waiting for her to perform, waiting for her to be Verity Driver, the town's talent show. In the distance, at the back, she could make out a red dot on Scott's camera.

Part of her was tempted to run off stage, but the greater part of her knew that was the cowardly thing to do.

She could feel Mr Peters's panic as he sat at the piano beside her. She couldn't let him down. The show must go on, she thought, as he played the introduction again. Somewhere out there in the hall was Jimmy. She opened her mouth and let the song soar above the heads of the audience, but her voice was destined only for Jimmy's ears. All the while, as she sang, she thought about being in the chapel with him and the way he'd been about Ryan when she'd questioned him on the path. For the first time, she finally understood the enormity of Jimmy's loss. The person closest to him had gone and he hadn't been able to do a thing.

She realised how strong Jimmy was and how much courage he must have had to have carried on and coped with Ryan's death on his own. He was amazing, Verity thought. Jimmy was amazing, and no one apart from her knew. She thought back to the film he'd made of her on the chapel wall, and how she'd felt when she'd seen it. She'd been shocked, but something inside her had realised what it had meant for him to have done that for her. And now she had to tell Jimmy. She had to tell him all this, before it was too late. As the final note hung in the air, she took no joy from the applause that greeted her.

Clive walked on to the stage, clapping with the audience. 'Thank you, thank you,' Clive said, breathily into the microphone. 'And thank you to the ever-talented Verity Driver.'

Verity dipped her head at the further applause and sat down near the back of the stage.

'Tonight, we are here to celebrate the life of one of our own,' Clive began. 'We all knew Ryan and on this, the anniversary of his tragic death . . .'

Verity scanned the rows further back, watching her mother nodding with false sincerity, her head cocked to one side. Moving on, she squinted against the light, searching each seat for Jimmy, but he wasn't anywhere to be seen.

By the interval, Verity knew in her heart that Jimmy must have left and she couldn't bear sitting still, but with the camera on the school orchestra there was no way she could leave her seat without everyone seeing her. Impatience filled every cell of her body.

She had to find Jimmy and she had to find him now.

When the school orchestra had finished, she was the first out of her seat. Seeing Denny get up, she hurried to the other side of the stage, where she knew there was a small space where she could jump down to the audience. She could see Jimmy's friend Tara standing and putting the programme back on her seat. She was wearing a black dress over jeans and she had a black hat on. As Verity got closer, she could see that she had a green sparkling stud in her nose. 'Tara?'

Verity asked, pushing through the crowd to get to her. 'Tara, have you seen Jimmy?'

Tara looked Verity over scornfully, her eyelids heavy with dark-grey eyeshadow. Verity wondered how much Jimmy had told her about their relationship and everything that had happened, but she didn't have time to worry about it now.

'He was here,' Verity explained, not having time to be offended by Tara's sullen manner. 'I need to talk to him, but I can't see him anywhere.'

Tara sniffed and folded her arms, slumping down on to one hip. 'Yeah, well, it figures,' she said. 'He's probably done a bunk. His gran died today. He's pretty chewed up.'

'I've got to go,' Verity muttered, hurrying away down the aisle. She felt an ache of sympathy spread through her. After what Jimmy had told her up at Appleforth House about his gran and how close he was to her, she knew that her death was going to have knocked him sideways.

She had to find him. She had to find him. Now.

People were already queuing at the counter for tea and she had to edge through the crowd to get to the central aisle. Everyone she passed wanted to pat her and congratulate her. She kept batting away compliments and forcing herself not to snap.

Finally, she made it to where Scott was checking a cable up to the stage.

'Hey,' he said. 'Nice singing.'

'Have you seen Jimmy?'

'He left,' Scott said, standing up.

'When?'

'Before your solo at the beginning.'

'But –'

'Around the same time you started kissing Denny.'

352

Verity turned away, not even able to look Scott in the face. The last thing he'd seen was Denny punching Jimmy, and now he thought . . .

But Verity felt sick with a greater horror than Scott's opinion of her. Jimmy had seen her kissing Denny. He must have thought she'd *wanted* to. He had no idea of the truth. He had no idea how she really felt and now . . . now he'd gone . . . Desperation swept through her. This was all wrong. It wasn't supposed to turn out like this.

'Verity, Verity, there you are,' her mother said, hanging on to her elbow.

Verity shrugged her away. 'Not now, Mum, OK?'

'Ellen has said she'd like to do an interview at the end with you and me,' her mother bulldozed on, and Verity could see her almost glowing with anticipation. 'She wants to end the documentary on a positive note and we thought that we could talk about the future hopes for the young people in Shoresby. And future hopes? Well, I said that's you, of course! We can talk about how we've nurtured your talents and how you feel –'

Verity felt an enormous surge of energy, as she looked at her mother with unbridled disgust. 'You know what, Mum,' she interrupted. 'I'm sick of people telling me how I should feel and what I should do.'

'There's no time for histrionics, Verity. You've got to think of your future.'

Future? What would her mother know about what Verity wanted for her future? Right now, all she needed for her future sanity was to find Jimmy, but Verity couldn't tell her mother this. And even if she did tell her, she wouldn't understand. 'Oh, for God's sake, Mum!' she said.

'Don't take that tone. Ellen is an extremely useful contact. Your future in –'

'Give me a break,' Verity said, her pent-up anger threatening to choke her. She lowered her voice ominously and glared at her mother. 'It's not about my future, is it?'

'Verity?'

'All this is about *you*, Mum. It's always been about you.'

'You can't say that! That's not true –'

'If you care so much about being on TV, then do the interview on your own. I'm sure you'll find plenty to say.'

Cheryl Driver gasped.

'You see, I don't give a shit,' Verity continued, speaking very slowly. 'Do you hear me? I don't care about any of this. I'm not doing an interview with you, because it would all be lies. I hate singing in public. Haven't you noticed that yet? I hate what you've forced me into becoming.'

'What you've become? What you've become? I'll tell you what you've become. Don't think I don't know you've been sleeping with that Denny Shapland –'

Verity willed herself to remain calm. 'And how do you know that? Been reading my diary, have you?'

Cheryl Driver reddened and patted her hair. 'No,' she said, but she was tipped off balance from her tirade for a split-second. 'It doesn't matter how I know, I just know and –'

Verity had heard enough. The enormity of her mother's hypocrisy overwhelmed her. Steeling herself, she forced herself to look her mother in the eye as she said, '*I know* some of your secrets, too, Mum. So before you continue making judgements about my life . . .' Verity could feel herself shaking. Her voice caught as she struggled to continue, her words coming out as no more than a whisper. 'I suggest you sort out your own.'

Then, before her mother could say anything, Verity turned her back and walked down the central aisle,

354

trembling with a strange kind of victory, hardly able to believe that for once in her life she'd silenced her mother.

'Verity, where are you going?' It was Denny who stood in her path now.

Why couldn't she get out of here? It was as if she were trapped in some kind of hellish obstacle course. 'Please, just let me go, Denny,' she begged, trying to push round him.

'Verity,' he whispered, as he stepped towards her. 'What's got into you? I've made a big effort to be here tonight.'

'Oh! Almost as big an effort as you made to call me over the past week?'

She stared at him, revulsion and regret raging inside her. Why had she ever found him attractive? Why had she ever let herself get into the situation she had? He'd disrespected her and hurt her feelings and now she wanted to hurt him back.

'I was busy,' Denny said, shrugging. 'I told you I was on business.'

'Poor you.'

Suddenly, she could hear her voice through the loud-speaker system. Scott must have accidentally turned on her microphone, which she'd forgotten to take off. But she didn't care. She didn't care who heard what she had to say.

'Come on, babe,' Denny said, glancing nervously around him. 'Maybe we should talk.'

There was ripple of laughter through the crowd, as people started to understand what was going on. Denny grabbed the top of Verity's arm.

'Let go of me,' she said, her voice booming out. 'It's over, Denny. Do you hear me? Whatever pathetic thing we had, it's over. I don't want anything to do with you. I've been such an idiot and it's taken me until now to realise that I don't even *like* you.'

'Go, girl!' Tara shouted, whooping over the crowd.

'You can't speak to me like that!' Denny said.

'Why not?'

'Because I'm your boyfriend.'

There was another ripple of laughter and Denny spun round furiously to try to catch the culprit.

'No you're not,' Verity informed him. 'You think you're so great. But you're the most conceited, arrogant pig I've ever met. And . . . and you're crap in bed,' she added, before she ripped off the microphone from her dress and ran down the aisle of the Community Hall, pushing people out of the way.

Verity didn't care. She knew she'd overreacted. Denny wasn't the most conceited, arrogant pig she'd ever met. Just one of them. No, the real reason she didn't want Denny Shapland any more was because she wanted someone else.

She could hardly believe how easy it had been to stand up to him. It was as if all the scales had fallen from her eyes. She'd finally snapped out of whatever spell she'd been under and now, at last, she could see the truth.

At the door, she handed Scott the microphone and he unclipped the receiver box from her waistband at the back. 'Thank you,' she said. Then she opened the door and ran out into the night, to find the only person who mattered, knowing where he'd be and hoping with all her heart that it wasn't already too late.

Chapter XXII

The freezing air bit like teeth into Jimmy's knuckles and the snarl of the scrambler's engine filled his ears. Switching gear, he twisted back on the throttle, taking the stolen motorbike past thirty miles an hour. Up ahead of him the beam of the headlight picked out rocks and sticks and potholes on the path. Jimmy swerved right, then left, then right again. Almost everything outside the headlight's reach was in silhouette. The barrier of brambles and holly to his left was nothing but a mass of moonlit purple, and the three feet of eroded scrubland to his right an uneven streak of black.

But beyond that – there, where the coastal path along which he was racing gave way to thin air – everything became clear. There, an infinity of starlit sky stretched away from him. There, the moon was a perfect circle. There, a million waves winked up at the sky. And there – if he were to skid sideways now, or get thrown by a rut from his seat – he'd disappear over the edge of the cliff and his future would become clear, too. Because he'd have none. Because he'd be dead.

Two red pinpoints flicked on in the hedgerow further down the path, the eyes of some animal transfixed by the headlight. But whether it was a fox or a stoat or an owl, Jimmy didn't know and couldn't care less.

He was blitzed, half a bottle of Smirnoff Red down. The vodka bottle was zipped inside his leather jacket, pressed up against his heart. He'd picked it up from the Wreck not five minutes ago, having ditched the bike as near as he could on the path, and walked the rest of the way and kicked in the door. The Smirnoff had been inside the rusted army surplus ammo box behind the altar, stashed alongside the sealed packet of Orkney Island smoked salmon, the loaf of brown bread and the mini-bottle of Moët & Chandon champagne. The salmon had passed its sell-by date and the bread was going mouldy. Jimmy had picked up the champagne bottle and hurled it against the wall. The vodka aside – which Ryan had left behind last year – Jimmy had got it all from the supermarket two days ago, before he'd taken Verity up to the Wreck to show her the projector and tell her how he felt. He'd planned on a picnic if she'd told him she felt the same way. But she hadn't.

Slumped against the wall of the Wreck just now, Jimmy had drunk as much Smirnoff as fast as he'd been able to without making himself sick. And with each bitter swig he'd pictured Verity kissing Denny in the Memorial Hall. So much for her having been confused . . . If she'd needed time to think, she'd had it, and she'd chosen not to be with Jimmy.

Everything he had, everything he'd shown her . . . his heart . . . his mind . . . what he liked . . . who he was . . . the plain truth was that she hadn't wanted any of it.

A low branch swept out of the night at Jimmy like a pinball arm. He ducked, pressing his head flat against the petrol tank. The scrambler kicked sideways beneath him. Fighting to straighten the handlebars, he forced himself back upright. He faced front again and the wind tore into his eyes.

Drunk was better than sober. He knew that now for sure. Just as riding like this with every nerve ending in his body screaming for him to stop was better than feeling dead. Dead was how he'd felt when he'd heard the news about his gran this morning. Dead was how he'd been feeling all year since Ryan had died. Only Verity had made him feel alive. But dead was how he'd felt when he'd seen her kissing Denny.

Everything ended, didn't it? Everything you gave a damn about finished sooner or later. So what was the point of caring in the first place?

Jimmy saw his gran's face for an instant, smack here in front of him as the bike hurtled on. Her eyes were closed, her mouth clamped shut. They'd have done that, made her look nice – the nurse or Dr Kennedy, or whoever else had taken her pulse that morning only to find that she no longer had one. They'd have done it to make it easier on Jimmy and Rachel when they'd gone in to the William Bentley Hospice after having been told on the phone what had happened.

As then, here in his mind's eye now, Jimmy's gran looked serene, at rest, asleep, at peace. Those were the clichés, weren't they? That's what he was meant to believe, wasn't it? That his gran had found peace at the end? There'd been no sign of suffering. There'd been nothing but the faintest trace of a smile on her still lips, as if death – the punchline of life – had been worth the wait after all. There'd been nothing scary about her face at all.

Not like Ryan's. No one had been there to close his eyes. He'd died with them open, wild and full of fear. And no one had been there to close his mouth. It had been as wide as the night sky, and it had been screaming Jimmy's name.

Jimmy pulled back harder on the throttle, challenging the bike now, daring it to show him what it was capable of. Once more he switched gear and once more the bike jolted. The needle on the speedometer flickered past forty-five.

'I'm gonna live for ever!' he bellowed up at the heavens, as Ryan had done a year ago today.

But at the same time he knew he wasn't Ryan. He wasn't dead. Not yet. Not him. Not Jimmy Jones.

The bike's engine was screaming like a cornered animal. Brambles cracked down hard on Jimmy's hands and legs. The suspension shuddered over another series of ruts and stones. Jimmy's whole body vibrated and his teeth clattered together as though they were about to drop from his mouth like so many dice. The speedometer needle was fixed on fifty-five.

Up ahead, the path widened out into the clearing in the gorse. Jimmy knew the place – Christ, did he know it! The tractor lane branched off to the left, leading back into the heart of the Appleforth Estate. And there to the right was Lost Soul's Point.

Who's not taking any risks now? he wanted to ask Tara.

Only she wasn't here.

Better than drugs, he wanted to agree with Ryan.

Only Ryan was dead.

The path was fast running out and Jimmy aimed the bike at the cliff-side edge of the clearing, wondering how near he'd get before he slammed on the brakes, wondering whether he'd slam them on in time to stop himself from flying over the edge, wondering whether he'd slam them on at all.

'For ever!' he shouted again.

Only this time it wasn't the throttle he pulled back on but the brake. Because there, straight in front of him, was Verity Driver.

Switch to slow motion: Jimmy cutting the throttle; Jimmy tightening up on the brake; a crazy wish entering Jimmy's head that he'd taken his bike test and knew what to do; Jimmy and the bike closing in on Verity now; Verity frozen to the spot; the noise of the engine dropping off; the sound of the bike's wheels hissing and grinding; the dirt rising up; a glimpse of the moon and the stars, but the angle all wrong; the bike skidding wildly now, on past Verity, over towards the edge; but Jimmy righting himself, heaving with all his might, his stomach muscles feeling like elastic bands about to snap; the bike veering away from the cliff –

Then smash.

Everything speeded up again: the sound of branches cracking; the hiss of leaves rushing by; the heat of the engine on Jimmy's legs and the smell of burning oil.

Then stop.

Jimmy found himself surrounded by foliage, but it was a miracle: he and the bike were still upright and the scrambler's engine was still running, not deafening any more, but low and easy, idling – so much so that Jimmy could hear shouting behind him.

'Jimmy!' It was Verity.

Jimmy tried to turn round to see but his hands wouldn't relinquish their grip on the handlebars, like they'd become autonomous and didn't trust the rest of his body's judgement any more. Jimmy looked about, left and right, but all he could see was half-dead bracken and fern, and the sinewy leafless limbs of some plant he couldn't name.

'Jimmy!' Verity called again. 'Are you all right?'

Jimmy jerked at the handlebars, trying to pull the scrambler backwards; it wouldn't budge. But he was thinking more clearly now. He switched off the engine, listened to it sputter and die, and then he clambered off.

He shook himself, waiting for pain to spear him, waiting for the realisation of a broken limb or rib to drop him to his knees. But instead he felt nothing, like this was a dream, like he could dive head-first off a fifty-storey building and pick himself back up the moment he connected with the street. It occurred to him that maybe none of this mattered: action and consequence, life and death and love. Maybe it was all just in the mind and he'd been crazy to give a toss about any of it in the first place, Jimmy lifted up the scrambler's back wheel, then hauled the bike backwards out of the thicket.

Which was when reality bit back, as he became suddenly aware of Verity at his side – nothing but a familiar silhouette – reaching out to touch him. 'Don't,' he told her, ducking out of her way, turning the bike round. He didn't want her here. He didn't want to see her ever again.

'But –' she began, reaching for him again.

'But nothing!' he snapped, climbing on to the motorbike. 'Leave me alone.'

Verity stood with one foot either side of the bike's front wheel. She seized the handlebars, gripping her hands on top of his. 'You're drunk,' she told him bluntly, glaring into his eyes. 'Get off the bike.'

He shoved the bike towards her, trying to start it but getting no response. 'Move.'

Verity shoved back, standing her ground. 'You're going to have to run me over first,' she told him.

He stared at her. Her hair was tied up, but some of her curls had escaped and hung down now at her shoulders. She was still in the long black dress she'd been wearing at the concert. Her make-up was smudged like warpaint beneath her eyes. He looked down at her high-heeled shoes that were making her so tall. Everything about her – from the way she was speaking to him to the way she was dressed – struck him all of a sudden as adult and unattainable. 'Go back to your stupid concert,' he told her. 'This has got nothing to do with you.'

'What hasn't?' she demanded. 'You deciding to run yourself off the cliff?'

'I wasn't –' he started to deny. But then he stopped. What *had* he been about to do? He wasn't sure. He was confused, disconnected, light-headed, shifting between reeling drunkenness and cold sobriety.

'What you saw,' Verity said. 'What you saw between me and Denny just now . . . it wasn't anything.'

What did she think he was? Stupid? But there wasn't any point in talking this through with her. He'd made enough of a fool of himself already. And he wasn't going to let her make this all about her. He wasn't going to throw the blame at her. He'd been teetering on the edge all year. All she'd done was give him that final push.

'Fuck Denny,' he said. 'I don't give a shit about that. And fuck you, too, Verity.'

She stared at him in disbelief, but then something in her expression altered, softening into compassion. 'I know about your grandmother, Jimmy,' she said. 'Tara told me what happened and, if that's what this is all about, then we can talk. *Whatever* it's about,' she added with increased urgency, 'we can still talk.'

Again, the image of his gran flashed up before him.

'She was a good woman,' he said, staring into Verity's eyes. 'I loved her. She didn't deserve to die, not like that: on her own in the dark.'

'I know, Jimmy. I know.'

'No,' Jimmy snapped, 'you don't know shit. You don't know the first thing about her. Or me. Or this . . . Or . . .'

Suddenly he became aware of Verity's hands tightening round his. 'I want to help you, Jimmy.'

'You don't get it,' he said, shaking her off. 'You weren't there. You didn't see what happened. You didn't see what I did.' His words were coming out in a rush now, like they'd burst through a dam inside him.

You're in control, a voice inside him screamed. *No one can see inside your mind. No one can make you speak about the things you saw or tell about the things you did.*

But he wasn't in control. He couldn't keep it all inside him any more. He couldn't face it on his own. He wanted to tell it to someone. He wanted to share it, to be told that he wasn't bad. He wanted to hear that from *her*.

His breath was shallow now, coming in gasps. 'All those people at the concert . . . None of them know what really happened . . .'

'What?' Verity asked.

'The night Ryan died!' Jimmy shouted.

He got off the bike, kicked it to the ground, careless of whether it hit Verity or not. He pushed past her and walked towards the centre of the clearing. 'Here.'

Verity moved towards him, but he wasn't looking at her any more.

He was staring up the tractor lane which led away from Lost Soul's Point. 'It was an accident. Ryan didn't want to die. It was a game,' Jimmy said. 'Just a stupid fucking game.'

'But I don't understand. How can you –'

'Because I was there all right!' Jimmy voice dropped to a whimper. 'Because I was fucking well there . . .'

He pictured the stationary stolen Mazda MX-5 down the track the night Ryan had died and, even as he did, the image blurred as tears welled up in his eyes.

Ryan had boosted the Mazda convertible from the car park of the George Inn, not ten minutes after he'd shouted 'For ever!' up at the sky. He'd been wasted, but not so wasted that he hadn't managed to wire the car and drive it up to the Appleforth Estate without being spotted by the cops.

It was a beautiful car all right: alloy wheels, an aluminium interior finish and heated brown leather seats. The top was down and its titanium-coloured paintwork seemed to shimmer and flow like mercury in the light of the moon. 'What a machine,' Ryan announced as he switched off the engine and let the car roll to a halt on the farm track that led to Lost Soul's Point.

Jimmy was sitting beside him in the passenger seat. His hair was shorter then and he scratched at his head, itchy from the open-topped ride. He looked around them, nervous as hell about being in a stolen car so near to home. He'd felt sick every yard of the journey up here from the town, paranoid about getting busted, terrified at how quickly his future (his way out of the flat and this tiny corner of the world, his film school ambitions, the rewards of the work he'd started putting in at school) might be snatched from him. His stomach was a yo-yo. He wanted to throw up. He couldn't deal with this shit any more. Driving around wasted in other people's cars no longer gave him a buzz. But Ryan was his best friend and he didn't want to let him down.

Almost as if he'd sensed Jimmy's turmoil, Ryan leant towards him, his breath heavy with booze fumes. He studied Jimmy through olive-black eyes. 'I think we've earned ourselves a joint,' he said, turning the Eminem CD down so low that it was barely audible. 'Shall I do the honours?' Without waiting for Jimmy to answer, Ryan pulled his gear from his jeans pocket and started to skin up.

The silence that followed was almost overwhelming for Jimmy. He tilted his head back and stared up at the night sky, breathing out with relief at the lack of any sound of pursuit. But even though the danger had gone, he remained drunk and the world felt unsteady beneath him, and the sensation of seasickness wouldn't go away. 'Hey, Ryan?' he asked, forcing himself to talk, forcing himself out of the sickly confines of his skull. 'Do you remember that time we swam out on to that motor boat moored out in the middle of the bay?'

'Kevin Watson's cruiser . . .' There was the click and whirr of a cigarette lighter being struck. 'Shit, yeah,' Ryan said with a chuckle. 'How old were we? Eleven and twelve? Thirteen tops? Bloody crazy, that was.'

'I was eleven,' Jimmy said, locating the Plough just before an ominous black cloud extinguished its seven-starred outline point by point.

'Yeah, but you swam as strong as if you were way older, didn't you? We both did.'

'We had to,' Jimmy reminded him. 'Otherwise we'd have drowned. It must have been half a mile out to that boat and half a mile back. And it was freezing. If we hadn't done it so fast, we would have seized up and that would have been the end of it. They'd have found us washed up on the shore, bloated and chewed on and dead.'

Ryan snorted with laughter. 'Christ, you've got some imagination, Jimmy. I'd have got you back safe and sound, you needn't have worried about that.'

Jimmy didn't comment, knowing that Ryan meant what he said, knowing that he'd risk his life for Jimmy, the same way Jimmy would risk his life for him. He felt Ryan nudge him in the ribs and looked across at him and accepted the spliff. Ryan's black jeans were ripped over his right knee and his left nostril was caked with freshly dried blood from where he'd slipped and fallen flat on his face, after chasing Tara up and down the street outside the George, before she'd had to go home. His bright-orange top was streaked with mud and the peak of his white Nike baseball cap drooped low over his brow, soaked from where it had landed in a puddle.

'What made you think about that?' Ryan asked, stroking his thumb thoughtfully down his left sideburn, which he'd trimmed long and triangular, like a knife.

'Seasickness.'

'What?'

There was the sound of thunder to the east, close and loud.

'Never mind,' Jimmy said.

Jimmy pictured him and Ryan climbing up the boat's anchor chain like a couple of skinny, exhausted rats. It had been a bright March day and seagulls had whirled above them in the white-blue sky, screaming like famished babies. Jimmy and Ryan had flopped down on to the pleasure boat's deck in their soaking boxer shorts, and had stared back at the beach. In the distance, Jimmy remembered seeing Carl, waving at them as he'd guarded their clothes. Carl had been their other great mate back then, but he'd moved with his family to London later that year and had never come back.

'We talked about the future,' Jimmy said, handing the spliff back to Ryan. 'There on the boat, while we were catching our breath before swimming back to shore. We talked about what we'd be doing by the time we reached the age we are now.' A spit of rain splashed off Jimmy's nose.

'I don't remember,' Ryan said. 'It was a long time ago.'

'I said that I wanted to have a boat of my own. I told you about what my dad had told me, about sailing off to see the world. I told you that if I could get myself a boat by the time I left school, then my dad would be happy to spend time with me, and I could sail away with him and my gran and we'd never have to worry about anything again.'

'And what did I say?'

'You said that you wanted a big house on a hill and a job in a city, but only so long as you could still have fun.'

'Sounds good to me,' Ryan said.

Jimmy cut the subtle approach. 'But don't you get it, Ryan?' he said. 'You never talk about the house or the job or the city any more. All you care about is the *fun*.'

'Stop being so bloody serious.'

All Jimmy wanted was to tell Ryan the truth: that he didn't find this *fun* any longer. He was trying to tell him that he'd grown up this last year and he wanted *out*, out of the car and out of this way of life. He was trying to tell him that he wanted them both to walk back into town together. He was trying to remind Ryan of the people they'd once hoped to be. 'I was just –'

But Ryan didn't want to know. 'Well, just don't, OK?' he said. 'I don't need anyone lecturing me. Ambitions change, Jimmy. You get older and then you realise that you're not going to get everything you want just because you want it. So you make the most of what you can have, OK? And don't go telling me it's any fucking different, because it's not.'

'But what if I want more?' Jimmy protested.

Ryan shrugged. 'I don't know, Jimmy. Maybe you need to work that out for yourself.' Ryan hit the eject button on the state-of-the-art sound system. 'Or maybe you just don't know what fun is, eh?'

'Maybe,' Jimmy said, because maybe Ryan was right. Maybe Jimmy was just stoned and he wouldn't care about any of this in the morning. Maybe fun was all there really was after all.

'So enough pretending,' Ryan went on, taking the Eminem CD and spinning it away like a frisbee into the bushes. 'Let's get ourselves some kicks for real.'

'Like what?' Jimmy asked, accepting the spliff and taking a deep drag.

'Chicken,' Ryan said, gazing along the track towards Lost Soul's Point and starting the car. 'I'll get us lined up nice and straight, and then I'll close my eyes and keep on accelerating,' he explained. 'And you – you shout stop. That's your job. And when you do, I'll slam on the brakes and we'll see how close we end up to the edge of the cliff. Can I trust you, Jimmy? Can I trust you to do that?'

Jimmy chucked the spliff away. He was stoned all right, but not *that* stoned. 'No,' he told Ryan, 'what you can do is forget it.'

'Too late,' Ryan said, slipping the car into first and putting his foot down.

The car leapt forward with such force that it pinned Jimmy back in his seat. 'Stop it!' he shouted above the engine, as Ryan slipped past second into third.

'That's your job!' Ryan shouted back with a laugh.

Already the speedometer was up past fifty. Already they were closing in on the clearing before the land dropped off into space. Already – Jimmy shifted sideways, glancing into the rear-view mirror – Ryan was shutting his eyes, a manic grin locked on to his face.

'Stop!' Jimmy shouted. Because this was too big a kick for him already. Because he was drunk and stoned, and so was Ryan and he didn't trust either of their reactions.

But Ryan didn't stop, because – Jimmy suddenly realised – he hadn't actually shouted at all. He'd been too frightened to shout. The word had caught in his throat. He'd been twisting sideways instead, away from Ryan, clinging on to the passenger door. He glanced forwards. They were about to enter the clearing.

'Stop!'

And this time the word *did* come out and this time – thank Christ! – Ryan did react. His eyes flicked open as they burst into the clearing. Emergency stop: he yanked on the handbrake. But they were going too fast and all he succeeded in doing was throwing the car into a vicious spin.

'Oh, Jesus!' Jimmy heard Ryan cry out.

Jimmy whimpered. They were still rushing towards the cliff. They weren't going to stop in time. The car's momentum was dragging them on. The ground was too wet. The tyres weren't biting. Under ten miles an hour now, but less than twenty yards to go. They were going over the edge. Jimmy knew it as fact.

Jimmy was on his knees. The night sky was spinning above him. Lightning flashed across it, splitting the darkness in two. He was on his feet now. He was crouched on the leather seat. The car spun on. Jimmy jumped, over the passenger door. The back of the car clipped him as he landed, knocking him on to his hands and knees. He looked up just in time to see Ryan staring at him through the windscreen as the car swung round one final time. Ryan's mouth was wide open. Jimmy's best friend was screaming his name.

And then the impossible happened: as the rain hissed down in a sudden torrent, Ryan and the car reached the edge of the cliff and were gone.

Chapter XXIII

The door creaking in the wind woke Verity. She came to abruptly, her intake of breath laced with cold fear at her unfamiliar surroundings, before she remembered what had happened and where she was. Quietly she exhaled, her mind alert and fresh. She was shivering, so cold that she couldn't feel her feet. Her body was stiff and sore from where she'd been lying on the damp mattress on the floor of the chapel. Her eyes darted around the solid dark objects in the shadows, but still she didn't move.

Jimmy was curled up beside her. His arm was heavy across her waist. She looked at his face, just inches away from hers. He looked so cute, she thought, longing to trace the line of his dark eyebrow. But she didn't want to wake him yet. She could see the deep shadows under his eyes and knew he would still be exhausted.

Now, as she stared at him, she realised that there were so many things about him that she wanted to look at. She'd never noticed before that he had patches of his jaw where the hair didn't grow. There his skin was pink and flushed, and she thought how sexy he was.

She could see his hand was cut and grazed, and he held it near to his face, and immediately she wanted to kiss it. The events of last night slowly came to her and her heart ached for Jimmy. The last thing she remembered, after she'd brought him back here, was holding him as he'd sobbed. They must have fallen asleep where they'd been sitting.

Now Verity could feel his warm, steady breath on her

face, as they lay side by side, their legs tangled together beneath Jimmy's leather jacket, and she was pleased that they'd formed a heart-shaped embrace in their sleep. Even though they were both fully clothed, she didn't want to break the seal of their bodies.

She turned her head a fraction towards the door. She'd wedged it shut with a packing crate last night, but she could see a band of silver daylight around the edge. So it was morning, she thought, and no one in the world apart from Jimmy knew where she was. She smiled to herself.

Quietly, a centimetre at a time, Verity slowly eased herself away from him. Stealthily she stretched, slowly grinding her neck around to crunch out the tension at the back. Her arms clicked as she circled them. She stopped, careful not to make any noise that might wake Jimmy. Carefully she eased off her shoes and picked them up, along with the half-empty vodka bottle. Tiptoeing through the chapel, she moved the packing crate silently and eased open the door just enough for her to slip through.

Outside, in the pink dawn, the grey clouds looked like leaping dolphins on the silver horizon. Verity took a deep breath, stunned by the magnificence of the view, her eyes narrowing at the brightness of the high undulating sea. She shivered, half with cold, half with exhilaration. She was still in her concert dress, but the full skirt was muddy and her tights were laddered. Her hair clips had fallen out in the night and her hair hung round her neck in messy curls, but she didn't care.

Above, the gulls soared in the thermals, laughing to each other, and Verity's eyes watered at the sharp saltiness of the air. Easing on her shoes, she tipped out the remaining vodka into the brambles, then made a guess as to the direction of Appleforth House and set off in search of some water.

She knew there was a tap in the kitchen garden, near where she'd filmed the scenes in the arbour. She quickly took the path round the side of the house and, even though it was Sunday, she kept near to the wall, careful to stay out of sight of any workmen who might be about. She didn't want anything to spoil this morning.

As she glanced at the house, she noticed that several of the windows that had been boarded up now had new glass and fancy curtains. It made the house look alive and Verity thought how beautiful it looked.

As she entered the kitchen garden and quickly walked up the path, she felt as if she, too, was opening herself fully to the world for the first time. It was almost as if she'd been standing in a dusty corridor inside herself and now she was flinging open the doors of her personality, discovering that she could be entirely new. As the arbour came into view, she felt filled with light.

She stopped and looked at the spot where Jimmy had kissed her. 'It was real,' she said aloud, claiming the memory for the first time, without shame or guilt. 'It was real.' Then she smiled and closed her eyes, recapturing the sensation of that gentle kiss and all she wanted was to be back near Jimmy.

He stirred as she came back in with the water, her breath quick from where she'd run back from the house. 'Here,' she whispered, kneeling down and offering him the bottle.

Seeing the label, he groaned.

'It's water, silly.' She laughed.

Jimmy took the bottle gratefully. Verity stood and, jumping up, grabbed a corner of the rag in one of the slit holes in the wall. As it finally came away in her hand, a shaft of dusty light angled down into the chapel and pulled everything into light-grey focus.

Jimmy blinked and rubbed his eyes. 'What time is it?' he croaked.

'Don't care,' Verity said with a shrug, before sitting down next to him. 'The sun's coming up, if that's any help.'

Jimmy took a deep breath and sighed. There was a long moment of silence between them. Verity sat down next to him and hugged her knees. The scratch of the glass bottle on the stone floor echoed as Jimmy put it down.

'I told you about Ryan, didn't I?'

Verity reached out and touched Jimmy's face for a moment.

'Shit,' Jimmy said, pressing his thumbs into the corners of his eyes.

'Don't say that.' Verity pulled his hand down and forced him to look at her. 'You've nothing to be ashamed about. It's OK.'

'Is it? You don't hate me?'

'Of course I don't! It was an accident! It wasn't your fault.' Verity extended her hand and put it on Jimmy's chest. It felt warm. 'I can't believe you've carried it around all this time.'

Jimmy slowly took her hand. He rested it on his scratched red palm and examined her pale fingers for a long moment. 'What do you think I should do?' he asked.

'You're going to have to tell Ryan's parents, I guess. Let them have some peace. You can't let them carry on thinking he killed himself when he didn't.'

Jimmy looked back down at Verity's fingers. Verity had never wanted to hug someone as much. 'It's funny,' he said. 'All year since he died, I've been frightened about getting caught for being there. Like everyone would blame me. Or the police would put me away.'

'Why's that funny?'

'Just because it doesn't seem frightening any more. Not

374

now I've told you.' Jimmy squeezed the top of her index finger. 'Why are you helping me?' he asked. 'You don't have to, you know.'

'I want to.' She gripped his hand so that he winced. 'Sorry,' she said, withdrawing and smoothing back her hair from her face. 'You didn't give me a chance to explain last night.'

'Explain what?'

Verity exhaled and took a deep breath. 'It seems ridiculous now . . .'

'No, go on,' Jimmy urged.

'I finished it with Denny. I mean . . .' Verity shook her head, exasperated at herself. She felt so foolish trying to explain this to Jimmy, but after what he'd confessed last night, she had to get it off her chest. It was horrible to soil these precious moments with Denny's name, but she felt compelled to go on. 'Last night at the concert . . . when I realised you'd gone . . . when I realised what you'd seen, I was desperate . . .'

Jimmy didn't say anything.

'It was as if nothing about that stupid concert made sense. Denny made the whole thing so much worse and I just sort of . . . lost it. I dumped him. In front of everyone. Scott put the whole thing on loudspeaker,' Verity said, and at last Jimmy started to smile. 'I told Denny that I didn't even like him and that he was crap in bed.'

Jimmy's smile faded and he let her hand go.

Verity stood up. She had to make him understand. 'He *was* crap in bed. Worse,' she said. 'It was awful, Jimmy. I hated every second of it. I shouldn't have done it, but I thought it would make everything OK. I was so hung up on some stupid ideal, making Denny into something he could never be –' Verity's voice caught as she looked at the wall

375

where Jimmy had projected her face and shown her how she looked to him. 'What you did . . . what you did was so beautiful. You asked me to make a choice, but you see . . . I'd already made the wrong one. I'm so, so sorry –'

Jimmy stood up. He put his arms round her and stroked her hair. Now, as he supported her, she realised just how much she'd been alone. She'd felt so sad and upset about Denny, but she'd had no one to share her grief with until this moment. But trusting Jimmy made it easy to let it go. It didn't matter any more. Nothing mattered. Only that Jimmy was holding her. She felt his body against hers and its gentle warmth seemed to fill her with strength.

Eventually, Jimmy pulled back and held her face. He smiled. 'If it makes you feel any better, that was his bike I was on last night.'

'The one we ditched in the undergrowth?' Verity remembered how she'd hauled the bike to the brambles, after Jimmy had told her about Ryan. She remembered now how she'd told him to leave it, and had put her arms round him, walking back in silence to the chapel, as Jimmy had started to cry.

'The very same.'

Verity laughed. 'Good. I'm sorry, Jimmy,' she said again. 'About us. I should have realised sooner.'

'It doesn't matter. That was yesterday.'

'What about today?' she asked.

'Today. Hm. Today, we have to clear this place out before Ned's guys get here.'

'Are you sad?' she asked.

He shook his head and looked around. 'No, not really. Not any more. I thought I would be.' Jimmy shrugged and smiled at Verity. 'But now I think it's time to move on.'

*

Jimmy talked about all the times he'd spent in the chapel with Ryan, as Verity helped him dismantle their hang-out. 'He was a daredevil,' he said, laughing, and Verity couldn't help smiling too.

'Better than not having the guts to do anything,' Verity said, standing back to survey their work. With all the rags out of the slits in the walls, she could see how beautiful the chapel must have been once. It was filled with shafts of dusty sunlight and the sound of seagulls.

'He scared me, too, though,' Jimmy said, his face serious.

'How do you mean?'

Jimmy fell silent. 'You know, sometimes it's been a relief that he hasn't been here.' Jimmy seemed to swallow hard. 'Is that dreadful?'

'No,' Verity said, and she thought about her mother and Denny, too. 'You can't live by other people's expectations, whether you love them or not.'

'He wanted me to be like him, but I wasn't.'

Verity shrugged. 'Perhaps you had more to lose.'

Jimmy shook his head. 'I don't know. I miss him. But then, I can't help feeling that if he was here, then you . . .'

He didn't say 'wouldn't be', but Verity knew what he meant all the same. She nodded and, after a while, he bent over and continued sweeping the floor with two bits of cardboard.

Verity glanced at him. In profile, she could see how slim and agile he looked. There was something so boyish about his face and she could see how he was going to look better and better as he got older. She realised now, as she looked at Jimmy, that she loved his face. She loved the variety of his quirky expressions – how he looked when he concentrated or when he was bored, when he was happy or sad, or how he looked now as he worked.

But it was more than his looks that intrigued her. She loved the way he thought, how he expressed himself and how, when she was with him, she didn't have to censure anything she said. She'd spent so long withholding information from her mother and working out how to sound sophisticated in front of Denny that she hadn't realised the joy of being able to speak freely. Just being with Jimmy made her feel as if there was so much to talk about and to discuss. Not like the stupid conversations she'd had with Denny about his shop and where he wanted to surf, but about real things that affected them both.

Now, as she slowly folded up the poster of Che Guevara, she thought about what Jimmy had said about if Ryan had still been around. She couldn't help feeling that unless she'd defied her mother and taken responsibility for herself, she wouldn't be here either. She thought back to the concert and the fleeting look of fear in her mother's eyes as Verity had confronted her. How ironic, Verity thought, that she was famous for singing and for having a big voice, when she'd only really found her voice last night.

'My mother's been having an affair!' She laughed, astonished at her outburst.

Jimmy stood up straight, dropping the cardboard and wiping his hands on an old cloth. His eyebrows drew together with concern. 'Your mother?'

'I know. Who'd have thought it?' Verity tried to sound flippant, but she still felt wobbly saying the words.

'How long have you known?' Jimmy asked.

'About a year. I haven't been able to tell anyone,' she admitted. 'And I hate secrets.'

'Everyone has secrets. They're part of life.'

'Well, I don't want to have them.'

'Then we won't.'

He said it so simply, as if it were a fact. And she knew that at that moment it was true.

There was a pause as Verity put the poster down. 'Do you think I should tell my dad?'

'Do you?'

'No,' Verity said.

Jimmy shrugged and smiled kindly. 'Well, then.'

Verity was silent.

'Everyone has their own love lives. You can never understand someone else's.'

'I guess not.'

'And you can't interfere, because you can't ever know all the facts. Maybe your dad knows already. Maybe they have some sort of understanding. You never know.'

Verity leant down, picked up a frisbee from the floor and dusted it off. Jimmy was bending down picking up a pile of newspapers. Feeling mischievous she threw the frisbee at his bum.

'Hey!' he exclaimed as it hit him. Jimmy's blue eyes were shining as he lined up the frisbee at her. But then, as she dared him to throw it, he suddenly discarded the frisbee with a growl and started to chase her. Verity yelled, jumping out of his way, as Jimmy darted after her. They chased each other all around the chapel, as Verity dodged out of the way, her stomach aching with laughter and breathless exertion. She scrambled up on to the altar.

'Not fair,' Jimmy panted. 'That's sacrilegious.'

Verity surrendered, leaning over to put her hands on Jimmy's shoulders. He put his hands on her waist and she jumped down on to the wooden floor. For a split-second, as he held her in mid-air and she stared down at his smiling face in the dusty sunlight, she was filled with happiness. Then she landed and the heel of her shoe broke through the floorboard. With a yelp, she fell away from him.

'Are you OK?' Jimmy asked, crouching down to help.

As Verity struggled with the heel of the shoe, she could see that there was a space below the rotten floorboard. There was something beneath it, just a few inches away. 'Look,' she said, their chase forgotten as she showed Jimmy the floorboard. 'I think there's something under there.'

Jimmy knelt down and put his hand into the hole. 'I've got it,' he said, his eyes connecting with Verity's as he pulled out a folded letter.

Verity got up hastily, brushing her dress down. Jimmy stood close, as he laid out the sealed letter on the altar. Verity blew away a small cloud of dust from the paper. It was brittle, with a brown wax seal keeping it closed. The imprint of a coat of arms was pressed into the wax. 'I wonder what it is?' she said, running her fingers over the seal. 'Shall we open it?'

Jimmy looked at her, then carefully eased up the seal. It made a crackling sound as it opened. Jimmy's eyes were wide with anticipation as he looked at Verity and back to the letter. Together they carefully smoothed it out. Dense ink handwriting covered the paper.

'Wow,' Jimmy said, his hand brushing lightly over the writing. 'We should show this to Ellen.'

'What do you think it is?'

'I don't know.' Jimmy traced his forefinger along the first line of writing.

Verity leant over, following his finger, but she couldn't read the words. All she could feel was Jimmy's face close to hers. She put her hand over his.

For a long moment neither of them moved, as they both watched their fingers clasped together on the dry parchment.

'I know they were filming,' she whispered. 'But our kiss was real. It was to me.'

Jimmy stayed still, their hands bathed in sunlight over the altar, and she felt a profound connection with him. As if some sort of unspoken promise had been made between them.

They both jumped as the door opened, springing apart as Ned came in.

'Morning,' he said, looking at them both. 'I didn't expect to find you here.'

'We've nearly finished clearing everything out,' Jimmy said, hastily leaving Verity and walking round the altar.

'Don't worry. There's no hurry.' Ned smiled, as a dog wandered in behind him and started manically sniffing along the bottom of the wall. 'Don't mind Wobbles,' he said.

'We found something,' Verity said, holding up the letter.

'Oh?' Ned enquired, coming forward.

'Under the floorboard.'

Ned rolled the paper out on the altar. 'Well, well, well,' he said, drawing away and staring at it. 'Like father, like daughter.'

'What?' Jimmy asked.

'Nothing,' Ned answered. 'Just that the Walpoles seem to have a habit of hiding stuff for us to find.'

'Is it important?' Verity asked.

Ned looked at her over the top of his glasses and then back down at the paper. 'I don't know yet. I'll have to take a closer look.'

'Yes, well, we'll be off now,' Jimmy said.

'Hm?' Ned looked up, clearly distracted.

'I've cleared all the stuff outside,' Jimmy said, shrugging on his jacket. 'I've decided I don't want any of it after all.'

Ned smiled. 'OK. I'll get the boys to come and put it in the skip.'

Outside, the sun had risen and the sky was now a clear bright blue. Verity looked at the pile of belongings by the door. The old mattress was slumped against the wall, as if surveying the view. Bottles, an old wheel, a bin bag of rubbish and old clothes were piled high next to it. 'You don't want any of it?' she asked Jimmy.

'It's all memories. I think I'll feel better if it's gone.'

'Let's keep the kite.' Verity said, picking it up.

'It's yours.'

Verity held the kite as they walked away.

'What now?' she asked after a while, smiling shyly at him. She meant 'about us', but she didn't want to say it, in case it ruined the moment.

But Jimmy took her literally. 'I've got gran's funeral to arrange with Rachel, and I guess I'll go and see Ryan's mum and dad. If they want to go to the police, then that's up to them.' Verity took his hand and Jimmy looked down at her, his eyes bluer than ever. 'And what about us?' he asked, his voice soft, and she loved him for mentioning the one thing that was on her mind.

Verity smiled and shrugged. 'I don't know. I suppose you could ask me out. Isn't that what people normally do?'

'OK,' Jimmy said, then he laughed.

'What's so funny?'

Jimmy shook his head, but he was still smiling. 'OK. Verity Driver, will you go out with me?'

'Yes, I will,' she said decisively. 'That wasn't so difficult, was it?' she asked, putting her arm round Jimmy.

'You have no idea,' he said, kissing the top of her head, as they walked down the path together.

Chapter XXIV

Ned stood in the doorway of the chapel, watching the two of them walking away from him until they disappeared through a gap in the bushes. He wondered if he should be feeling guilty for turfing them out like this, but was quick to dismiss the thought. They looked happy enough and besides, that's what growing up was all about, wasn't it, letting go of your past and moving on? Everyone had to do it sooner or later. That was life. He glanced down at the pile of junk they'd dumped up against the wall: broken CDs, empty bottles, torn posters and – bizarrely, he observed – an unopened packet of Orkney Island smoked salmon. Unsurprisingly, there wasn't anything of any worth.

He weighed the letter they'd given him in his hand. He'd seen the date at the top, the day, the month and the year: all of them matching the week Appleforth House had been burnt down. And he'd seen the signature, too – undoubtedly that of Alexander Walpole.

He remembered Ellen quoting him the last words Caroline Walpole had written in her secret diary. He remembered how her eyes had shone with interest, and how she'd spoken of Caroline as someone who'd been truly alive and not simply lived. She'd be thrilled by this latest discovery as well, Ned knew. And even though it was too late in the house's restoration for any new historical evidence to be of any practical use, Ned felt a flame of anticipation flicker inside him. It was as though Ellen's own enthusiasm over the human story behind the house had rubbed off on him. Unfurling the letter, he wondered if its contents would finally explain why Alexander Walpole had taken his own life and burnt down his beautiful home.

But before he'd read so much as a word, he was distracted by a sudden snapping noise. Careful not to crease it, he slid the letter safely into his jacket pocket and stepped back inside the chapel. The cause of the noise was immediately apparent. Wobbles was hurling himself up against a marble plaque on the wall, attempting to devour a large spider, which clung tight to its web just beyond his reach. Ned walked over and pulled the dog firmly out of the way before he injured himself. Leaning forward and adjusting his glasses, Ned then drew the cobweb clear of the plaque and let it drift to the floor by his side. He traced his fingers across the plaque's neatly engraved lettering. Each line bore the name of one of the people buried here, as well as their dates of birth and death.

There were only nine names here, which made sense to Ned, since the chapel had been built in 1804 (if the mark he'd noticed on the lintel above the door was to be believed) and the house had been destroyed by Alexander Walpole in 1871. The last three members of the Appleforth family were listed first, but then the name of the estate's founding family halted, its male lineage at an end, and the Walpole branch of the family took over. The last name on the plaque was that of Caroline Walpole, although Ned knew full well that her body had never been found, and any implication of its being here had been little more than wishful thinking on the engraver's behalf – or that of his likely employer, Alexander Walpole, at any rate.

Alexander Walpole's name wasn't listed here. Given the manner of his demise, this came as no surprise to Ned. Alexander's youngest daughter and heiress, Henrietta, had been in no fit state to oversee such a memorial. Alexander had sent Henrietta into the town along with the servants the night he'd set fire to Appleforth House, and the news of her father's death had so traumatised the fifteen-year-old girl that she'd never set foot on the family estate again, emigrating almost immediately to America to be with her uncle and temporary guardian.

But Ned knew of a further reason – other than trauma – which accounted for Henrietta's willingness at the time to abandon what little had remained of her family home: guilt. Jonathan Arthur (who was Henrietta's grandson, as well as being Ned's employer) had shown Ned a letter, which explained how it was that Alexander had been able to intercept Caroline's lover, Leon Jacobson, and pay him off. Caroline, so the letter detailed, had confided in her younger sister, Henrietta, about her plans to elope. But Henrietta, rather than keeping this secret, had been so frightened of what might have become of Caroline once she left the family home that she'd told her father everything. She'd gone on, of course, to regret this decision, knowing that, if she'd only kept quiet, both her sister and her father might have gone on to live long and happy lives.

'Come on, you,' Ned told Wobbles, eager now to discover if Alexander Walpole had left a different version of events in his letter. He led the dog outside into the stark early-morning sunshine. Across the clearing he spotted a huge grey tree stump, black as tar around the top from where it must have been struck by lightening. He slipped Wobbles's lead on before the dog had had time to think about pulling a vanishing act, then walked over to the trunk and sat down. The instant Ned had finished knotting the dog's lead over a protruding shard of burnt bark, Wobbles started to whine.

'All right, all right,' Ned said impatiently, digging deep

into his coat pocket and feeling his way through the sweet wrappers, tiddlywinks counters, playing cards, lollypop sticks and other juvenile detritus that had accumulated in there for no reason other than he was a dad, until he finally located what he was after. 'This is a bribe,' he told Wobbles as he unwrapped the biscuit. 'I'll give you a chocolate biscuit if you give me some peace and quiet. Do we have a deal?'

Wobbles stared unblinkingly at the biscuit in Ned's hand.

'I'll take that as a yes,' Ned said, dropping the biscuit and watching Wobbles snap it out of the air and swallow it without even tasting it.

Ned took the letter Jimmy and Verity had found from his other pocket and rested it on his lap. Here, in the daylight, repositioning the letter's broken wax seal so that it became whole again, he saw that the initials stamped into it – *A. S. W.* – were indeed Alexander Walpole's, as were the remains of his signet ring's design beneath them, which consisted of the Walpole family crest. There was no doubt in Ned's mind, then: the letter was genuine.

He began to read and, as he did so, his eyes grew wider with every second that passed.

'Thank you, Ned. I've got a meeting in Chicago on Tuesday, but I'll be on the next available flight after that.' The phone went dead. Jonathan Arthur wasn't one for protracted goodbyes. Nor was he one for overt shows of emotion, which left Ned clueless as to how he felt about what Ned had just told him. And what he'd just told him was this: Jonathan Arthur's great-grandfather, Alexander Walpole, had committed not only arson and suicide, but murder as well.

Ned stared out of the Portakabin window at the east wing

of Appleforth House. Its sandblasted stone looked as ancient and immovable as the pyramids. It was impossible to imagine it on fire, with flames leaping outwards from its windows and its timbers collapsing into ash. But that's what Alexander Walpole had been the catalyst of. With one great and deliberate effort of will, he'd brought that roof crashing down on his own head – and, finally, Ned knew why. The letter on the desk before him, which he'd just read aloud to his boss, was a confession. Alexander Walpole had written it the night before he'd burnt himself to death, and he'd then hidden it from all but the eyes of God in the cliff-side family chapel. It had been his mortal explanation for what he'd thought he would have to answer for in eternity.

In contrast, what he'd told the earthly authorities (in the shape of the local magistrate) concerning the circumstances surrounding his daughter's death had been a lie.

What had actually happened had been that, on hearing from Henrietta of Caroline's plan to elope with Leon Jacobson, Alexander Walpole had gone to the clifftop rendezvous to intercept them. Walpole hadn't succeeded in paying Jacobson off, as he'd later told the magistrate. Rather, he'd discovered Jacobson already with his daughter at the clifftop, about to leave. He'd told them the game was up, but they'd refused to obey him, remaining adamant about their love for one another and their intention to marry. Alexander Walpole had then flown into a rage, first pistol-whipping his secretary, then shooting him dead when he'd still refused to yield.

That was why Caroline Walpole had thrown herself off the part of the cliff which later became known as Lost Soul's Point: *not* because she had been betrayed by her lover; and *not* because, as Ned had thought, of her naïve notions concerning love. Caroline Walpole had thrown herself off

Lost Soul's Point because she'd watched her father shoot her lover dead and she had chosen to die with him.

The remainder of Alexander Walpole's confession and the reason Ned (with Jonathan Arthur's complete agreement) was about to call the police gave the details of where Leon Jacobson's body lay.

Walpole had been too frightened to risk simply throwing the body off the cliff, in case it had washed ashore and the bullet wound had been identified. Instead, he'd buried Jacobson along with his belongings (already in the leather travelling case Leon had planned on taking with him). Walpole had then returned to Appleforth House and concocted the story concerning Jacobson's betrayal, so that no questions about his actual whereabouts would ever be asked.

Ned folded the letter closed. So there it was. He'd been wrong about Caroline Walpole all this time, as *everybody* had been wrong about her. She hadn't been a victim of her belief in love so much as a victim of her father's belief in hate. Something about this realisation filled Ned with confusion. Ellen had been right to say there'd been nobility as well as stupidity to Caroline's death. But the real stupidity had been her father's, in his determination to tear her and her lover apart. That was the true evil at the heart of the story. And that was its moral, too: passion was rare; love even more so; and neither should ever be wasted or destroyed.

He heard the sound of the Portakabin door clicking open behind him. 'Ned?'

Ned turned in his chair and saw Debs standing in the open door. Her auburn hair was tied up, held in place with a black lacquered Japanese comb. She wore sharply creased fawn trousers, an ironed black shirt and black shoes. But all her immaculate appearance served to do was to highlight the look of concern on her face.

'Where's Clara?' Ned asked, suddenly fearful of the power of the nearby cliffs.

'Outside with Scott.' Debs stepped inside and closed the door behind her. She stared at him awkwardly.

'What is it?' he asked.

'There's something I need to say to you.' Debs studied her fingernails. 'This isn't going to be easy for me to say, Ned . . .'

'Which means it won't be easy for me to hear, I suppose?' Ned guessed.

'You lied to her, didn't you?'

'Who?'

'Ellen Morris. You lied to her about how Mary died. You told her it was because of a brain haemorrhage.'

That afternoon in the Hope and Anchor when he'd spoken to Ellen about Mary . . . Two weeks had gone by and he remembered it now as though only seconds had passed. He remembered everything they'd spoken of, every expression on her face. He even remembered the way she'd sipped at her drink. 'A brain disease, actually,' he said, keeping his voice deliberately flat and emotionless, because he wasn't about to go losing control, not here in front of Debs. 'I was never any more specific than that.'

Debs's brow creased into a frown. 'A brain disease, then . . .'

'What of it?'

'Why?' she asked.

'Why did I choose brain disease and not, say, cancer, or a road accident?' he asked, disingenuous now, angry over having been put on the spot.

But Debs wasn't being drawn. 'No,' she said, 'I mean why lie at all?'

'I just did,' Ned answered.

Turning round, he pressed the space bar on his laptop, which had been idling on sleep mode since he'd forgotten to shut it down on Friday afternoon when he'd slipped off into town for a drink. The blue sky screensaver disintegrated, revealing the spreadsheet he'd been working on last. He glanced back at Debs, who hadn't moved a muscle. 'If there's nothing else,' he said, 'there's some accounting I need to be getting on with . . .'

'I don't believe you *just did* anything,' she said, a note of challenge in her voice, which he'd only ever heard her use with Clara.

He swivelled fully round in his chair to face her. 'What?'

'You lied to protect yourself.'

Ned bristled. 'Oh, really' he began, 'and since when did –'

'Ellen's not a kid, Ned,' she interrupted. 'Not like Clara. She's not someone you need to tell fairy tales and fibs to because they're too young to be able to understand the truth.'

'I don't see what Clara's got to do with any of –'

But Debs wasn't listening. 'So you can't have been lying to Ellen for Ellen's sake,' she reasoned. 'You can't have been doing it to protect her. Which means you can only have been doing it to protect yourself.'

How dare she try to browbeat him like this, over something that was essentially none of her damn business? 'What is this?' he demanded. 'Let me guess: you've been taking a correspondence course in armchair psychology, right? Because that's what it sounds like to me: a load of old –'

Again, she cut him off. 'You don't need to go on a course to see what's there right in front of your eyes,' she said. 'And do you know what I've seen every day since I started working for you three years ago? I've seen you pushing people away, Ned, anybody who tries to find out anything

390

about you and what makes you tick. You do everything you can to put them off the scent. You keep them out. You've done it to Ellen. You do it to everyone.'

'Everyone?' Ned scoffed. 'There is no everyone. None of what you're saying makes any sense. Everyone, who?'

'Exactly, Ned. That's the point. The reason there's no everyone in your life is because you've already locked them out. I found six wedding invitations in the kitchen table drawer. Six, Ned . . .' She slowly shook her head. 'That's six couples whose friendship you've rejected. And then there's your parents. You never call them, do you? And whenever they call you, you answer their questions like a robot and don't ask any in return. And it's me who always has to drive Clara over to see Mary's parents and me who has to pick her up afterwards – because you act as if they don't even exist.' Debs's eyes didn't falter from his for so much as a second. 'It's like there's this huge part of your life that you won't let go of and won't show anyone, Ned . . . But don't you get it? It's not even life, it's death . . .'

Ned knew he should be shouting at her. He should be telling her she was wrong, *proving* to her just how wrong . . . And yet . . . and yet he said nothing, because he'd run out of words to defend himself with.

'I'm not doing this to hurt you, Ned,' she then said, the harshness now gone from her voice. 'I'm doing this because I care. You're thirty-six years old. Not ninety-six. I see you with Clara. I see how much love you've got to give. You're a wonderful man, Ned. But you've to get over what happened and start a new life.'

Ned felt as though the room were darkening, as if a cloud had slid in front of the sun. Suddenly, all he wanted was for this confrontation to be at an end. He wanted to be buried in his work, or drinking from a bottle, or back in his bed in the

391

cottage, lying in the silence and the dark, not having to justify himself or his behaviour to anyone, not even having to think.

'People can change their lives for the better, Ned,' Debs said. 'It happens every day. Look at Ellen. Look at what she did. Look at the future she opened up for you both, which you then chose to shut down.'

Ellen? What future? 'What do you mean?' he asked.

'She risked everything for you, Ned,' Debs told him. 'She looked at her own life and she looked at you and she chose you. She finished with him, you know, her boyfriend. She broke it off with him, because you'd made her see that there were better lives out there to build.'

Ned couldn't listen to this any more. 'Leave,' was all he managed to say.

He glanced across at Alexander Walpole's confession, at the story of wasted love, the story he now so wished could have ended happily. He waited for the sound of the door being opened and closed behind him, the sound of isolation.

'She's finished her work here now, you know,' Debs said. 'She's going back to London and you haven't even bothered to say goodbye.'

Ned felt the news almost as a physical wrench. For the first time he allowed himself to face the possibility of never seeing Ellen again, to focus on this fully and accept what it would mean. It filled him with hopelessness and dread.

This was how he'd felt when he'd seen the electric cable leading into the bathroom and had known that Mary had killed herself: like death, like he'd been dying himself, like his whole world had started slipping from his grasp, sliding out of focus, ceasing to exist. Only this was even worse. Because it had been him who'd driven Ellen away. Because he could have made it all so different.

The door clicked shut behind him.

He turned to the evenly spaced columns of figures on the screen. But he couldn't read them any more. The numbers seemed to be melting on the screen, as if they were made of ice. Holding his hand to his face, he felt the tears trailing down his cheeks. But instead of feeling bad, it felt good. He felt lighter by the second, as though the tears he was shedding were made of lead.

And then the great knot of confusing, conflicting emotions he'd been feeling for Ellen – his desire, his fear, his hope, his sadness and his joy – all at once started to make sense. Because, suddenly, Ned realised that what he felt for her wasn't a tangle of emotions at all, but one emotion. And what's more, it was the one emotion he'd told himself he'd never feel again.

Standing, he wiped his face on the sleeve of his shirt, then turned and walked towards the door, knowing exactly what he had to do next.

Chapter XXV

Ellen's head was throbbing as she drove up to the Appleforth Estate for the last time on Monday evening. She scowled as she turned the Land-Rover into the lane leading to the gate, noticing that a new brown heritage sign had been driven into the ground next to the hedge.

She'd been trying to leave Shoresby for hours. She'd wanted to drive back to London in daylight, but despite helping her load everything into the Land-Rover, Scott had kept stalling her until he'd eventually insisted that she come up to the house to collect a monitor he'd left. Ellen had muttered under her breath the whole way up to the house. Scott knew things were difficult for her, so why couldn't he have had the courtesy to be organised today of all days? As if she didn't have enough on her plate without coming to the one place she didn't want to be. And now it would be gone midnight before she'd finally make it back to London.

Ellen was desperate to get away, not least because Scott had been annoying her for the last couple of days. He'd decided to stay on for a few weeks in the cottage so he could be near Debs. Ellen didn't blame him for it, but she'd felt invaded and taken over. Feeling as fragile as she did, she couldn't cope with Scott's relentless optimism and cheeriness. And Debs? Debs was altogether too much for Ellen. Too young, too in love. But most of all, too connected to Ned.

She hated to be bitter, but she couldn't help it. She'd been trying not to think about Ned, but it was impossible. She could still barely credit how much he'd hurt her. There'd been the shock of what he'd actually said to her, the callous way in which he'd let her know how little he'd felt for her, but worse, she'd finally seen the terrifying gulf between her expectations and his. And the pain of that knowledge had multiplied with every minute that had passed since.

Ellen had even shocked herself at the strength of her feelings. When she'd gone to see Ned on Monday, she hadn't had any inkling of the depths to which they ran. But now, now it was even worse. Because what Ned had told her, the way he'd done it, well now, she couldn't even fight for him. Because she was nothing to him. He felt nothing for her. He'd made that quite clear. He probably didn't even care if he never saw her again in his entire life.

Ellen turned off the engine and sat in silence for a few moments, looking out into the dark night. I'm a mess, she thought. I'm a mess and a dreadful person. Steeling herself, she forced herself to look towards Ned's Portakabin. Not that it was any use. He'd dashed her final hope. He hadn't even bothered to turn up to the concert to say goodbye. Now she just wanted to leave, to give him what he so obviously wanted and put as much distance between them as possible.

Just sex. Ned's words echoed in her head. How could she have been such a fool? What had happened had been her fault. She'd instigated it. Ned had told her all along that he wasn't available and she hadn't listened. She was the one who had stacked up their relationship with misconceptions and exaggerated feelings. But she'd only fooled herself. Ned didn't trust her. He never had. He hadn't even trusted her with the truth about Mary – even when Ellen had slept with him.

The lights were off in the Portakabin. Ned would be at

home with Clara, where he belonged. How long would it be, Ellen wondered, before he realised that she'd left for good? Would it even bother him?

If there was one thing she was thankful for, one small glimmer of salvation, it was that she hadn't told Ned that she'd finished with Jason. So at least she could still hold on to that one shred of dignity. Even though Ellen had confided in Scott, she'd sworn him to absolute secrecy and made him promise that he wouldn't breathe a word about her break-up with Jason. She wanted to make sure that Ned never found out. She didn't want Ned to have the satisfaction of knowing he'd completely ruined her life.

Wearily, Ellen pulled out her mobile phone and, steeling her nerves, dialled Beth's number. Sim, her husband answered. 'Sim, it's Ellen. I –'

'I'll get Beth,' he said, a horrible rude taunt in his voice. Ellen physically recoiled at his tone. She knew that Jason and Sim were friends, but surely she could expect a little bit of loyalty from her best friend's husband.

'Where are you?' Beth asked after a second. 'George and Harry have been waiting for you to have supper.'

Ellen rubbed her eyes. She'd entirely forgotten that her godsons would be excited about seeing her. 'Oh, God,' she groaned. 'Beth, I'm sorry. I'm still in Shoresby.'

'Still there!' Beth exclaimed. 'You could have called earlier.'

'I know, I know. It's just been so hectic packing up. I'll get there as soon as I can. I'm sorry. Give the boys a kiss from me and tell them I'll see them in the morning.' There was a pause and Ellen knew that she hadn't been forgiven. 'Oh, please don't be cross,' she begged. 'I'm so grateful you're putting me up. Really. I'm sorry.'

'Jason came round today with your stuff,' Beth said

stiffly. 'Your clothes . . . things . . . they're all in the spare room.'

Ellen blinked back tears. Even though she owned the flat with Jason, it had been she who had decorated it and looked after it, and it had always felt more like hers than Jason's. They hadn't even discussed her moving out of the flat. But now Jason was moving her things out and they'd hardly spoken. She didn't have to, to know how upset he was. 'How was he?'

'Devastated would cover it.'

Ellen closed her eyes. She felt appalling about what had happened and Beth's anger made her feel worse.

'I just don't know how you could . . .' Beth continued.

'How I could . . . what?'

'Throw away the best thing that ever happened to you, over some idiot you've known for five minutes. Well, I hope he's worth it.'

'We're not together, if that's what you're thinking.'

'Then *why*?'

'Beth, do we have to discuss this right now?'

'You were our best friends,' Beth said and Ellen could hear tears in her voice.

Ellen had turned to Beth because she was her oldest friend and ally, but in the ten years that she'd been with Jason he'd become Beth's friend and ally, too. Now Ellen realised that she didn't have exclusive rights on Beth's friendship and, what was more, Beth wasn't offering them. 'I'm sorry,' she whispered.

'Just get here as soon as you can,' Beth said, ringing off.

Ellen opened the car door and stepped out into the wind, savouring the salty breeze for the last time. She knew it would take every ounce of her remaining strength to go back and face Jason.

She knew that he was angry and hurt, and it would take him a long time to calm down. She also knew that telling Jason that she and Ned were never going to be together wasn't going to help. There was no way Jason would ever forgive her, and anyway, she'd come to realise that she didn't want to go back to him. She cared about Jason still, loved him probably, in the way that she always would. He was a part of her, her history, her one formative relationship. But the love she felt for him was no longer an active kind of love. She'd spent too much time waiting for him. Waiting for him to be there for her, waiting for him to give her some sort of signal that he was hers. And when he had, it had simply been too late. Even if she could skip back in time to Jason's proposal on Sunday, in the full knowledge that she and Ned were over, she still wouldn't have accepted. How could she live with Jason, when she knew that potentially there could be someone else like Ned, who could make her feel that kind of passion?

But the thought of being single in London filled her with dread. What if she never met anyone like Ned ever again? Maybe she'd turn into one of those clichéd thirty-something women with cats that everyone talked about. And what if she grew old alone and became a wizened old spinster, who lived for the memory of one night of passion?

Ellen shivered. Concentrate on the present, she told herself. She would have enough time to contemplate the future once she was back in London. Right now, she might as well get this over and done with, she thought, forcing herself to walk towards the house. Scott had assured her that one of the workmen would be up at the site and would be able to give her the monitor. It should only take a few moments.

Ellen pulled up the brand-new brass knocker that had

398

been fitted to the front door and banged it several times. She'd never been into the house via the front door and it struck her that this would be the last time she would ever come here. She looked up at the window above the door, with its fan of ornate glass. She would so loved to have seen the whole place finished and to have met Jonathan Arthur when he came to inspect Ned's handiwork. But she knew it was never going to happen. Her time here was over. She would never see the house finished.

For a while nothing happened, and she was about to knock again when she heard footsteps. Slowly, the door opened.

Nothing could have shocked her more than the sight that greeted her. Scott was dressed in Jimmy's costume from the shoot. Ellen stood dumbfounded. She'd spent ages saying goodbye to Scott, not an hour before. Why and how was he here? 'What are you doing?'

'This way, madam,' Scott said in an absurd attempt at a posh English accent, sweeping back the door and bowing her inside the house.

'What?' Ellen asked, confused. Oh, God, she thought, with an inward groan. What if Scott has organised some kind of wrap party? Surely, after everything she'd confided in him over the last week, he couldn't be that insensitive. Could he? Confused, Ellen cocked her head and stared at Scott, but when he still didn't react she stepped inside.

The hallway was festooned with tea lights, the tiny metal candles flickering up the staircase. Debs was standing by a set of double doors, in Verity's costume. She bobbed in a curtsey when she saw Ellen. 'May I take your coat, ma'am?' Scott asked.

Truly alarmed now, Ellen hardly felt it as Scott gently took the ripped fake fur coat from her shoulders.

'This way,' Scott continued, walking past Ellen towards Debs. Together they took one door each. Ellen stared between them, her heart pounding.

Then they opened the doors.

Inside the dining room the billiard table was covered by a cloth, with a vast silver candelabra in the middle, bathing the half-decorated room in soft candlelight. The table was laid up with silver cutlery and china place settings at either end.

'This way,' Scott urged, guiding Ellen towards the table. He pulled out a packing crate with a cushion on it and she sat down.

Ellen looked at Scott, but he was keeping up the charade. 'Is this . . . is this . . . a joke?'

Scott didn't say anything, but as she looked into his eyes she could see that he was smiling. Scott poured her a glass of wine, then bowed his head and walked backwards away from her. A second later Ellen heard the doors close.

Unable to breathe, Ellen sat alone in the vast room, watching the tall candles. Could this really . . . could this really mean . . .

'I thought you might like some dinner.' It was Ned's voice.

Ellen looked around the candelabra to the other end of the room, where Ned was standing in the shadows. Then he stepped into the pool of candlelight and Ellen gasped. He was dressed in black tie and he looked handsome in a way that he'd never looked before. Ellen was so used to seeing him in old work clothes or his scruffy corduroy jacket that she was amazed by how sophisticated and debonair he looked. He looked younger, too, without his glasses and Ellen remembered how he'd looked in the cottage the night they'd nearly kissed. As he gave her a

400

suave smile, something inside her began to flutter with excitement.

Then the side door opened and Debs and Scott wheeled in a trolley.

Without a further word, Debs brought a plate of smoked salmon and asparagus to Ellen.

She gazed up the table to where Ned had been served by Scott. He seemed so far away.

'I hope you're hungry,' Ned said, nodding to Scott and Debs, who withdrew silently.

Ellen stared at Ned and then down at her plate. What was this all about? Was this Ned's excuse for an apology?

'Ah, sod this,' Ned said, standing up. 'I can hardly see you!'

Ellen let out a short burst of laughter and covered her mouth, as Ned dragged a packing crate across the floor to her end of the billiard table. He was wearing work boots with his dinner jacket and she realised she loved him more right now than she ever had.

'I meant to get some music,' he said, sitting down next to her. 'Sorry.'

For a long moment she stared at Ned. There was something so different about him. Something soft as he stared at her. 'Ned, if this . . .' she began '. . . if this is some sort of –'

Ned silenced her, putting his hand over hers. 'I owe you so many apologies,' he said, 'but mainly I'm sorry because I lied to you. I lied to you about Mary.'

Ellen looked down at his hand over hers.

'I know you know,' he said, 'but I wanted you to hear it from me.'

Ellen looked up into his eyes, as Ned sighed.

'Mary committed suicide four years ago. She had post-

401

natal depression. She was ill and . . . and it's complicated . . . how I feel about it is complicated. I'm not sure I've worked any of it out yet.'

'I see,' she said.

'I don't want to talk about it tonight,' Ned said. 'I want to talk about it some other time, but tonight is about us.'

'But I don't understand,' Ellen said. 'I didn't think you –'

'You know I told you I didn't believe in second chances?' Ned asked.

Ellen nodded.

'Well, that was until I realised how much I wanted one. With you.'

Ellen couldn't believe what he was saying. She watched as he took his hands away from hers and rubbed them over his face.

'I know I've been horrible to you, Ellen. I know I've snubbed you and lied to you and hurt you. But please, you've got to hear me out.'

'I'm listening.'

Ned stood up, as if he hadn't really been expecting her to agree to his request. He looked as if he was expecting a fight and now he looked at a loss.

'Why don't you start at the beginning?' Ellen said gently. 'Just tell me how you feel. That would help.'

Ned nodded, but it took him a while to say anything. Then he stared at her, taking her aback with the forcefulness of his look. 'You know, the very first time I laid eyes on you something inside me told me you were special. That you had blasted into my life for a reason. But then I ignored it. I've spent so long not trusting my instincts, not daring to listen to any feelings inside . . . that I pretended nothing was going on, that I didn't feel anything at all.' Ned let a breath out, but he hadn't finished. 'But the point is, I do have feelings. Lots of them. I'm not sure they're all good, but they're all there.'

Ellen looked down at her hands.

'You made me see that I haven't been living until now. I've just been going through the motions, because a bit of me died with Mary.'

'And now?'

'Oh, Ellen, you have no idea . . .'

'I don't know what to say,' she said. 'I'm glad if I've helped. That makes me feel better.'

Ned dropped to his knees next to her and grabbed her hand, forcing her to look at him. 'Oh, God, I'm doing this all wrong. This isn't about me getting over Mary. This is about you. This is about me and you.'

'It is?' she whispered.

'I love you, Ellen Morris. You must know that. I love everything about you. I love the way you're strong and you stand up to me, I love the way you're gentle too, that you're wonderful with Clara. I love the way you make me feel special to be alive and happy to be near you. I love the fact that you're beautiful and clever and smart. I love it that you made me feel passion that I didn't know was possible –'

'So it wasn't just sex,' Ellen said, choking back tears, but she was smiling too.

Ned shook his head. 'Please give me a chance, Ellen,' he whispered. 'I can't let you go.'

'Oh, Ned,' Ellen cried, reaching out to him and touching his face. 'Of course I'm not going to go. I'm not going anywhere.'

'I'm sorry,' he said. 'I'm so sorry that I hurt you.'

Ellen put her fingers on his lips. 'You're here now. That's all that matters.'

'Don't cry,' Ned said, kissing her fingers gently. 'Eat.'

'I can't eat! How can I eat?' she wailed.

Ned laughed, lifting her up into his embrace. 'But I thought you wanted romance?'

Ellen held him tight. 'And I thought you didn't believe in it.'

'Well, let's just say that you made me a believer again.'

She stared into his eyes, thinking how beautiful he was. Here he was, the man she loved. Her Ned. Wordlessly, he leant down and kissed her.

Ellen felt as if she were levitating as her whole being dissolved into him, until she didn't know who or where she was. Every fibre of her being felt as if it was fizzing with love. She realised, now, that this kiss marked the very start of her future. That from now on she could live every moment to its full potential, because she wasn't waiting any more. It had happened. The impossible had happened. Some benevolent God had seen into her soul and had granted her heart's desire. She could scarcely comprehend how lucky she was, or how blessed she now felt. The one thing that she wanted more than everything else had happened. She had found Ned.

Ned rested his forehead against hers.

'Hello,' she whispered.

'You'll stay for dinner, then?' Ned asked.

'What do you think?' she answered, smiling. Then she looked at the table. 'I can't believe you organised all this. How?'

'Let's just say that Debs put me straight about quite a few things.' Ned pulled away. He put his arm round Ellen's shoulder. 'And he's a damn good mate to you, that Aussie.'

'And to think . . . I've been cursing him all day,' Ellen said, wanting to hug Scott.

Ned smiled and turned to look out of the windows. Ellen

404

followed his gaze to the lights of Shoresby twinkling in the distance. It was the most romantic sight she had ever seen. 'It's beautiful,' she sighed. 'This house is beautiful. Alexander Walpole would have been proud of you.'

'Ah,' Ned said. 'Yes, about the Walpoles . . .'

'What?' Ellen asked, alarmed at his tone.

'Well, you might want to consider a rethink on their story.'

'Why?'

Ned reached inside his jacket and pulled out an old faded letter. 'This,' he said.

Ellen tried to take the letter, but Ned held on to it. 'What does it say?' she asked.

'Well, how about . . .' Ned folded her into his arms again '. . . we discuss it tomorrow. When we wake up. Or the next day. Or the day after that . . .'